LOST COAST

BOOK 3 OF UNDEAD ULTRA

CAMILLE PICOTT

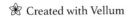

ACKNOWLEDGMENTS

I had so many awesome people help me with this book! From website ninjas, to firearm and explosive experts, to generous beta readers, and to a fellow ultrarunner who wasn't afraid to tackle the Lost Coast's impassable zone at 2:30 in the morning, this book could not have come together without them. Thank you!

Lori Barekman
Linda Bellmore
Lan Chan
Victoria deLuis
Joe Dulworth
Jayson Fowler
Chris Picott
Andy Salas
Jon Theisen
Sandra Winn

FREE BOOK

PROLOGUE
MASSACRE

BEN

Six months ago ...

That rat bastard Johnson was up to something. Johnson and his little weasel, Ryan. Ben was certain. Those boys had a charisma inherent to high school bullies.

Ben was convinced they were going to go for the food. For the past week, Johnson's lackeys had been sneaking off in the middle of the night in pairs. He suspected they were setting up a new headquarters and planned to steal all the supplies for themselves.

Ben saw the way Johnson looked over the rations, at the way he leveraged the best food for himself and the soldiers. He liked having power over people.

Just last week, he'd bullied the college kids into smaller rations.

"Who's going to keep you safe?" Johnson had reasoned. "If you don't have us to protect you, the zoms will get you."

The rest of the soldiers were just as bad. They were all obnoxious pricks who subscribed to pack mentality. And Johnson was the leader.

Ben was going to make sure the college kids weren't left high and dry when Johnson made his move. In fact, if everything went according to plan, Ben didn't intend for any of them to be around come tomorrow night.

He made his way through the dark hallway and slipped into the dorm that had been converted to a stores room. He looked for things that could be carried easily. Powdered soup mixes and packets of Top Ramen. Bottles of aspirin. He scribbled a list with a broken pencil on a Post-It Note, making note of everything he planned to steal.

He'd lead the kids away tomorrow night. Sneak out all the ones who hadn't thrown their lot in with Johnson. Five miles north of here was a town. McKinleyville. He didn't think Johnson would follow them all that way. Ben just needed to make sure they had enough supplies to hold them over a few days until they found a new home base.

He considered recruiting other soldiers to join him. There were two on the outside of Johnson's gang. The first was Ash. The fact that she was female put her at a disadvantage with Johnson. He respected her because she was tough, but she wasn't part of the inner circle.

The other was Caleb. The young man was close to Johnson for reasons Ben couldn't fathom, but he wasn't like the rest of the soldiers. He knew the way they bullied the college kids was wrong. But he didn't do a damn thing about it, which in Ben's mind made him as guilty as the rest.

In the end, Ben decided it was too risky to trust Ash and Caleb. They spent too much time with Johnson. Ben had to pull this off on his own. He—

"Stop!" someone yelled. It sounded like Caleb. "Don't do this! Johnson, *stop!*"

The sound of shattering glass sent a spike of adrenaline through him. Ben jumped to his feet just as gunfire peppered the air.

No.

He tore out of the room and sprinted to the stairwell, taking the steps two at a time.

No.

He flung open the door, running full tilt toward the sound of battle. Screams clawed at him, urging him onward.

It wasn't the screams of zombies. It was the screams of people. Of college kids.

The double glass doors leading out into the courtyard were shattered. Ben threw himself through the opening, not feeling the shards that tore right through his clothes and his flesh.

He burst into the courtyard, confronted by the sight of blood. So much blood. It ran toward the large drain near the center of the open area, bright red slashes against the gray pavement.

His brain flashed through a sequence of scenes. Blood on the hard-packed ground in an Iranian village. Blood spurting through his fingers as he tried to staunch a bleeding friend on the desert ground. Blood spraying like a popped soda can when the grenade went off near the meat shop in Somalia.

His life could be painted in a series of blood patterns.

It took him several heartbeats to wrench himself free of the memories. He careened back into the present just as a bullet grazed the tip of his ear, sending a burn up and across his scalp.

Ben leaped for cover in the doorway's alcove. He gripped his Sig and peered around the corner.

That's when he finally saw past the blood and registered the bodies. The youthful bodies in brightly colored clothing.

Erin. Jason. Scarlet. Andy. Ted. Ginger. What's-his-name who never shut up.

Their names scrolled through his brain in red kiosk lights. Red like the blood that matted their hair, marred their clothing, and drizzled across their skin.

"Come out, come out, wherever you are," sang a voice.

Johnson. That motherfucker.

"Come join your friends, Benny."

"What the fuck have you done?" Ben bellowed.

"I just expanded our rations," Johnson drawled.

That's when Ben saw Caleb. The tall, handsome African American kid from San Diego crouched behind a pillar, gun in hand. He had a clear shot at Johnson.

"Come on, Benny," Johnson said. "You know that crew was just dead weight. All they did was take, take, take."

"You murdered them!"

"Watch your voice, Benny. You'll bring the zoms."

"I'm going to make you a zom, you sick fuck."

Johnson sighed loudly. "That's why I didn't ask you to join us, Benny. You pull your weight, but you're a cranky fuck. Isn't he, guys?"

A chorus of voices answered in the affirmative. Ben saw them. The young soldiers and the college kids who had thrown their lot in with Johnson. They clustered around him like high school bullies guarding their ringleader.

Ben counted them off in his head. Every last murderer. Every last fucker who was going to die for what they'd done.

Across the courtyard, Caleb raised his gun. Ben watched him take aim at Johnson.

Do it, he urged silently. *Put that fuckhead in the grave.*

But Caleb only stood there, gun raised. And stood, and stood, and stood.

With a sinking feeling, Ben realized he wasn't going to shoot. The fucker was going to let Johnson walk.

Rage clouded his vision. Ben leapt out, a gun in each hand. He fired blindly in the direction of Johnson and his lackeys, then dove back toward the safety of the building.

Miraculously, he wasn't hit. Sheer dumb luck. He charged back through the shattered doors and made a break for freedom. Gunfire followed him.

As he fled, the last thing he saw was Caleb, still standing behind the safety of the pillar like a coward.

1

SHIFT CHANGE

BEN

The sun comes up, staining the sky a deep pink. The clouds are dark puffs of gray, promising rain sometime today.

It always rains in this fucking place. Ben is sick of it. Even if rain is one of the few things that anchors him when the flashbacks come.

Like now.

Like when the sky is a deep pink at sunrise.

The color sucks him back thirty years, when the ink of his signature was still wet on the army enlistment papers.

A similar pink sky stretched over him as his ground unit entered Kuwait to drive out Iraqi forces. He feels the vibration of grenades under his feet. His ears sting from the machine gun chatter. He feels the suffocating hot air of that desert hell.

The fear of that day sucker punches him. It fills every segment of his body, making his hands shake. He's a fresh recruit in Kuwait all over again, wondering what the fuck he's gotten himself into.

Ben never has been able to stomp out that old fear, no matter how old he gets or how many wars he fights in.

He grinds his teeth and tries to focus on the smell of the rain clouds. It never smelled like this in the Sandbox. Ever. Just black plumes as petroleum fields burned.

Ben stares at the clouds, willing himself to return to Arcata. Willing himself to leave the hell of Desert Storm and come back to the hell of the present apocalypse.

Gunfire fades in his ears, replaced with the soft, distant moans of zombies. The explosions from rocket launchers and grenades diminish, leaving the roof of the Creekside dorm building in Humboldt State University solid beneath his feet.

Somewhere nearby, a bird chirps.

It chirps a second time, then a third. By the time the third chirp sounds, he's returned to the present.

His hands stop shaking. The old fear recedes, disappearing back into distant memory where it belongs.

Ben wipes sweat off his forehead with the back of his hand.

Fuck. That was a bad one.

He's always dealt with flashbacks, mostly at night. It's fine. Sleep is overrated, anyway. Shit, PTSD is practically a surrogate brother to him.

He always shoulders the shit and moves on. But this fucking zombie apocalypse keeps triggering old memories. It's a new card surfacing from an old deck every fucking day.

He runs a hand over the familiar handle of his Sig. The weapon further grounds him, helping him focus on his mission for the day.

This is how he survives. One mission at a time. Kate tells him what to do and he does it. The work keeps him sane. One job after another, until he's so exhausted his mind can't help but fall into a few precious hours of dreamless sleep.

The hair on the back of his neck prickles, alerting him to an approach. Even though he's expecting the shift change for watch, he can't erase thirty years of paranoia learned in combat. He eases the handle of the Sig out of its holster and turns toward the hatch in the dorm rooftop, ready for anything.

A lean woman with a ponytail climbs out. Kate.

His slips the Sig back into place.

He takes advantage of the thirty seconds it takes her to climb all the way onto the roof, admiring her lean muscles.

She wears a tight tank top with a light jacket and running shorts. She's always in those fucking shorts, even when they go out with the zombies.

He has a love-hate relationship with her shorts. When he isn't scared to death that she's going to get herself bitten, he can't stop staring at them. Or more precisely, at the legs revealed by those shorts.

He's never seen a pair of legs like Kate's. She has leg muscles he never knew existed. Which is saying something; he's spent his entire life with men who powerlift and do other shit meant to build muscle and decrease body fat.

She's wearing a new pair of shorts today. He knows this not because he pays any attention to the color or the design on the various things she wears. He knows this because an extra two inches of leg is exposed above her tan line.

Honestly, he'd been pretty sure the only way her shorts could get any shorter would be if she dispensed with them altogether and started running around in her underwear. Which he wouldn't put past her, if she thought it would serve some greater purpose. The crazy woman is always putting herself at risk for all the little shitheads she's adopted.

"Hi." Kate gives him a tentative smile as she emerges fully onto the rooftop. Her body is haloed by the rising sun, which accentuates those perfect leg muscles.

He stares at her. She looks so damn good.

He wants to tell her this. In truth, he's been looking forward to this very moment for days. This exact moment of the shift change, when he knew he'd be with Kate and she wouldn't be surrounded by one or more of the little shitheads who all adore her. A moment when he could talk to her without anyone being there to watch or eavesdrop.

The problem is, he hasn't worked out what to say. Even though he's had days to plan. Days to come up with some clever conversation starter.

A dent appears between Kate's brows as she watches him watching her. "Ben? You okay?"

He wants to tell her that he's more than okay whenever she's around. He wants to tell her that he could watch her run for hours without getting bored. He wants to tell her she's the craziest fucking woman he's ever met, and when he lies in bed at night unable to sleep, he likes to recall the night he watched her take out Johnson's entire poisonous nest with a bottle of laced brandy and three zombies. Thinking about that is more restful than sleep.

God dammit, he'd settle for *any* comment civil and uncomplicated. Anything for a chance to talk to her, to keep the conversation going.

Anything except for the words that actually come out of his mouth, which are: "Nice tan line."

Her frown deepens, sliding from her brow down to her mouth. He hates this look, mostly because it's the only one he can seem to get out of her when he works up the nerve to talk to her.

"I have to wear what I can find, okay? I ripped my favorite pair on that door hinge when we cleared out those zombies that congregated in the Depot. Jenna found these in a room on the third floor and they fit."

He should explain that he didn't mean that the way it sounded. He should explain that she looks damn fine in those shorts.

But she brought up the incident in the Depot, when she'd

had a near-miss with a zombie. Just thinking about it pisses him off all over again. She risks herself too often.

"You shouldn't wear shorts when we leave Creekside. It's too risky. I've told you that before."

"What's risky is having to run hard and fast in jeans or stuff like *that*." She gestures to his sturdy military fatigues. "It's not the right gear for our lifestyle here."

"I run in these just fine." He won't budge on the fatigues. He can't. He was practically born in them. He never liked wearing civvies even when he was on leave. "I do your four-hour workouts like everyone else."

She pokes a finger in the direction of his waist. "Yeah, and I know you've got blisters and chafing. I've seen the bandages. Don't try to deny it."

He's torn between pleasure that she's paid enough attention to notice the bandages and irritation that she's seen through his bald lies regarding fatigue pants.

He learned the hard way that there's a big difference between clothes suitable for five miles of running and clothes suitable for twenty-five miles of running. Even so, the last thing he wants to do is wear a pair of those flimsy running shorts. He made up his mind weeks ago that he'd suffer in silence and keep his fatigue pants. That's exactly what he's done.

She arches a brow at him. "Go ahead. Tell me those things are comfortable to run in."

Ben knows a challenge when he sees one. He wants to point out he *did* agree to the fluorescent orange and yellow running shoes she picked for him. Ben has never done fluorescent. Not ever.

Those shoes make him look like a washed-out old man trying to be a Millennial. All he's missing is ten pounds of hair gel. And maybe half a dozen piercings in odd places.

All because of the apocalypse. And Kate.

He wishes he could rewind the last sixty seconds and start

over. Since he can't, he does the next best thing; he changes the subject.

Grabbing a thermos off the small table they keep on the roof, he holds it out to Kate. "I made you coffee."

She blinks. "When did you make me coffee?"

"Last night, before my shift."

"Four hours ago?" Now she's really frowning.

She thinks he's offering her cold coffee. "This is a Yeti thermos," he explains.

That doesn't clear up her frown. Maybe she doesn't know about Yeti thermoses. She barely knew the front end of a gun from the back when he met her a few months ago. Why would he assume she knows about Yetis?

"This is the best thermos on the face of the earth. A friend of mine in the service was a hunter. He went on a hunting trip every time he was on leave. He'd go out into the backcountry for days. He always took a Yeti and kept ice cream in it."

"I'm confused. I thought we were talking about coffee?"

Ben wants to kick himself. His mouth very rarely cooperates with his brain. Especially when Kate is around. He decides to dispense with the Yeti explanation altogether.

"The coffee is still hot." He holds it out to her like a peace offering. "The coldest time of day is always at dawn." Which is the exact time of her shift.

"Thank you." She takes it from him, studying his face. "That's really sweet of you."

He looks at her. She looks back.

He wants to share the coffee with her. That had been his original idea. Strike up a conversation and share a cup of coffee with her. He'd even brought two cups up to the roof.

Except he's fucked things up. How's he supposed to segue into coffee?

"Frederico and I often went running before the sun came up." Kate's voice is a reprieve to the awkward silence. It feels like an olive branch. "He always groused about the temperature drop at dawn."

She doesn't talk about Frederico very often. Ben's listened to enough conversations at mealtimes to know he'd been her best friend. She'd lost him on her run north to find Carter.

If she'd been a soldier, he'd get out a flask and share a swig in memory of one who had fallen. But Kate isn't a soldier and Ben doesn't carry a flask these days. Kate keeps the alcohol they find in a special cabinet in the supply room and rations it out for special occasions. He respects her too much to make himself an exception to her rule.

But the fact that she's sharing a little bit about her lost friend means something. Or at least, he *hopes* it means something. He latches onto this idea and plows ahead.

"Did you run a lot before dawn? Before the apocalypse, I mean?" He doesn't have to feign interest. Ben is fascinated by her pre-apocalypse running life. The bits he's gleaned over the past few months are like glimpses into the journal of an exotic explorer.

"When Carter was young, we started long runs before dawn," Kate says. "Four or five in the morning, usually. That way I didn't blow the whole day running and still had time with Carter and Kyle. Frederico was always at our house anyway." A long breath escapes her as she settles into the chair he recently vacated. "I miss him."

He isn't sure if she's talking about Frederico or her late husband. What he does know is that she's talking to him, and he's talking to her, and he hasn't said anything idiotic in the last forty-five seconds. He's not on a roll, but he isn't eating his shoe, either.

He inches toward the empty chair next to her, hoping he doesn't look like an awkward idiot. He *feels* like an awkward idiot.

"Here's a coffee cup." He hands her a mug, picking up the second one he'd brought to the roof. "Mind if I—"

"Did someone say coffee?"

Paranoid reflex kicks in. Ben drops the second mug and snatches his Sig. The porcelain shatters on the rooftop as he spins around. A handsome young man climbs into view.

Caleb. Irritation prickles up the base of his spine. Leave it to this little shit to ruin his moment with Kate.

Caleb is everything Ben is not. Young, good looking, and— most irritating of all—good with words. Whereas Ben always struggles to find ways to talk to Kate, Caleb never has trouble slipping into conversation with her. Their mutual affection rankles Ben.

"What do you want?" he snaps at the younger man.

"Good morning to you, too, old man." Caleb takes in the ruined coffee cup. "Sorry if I startled you. I was just bringing Kate some breakfast."

Irritation turns to seething anger. *Startled?* Like Ben is a jumpy recruit. He'd fought in at least two wars before Caleb was in diapers.

Ben doesn't like many people, but there are very few he loathes. Caleb tops that short list.

"Breakfast?" Kate turns. The smile she has for Caleb is wide and genuine. Much wider than the one she had for Ben a few minutes ago.

She wouldn't have such a ready smile for the younger man if she knew what he'd done. Of the innocent people he'd let die. Of all the blood on his hands.

"What's cooking today?" Kate asks.

"Mmm." Caleb slides into the empty chair—the very one Ben had been angling for. "Well, Lila is up to her usual magic in the kitchen."

Kate coughs. It's Caleb's turn to grin.

Lila's cooking is a constant topic of conversation among the residents of Creekside. Ben is the only one who doesn't find it amusing. The girl has shit to work with and still manages to be creative. So what if not everything tastes good? If these guys had eaten half as many MREs as he's eaten, they'd love Lila's cooking.

"We found some oats in the supply room," Caleb says. "They expired *before* the apocalypse. Lila whipped up some powdered milk and let the oats soak overnight. They're bland and stale so she added some jam." Caleb pulls a small container out of his coat pocket. "They don't taste so bad when they're hot so I figured I'd bring them up for you."

"Thanks. Ben made some coffee. Want some before you head back down?"

"The other cup broke." Ben looks pointedly at the ground, knowing he's being petty but unable to stop himself. He's rankled by the idea of Caleb sharing the coffee he'd made to share with Kate.

"No prob," Caleb says. "I have one." He pulls a collapsible silicone cup out of his cargo pants.

Kate fills the cup and glances up at Ben. "Want to join us?"

Ben doesn't want to go, but nothing good will come out of his mouth while Caleb is around.

"I have work to do before target practice later today. Enjoy your breakfast."

You'd have to be deaf to miss the rancor in his voice. By the look on Kate's face, it's clear she isn't deaf. He retreats before digging his hole any deeper, leaving the splintered remains of the coffee mug behind.

2

CAFFEINE

KATE

CAFFEINE.

Some days, there isn't enough of it in the world.

Like today.

I down the last of the coffee, marveling that it stayed hot in the thermos for so long. I turn the black cylinder over in my hands, tracing an idle finger over the logo. *YETI.*

Sleep deprivation coupled with four hours of sitting on a roof in the cold morning has left me exhausted. I could have used three Yetis of coffee today.

I'm no thermos aficionado, but Ben clearly is. Why someone named a hot beverage container after the abominable snowman is beyond me. Ben did say something about Yetis being used for ice cream, so maybe that was the original intent.

I try not to think too hard on the fact that he thought far enough ahead to make me a thermos of coffee. We almost had a normal conversation before Caleb interrupted us. Ben often says rude and off-the-wall stuff—like that comment about my tan line—but then he counters it with sweet gestures, like the coffee.

I'm pretty sure there's a nice man underneath the profanity

and monosyllabic grunts. I'm drawn to those little bits of kindness I see. I wish Caleb had waited another five minutes, if only so I could have proof that Ben *was* capable of normal conversation.

"Hey, Kate." Lila's dark head pops into view as she climbs the ladder onto the roof. "My turn for watch. Ben says it's time for you guys to go shoot things."

I smile at the younger woman. Her dark hair hangs in a long braid down her back, a smudge of something on her cheek. It might be strawberry jam from her breakfast concoction.

She steps onto the roof, shoulders hunched. Even though there's no way zombies can get her up here, she still looks around like a hunted animal.

"Ben really did say that." Lila takes the chair next to mine, her tone dropping to mimic Ben's deeper voice. "Tell Kate it's time to shoot some zoms." She frowns at me. "You look like shit. Did you sleep at all last night?"

I shake my head with a dry laugh. "Ben brings me coffee. Caleb brings me breakfast. You bring me a 'you look like shit.'"

"I only mean that you have dark circles under your eyes. You don't look like you got any sleep."

I shrug. "It's been warm. I'm still getting used to falling asleep without an air conditioner." It's partially true. Except that it never gets that hot in Northern California, not even in the summer.

In truth, I wouldn't be sleeping well even if I had a pre-apocalypse air conditioner. Every time I close my eyes, my brain travels back to the night I murdered Johnson and his people. I see the ravaged bodies of those young, twenty-something men I drugged and killed with zombies.

Looking at Lila reminds me it was worth it. I did it for her. I did it for Carter, Jenna, Reed, Johnny, and Eric. I did it so they could live without the threat of Johnson hanging over them.

"I could make you some tea that would knock you out for a full night," Lila offers.

I shake my head. "I prefer to stay away from *that* kind of tea." Lila specializes in marijuana concoctions. Some of the other kids—mostly Reed and Eric—indulge in pot, but I prefer not to. "I have my own personal sleeping medicine. Have you seen the stack of books on my nightstand?"

Lila wrinkles her nose. "All that old stuff?"

"They're called *classics*. Two pages in one of those books and I pass out cold."

"If they're such a good sleep aid, why didn't you sleep last night?" Lila asks with an arched eyebrow.

Damn. Caught in a lie. I shrug with nonchalance. "I've finished all the ones on my nightstand. I need to get some new ones."

Lila studies me with narrowed eyes, as though trying to ferret out my lie. I look back at her, determined not to reveal the real reason for my insomnia. No one made me kill Johnson. His death, and those of his people, are on my conscience. The weight is for me to bear.

Lila breaks eye contact, shrugging. "Suit yourself. You know where I live if you change your mind. Speaking of which ..." She fishes a small glass jar out of her backpack and holds it out to me. "Need some? It's a fresh batch. The guys say you have a two-hour run planned today after shooting practice."

"I'll take it with me. Ash and Eric have both been complaining about sore muscles." I take the jar of homemade cannabis salve that Lila made.

We all used to tease her about the stinky stuff. Now, after months of using it on our various achy body parts, we're all fans of it.

"Did you give some to Johnny?" I ask. "He needs to keep it on his Achilles."

"Yeah, I lathered him up as soon as I finished mixing this batch. He should be back to running in no time."

I don't reply. From my own list of extensive running injuries over the years, I know Johnny will be laid up at least six weeks with his Achilles tendonitis. The only time he gets to go out these days is for shooting practice.

I look across at the college campus of Humboldt State University. From up high, I can almost imagine the world hasn't ended, that the world below isn't filled with the undead.

But the sound of the zombies is constant. The moaning, the keening, the snarling. It never ends. New zombies arrive every day on campus. No matter how many we kill, there are always more.

Which is why Ben insisted we institute a twenty-four-hour watch post on top of Creekside. Remembering Johnson and the night his people found us and robbed us, I didn't have to be asked twice before agreeing.

"You'd better go," Lila says. "The sooner you go, the sooner you'll finish and someone else can take over the watch."

The only time Lila keeps watch is during shooting practice. Only because she refuses to leave Creekside. Hell, even getting her to agree to that had taken some persuasive powers. Johnny, with his injury, keeps watch when we train at the campus track.

"You should come with us one day. Just walk with us to the track. You know I wouldn't take you there if it wasn't secure." It had taken us two entire days to clear the track and zombie-proof it.

Lila wrinkles her nose and looks away. "You just want to trick me into running."

"Running would be good for you," I agree. "We both know that." But Lila refuses to exercise. All she likes to do is cook and tend to the indoor garden she and Eric built. She keeps watch now only because there's no one else to do it, and her fear of someone sneaking up on us is greater than her fear of being on the roof.

"It's not a way to live. Lila, I know it's scary out there, but locking yourself up in Creekside isn't the answer. You have a life to live. It shouldn't be within the confines of this single building."

She shrugs, still not looking at me. "It's not the answer for you. It's working alright for me."

"Just think about it." I reach across the distance separating us and squeeze her shoulder. "Think about coming out with us one day. We'll keep you safe. You'll see it's still worth being a part of this world." I raise a teasing brow. "There's a big marijuana plant growing beneath the bleachers at the track. Just think of all those buds waiting to be harvested for your salves and concoctions."

"I'll think about it." Lila's eyes flick in my direction then back out to the campus. "You'd better go. The troops are no doubt getting restless. You know how they are when they want their Mama Bear." She gives me a quick smile at the use of my nickname.

I give her shoulder one last squeeze before heading to the ladder.

"Kate?"

I pause, turning to look back at Lila.

"I know I'm fucked up," she says. "I know a screw came loose in my brain when the world ended. Thanks for giving a shit."

I smile warmly at her as I step out onto the ladder. "You're part of the Creekside Crew, Lila. I'll always give a shit."

3

PACK
KATE

Everyone is assembled on the bottom floor of Creekside.

Carter, my son. Johnny, our writer and ham radio extraordinaire. Reed, one of the resident stoners who just so happens to have turned into a damn good runner. Eric, our engineering genius and resident stoner. Jesus, a former drug mule who is as good with a gun as our soldiers. Ash and Caleb, the two soldiers who joined us after I killed their psychotic leader, Johnson. And Ben, who had once been allied with Ash and Caleb before breaking off on his own.

I pretend not to notice him as I enter what had once been a dorm building lounge. He's counting a stack of magazines, placing them into a large pack.

Since we commandeered this place and made it our home, the bottom floor has been converted into an indoor garden. The solar panels on the roof power the grow lights. More than two dozen sturdy plastic garbage bins scavenged from around campus collect rainwater on the roof.

A clever gravity hose system designed by Eric makes it easy to drain water from the bins to the garden beds. The kid is a genius. I can only imagine what he'd come up with if he laid off the pot. He doesn't smoke as much as he used to, but I know not a day goes by that he doesn't take a few hits at night.

"Sorry to keep everyone waiting," I say.

"Time to shoot some zombies!" Reed slaps high-five with Jesus.

"Don't let yourself get too reliant on guns," I say with a frown. "They're zombie magnets without the silencers. You—"

"Yeah, yeah." Jesus cuts me off with a grin. "We know. We can't rely on fire power for defense against the zombies. Mama Bear, check this out." Jesus produces a scratched aluminum bat.

I grin as he hands me the bat, running my hands over the metal. "Where did you find this?"

"Not just one," Reed says. "We broke into one of the locker rooms and found two dozen of them."

He throws back a tarp, which is normally used for storing extra gardening supplies. Beneath the crinkly plastic is a pile of aluminum bats.

"Zombie swatters for everyone," Jesus declares, throwing his arms open wide.

"That is awesome." Carter hefts a bat in one hand. "Think we could add spikes or something to the end?"

"Yeah," Jenna says. "I took a welding class last year. I bet we could get supplies from the metal shop."

"For you, *mi hermosa flor.*" Jesus presents a bat to Ash with a flourish and an open, flirty smile.

Caleb, who's never more than a dozen paces away from Ash, stiffens. Emotion disappears from his face, only his dark eyes revealing how much he dislikes the other man.

If Ash notices the silent battle waging between Caleb and Jesus for her attention, she pretends not to. "*Gracias, mi amigo.*" It doesn't help Caleb's case that both Ash and Jesus are fluent in Spanish.

"Don't get caught up in the show." Ben stomps over to me,

shouldering the pack full of ammunition. "There's no substitute for a Sig." He holds a handgun and holster out to me.

I wave away the weapon. We go through this almost every time we leave the building. "You know I'm not comfortable with guns."

"You're not going to get comfortable if you keep avoiding them." He shoves the thing into my hands. "It's not loaded. Just wear it and practice getting used to it."

I roll my eyes. I've taken to wearing a loose belt over my running shorts these days. The belt holds a knife, a screwdriver, and now a gun. And a baseball bat, which wedges perfectly on my lower back.

Jenna fidgets with the bat, trying to find a comfortable angle for it in her belt. "It's a bit clunky," she says. "Did you know these things are hollow? We could cut off the big end, fill the handle with sand, then weld a cap on the top. That would make it compact and easy to carry, but it would still pack a punch."

"That's your project for next week," I say. The bats are too good to pass up. We can use all the viable hand weapons we can get. "You and Carter figure out a way to convert these into portable zombie-killing clubs."

"But it was my idea," Jesus complains. "Jenna isn't the only one who took a welding class."

"You can help them," I reply.

"If you'll all stop drooling over the baseball bats like cavemen, it's time to practice with real weapons." Caleb steps between Ash and Jesus, staring coldly at the other man.

"Amen to that," Ben mutters. "Let's get the fuck out of here."

"Wait, I have one more thing to show you guys." Jesus fishes a thick gold chain out from around his neck. Dangling from the end is an even thicker gold pendant. "I found this yesterday on a zombie in the locker room."

Everyone leans forward to look at the pendant. It's a haloed man in a robe with a dog at his feet. He looks like every other saint image I've ever seen.

"Is that a saint?" Jenna asks.

"Bingo." Jesus grins. "This is St. Roch. He was the patron saint of dogs, the falsely accused, bachelors, and—get this— he's invoked during times of the plague."

His words hang in the air.

A plague saint? It never occurred to me such a thing existed, but why not?

"St. Roch is going to look over the Creekside crew from now on." Jesus tucks the necklace back into his shirt. "I'm going to build a shrine for him."

"Dude, " Reed says, "you and your shrines. You already have two in our room."

"Those are for our mother, Guadalupe," Jesus replies. "This one needs to be in a central location. I'm going to build in it in the kitchen."

"You'll have to clear it with Lila," Reed replies. "The kitchen is her domain."

Jesus waves a dismissive hand. "I got her number, bro. All I have to do I pretend to like her food."

Ben frowns. "You're going to lie to her to get something you want."

"I'm doing her a favor," Jesus replies. "Lies are okay when they make someone feel good."

"She'll see through your bullshit," Ben says. "You haven't said a single nice thing to Lila about her food since you got here."

"Don't hate me for playing the system, man."

Ben's expression darkens. Everyone knows he gets prickly around insults to Lila's kitchen experiments. I find this sweet, even if I can't understand it. Lila's food makes me gag on a good day.

I decide to break up the banter before things go south

between Jesus and Ben. "Jesus, you can take up this conversation with Lila when we get back. Everyone, outside. We're leaving now."

No one argues. We troop outside, locking the door behind us. What was once a swinging glass door has since been converted in what Lila likes to call a wood-and-metal monstrosity, built to withstand zombies and humans alike.

I lead the way, my people spreading around me in a loose circle. Ben shadows me much the way Caleb shadows Ash. He's been doing this for a while now. Jenna says it's because he's taken it upon himself to look out for me. I pretend not to notice. Unfortunately, feigning ignorance with Ben is easier than having a conversation with him.

We've cleared the campus as much as possible. We hunt zombies every time we leave Creekside, killing those we come across. One day, the campus will be completely free of zombies. Hell, maybe St. Roch will be up to helping us with the task.

As we pass the university bookstore and enter one of the campus quads, we find a cluster of zombies. They squat around the remains of some poor animal, likely a cat or a raccoon.

I hold up a fist to signal silence. Not that my people talk or make a lot of noise. They know better than to do anything that might draw attention to us out here.

I draw to a halt, counting the undead. Seven in all, against ten of us. I like those odds.

I flick my fingers, indicating we're to separate into two groups. Ben and Jesus instantly glue themselves to me. The two of them have a protective streak when we're out here. Eric and Johnny join us. The five of us circle around to the right side of the zombies. The rest of the group circles left.

This is a maneuver we've rehearsed countless times. Split up, come at the zoms from two sides, and take them out. It's not flawless, but it's effective.

A zombie near the edge of the group straightens as we

approach, head cocked in our direction. Its blind white eyes roll in the sockets, as though searching for us. Longish brown hair is ratty and matted with dried blood. Its nostrils flare, neck craning in our direction as it sniffs the air.

I pause, the rubber soles of my running shoes poised on the concrete. My group stills with me. I watch the zoms, well aware of the keen hearing they possess.

On the other side of the quad, Caleb leads the other group. They ease closer to the zombies with weapons in hand. Ash and Jenna both have their new baseball bats out. I follow suit, pulling out my bat.

Across the quad comes a snapping sound. Carter grimaces, shifting away from a tiny twig.

The ratty-haired zombie jerks in the direction of Carter. Its mouth opens, emitting a series of keens and clicks.

Then something happens that I've never seen before. The other zombies straighten and turn toward the ratty-haired one as it continues to click and keen.

Its head turns in the direction of Carter. The rest of the zombie heads follow suit. Seven sets of dead white eyes home in on my son. A chorus of moans and hisses drifts up from the group.

My eyes involuntarily flick in Ben's direction. He exchanges a tight-lipped look with me.

The lead zombie clicks again, then lets loose a long, low keen.

It charges straight at Carter. The rest of the zombies follow, all of them snarling as they surge after their leader.

Fuck. I break into a sprint, the bat raised over my head as I rush across the quad. Ben, Eric, Johnny, and Jesus are hard on my heels.

We don't make a lot of noise, but we aren't completely silent, either.

The lead zombie releases another string of keens and clicks. Half the zombies spin in our direction.

My new bat smashes through the skull of the first one. The others fall in with their weapons, cutting and smashing with knives, bats, and screwdrivers. Carter's group attacks from the other side, also closing in with bats and knives.

The battle is over in less than ninety seconds. I suck in gulps of air, hands sweaty around the handle of my bat. We stand in a loose circle, staring down at the dead zombies.

Caleb is the first to break the silence. "What the fuck was that?"

No one replies. I approach the lead zombie, the ratty-haired man with the blood-stained head. Using my bat, I flip over the body. The face is a mess, having been smashed in by Ash's baseball bat.

Ben eases up beside me, scanning the body. "He doesn't look any different than the others."

But he was different. We all saw it.

I swallow, trying to work moisture into my mouth. "It ... communicated with the others."

"It issued orders," Ben states.

The back of my spine prickles. It's bad enough that we're outnumbered by the undead. But up until two minutes ago, we had the advantage of organization. Of skilled counterattacks.

"They acted as a unit," I say at last. "Like a hunting pack."

"A fluke," Reed says. "We've never seen them organize before. That's not how they work."

"That's not how they've worked up until *now*," Johnny counters. "We may be witnessing an evolution."

"Evolution?" Eric asks. "Fuck that. This was a fluke."

"Maybe," Johnny says. "But let's take a brief walk through the history of man. We started as apes. Over the years, we learned how to hunt, talk, and organize. Who's to say zombies won't undergo a similar evolution?"

"The explanation might be even simpler than that," Jenna says. "Maybe the virus mutated differently in a small percentage of those who have turned. Maybe there's a small percentage who are intelligent."

"St. Roch looked after us." Jesus fishes the saint out of his shirt and plants a kiss on it. "He kept us safe."

"We need to get on the ham," Ben says. "Find out if this is an isolated problem or if other people are seeing the same thing. We're in serious fucking shit if this is happening in other places."

"I don't buy any of that," Reed says. "I'm not freaking out over one incident."

"No one is freaking out." I wipe my bat clean on the shirt of one of the dead zombies. "We'll have Johnny reach out to his contacts on the ham. In the meantime, we need to be vigilant. This may or may not be a fluke. We need to be prepared for anything."

"Amen to that," Ben says.

4

PRACTICE

BEN

BEN FINDS COMFORT IN *PSST-PSST* OF THE HANDGUNS AS THEY SPIT bullets on the zombies below. To him, it's the sound of self-preservation. Of survival.

College Creek dorm, for all the bad memories it holds, has proven to be a perfect place for target practice. The long balcony across the second floor, connecting three dorm suites, is perfectly positioned above the athletic field. There are plenty of zoms to shoot without fear of being bitten or swarmed in the process.

"You're leaning backwards. Your shots are punching holes in the clouds," Ben tells Kate. "Bend forward at the waist and lower your arms. Better. Try again."

"I suck at this shit." Kate heaves a sigh. The dark circles under her eyes are more pronounced than usual today. He hadn't noticed them in the smudged light of dawn this morning. She could have used a bigger thermos of coffee.

"Like this." He takes her by the shoulders and adjusts her stance. He does his best not to notice her warmth beneath his hands. "Try again."

Brow furrowed in concentration, she once again raises the

Sig and takes aim. This time, she hits a zom right between the eyes. Granted, it's only twenty yards away, but this is a vast improvement over a few weeks ago when all she could hit was dirt.

"Good work, Kate. Keep it up."

She responds with a small, tired smile. A sense of contentment fills him. He likes knowing she won't be defenseless if she ever gets caught in a bad place. With the way she plunges head first into things, that's likely to happen sooner or later.

He continues down the row, critiquing people as needed as they fire down into the athletic field.

"Your thumb is too low on the grip," he tells Reed. "It should be parallel to the ground."

"Two hands," he tells Carter. "That shit you see in the movies with cops shooting one-handed is just that: shit. If you want to kill zombies, hold your gun with two hands."

"Feet shoulder-width apart," he reminds Johnny. "You look like a frog."

The kids don't argue. They take his instruction, do their best to make corrections, and keep practicing.

Shooting practice is the only time they aren't all flapping their jaws. Couple the lack of chatter with the silencers on the guns, and it's bliss out here for Ben. No wonder he looks forward to practice sessions.

The silencers were a score. Ben managed to scavenge several dozen sound suppressors when he first raided the army's weapon's cache. It was a good thing, too. Without those silencers, Kate would never have agreed to their weekly practice sessions.

You'd think anyone who found herself in the middle of a zombie apocalypse would welcome guns and the chance to learn how to use them. Not Kate. Nope, she was happy with her knives and screwdrivers. And now, he supposes, her aluminum baseball bat. He wouldn't put it past her to pick running shoes as a preferred form of defense over a firearm.

But he'd won her over. Eventually. With lots of pestering that earned him frowns. In the end, he'd gotten his way. Sort of. She'd consented to target practice two days a week.

"Our two-hour runs are scheduled on Wednesday and Friday," Kate told him. "We can add target practice to those days."

Of course, she wouldn't dream of cutting a running workout. He would have to make do. Consistent practice two days a week was better than nothing.

Kate almost put the kibosh on the whole thing as soon as she figured out silencers don't really make guns silent. Like most people, she'd been misled by the movies. Silencers drop the overall decibel of a weapon, but guns still make a healthy amount of noise. Enough that they attracted new zoms to the wrought iron fence around the field every practice session. It wasn't until Ben convinced her the newcomers were good for long-range target practice that she reluctantly agreed to allow the lessons to continue.

It was paying off, as evidenced by the fact that Jenna and Carter, who never held a gun before the apocalypse, were hitting their targets eighty-five percent of the time. Only half of those are headshots, but he doesn't expect miracles.

Ben stops beside Jenna as she fires at a senior citizen zombie on the athletic field below. "You're flinching right before you pull the trigger. It's messing with your aim. Don't flinch."

She wrinkles her nose, raising the Berretta as she again takes aim at the senior zombie. This time, when she fires, her bullet sinks into the shoulder of the creature.

"Nice work. Bend your knees a little. You're too tense." He takes her by the shoulders and adjusts her forward a few degrees. "You want a slight tilt at the waist. Try again. This time aim for the head."

Jenna nods, her body locked in place, and fires. Her shot brains a zom and drops it.

"Nice. Keep it up." Ben continues down the line.

Jesus is a good shot. The man is open about his pre-apocalypse days as a drug dealer, which no doubt plays into his proficiency with firearms. Caleb and Ash are more than proficient, of course. They both had professional training.

Then there's Eric. Ben stops beside the young man. More than two dozen zombies lie dead on Eric's end of the field, the result of the young man's handiwork.

Not bad for two fifteen-round mags.

"Nice work." Ben gives him an approving nod. "I have something new for you to try."

Up until now, he's kept their practice sessions to handguns. He wanted them to feel comfortable with smaller weapons before pulling out the rifles.

Ben unslings the AR-15 from around his neck.

"No way," Caleb protests. "You're letting the rookie fire the AR-15 before me and Ash?"

Ben scowls at him. He'd prefer not to give Caleb any firearm and let the asshole test his luck.

"Want to test yourself against the rookie?" Ben jerks a thumb at the tactical bag he carried here. "Knock yourself out." Maybe he'll get lucky and the shithead will shoot off his own foot.

Caleb gives him a dirty look and resumes shooting with his Berretta.

Ben spends the next fifteen minutes with Eric, showing him the ins and outs of the rifle. When the young man raises it to his shoulder and takes the first shot, the recoil rocks him backward. He adjusts his stance and tries again.

"Keep practicing," Ben says. "Try not to fall on your ass."

He continues his patrol up and down the second-floor balcony, eyes flicking out to survey the zoms in the field below.

He tries not to recall why there are so many trapped there, but the memory shoves its way forward. Sometime in the early days of the outbreak, some genius had come up with the idea to lead a bunch of zombies into the field, which was surrounded by a wrought iron fence. Ben had watched the idiot First Sergeant do it. Right before he'd gotten himself swarmed and bitten.

Ben feels the claws of a flashback creeping up on him. He forces himself to look away, to break from the memory

His eyes land on Kate. Her incredible legs are enough to make him forget all about the overturned jeep and his long-lost First Sergeant. For a good ten seconds, he allows himself to absorb the sight of her.

The way her brow wrinkles in concentration. The tight tank top. The damned tan line on her legs.

Then he takes note of her hunched shoulders. Her posture has gone to shit in the five minutes since he last critiqued her. Irritation and anxiety prick him. She's the worst shot out here. The idea of her failing to properly defend herself due to his poor training does not sit well with him.

He steps up behind her, pressing down on both her shoulders with his hands. "You're too tense. Drop your shoulders. All the way."

She gets them in place.

"You're leaning over too far—" he begins.

She fires mid-sentence, her bullet flying to the side and burying itself in the grass. "Dammit," she snarls.

Ben swallows back his impatience. "Just wait a sec. Your posture is all wrong."

"You said to bend my waist."

"I said *slight* bend."

"You never said *slight*. You said *bend*."

Her obvious annoyance irks him. Words run out of his

mouth like a freight train on autopilot. It's with an effort that he manages not to snap at her.

"You make us run because you don't want us to die out there. This is no different. I want you to survive whatever this fucking world throws at us."

He means that last part more than she knows. Just to cover his tracks—in case anyone is listening—he turns a glare on the rest of the pack. "I want all you little shitheads to survive, okay? Now get back to practice."

Said shitheads keep firing.

Kate adjusts her body into a semblance of a proper stance. "Is this what you meant?"

He swallows, doing his best to let go of his anger. "Almost. Straighten up another two degrees. There. That's good. Try again."

This time, when she fires, her bullet hits a zombie in the lower sternum.

"Nice," he breathes. "Again."

She fires three more shots. The third one goes straight into the head of a zombie and drops it.

Ben folds his arms in satisfaction. The tension within him eases. "Nice work. Just keep working on your stance. That's half the battle."

Kate nods, giving him another small, tired smile. "Thanks."

Her exhaustion is evident. If he wasn't afraid for her life, he'd tell her to skip practice and take a nap.

He wants to say this to her, but has no idea how to shape these thoughts into words. So he does the next best thing. He gives her a curt nod and moves on.

Maybe tomorrow he'll make her another thermos of coffee and sneak in an extra spoonful of grounds for a caffeine boost.

5

HAIR
KATE

A WEEK LATER, I STARE AT MYSELF IN THE MIRROR.

I hardly recognize the face that stares back at me. Lean bordering on gaunt. Brown ponytail with a solid five inches of gray roots. The skin around my eyes shows the beginnings of crow's feet.

"God," I say. "You'd never know I'm turning forty next month. I look fifty."

"Your birthday is next month?" Jenna, who stands beside me in the bathroom, frowns at me in the mirror. "Carter didn't say anything about your birthday."

"You may have noticed my son is short on details."

Jenna's mouth twists in an affectionate grimace. "Yes, I've picked up on that once or twice."

"His father was the same way."

"For the record, you don't look fifty. You look like someone who does CrossFit at the beach."

Jenna is being nice. I appreciate her kindness. My son snagged himself a great girlfriend.

"So, what will it be? Cut or color?" Jenna picks up a pair of scissors with one hand. With the other hand, she hefts a bottle of brown hair dye.

It turns out brown hair dye isn't the easiest thing to find on a college campus. Green, yes. Blue, yes. We even found pink and red and purple in one room, but no brown. If the apocalypse had stranded us in an old-folks home, I'm sure there would have been brown hair dye in every other bathroom.

When I happened across this bottle yesterday while scavenging in a nearby dorm building, I'd been ecstatic. Now that I have the dye, it seems stupid. What's the point of dying my roots if they're just going to grow out again? I don't have time to spend messing with my hair.

"What do you think Ben would like?" Jenna asks.

"Why does that matter?"

Jenna shrugs, giving me a look of wide-eyed innocence. "I don't know."

Without a doubt, I'd look better with dyed hair. I'd look younger. Not haggard. Borderline okay-looking. Not attractive by any sense of the word, but not a she-got-run-over-by-a-truck look, either.

"I think he likes you," Jenna says.

"No." I shake my head. "He barely talks to me." Which is technically true. Ben doesn't talk much to anyone.

"He spends more time with you on the firing range than anyone else."

Target practice. I wish she hadn't brought that up. I didn't know it was possible for someone to get worse at something with practice, but over the past week my already nonexistent shooting skills have declined.

Ben is so different when he's patrolling the balcony and critiquing us. Yeah, he's still gruff and curt. I don't think anything will ever change that. But he's a good teacher. No, scratch that. He's a *great* teacher. Give the man a gun and he's completely in his element.

I like seeing that side of him, but it's distracting. It's even worse when he starts prodding me to stand correctly. I pretend not to be hyper aware of his small touches as he corrects my stance. He has no idea how hard it is to get everything right when he's standing two feet away scrutinizing me. I hate looking like an inept idiot in front of him.

"The only reason he spends extra time with me on the shooting range is because I'm a terrible shot," I tell Jenna.

Jenna just looks at me and says, "Uh-huh."

I decide not to tell her about the thermos of coffee left just outside my bedroom door every morning for the past week. Ben has never said anything to me, but I have no doubt he's my coffee fairy. Seeing the Yeti thermos there every morning warms me more than the coffee.

But my hairstyle is not about Ben. His theoretical opinion doesn't have any bearing on my decision.

"Cut it all off," I say. That's the practical thing to do.

Jenna's bottom lip sags open. She snaps it back shut. "Are you sure?"

I nod. "I can't be worried about my hair." Or about Ben's opinion. "There are too many other things to worry about."

Such as the evolution of zombies. Johnny spent the last week on the ham talking to every person he could find. Three reported seeing organization among the zombies. It's a small percentage, but it's enough to make me think our post-apocalyptic world might be on the brink of a major shake up. Practical hair is the only way to go.

"Are you sure, Kate? You want to cut it *all* off?" Jenna's discomfort is not making this any easier.

"Yes." To emphasize my decision, I plop down on the lid of the toilet seat. "Chop it all off."

Jenna picks up the scissors. "You should know I've never cut hair before. I'm an experienced dyer, not a cutter."

"How much talent does it take to hack off someone's hair?" I position myself so that my back is to the mirror. So I won't have to watch my transformation. I yank out the rubber band holding my hair in place. "Go for it."

Licking her lips, Jenna picks up a strand of my hair. It hangs well past my shoulders.

I force myself to stare at the shower curtain. The cheery cloth with pink, yellow, and orange flowers is now tarnished with gray splotches of mold.

I feel like that shower curtain.

Snip.

The first chunk of hair falls to the floor. I see it out of my periphery and make it a point not to look at it directly.

Snip. Snip.

My vision blurs. The shower curtain flowers swirl before my eyes.

Twenty minutes later, Jenna steps back. "That's it. It's all gone."

The smile she gives me eases the tension gripping my chest. I hate the fact that cutting hair produces anxiety. In a world where stepping outside can result in death, I shouldn't give a shit about my hair.

"I like it," Jenna says. "You have nice cheekbones."

More like gaunt cheekbones, but I don't say that. Jenna was nice to help me. I shouldn't ruin it by complaining.

"Turn around," she urges.

I turn.

I hardly recognize the women in the mirror. If not for the sports bra, I could almost imagine myself as a no-nonsense businesswoman. The pixie cut lends youthfulness to my face and eases the weight of my impending fortieth birthday.

"I was worried." Jenna grins at me in the mirror. "But love it."

I can't help but grin back at her. "Me, too."

"Maybe I should cut mine." She pulls back her long tresses,

studying her face in the mirror. "One less thing for zombies to grab."

"If you, me, and Carter all cut our hair, people are going to think it's a conspiracy," I say, referring to the time a few months ago when my son abandoned his lumberjack look by shaving off his beard and hacking his hair short.

Jenna cocks her head. "Maybe it's an indoctrination thing. Like, you can't be an official Stevenson family member unless you shave off your hair."

I rest a hand on her shoulder. "You're already an official family member as far as I'm concerned."

We share a moment in the mirror, the two of us looking at one another. It's hard to remember a time when I resented Jenna's very existence. Now I think of her as a daughter.

Jenna looks away first. "Come on. Let's go show everyone your new look."

We exit the dorm bathroom and enter the sitting room. The whole Creekside crew is gathered there, except for Reed, who's on watch.

This is the original dorm where I lived when I first arrived in Arcata. We've since branched out into other rooms. I now share a four-room dorm suite with Carter, Jenna, Ash, Caleb, and Ben. The rest of the kids live here.

Eric is currently commanding everyone's attention. He stands on a chair, one hand grasping the front of his pants.

"Watch this, everyone!" He flashes me a grin as Jenna and I enter the room. "Wait for it." He pauses dramatically, making sure all eyes are on him.

Then he releases his waistband. His pants fall, puddling around his ankles and revealing blue-striped boxer shorts.

Eric holds up his hands in triumph. "No more beer belly!" he exclaims.

Carter stands up and applauds. Everyone else groans, myself included.

"*Mi amigo*," Jesus says, "there's no one here besides Lila who wants to see that."

Lila colors, then rallies. Straightening her spine, she levels a glare at Jesus.

"You've been buttering me up for the last week," she says. "I don't know what your deal is, but right now you're doing a good job of *un*buttering me."

"Told you she'd see through the bullshit," Ben says.

"There's no buttering going on in this corner," Caleb says. "Pull up your pants before we go blind."

Eric remains nonplussed, propping his hands on his hips. "Guys, this is a miracle. Before the zombie apocalypse, I thought I was destined to be a fat guy forever."

"It's not the apocalypse that made you skinny," Ben says. "It's Kate's hard ass workouts."

"I know, but I wouldn't have to run every day if the apocalypse hadn't happened. I call this my apocalypse bod." Eric rotates on the chair with his arms up. Somehow, he manages to do this without tripping on his pants and falling. He also flashes a bit of his stomach. It's covered in light brown hair.

"Dude," Caleb says, "I wasn't joking about going blind. Put that shit away."

"Mom, you cut your hair!"

Every head in the room turns in my direction. Eyes widen.

Eric falls off the chair. "Ow," he complains.

Everyone ignores him, except for Lila. She helps him get his pants from around his ankles back up to his waist.

"You look like a hot biker chick," Ash says.

"You've always been kind of scary," Caleb adds, "but I think you just managed to make yourself scarier."

Ash slaps him. "Caleb!"

"I meant that as a compliment," he grumbles. "She looks badass."

"Our Mama Bear would be beautiful with green skin and purple hair," Jesus declares.

"You look like a wannabe G.I. Jane." This comment comes from Ben. A dent mars his brow as he studies me.

His comment makes my stomach sink. I cover the disappointment by wordlessly flipping him the bird, which gets hoots of approval from everyone else. Ben reddens and looks away.

Jesus turns to Ash. "*Por favor, no te cortes el cabello bella dama.*"

Ash rolls her eyes.

"Hey, we've talked about this," Caleb says. "No speaking Spanish when the rest of us are around."

Jesus smirks, folding his arms across his chest. "What are you going to do about it?"

"Everybody up," I say, attempting to turn the tide of the conversation. "Time to go for our run."

Everyone shifts into action, not a single argument among them.

"You." Ben flicks a hand at Johnny. "It's your turn to keep watch."

Johnny grumbles, but plods toward the door. He detours by the kitchen table, grabbing a notebook and a pencil. "At least I can work on my *Thrive* book if I'm going to be stuck on the roof for the next few hours."

"I thought you were writing something called *Dorm Life*," Lila says.

"I am," Johnny replies, "but that's the blue notebook. The red notebook is *How to Thrive in the Apocalypse*."

"Here are your snacks." Lila hands me a Ziploc filled with granola bars. "I'll have lunch ready when you guys get back. I'm making vegan mac 'n cheese today."

"It's not vegan if you use powdered cheese," Caleb says.

"It's vegan," Lila insists. "We don't have any milk or butter, which makes it vegan in my book."

I give Lila props for her enthusiasm. Unfortunately, enthusiasm doesn't always equal flavor. I'd never tell her that, though.

Twenty minutes later, we march down the stairwell in a group. Lila holds open the door, security bar in hand as she prepares to lock it after us.

"Come with us," I urge. "Some fresh air and sunshine will do you good."

She shakes her head. "I have to check on my plants." She gestures to the indoor garden beds. "The zucchini and tomatoes are almost ready to harvest. Besides, someone has to stay behind and cook lunch for all you losers."

I stare at her until she looks away. We both know she's full of shit.

I wait until everyone else files out. I lower my voice so only Lila can hear. "This isn't living. You weren't meant to spend your life in a cage."

"It's good enough for tigers in the zoo," she replies with a forced laugh. "If it's good enough for them, it's good enough for me."

I give her shoulder a squeeze. "Think on it. Just come with us to the track and sit in the sun one of these days."

Lila shrugs and falls back. "I'll see you guys after your run." As she closes the door, I hear the bar and several bolts sliding into place.

6

SPAM

KATE

As we return to Creekside after our track workout, I run through the list of things we need to get done today. We're in the process of mounting several more solar panels on our roof. With any luck, we'll have grow lights for additional garden beds soon.

And, most importantly, a solar-powered water heater.

Eric spotted one on a recent trip into town. It took us three trips and a few run-ins with zombies, but we managed to get it dismantled and transported back to Creekside.

Now we just have to figure out how re-assemble it. And get water into it. We may be able to divert some of the garden's water supply. Whatever the case, I'm confident we'll figure it out. We have the university library at our disposal. And Eric. He's our secret weapon. He might be a pot head, but he's an engineering genius.

As we reach Creekside, Ash puts two fingers to her lips and whistles. Johnny's dark-haired head appears on the edge of the roof.

"Be right down," he calls.

A few minutes later, the metal bar protecting Creekside slides aside. Lila and Johnny throw open the door. They jostle each other, Lila glaring

"We need to take a poll," Johnny announces.

"Fuck you and your polls," Lila says. "I get to say what it is. I'm the chef."

"That's a generous appropriation of the word," Johnny replies.

"I'd like to see you do better," Ben snaps.

But Lila doesn't need Ben's defense. She's more than capable of sticking up for herself. "If you don't like it, you can go to bed without supper. Your loss. I found a tub of vegan protein under a bathroom sink upstairs. Everyone is getting an extra dose of good health tonight."

She spins on her heel, marching toward the stairwell as the rest of us file into Creekside.

"It's not vegan just because it has vegan protein powder in it," Johnny calls after her.

"I used soy milk, dick wad." Lila punctuates this sentence by flipping him off.

"Yeah, with Spam," Johnny hollers. He turns to us, palms up. "She insists the mac n' cheese casserole she made is vegan because she used soy milk and vegan protein powder. Even though she threw in a can of Spam and used the powdered cheese."

I drop the security bar into place and slide the three bolts into the locked position. "Does it really matter?" Whatever the case, it sounds awful, though my criticism of Lila's cooking never leaves my mouth.

The others don't have the same standards.

"I'm less worried about the description and more worried about the fact that Lila put protein powder into a mac n' cheese casserole," Carter says. "Hopefully it's not something weird like chocolate protein powder."

A collective groans goes up.

"You're all a bunch of ingrates." Ben scowls. "That young lady works hard to make sure we get nutrition. She has shit to work with and look at the things she makes for your ungrateful asses."

"Vegetable soup with canned tuna is not earning anyone a Michelin star," Johnny says. "Especially when you consider the fact that she put spam in that, too."

"What about that three-bean salad she tossed with the blue cheese dressing?" Reed chuckles. "That was nasty."

"Beans are a great source of protein. You guys should try eating beef stroganoff MREs for thirty-two meals in a row." Ben's face is flushed with irritation, his mouth pressed into a hard line. "None of you guys would complain about anything after that."

He shoulders to the front of the pack, stomping ahead and slamming open the door to the stairwell before disappearing.

"Beef stroganoff MREs for thirty-two meals in a row? That must violate some sort of regulation," Ash says.

Caleb shrugs. "I don't know. Maybe someone fucked up on a requisition and shipped too many of the same thing."

The debate continues as we file upstairs. Since the university-issued table was only built for six people—and moving in an extra table would mean getting rid of the couch—we don't have a formal eating arrangement. With eleven of us, we sit wherever we find a spot. Despite this, I take pride in the fact we eat three meals a day with each other.

I get comfortable on the floor, holding a bowl of Lila's afternoon concoction in my hands. I scrutinize the lumpy mess in my bowl. The base is mac 'n cheese from a box. The cheese sauce, according to Lila, is made of powdered cheese, soy milk, and protein powder. The smart thing would be to spoon the food straight into my mouth with my eyes closed.

"What's with the Spam?" Caleb asks. "You put this shit in everything."

Lila plants her hands on her hips. "What's wrong with Spam? I'll have you know that a hundred million pounds of spam were consumed by the Allied troops during World War One."

"What she means," Ben says, already shoveling food into his mouth, "is that Spam was partially responsible for the defeat of Hitler. All you little shits would do well to remember that." He jabs his fork at our collective group for emphasis.

"Thank you, Ben." Lila draws herself up, beaming at the older man. "At least *someone* appreciates Spam. My mom always put Spam in our spaghetti when I was a kid."

"Dude, I'm pretty sure the nukes were responsible for the defeat of Hitler," Reed says.

"I said *partially* responsible," Ben retorts. "You think our soldiers would have stood a chance if they didn't have Spam to fill their stomachs?"

"Okay, we get it," Caleb says. "Spam saved us from the Nazis." He rolls his eyes, popping a bit of the casserole into his mouth. "What kind of protein powder is this?"

"Plain." Lila, from her seat besides Eric, spoons a heaping amount into her mouth. "It gives the cheese sauce a nice texture."

A few people cough. Ben says, "Good stuff."

I stir the stuff around in my bowl, working up the courage to try it. "If Spam is responsible for the defeat of the Nazis, what do you think are the chances of it defeating the zombies?"

Ben glances up from his bowl. He looks at me like he can't tell if I'm serious or not.

Best not to leave that open to interpretation. "I'm joking."

"Thank God. I was trying to figure out the best way to answer that from a logistical standpoint."

I do my best not to laugh in his face. Only Ben would use

Spam and *logistical* in the same sentence. I look away before the conversation can deteriorate, as it often does between us.

I venture to put a spoonful of the stuff into my mouth. My gag reflex works in the back of my throat. The cheese sauce has a gloppy texture, but not in a nacho-cheese sauce sort of way. More in a runny-with-chunks way. The supposed plain flavor of the protein powder has a distinct earthy flavor that lingers long after I've swallowed.

It's amazing than even Kraft mac n' cheese can be thoroughly ruined, even in the apocalypse. Straight water with the cheese powder would have been better than the sticky mess that's in my mouth right now.

"I did the calculations," Lila says. "We each have about twenty grams of protein in this meal. It's good for us."

"Twenty grams?" Jenna's mouth sags open. "How do you figure that?

"I calculated the serving ratio of the protein powder and added that to the protein in the mac n' cheese. I added a little more for the soy milk. The apocalypse is treating us well."

"It's the best damn thing I've had since the world ended," Jesus says. "Can I have seconds?"

Lila narrows her eyes at him. "You've been complimenting my food for the past week. Why?"

Jesus's eyes widen with innocence. "Can't a man compliment the chef?"

Ash snorts. "*Mentiroso.*"

Lila doesn't buy it. "In all the months you've lived with us, you've never said one nice thing about my cooking. In fact, I believe I recall you saying something along the lines of my stew tasting like roadkill."

"I didn't say that."

"Yes, you did."

"What I meant is that maybe we should find some roadkill for snacks."

"You are so full of shit."

"No, I mean it. Roadkill could make nice jerky."

"I can see why you and Reed are besties," Lila says. "You're both full of shit."

"Hey, don't drag me into this," Reed says. "I don't fill your ears with lies. This casserole makes me want to yack, Lila. But I'm going to eat it because I know it has nutritional value and Mama Bear made us run for two hours today. Then she made us run up and down the bleachers for another thirty minutes. So I'm hungry and pretty much up for anything. See? Truth."

"Thank you, Reed." If Lila is offended by anything he's just said, it doesn't show. "I'm glad you appreciate the nutritional value. I work hard to find ways to get you all extra protein." Her gaze swings back to Jesus. "Out with it. What do you want from me?"

"Want from you?" Jesus protests. "Why do you think I want something?"

Lila stares at him, refusing to answer. She stares at him until he squirms and throws up his hands.

"Okay! I admit it. I was trying to soften you up."

Lila narrows her eyes. "For what?"

"For St. Roch." Jesus fishes the necklace out of his shirt, holding it up for Lila to see. "He's the patron saint of plague victims. I want to build a shrine for him in this room."

"Why here?"

"Because this is where the Creekside crew gathers," Jesus replies. "St. Roch can look over all of us this way. And we can pay him respect."

Lila considers this. "If I let you have space, will you continue to tell me my food is good?"

"If you will grant me a place for a tribute to St. Roch, I will gladly tell you every dish you serve is worthy of French royalty."

"I'm pretty sure France hasn't had a monarchy in over a hundred years, but whatever. You have yourself a deal, Jesus."

Jesus kisses the pendant and crosses himself. "Thank you, *mi chef*."

By the end of this exchange, most of us have finished eating. I drop my empty bowl and fork into the sink, glad I don't have dish duty today.

"Babe," Eric says, "we gotta go back to that part about you calling this a vegan meal. I could ignore that statement if we were just talking about cheese powder, but it has Spam. It can't be vegan if it has Spam."

"Don't be a dick," Lila shoots back, her eyes brightening. For some reason, these two love to bicker with one another. "It has vegan components. I mean, *soy milk*, Eric. That's as vegan as it comes."

Eric is grinning now. "That's like saying a chicken Caesar salad is vegetarian because it has lettuce in it."

"I'm the chef. I get to say what it is."

"You can say whatever the hell you want. That doesn't make it factual."

Lila huffs. "Go fuck yourself, Eric. You try cooking for eleven picky people when there are no grocery stores and see how well you do." She makes a show of stalking out of the kitchen, loudly slamming the door to her bedroom.

"Here we go," Carter mutters, rolling his eyes. Jenna elbows him.

Eric waits sixty seconds before following. Another sixty seconds later, rhythmic banging sounds from the bedroom.

Another collective groan rises from us. Lila and Eric never seem to care if any of us are around when they get busy.

"I'm going to go in there with a hacksaw and remove their headboard." Johnny pushes an empty bowl away. "I have to say, that was weird as shit but not terrible. Maybe I'll pass the recipe on to Alvarez."

"You and I have different definitions of the word terrible." Jenna stares forlornly into her bowl. "My mother would roll over in her grave if she saw me eating Spam. She'd probably give me a sermon on what this stuff does to my colon."

"Ew." Carter makes a face at her. "You couldn't have waited until after I finished eating?"

"Anyone gonna eat the rest of this?" Ben prods the casserole. When everyone declines, he spoons the rest of the mixture into his bowl. "Your loss," he says to no one in particular.

7

MAYDAY

KATE

"To the left," Jenna calls. "Kate, dip your side!"

"I'm trying!" I'm on the bottom corner of the new solar water heater we're installing. If I get any lower, my hand is going to get crushed.

"Use those killer leg muscles and squat," Johnny says.

Jaw tense, I take his suggestion and shift my weight, straightening my back and sinking into a crouch.

"Perfect!" Eric crows. "Hold it right here."

"Nice work, Mama Bear." Caleb, holding the other bottom corner of the solar water heater, flashes me a grin.

"Easy for you to say," I reply. "You're buff. How did I get stuck on this end with you?"

"Luck of the draw." He winks at me.

"You can set it down now," Eric says.

I let out a breath and ease the solar panel into place. Eric gets to work bolting it down.

"I've been fantasizing about this moment since the world ended," Jenna says. "Hot shower." She smiles, face tilted toward the sky.

"I thought I was the only thing you fantasized about." Carter slings one arm around her waist, pulling her close.

Jenna snorts. "You're hardly a fantasy. I get you whenever I want."

"Guys, let's keep this G-rated," Reed says. "There are sensitive ears present."

"Who gets the first shower?" Ash asks.

"We still have to design a catch basin for water to fill the pipes," Eric says. "We haven't crossed home plate yet."

"Yes, but when we do," Jenna says, "one of us will get to go first." She narrows her eyes at Ash. "I'll thumb wrestle you for the rights."

"You're on," Ash says.

"Oh, hell no," Jesus says. "The only kind of wrestling I want to see is mud wrestling." He points both index fingers at the girls. "You two. In the mud. That would have been some quality pay per view back in the day."

"Dude." Carter tightens his arm around Jenna's waist, frowning. Caleb mirrors his frown, though he doesn't say anything.

"Don't blame me." Jesus holds his hands up. "Your woman is hot. That's not my fault."

Carter opens his mouth to retort, but he's cut off by Lila's unexpected voice. It drifts up through the roof access hatch.

"Guys! Come downstairs." The urgency in her voice stills me. "You guys have to hear this."

"What is it?" I hurry across the rooftop and scramble onto the ladder.

"I was flipping channels on the ham," Lila says. Her eyes are wide, her lower lip lodged between her teeth. "Someone is in trouble."

I frown, unsure why this has her riled up. We're six months into a zombie apocalypse. Of *course*, people are in trouble. It isn't the first time one of us has met someone over the ham in a dire situation. Just last week we talked to a man caught in the cab of a semi at a monster truck rally somewhere in Texas.

"Trust me. You guys need to hear this," Lila says.

We reach the second floor where we live. Ben comes out of the weapons room as we file past. It's a dorm suite we converted to hold all the weapons we've scavenged. Half the supplies were brought by Ben when he joined us. The rest were taken from Johnson's lair. Ben has been in there cleaning since lunch.

"What's going on?" he asks.

"Come in here," Lila replies. She ushers us into our main sitting room and cranks up the volume on the ham. "Listen to this."

A woman's voice bursts from the tiny receiver, filling the room.

"Mayday, mayday, mayday. Can anyone hear me? Boat grounded in Humboldt Bay. My husband was attacked by a great white. His condition is critical. Is anyone out there? Can anyone help us? Mayday, mayday, mayday. Our boat is a blue charter boat named *Fairhaven*."

The message repeats three more times, the woman's voice becoming more and more despondent with each one.

Lila turns down the volume after the third desperate message. She stares at us, lips compressed in a thin line.

"We need to help them." Carter shoulders up to the table, reaching for the receiver.

Ben's hand whips out. His big hand covers the receiver. "It could be a trap. It's not safe."

Carter frowns at Ben. "She said her husband was attacked by a shark. That's not the sort of thing you say if you're setting a trap."

"It's gotta be real," Jesus says. "Who the hell says her man got attacked by a shark in the zombie apocalypse? No one would believe that."

To my surprise, Caleb sides with Ben. "Someone just so

happens to ground a boat in Humboldt Bay? It wasn't exactly filled with boats before the apocalypse."

I glance at Lila. "Have you spoken to her?"

Lila shakes her head, dark eyes still wide. "I had a meeting scheduled with Alvarez to go over composting techniques. He wasn't there so I was just scrolling through the channels."

Alvarez wasn't there? It wasn't like him to miss a scheduled ham appointment. I file the worry away to examine later.

"Turn it back up," I say. "I want to hear the message again."

"Mayday, mayday, mayday." The woman on the other end of the receiver chokes on a sob. "Can anyone hear me? Can anyone help us?" She breaks down into tears.

It's the sound of her sobbing that solidifies my decision. That is a genuine sound of someone who needs help.

Ben must see the decision on my face. His mouth opens, an angry furrow between his brows. I can practically smell the argument.

I cut him off. "That crying"—I jab a finger at the ham—"is not fake."

He purses his lips, scowling at me. We lock eyes. I don't look away.

"How many times have we talked to people we can't help?" I say. "Just a few days ago there was that officer in Oregon. He was barricaded in a police station closet and slowly starving to death. And what about that woman whose semi was swarmed in Southern California? She was surrounded by zombies with no way out. All these people out there talking to us on their ham radios and we can't do a damn thing to help them." I rest my hand on the receiver. "This time, it's different. We have the chance to help someone in our backyard. This woman, whoever she is, is asking for our help. I'm going. It's the right thing to do."

"Fine," Ben snaps. "But we do it carefully. Recon the ship. Don't show ourselves until we're sure it's safe."

"We?" I raise an eyebrow at him.

"Did you think you're going alone?" He stomps over to the door, sifting through the rack of weapons we have mounted on the wall.

"I'm going, too," Carter says. "We don't know what sort of shape this guy is in. You'll need at least four of us if he has to be carried out."

"I'll go, too," Jenna says.

"I'm the medic," Ash says. "If the husband really has been attacked by a great white, I should be there to help."

"Do great whites even live around here?" Eric asks. "I tend to be on Ben's side in this argument. I think it's a trap."

"San Diego is home to the largest population of great whites in California," Caleb says. "Humboldt County is the second largest population."

"How do you know that?" Ash demands.

"I made it my business to learn about great whites the first time I saw Jaws as a kid," Caleb says. "I'll go with you guys. Ben and I are best suited to recon the boat. Assuming it's even there."

I'm grateful for the help. I run my eyes over the group, wanting to make sure we truly have everyone we need.

"Reed, suit up," I say. He's the fastest. I don't know what we're going to find out there, but there's always the chance we might need a sprinter. "Jesus, you, too." The man is a good shot.

That leaves Johnny, Lila, and Eric at home. Enough to keep an eye on Creekside until we get back. Ben is adamant about never leaving Creekside empty.

"Are we going to stand around and stare at each other, or are we going on a suicide mission?" Ben glowers. He has a rifle over his shoulder, a gun on either hip, and an ammo belt slung across his chest. I wish he didn't look so good.

"I'll finally get a chance to try this out." Ash grabs the first aid backpack she assembled a few months ago from our supply cache. She takes it on supply runs, but until now she's never had a real reason to use the things inside.

I move toward the weapons rack. The rest of the group mobilizes with me. I already have a knife and a screwdriver on my belt. I pick out one of the smaller handguns, a glock that I've been practicing with.

"Take one of the rifles," Ben says.

I shake my head. "I've never used one."

"Take it anyway. It could save your life."

"At the very least," Reed says cheerfully, "you can smash a zombie in the face with it."

"We all know Mamita is good at smashing things." Jesus touches the dent on his forehead. "Speaking of which, we should try out our new zom bats."

He grabs a box filled with modified baseball bats. The handles have been sheared short and the bottoms welded closed with the original ends. Jenna, Jesus, and Carter have been working hard to assemble these new weapons.

"What do you think?" Jesus hands me one of the zom bats.

"Nice." I give it an experimental swing. I can already tell it's going to be better than the regular baseball bat. The others show similar appreciation as they receive their new weapons.

"We could get rich selling these things on eBay," Carter says.

"Heck, yeah." Jenna grins at her boyfriend. "We could finally afford our own place and move out of this dump."

"Creekside is not a dump," I say loudly, right as Jesus says, "Don't forget who's the master with the soldering gun. Half those eBay profits are mine."

"One-third," Jenna counters. "Or I'll solder your hands together."

"Ouch." Jesus feigns wounded hands. "Carter, your woman is ruthless."

"I know." Carter slings an arm around Jenna. "It's hot, isn't it?"

"Okay, time to focus," I cut in. "We need to move out. There are people who need our help."

Ben blocks the door, preventing us from leaving the apartment. "We need to agree on a few things before we go out there."

I put my hands on my hips and face him, ready for whatever argument he has in store. "Such as?"

Ben jabs a finger in the general direction of the group. "When we find the boat—if we find the boat—everyone else stays in hiding until Caleb and I give the all clear. No matter what happens, you wait for our all clear."

I can't argue with this logic. "Agreed."

"Should we tell them we're coming?" Jenna asks.

Ben shakes his head. "No. If it is a trap, we don't want to alert them."

"If it's a real emergency, knowing help is on the way might give them the strength to hold on," Carter argues.

My son makes me proud, but in this case, I think Ben is right. "We don't alert them. We find them, recon, then decide our next steps."

Three minutes later, we're out the door and heading down Granite Avenue.

Running.

8

HORDE

BEN

Granite Avenue is the street that runs along the north side of campus where most of the college dorms are. Creekside is nestled at the very end of Granite Avenue among the towering redwoods of Northern California. To most people, it's a beautiful, picturesque road.

Ben hates it. It's the place that holds the culmination of the worst moments of his life. It's the place where he had been ordered to open fire on kids.

Kids.

Granted, some of them—a lot of them—had been infected. But a full-scale offensive on the college had been nothing more than mass murder.

That wasn't even the worst part. This had been the place where Ben disobeyed a direct order and went AWOL. He scooped up half a dozen students and hustled them to safety. Away from the gunfire, away from the infected.

Ben had never, *ever*, disobeyed a direct order from a commanding officer. Sure, there had been moments when he'd had to grit his teeth and mentally cuss someone out for a stupid order, but he always followed through. It's what a good soldier did. He'd always taken pride in being a good soldier. Of doing the right thing for his country, even when it was hard.

All that was shattered on this godforsaken road.

As he runs down it with Kate and the others on their fool-hardy mission, it takes all his focus not to fall back to that night of gunfire and madness.

Usually, he focuses on the swing of Kate's ponytail. It's a good anchor. Keeps his brain from spinning out of control.

Now that she'd gone and hacked her hair off—which looks damn good, even though he'd fucked up trying to tell her that —he isn't sure where to look. The natural thing to focus on is her ass in those skin-tight running pants. He's grateful she swapped out the tiny running shorts for the mission, though in truth they aren't much more protection. If any of the little shit-heads catch him looking, he'll never live it down. He settles for watching the sweat spot forming between her shoulder blades.

Granite Avenue, for its part, is indifferent to his PTSD bull-shit. The place had been akin to a Sandbox warzone a few months ago. Rotting corpses strewn across every conceivable surface. Feasting carrion birds. Maggots and flies everywhere. The smell of death had been inescapable.

Then Kate got it into her head that she wanted to clean up the neighborhood. She took them all to the campus green-house. Goddammit if they hadn't unearthed five wheelbarrows.

It had taken them weeks to cart away the bodies. Jenna was the one who came up with the idea to cut a hole in the fence separating the college from the freeway—and the twenty-foot drop to the once-busy road. After that, it was only a matter of collecting the bodies and dumping them over the side.

These days, Granite Avenue is stink-free, fly-free, maggot-free, and vulture-free. The same can't be said for the rest of the campus, but if Kate has anything to say about it, she'll have the entire campus cleared one day.

He loves that she thinks she can do it. That *they* can do it. Where everyone else sees death, she sees hope.

Ben keeps his focus on Kate's shoulder blades. Her sweat spot expands from a few dots to a large, lopsided circle about the size of a fist. He exhales in relief as they hit the main road and turn south. This street is sandwiched between the western perimeter of campus and the drop-off down to the freeway. The memories aren't so thick here.

They soon reach the vast wrought-iron fence that surrounds the athletic field where they come for target practice. The field most definitely is *not* fly- or vulture-free.

They leave campus and turn west across the bridge that takes them over the freeway and into downtown Arcata. He watches the others transform, muscles tensing and eyes scanning. They kill their fair share of zombies every time they make a trip into town, but there are always more to deal with.

As they crest the top of the overpass, Ben glances to the freeway below. It's a mess of cars and zombies, even more so since they started dumping bodies down there. He'd like to dump kerosene over the entire scene and drop a match to it.

"We should run south along the freeway," Jenna says as they exit the overpass. Her voice low so as not to attract any undead. "It's a straight shot to Humboldt Bay."

Kate nods. "Good idea. Everyone, stay alert."

Ben maintains his position at the back as Kate takes her position at the front. He doesn't trust anyone else to do a proper job of rear guard.

"Bro." Ahead of him, Jesus nudges Reed in the arm. "Remember this place?" He points to a small blue house they pass.

Reed smirks. "Totally. That's where we delivered the E."

"And scored ourselves an invite to a par-*tay*."

"That was some good E." Reed sighs.

"Those were some horny chicks," Jesus adds, nostalgic.

"Yeah, that too."

The conversation makes Ben want to bash their heads together. Everyone is out here putting their lives on the line, and all they can do is reminisce about fucking and doing drugs? Is it any wonder living around these kids makes him insane?

Something crashes with a hollow thud. It sounds like a trashcan just went over.

More than a dozen zombies shamble onto the street in front of them. They're a mere two blocks away. There are so many they clog the road, creating a solid barrier blocking their way. Soft moans pepper the air.

Not good.

Kate cuts away from the frontage road, turning right at a cross street. It's residential, lined with colorful bungalows and an auto repair shop. Several blocks ahead of them is a worn-out strip mall

Their fast jog turns into a run. Fluorescent orange running shoes might be the most despised thing he owns, but right now he's grateful for their quiet rubber soles.

Kate ducks behind the corner of the auto repair shop. They pile after her, all of them breathing hard.

Breathing hard, but not out of breath. There's a difference. They have Kate to thank for that.

Ben peers around the corner, looking back up the way they came. The first few zombies stagger into view. Hard on their heels are more. And more.

And more.

"*Follame*," Jesus mutters, squinting down the road beside Ben. He often defaults to Spanish when he's stressed.

"How many are there?" Carter whispers.

No one answers him. Ben stares, his eyes resting on the zom that stands in the center. It's a nondescript man in his forties, clothing torn and gray from long months of exposure. It wears

a baseball cap that was once bright red, but is now a dull
maroon.

It works its jaw, letting loose a series of keens and clicking
noises. The rest of the zombies swirl around it, heads cocked as
they listen. They click and keen in response.

A shiver travels down Ben's spine. He swings around, his
eyes meeting Kate's. "We have to get the fuck out of here. It's
another alpha zom." The name rolls off his tongue without
thought.

Kate's eyes widen. "Alpha zom?"

"Yeah, like the one we saw on campus the other day. The
kind that issues orders to the rest of the zombies. There's a good
two dozen of those fuckers around the alpha."

"*Follame,*" Jesus mutters again.

Kate leads them away from the herd, pushing hard through
town. They barrel past the strip mall, working their way deeper
into the streets and away from the pack.

They pass a few lone zombies, which are dispatched with
knives and screwdrivers. Kate sticks to the narrower streets and
alleyways. Ben spots a few other large clusters of zombies, but
Kate steers wide of them.

Fifteen minutes later, she draws to a halt on the side of a
warehouse building. They clump together without speaking,
everyone breathing hard.

"Evolution," Carter breathes. "They're evolving."

"Learning to communicate with one another." Kate bites
out the words.

Jenna rubs her arms, looking over her shoulder as if
expecting to find the pack there. "Do you think we lost them?"

"I think so." Jesus runs his thumb over the hilt of his gun.
"Unless they can track. Then we're fucked."

"We should scrap the rescue mission," Ben says. "Fall back
and regroup."

Kate shoots him an irritated look. "No such luck, soldier."

He tamps down the urge to list out all the reasons why this is a bad idea. If it's one thing he's learned about Kate, it's that she'll lay it all on the line to help people. Up until today, he thought that only applied to the residents of Creekside. Apparently, that extends to complete strangers in Arcata, too.

"Come on," Kate says. "It's not far. We should be able to see the bay as soon as we get past this row of warehouses."

Ben resigns himself to the mission. He might think it's idiotic, but there's no way in hell he'll turn his back on Kate.

9

ROAD CROSSING

KATE

The fastest way to reach Humboldt Bay is across Samoa Highway, a four-lane country highway. Until now, there hasn't been a reason for us to push this far south to the town's boundary. There are cars everywhere, most of them abandoned. Many have plowed across the narrow margin between the east- and west-bound lanes to crash into other cars.

The undead are everywhere. They meander in small circles, clogging up nearly every passable space between the vehicles.

This must be one of the routes people took when they fled in the early days of the outbreak. Then they zombified behind the wheel and everything went sideways.

"How are we going to get across the road?" Reed whispers.

I study the scene. On the other side of the highway are native grass fields that transition into marshland. The marshland rings Humboldt Bay.

I replay our run-ins with the alpha zombies, both here in town and back at the university. I can't write them off as isolated incidents, especially since Johnny has confirmation of it happening in other locations.

We could very well run into alphas on Samoa Highway. There are, quite literally, hundreds of zombies out here. If one or two of them step up as leader and get wind of us, we're fucked.

Stealth is the only way to get to the other side.

Fifty yards up the road is an abandoned semi. Its length spans two lanes before the front end pierces the muddy margin. Several cars have plowed into its side, effectively creating a barricade against zombies. I gesture, leading my people toward it.

"We go in groups of two," I whisper. "Under the semi and out the other side. No one make a sound. If there's another alpha out here ..." I leave the rest of that thought unspoken. By their expressions, they're as rattled by the alpha zombies as I am. "Everyone understand?"

I make eye contact with each person, waiting for nods. Unease crawls through me. Is this a mistake? Am I an idiot for risking my people to save two strangers?

Maybe. But there aren't all that many people left in the world. We need to help each other if we want to survive.

I can't help thinking about the houseful of soldiers I murdered a few months ago. *Hypocrite.* I'm stained by that action, even though I'd do it all over again to keep Carter and the others safe. Maybe I can diminish some of that stain by helping others—people who aren't sadistic, rapist, murdering assholes.

"Ash, with me," I say. "We're going first." I take my screwdriver in one hand and my new zom bat in the other.

Ben opens his mouth. I silence the argument on his face with a single shake of my head.

"You bring up the rear," I tell him. "Watch our backs."

He hesitates before nodding. "Prove me wrong out there."

I grunt. He wants me to prove this isn't a suicide mission? That makes two of us.

I steal to the edge of the roadway with Ash by my side, eyes darting left and right. She carries a military-issue knife in either hand. On a bad day, Ash looks like a poster child for CrossFit. On a good day, she looks like Xena's little sister.

Like now. Her eyes glow with inner ferocity. I don't envy the zombies that come up against her.

We slip between a narrow gap formed by two cars that collided with the semi. There are no bodies inside either of the vehicles, dead or undead, but the force of the impact left shattered glass all over the pavement.

Our running shoes crunch on the glass. The nearest undead is two hundred yards away. It's a thirty-something woman with long hair that had once been thick and lustrous. The months exposed to the elements have turned it grimy and lank.

It turns in our direction, nose scenting the air like an animal. We dart underneath the semi and pause. Shade blankets us. The smell of gasoline is strong. A breeze wafts in from the ocean, carrying with it the scent of saltwater and rot.

I scan the path on the far side of the semi. There's an undead wedged between the front bumpers of two collided cars. Both legs are crushed, leaving the undead man splayed on the hood of one car. White eyes roll in its head as it bobs back and forth under the summer sun.

"I'm going to stab the one on the hood," I whisper. Better to take it out so it doesn't alert any of its brethren. "Cover me."

Ash nods, knuckles tightening on her knives.

I dash forward, my blade outstretched. The zombie crushed between the cars stirs as my feet whisper over more crushed glass. I pour on a burst of speed and slam the knife into its ear.

Yanking it free, I keep moving. Ash comes up behind me, her eyes never ceasing their constant scan of our surroundings. We slip around the cars and into the margin.

The eastbound lane isn't as clear as the westbound. I search for a kink in the armor, but it's no use. There is no clear path from one side to the other. We're going to have to make a path.

I sense movement behind us. Turning, I see Reed and Jesus dart through the underbelly of the semi and sprint toward us.

"Ben sent us," Reed whispers. "He said you'd need help to clear a path."

Through the corridor beneath the semi, I see Ben crouched down and watching. I nod to him in thanks. His decision was a good one.

Jesus flips the knife in his hand. "Let's do this, Mamita." The guy is a pro with a blade. I've seen him target practice with the wooden benches on the inside of the track; he can sink his knife into them from twenty feet away.

"See that yellow car?" I point. They lean in to hear my words. "We cut left around it. Jesus and Reed, you two take the three zombies on the left. Ash and I will take the two on the right. That will leave an opening for the others. Remember, the priority is to minimize noise."

We sprint forward, heading for our respective targets. My new zom bat finds the forehead of a senior citizen zombie. The skull collapses with satisfying speed beneath the force of the small bat.

Ash, Reed, and Jesus fell their targets just as quickly. Jesus takes out the fifth one with a knife thrown expertly into the undead's forehead.

A thumping sound to my right makes me jump. I spin around in time to see Ash backing away from the yellow car. Inside, a woman beats her fists against the glass. Smears of blackish-red blood streak the window. The zombie lets up a keen that can be heard up and down the highway, even muffled as it is by the car.

All around, zombies turn in our direction.

Dammit!

Ash yanks on the door handle. The door is unlocked. The zombie inside tumbles out. I dart forward and whip my bat against the side of her head.

The four of us crouch in a small circle between the cars, not daring to move. All around us, the zombies moan and scent the air.

I hold up a hand, indicating everyone to stay where they are. Any sound we make could bring them on us in a rush. I watch those zombies nearest to us, looking for sign of another alpha.

The zombies shift and moan, shuffling about. None of them emit the combination of clicking and keening that seems to initiate an order.

I look back and see Carter, Jenna, and Caleb still crouched on the far side of the road, watching our progress through the gap beneath the semi. Ben is nowhere in sight. Shit. Where did he go?

A second later, I get my answer.

A car alarm goes off somewhere to the west. Every zombie whips toward the sound.

Ben. He's clearing a way for us.

I don't hesitate. I break into a sprint, peeling for the open grass on the far side of the eastbound lane. Reed, Jesus, and Ash run in a tight circle with me.

We hit the grass and keep running, putting as much distance between us and Samoa Highway as possible. Ben is still nowhere in sight. Carter, Jenna, and Caleb have already made it to the eastbound lane.

I draw up short as a pack of zombies lumbers in their direction. Their blindness will buy Carter and the others precious seconds, but not much more than that.

Jenna leads them forward in a blind sprint. After Reed, she's the fastest of our group. She's the first to break past the pack and reach us. Carter is right behind her.

Caleb brings up the rear, wielding his rifle like a club. A zombie lumbers in front of him, coming between Caleb and the rest of us.

The young man doesn't hesitate. He slams the butt of the rifle into the face of the zombie. Blood sprays. Caleb leaps over the body as it falls and sprints the rest of the way to us, leaving the rest of the pack behind.

"Where's Ben?" I hiss as he joins us. We huddle in a tight cluster five hundred yards from the highway. The car alarm still wails. Zombies bump and flounder their way through the tangle of cars, fighting to reach the noise.

I scan up and down the highway, my chest clenching. There is no sign of Ben anywhere.

"He left to set off the car alarm," Caleb whispers. "Don't worry, the guy is as tough as shoe leather. He'll make it."

Tough or not, it only takes one slip out here to get you killed. And with no one to watch his back, the danger only increases.

And what if there's an alpha out here? Dread settles on my shoulders. The thought of something happening to Ben makes me feel sick.

I scan the zombies amassing around the car alarm. They're in a frenzy, pushing and shoving one another in their desperation to get to the source of the noise. More zombies stream in every second.

If there is an alpha in that mess, it's impossible for me to pick it out. There are too many bodies crammed together.

Where the hell is Ben?

"There." Carter points off to our left. "He's okay."

I follow the line of Carter's hand. At first, I don't see anything except tall grass bent by the breeze.

Then I notice a shape low to the ground headed straight for us. It's Ben, army crawling his way through the grass. Dressed in his camo, I hadn't been able to pick him out. I start breathing again.

"Next time, I'm going to make him wear fluorescent orange," I mutter.

"Good luck with that," Ash replies. "Even before the end of the world, I doubt the guy even owned a regular pair of jeans."

10

MARSHLAND

BEN

Ben is proud of the years spent in service to his country. He'd spent his entire adult life fighting wars. Every tour had been someplace hot and dry.

Afghanistan. Pakistan. Iraq. Somalia.

If he'd been born two decades earlier, he'd have spent time in Vietnam like his old man. He remembers his father cursing the humidity and the swamps of the rice paddies.

Now, as he and the others follow Kate toward Humboldt Bay—ankle deep in murky marshland—Ben wishes he'd paid more attention to his old man when he talked about the rice paddies. No doubt his rants contained tidbits of info Ben might have found useful in his current marsh-filled situation.

"That's the *Fairhaven*." Caleb lowers a pair of binos, gesturing to a charter boat with a blue roof grounded half a mile east in the marsh grass.

"Fuck," Ben grumbles. "There is no good way to recon that thing."

Caleb gives him a tight look. "We're going to have to get muddy."

"No shit." Ben huffs out a breath and looks at Kate. "You still gonna to let us recon before going in?" He says this just in case she's thinking of changing the plan. Kate's been known to do that.

Like the time she said they only had to run for two hours. Which was fine, but when she realized it was going to be a hot day, she moved the workout to the middle of the day. She had some long explanation about the importance of heat training. He would never complain in front of her, but that had been one of the shittiest workouts ever. He'd taken several large bottles of water into his room that night to rehydrate, and his piss had still been dark yellow the next day.

He looks into her eyes, waiting for her nod. It's reluctant, but it comes.

Ben shifts his gaze to Carter and Jenna. "I don't suppose either of you were science majors? Anything useful you can tell us about the environment that could help us on the recon?"

Jenna grimaces. "Sorry. Art and business major."

Carter adds his grimace to Jenna's. "I took a general science class that focused on local ecosystems. All I remember is that Humboldt Bay is responsible for more than half of the United State's oyster production."

The fact doesn't do shit for their current situation, but he files it away for later. Oysters may be a reliable food source for them at some point, especially if they can ever get Arcata cleared to the point that travel isn't so treacherous. Shit, he'd just love to get to the point where they could ride bikes instead of going everywhere on foot.

"Wait here until we give the all-clear." Ben adjusts his rifle and drops into a crouch.

Caleb joins him. Ben would rather have anyone else with him on this mission, but Caleb is the most qualified. He resigns himself to running side by side with the younger, stronger man.

Cold water sloshes around their ankles, soaking them up to the knees within seconds.

A hostile truce hangs between him and Caleb. They co-exist by avoiding and ignoring one another.

When they're a quarter mile away from the charter boat, Ben drops to all fours. His elbows sink into mushy mud. Water laps across his torso, soaking his clothing.

All this to save a man supposedly stupid enough to get himself attacked by a shark.

"Do you think it's a trap?" Caleb whispers to him, dropping into the water beside him.

"Yep." He said as much in the beginning.

"You're just doing this for Kate?"

Ben doesn't answer. There's something about that question that feels like a trap.

"For what it's worth," Caleb says, "I think she might like you."

Ben draws up short, momentarily frozen by the younger man's words. Caleb arches an elegant dark brow at him in silent question.

Ben snarls and turns away, refocusing on the charter boat. He can't afford to be distracted right now.

What did Caleb mean by that statement, anyway? Ben knows what it means in the junior high sense, but he isn't sure what it means with Kate. Most days they barely speak.

Charter boat, he reminds himself. *Focus on the charter boat.*

Fifty yards from the boat, he and Caleb draw to a halt. His body is already chilled from contact with the marsh water. From this distance, he can see the name *Fairhaven* scrawled across the side of the boat.

Caleb lifts the binos and studies the boat. After a few minutes, he passes them to Ben.

Ben has to prop both elbows in the water to hold the binos in place. There is no movement on the *Fairhaven*.

"Blood," Ben murmurs. There's a big smear of it on the side of the ship and part of the railing.

"From the guy who was attacked by the shark?" Caleb asks.

"Or the last idiots stupid enough to '*help*'."

Caleb lets out a huff. "You always assume the worst about people. Not everyone is out for blood. I'm going to circle around the *Fairhaven*. Be back in five."

Ben glares as the other man slips away. "Paranoia will keep you alive, motherfucker," he growls under his breath, too soft for Caleb to hear. Paranoia had kept his team from blundering straight into a landmine field in Pakistan. Paranoia had kept his men out of a house rigged to blow in Afghanistan.

Caleb is young and stupid. He'll learn. He'll learn, or he'll die. Ben doesn't give a shit either way.

He keeps the binos in place, watching the ship. He tenses as a tanned woman with a messy red bun comes up on deck. Her face is drawn, her eyes exhausted. Blood is smeared on her cheek and neck. When she brings up a hand to brush errant strands of hair from her face, he spots more dried blood on her fingers and forearms.

Ben studies her face. He expects to see the eyes of a woman who's set a cunning trap for softhearted idiots. Instead, he sees a woman who looks like she's going to collapse from exhaustion. As he watches, she buries her face in both hands, shoulders shaking with sobs.

Dammit. Maybe her husband really was attacked by a shark. Maybe she really is as desperate as she'd sounded on the ham.

Caleb returns a few minutes later, crawling up beside him. Even the mud splashed on his face can't diminish his pretty boy features.

"I saw the woman," Ben says.

"Me, too. I think her message was real. I think she needs help."

Grudgingly, Ben nods his head in agreement. "We go in together. Make sure it's all clear before signaling the others."

Caleb doesn't argue. He and Ben rise out of the marsh, lifting rifles to their shoulders as they advance on the *Fairhaven*. They make just enough noise to alert anyone on the boat paying attention. They don't want to board the *Fairhaven* in stealth mode and give the woman a heart attack. Or worse, scare her badly enough that she shoots at them.

Their splashing pays off. Her feet echo on the deck as she rushes to the starboard railing. She lets out a cry of joy at the sight of them.

Ben's not sure what he thinks of a woman crying in joy at the sight of two men pointing rifles in her direction. Women make no sense. At least, not to him.

"I need help," she cries. "My husband, he—"

"We received your distress call, ma'am," Caleb says.

The young woman practically melts at Caleb's words. "You're here to help?" she asks.

"Yes, ma'am."

She stares at them, her mouth hanging open. Tears stream down her face as she drops a rope ladder over the side of the vessel, no questions asked.

Ben trades his rifle for his handgun, making sure the woman sees the weapon. She does. And she shows no fear or trepidation. Either she's stupid or desperate. Maybe both.

On board the ship, Ben spots more blood. Big smears of it that could only come from a severe wound.

"My husband is in the hold. Do either of you have first aid or medic skills?" She wrings her hands together.

"Ma'am, we need to assess your husband." Caleb's voice is strong and reassuring.

She flashes him a grateful smile and hurries first into the hold.

They follow her down. The smell of blood hits Ben. The metallic stench of it is strong in the small, dark space.

On the starboard side is a small table for two, a tiny sink, and counter for food prep. On the port side is a bunk and a tiny bathroom.

On the lower bunk is an unconscious man. His legs are wrapped in bloody clothing. Wads of bloody bandages and towels are piled in one corner. It looks like the woman used every scrap of fabric in this place to staunch the bleeding.

The man is in bad shape. Real bad shape. There is no deceit here, only miserable desperation. He finally understands why Kate made them come.

Ben turns on his heel, heading back to the deck.

"Where are you going?" the woman asks, voice heavy with desperation.

"To get reinforcements. We have a trained medic with us."

The sob of relief that tears from her throat follows him upstairs.

11

FAIRHAVEN

KATE

The woman's name is Susan. Her husband is Gary. The two of them are high school sweethearts who grew up in Eureka, the aging crown jewel of the logging era of Northern California. The city is ten miles south of Arcata. They graduated from Humboldt University and took out a loan to buy their charter boat. They've spent the last eight years catering to the tourist industry: deep-sea fishing, kayaking, diving, and whale watching.

"We've been living at sea since the beginning," Susan tells us, eyes glassy as she watches Ash tend to Gary's leg.

The man looks like he was fed to a paper shredder. It's hard to believe he's still alive.

"We came into the bay to siphon gas from other boats," Susan tells us. "There were bodies floating in the water but we didn't think much of it. They were real dead bodies, not zombies, so we didn't worry. Gary climbed out on the rope ladder to pull us in close to another boat. He was in the water up to his knees." She swallows, wiping tears with the back of her hand. "It all happened so fast. I saw something big moving through the water." She gives a shaky laugh. "Have you ever seen a great white in the wild?"

We all shake our heads. Jenna pulls a bottle of water from her backpack and passes it to Susan.

"The one who attacked Gary was bigger than any I've ever seen. Like a small car. He came out of the water so fast. I was standing there with Gary. I grabbed his arm. We both went down, but I had my feet wedged against the inside of the boat." Her eyes glow with exhausted ferocity. "No way in hell was I letting go of my husband." She takes several gulps of the water from Jenna. "It all happened in less than thirty seconds. The shark swam away and I pulled Gary to safety."

Susan wraps her arms around her knees. "That was yesterday. I bandaged him up as best I could. We're low on fuel but I was too afraid to try and get more by myself. From all the reports we'd heard, Eureka is overrun with zombies. I figured Arcata was my best chance at finding help. Besides, it was the only place I could get to with the fuel we had. So here we are." Her laugh is shaky, tinged with the trauma of her experience.

Jenna makes a soft sound of sympathy in the back of her throat, kneeling down to put an arm around Susan. The other woman leans into her embrace, but her eyes travel to the bunk bed.

"Is he going to make it?" she whispers.

Ash doesn't look up from where she stitches one of the nasty tears in Gary's leg. "I'm going to do my best, ma'am. Once I get him sewn up, we need to get him back to Creekside."

I'd known there was a high probability we'd have to transport an unconscious man through Arcata all the way back to Creekside. Which is why I brought such a large party of strong young men. But I hadn't factored in the danger of the alphas.

"Bro, remember that time Jason got shot in that drive-by on Seventeenth?" Jesus asks.

Reed lets out a long whistle. "That sucked. Our car was, like, ten blocks away."

"But remember when we stole those shovels out of that shed and made a stretcher?"

Reed's eyebrows fly up. "Yeah."

The two of them turn to Susan. "What do you have around here that can be made in to a stretcher?" Reed asks.

Thirty minutes later, we have a makeshift stretcher cobbled together from boat railing and rope.

"Who would have thought first-hand experience in a drive-by shooting just might save the life of a man attacked by a shark in a zombie apocalypse?" Carter says as Reed and Jesus take the stretcher into the hold to retrieve Gary.

"Johnny is going to have a field day with this," I reply.

"He's going to be pissed he didn't get to come," Jenna says.

Most likely. Johnny is always up for an outing when he thinks he has a chance to experience something exciting enough to go into the book he's writing. *Books*, actually. He's writing at least two about the apocalypse, maybe three. It's hard to keep track.

I stand at the railing of the *Fairhaven*, staring back in the direction of Arcata. "We can't go back the way we came." In my mind's eye, I keep seeing the swarm of zombies we encountered with the alpha in its midst. "The risk is too great. We won't be able to run fast with the stretcher. We could lose Gary if we get ourselves into a position where we have to sprint."

We could lose Gary anyway, though I keep this to myself. I'm going to do everything I can to get him safely back to Creekside.

"You think we should head west and go the long way around?" Carter asks.

"No." I shake my head. "The stretcher is heavy. The shorter the distance we have to travel, the better. I think we need to try and get across Highway 101." I try not to flinch as I say those words. "It's a straight shot back to campus once we're on the other side of the freeway."

Jenna and Carter look at each other, then at me. Neither of them says a word.

"It's risky," I admit.

Carter heaves a sigh. "We just made it across Samoa Highway. We're practically lane jumping pros now." Despite his attempt at levity, it falls flat. The seriousness of our situation has us all on edge.

"Ben's car alarm trick was a good one," Jenna says. "He went for one of the shinier, newer cars to make sure it had one. We can do the same thing to get across 101. It's a solid tactic."

I resist the urge to wring my hands. I can't let my kids see how worried I am about this mission. It was my idea to come out here to help Gary and Susan in the first place.

Jesus and Reed bring the stretcher out of the hold, Gary's slack body secured in place with ropes.

Seeing Susan's pinched, exhausted face, I know we did the right thing. Good people are worth fighting for.

Once everyone is assembled on the upper deck, I say, "I have a plan for getting back to Creekside."

As I lay out the details, I watch Ben's mouth twist into a grimace. To my surprise, he doesn't insult the idea or even argue. Rather, he stomps to the side of the boat and climbs over the edge.

"We're burning daylight," he calls. "Let's get moving. I'm pretty sure none of us wants to cross 101 in the dark."

No one has anything to say to that. We gather our belongings and exit the boat. As I swing down onto the rope ladder, Susan lightly brushes my hand.

"Thank you," she whispers. "I know how much you all risked coming here to help us."

I give her what I hope is a reassuring smile, even though my stomach is already lumpy with anxiety over the mission. "Good people need to help one another," I reply. "It's the only way we're going to survive."

And even though I truly believe that, I wish helping good people wasn't so damn scary and dangerous.

12

HIGHWAY 101

BEN

If there's a crazy idea to be had, Kate's going to find it. It's that simple.

Not only did she propose they cross over Highway 101—the goddamn, motherfucking road of death—but she logically pointed out that the best way to get to it was to hike all the way through the marshland and bypass the southern part of Arcata all together.

Ben tries to imagine his old man fighting the Viet Cong. He often carries thoughts of his dad with him on missions. It helps him when things get hard and uncomfortable. He tells himself that if his old man could survive the paddies of Vietnam, he can survive the marshland of Arcata.

The one thing going for the chill, sticky mud he currently tromps through—in his neon running shoes—is that it was uninhabited by people before the apocalypse. The powers that be had set this land aside for birds and fish. And oysters, according to Carter. All that means there are no zombies to contend with out here.

But fucking shit, there are few things in life he hates more than wet shoes, wet socks, and wet feet. The one thing he detests even more than all that is shoes, socks, and feet that are wet *and* muddy. He'd had athlete's foot more times than he could count during his years in the service. That shit itches, stings, and burns to high hell.

"Ben, your turn." Kate indicates the stretcher.

Ben takes the front end from Ash, waiting as Jenna swaps out with Carter. They resume their sloshing through the marsh.

From the angle of the sun, he judges it to be around four in the afternoon. It doesn't get dark until nearly eight o'clock this time of year. They still have ample time to make it back to Creekside in the daylight. If things don't get fucked up between now and then. That's one really big *if*, in his opinion.

He glances back at the unconscious Gary once or twice as he huffs along with the stretcher. Poor bastard. Fucking great white. That was just as bad as getting bitten by a zombie.

His wet shirt and pants stick to his skin. The breeze from the bay chills the fabric. He supposes it's better than being too hot, but all it does is reinforce how much he hates marching through marshland.

Susan hovers beside her husband's unconscious body, her hand reaching out at regular intervals to touch his hand, his arm, or his face. Ben wonders what it would be like to have someone to care about like that. He's never had a relationship longer than a few months. Even his son's mother had only been a fling between tours.

"Is it me, or is the water getting deeper?" Ash asks.

"We're in the Brackish Pond," Carter replies.

"I can see that," Ash says, sarcasm thick in her voice.

"No, he means it's called the Brackish Pond," Jenna replies. "It's part of the protected marshland."

"There's high ground over there." Kate points to a levee. "Let's get out of the water."

Ben seconds this notion by picking up the pace. Caleb and

Ash push past him, rifles up as they scan the area for threats. They signal the all-clear.

Ben climbs the embankment, walking backward to handle the stretcher. Water streams off his fatigues in heavy rivulets. Once up on the levee, he and Carter relinquish Gary and the stretcher to Reed and Jesus.

"I want to go ahead of the group and scout the freeway," Ben says to Kate.

"Good idea," she replies. "I'll go with you."

He opens his mouth, ready to insist she stay with the group. Except that Kate is a fan of the buddy system. If he pushes her off, she'll just saddle him with someone else. Just his luck, it would be Caleb. He'd take Kate's company over the pretty boy anytime. Besides, hasn't he spent the last few weeks trying to work out a way to talk to her without any of the little shitheads around? This is his chance.

"Let's move out," he says to Kate.

"Make your way to the recycling center on G Street," Kate tells the rest of the group. "Ben and I will circle back and meet you there after we check out 101."

A small thrill goes through him as he sets out on foot with her. He lets Kate set the brisk jog, falling into step beside her. They move faster on their own without the stretcher and soon leave the others behind. He keeps his rifle at hand, ready to bring it up at a second's notice.

"Am I going to have to start making us work out on the track with rifles on our backs?" Kate asks softly. Her feet barely make a sound on the hard-packed dirt of the levee.

"In boot camp, we trained in full gear. You have us running with packs. Adding rifles isn't a bad idea."

"I just worry we could end up shooting one another on accident."

"The rifles don't have to be loaded."

"I mean when we're not training. If we're actually running with loaded weapons."

"You prefer your knife and screwdriver. Or Jesus's zom bat." His eyes flick to the silver club in her hand that's currently stained with zombie gore.

"Yeah, I do."

He wracks his brain, trying to think of something to say to keep the conversation going. He doesn't want to squander this rare opportunity to talk to her.

His mind flashes to her strange bedroom, a single dorm once occupied by a Grateful Dead fan. Posters still cover the wall and ceiling. Concert tickets are tacked over the headboard. Ben once even glimpsed clothing that belonged to the previous owner still hanging in the closet.

There was very little about the room that spoke of Kate, but Ben had noticed a rusty railroad spike sitting on the windowsill. It was the only thing in the small space that didn't reek of stoner college kid.

Maybe it was the bits of dried blood stuck to it, along with the dirt and grime. Maybe it was the way it seemed to have a place of honor in the room, perched all alone in the middle of the windowsill. Whatever the reason, when he first laid eyes on the spike, he'd known it was Kate's.

"What about that railroad spike?" he asks.

Kate looks at him sharply. "What do you mean?"

"The railroad spike on your windowsill. Why don't you carry that? It's as good as the screwdriver. Better. You don't have to worry about it snapping in half."

Her face closes down in a way he's never seen before. She grunts and picks up the pace.

Ben has never been great with people, but he's smart enough to know he just said the wrong thing. *Dammit.* He resolves not to speak until she does.

So it is that they continue to run in silence.

The longer the silence stretches, the more he agonizes over his words. Why did he ask about the railroad spike? Couldn't he have led with something more benign?

He's terrible at this stuff. All the normal small talk he'd used before the apocalypse doesn't apply to the current situation.

Where do you live?

What do you do for a living?

Come here often?

Can I buy you a drink?

This is the extent of his skills at making conversation.

Is it any wonder he's a bachelor?

"We're almost there," Kate says, breaking the silence.

"Sorry if I upset you." The words come out all by themselves. "Asking about the railroad spike, I mean."

She shakes her head, blowing out a long breath. "You didn't do anything wrong. I just don't like talking about it."

Now *that* is something he can understand. There are plenty of things he's seen and done that he has no desire to think about, let alone speak about.

"I won't bring it up again."

She gives him a small smile, making him think that maybe he's just said the right thing.

Now if only he could do that more than one time in a row.

"There's the recycling center," Kate says, pointing. "101 is just on the other side."

Technically, 101 isn't "just on the other side" of the recycling center. Ben refrains from pointing out that another quarter-mile of open marshland lays between the recycling center and the road. The only good thing is that they have a clear view of the freeway from the front of the building.

101 is a cluster fuck. No way to sugarcoat the mess of cars and undead tangled on the freeway.

"At least we don't have to worry about scrambling down a

twenty-foot embankment to get to the freeway," Kate says. This part of the 101 is level with the land around it.

"That's a shitload of undead down there," Ben says. "We're going to have to set off at least two car alarms if we want to get across that mess without getting killed."

She nods in agreement. "Let's go in closer for a better look."

They cross the two-lane road that services the recycling center, stepping into the open marshland on the other side. The land starts as hard-packed mud before sloping down into cold water once again.

"Loving the hike through the marsh?" Kate murmurs, looking at him out of the corner of her eye.

He's pretty sure that's sarcasm. He proceeds cautiously just in case. "I used to get athlete's foot in the Sandbox. I don't like having wet feet."

She turns, looking him full in the face with a frown. "The sandbox?"

"Iraq. Kuwait. The Middle East. You know, hot places with lots of sand?" He feels like an idiot for using military slang.

"Oh." Her eyebrows lift in surprise. "Where else have you served?"

"Afghanistan. Somalia. Pakistan. A short stint in Ecuador." He looks away, not sure how to meet her direct gaze. "I enlisted when I was eighteen. Served right up until the night they ordered me to kill college kids."

Silence drops between them like a wet blanket.

Fuck. Why did he have to bring that up?

"I went AWOL that night," he tries to explain. "I saw a group of scared kids. I got them out of the hot zone. Took them to College Creek dorm. Tried to protect them and keep them alive . . ." His mouth goes dry as he remembers the massacre spearheaded by Johnson and Ryan. He'd saved Ryan, that little fucker.

Kate gives him a sad look. He doesn't know what else to say, so he keeps his mouth shut.

One hundred yards away from the freeway, they stop. Ben pulls out the binos and sweeps them up and down the scene.

Fuck. It looks even worse up close.

"I see two fancy SUVs," he says. "They're close to each other and should both have car alarms. That's the good news."

"And the bad news?" Kate asks. He senses her tense beside him, bracing herself for the other shoe.

Unfortunately, he has more than one shoe to drop. "There are hundreds of undead out there. And the cars are a mess. There's no obvious egress."

They continue forward. The water forces them to move slowly lest they make any noise to alert the undead. At least they don't have to crawl on all fours through the cold sludge currently sloshing around their ankles. There are occasional perks to dealing with blind zombies.

Kate has a light step, the water making the barest ripple around her feet. He realizes he's looking at her legs again and returns his attention to the mess of cars. Getting distracted by a nice pair of legs is a good way to end up dead. He won't think about how good the whole GI Jane look is on her.

"There's a thing in ultrarunning known as a road crossing," Kate says. "Most ultras are run on dirt trails, but sometimes we have to cross roads to get from one part of a trail to another. Those are road crossings." She doesn't look at him when she speaks, her gaze focused on the freeway.

Even so, Ben gets the sense that she's sharing something with him. He stays quiet, willing her to continue.

"I ran a fifty-miler in Oakland in a park called Lake Chabot," Kate continues. "There's a gun range in the park. A bunch of gunfire went off and startled us as we crossed one of the roads. I tripped in a pothole and scraped the hell out of my knees, elbows, and palms on the pavement. I was so pissed."

Her lips pull back in a thin smile, though she still has yet to look at him. "I groused about road crossings for years after that. It feels stupid now when compared to this. Who ever thought I'd make a road crossing with zombies?" Her gesture takes in the long ribbon of asphalt cluttered with the dead and undead.

He knows he should respond. She's sharing something with him. He's supposed to say something, but damned if he knows what.

The seconds drag, becoming awkward. He's blowing it. Completely fucking blowing it.

"I went into a pothole once," he says, grabbing at the first thing that comes to mind. "In a jeep in Iraq. We broke an axel. Had to hoof it all the way back to camp through a hot zone. Had a shootout with some hostiles halfway home."

The memory washes over him with hot poignancy. He feels the bitch-hot breath of the sun burning the back of his neck and sucking moisture from his body. He remembers the fear that rode his shoulders even as he tried to ignore it and focus on the mission of surviving. It hits him so hard he stops mid-step, eyes going hazy at the memory. He'd lost two friends on that shitty day under that shitty sun.

"What happened?"

Kate's voice snaps him back into the present. He recalls he's having a conversation with her. Or at least, attempting a conversation.

He forces himself to meet her eye. "We lost two of our own in the shootout." He swallows, his spine hardening. "But we got those motherfuckers. And we got the bodies of our friends back to camp so they could go back to their families."

She stares at him, eyes wide. "I thought my running stories were messed up."

He barks a laugh. It flushes away some of the turmoil.

"I like your running stories. I'd rather hear about you eating it on a road crossing than talk about my shit."

Her eyes widen even more. "Really?"

He blinks. Now he's supposed to respond. Again. He's never liked talking about himself. But if he wants to get to know Kate, he can't do it by just staring at her and grunting. Even if that's his preference to meaningful conversation.

"Yeah. I like your running stuff." It's the best he can come up with. At least it's true.

Something catches in his peripheral vision. He turns, their conversation sidelined.

"Right there." He lifts a finger to point at two blue sedans that collided head-on in the margin between north and south-bound lanes. "That's our best way through."

A dent creases her brow. "I don't see how ... oh. You mean just to the left of that Dodge Caravan?"

"Exactly." He lifts the binos and inspects the scene. "There's a good six-foot gap between the Caravan and the back bumper of the blue Charger. Our people will fit through there. All we have to do is clear it out."

Kate flashes him a big smile. The first since they set out together. He blinks, taken aback.

"What?" he asks.

"You said 'our people'."

"Well, yeah," he answers. "Isn't that what they are?"

"That's what they are to me." Her smile deepens. "It's nice to hear you feel the same way. Come on, let's go get the others."

13

THE DODGE GAP

KATE

I'd rather hear about you eating it on a road crossing than talk about my shit.

Ben's words repeat in my mind. I think, in his own weird way, that may have been his way of saying something nice. Hearing him talk about his experience in Iraq had been both chilling and heartwarming. Chilling, because the experience sounded awful. But also heartwarming, because it was clear the memory caused him pain and he shared it with me anyway.

Knowing how hard it is for me to talk about Frederico—let alone even think about him most days—Ben's loss makes me appreciate his openness on a deeper level.

As I stand ankle-deep in chilly water, surrounded by my kids, Susan, and Gary on the stretcher, I push my thoughts away from Ben. I think about him too much as it is. I need my head in the game if I'm going to get everyone across the 101 to safety.

"It's the Dodge Gap," Reed says as he surveys the six feet of space we've chosen for our group to maneuver through.

"Tell that to Johnny," Jesus replies. "He can use it in his book."

"Quiet." I cut off Reed as he opens his mouth to reply. "Your job is to get the stretcher as close as you can to the gap between the blue Caravan and the blue Charger. Ben and I are going to set off the car alarms on two SUVs a quarter mile down the road. That should be enough to draw them out of the gap. When it clears, make a run for it. Ben and I will catch up. Everyone understand?"

Carter raises his hand. "I understand everything except the part about you and Ben risking your lives a quarter mile away from our opening."

"Nothing to be done about it," Ben cuts in. "This is the best way to draw them away from the opening."

"Your job is to get Gary and Susan back to Creekside," I tell Carter. "Understand?"

Susan wrings her hands, eyes flicking between Gary's prone form and the SUVs Ben and I targeted for the distraction. "You guys are helping us. I should be the one to set off the car alarm."

We can't stand here all day arguing the finer points of this plan. I decide it's time to pull out my trump card: my mom voice.

"This is not up for discussion." I sweep a firm gaze across the group and give them my best no-nonsense mom look. "You all know what you're supposed to do. Stick together. Watch one another's back. Get our new friends back to Creekside. Ben and I will be right behind you."

As if to back me up, Ben brings up his rifle. Without waiting for any more argument, we break away from the group

"I like how you do that," he murmurs as we make our way to the SUVs.

"Do what?" I eye a clump of undead that cluster near the side of the road. There are so many of them.

"That mom whoop-ass thing you do." Ben chuckles without sound, his chest and shoulders shaking with silent humor. "You're like a drill sergeant, only with kindergarten kids instead of adolescent recruits."

I wrinkle my nose in good humor. "I hope you're the only one who's onto me."

"No, they're all onto you," he replies. "They're all just so damn loyal they put up with it. They know when you mean business and when they can wheedle you."

"They do *not* wheedle me."

"Sometimes they do. Like when we had sleep deprivation training two weeks ago and you let Johnny talk you into giving out caffeine pills to everyone."

"Caffeine pills are bona fide ultrarunning fare," I argue. "They've gotten me through more than one hundred-miler. It's good for them to know how their bodies feel with the extra kick."

Ben raises an eyebrow at me. I huff again in annoyance. I was *not* wheedled. I am immune to wheedling.

"This is a good spot." Ben draws to a halt.

Separating us from the two SUVs is fifty yards of open marshland. It's a straight shot for Ben. We discussed the option of blowing out the car's windows from a farther distance—preferably closer to the Dodge Gap, as Reed aptly named it—but in the end, decided it was better to shoot closer to the SUVs. That will narrow the focus area for the zombies, which will be especially important if there are any alphas out here.

"Try shooting out a tire or two after you hit the windows," I say. "The deflation will make extra noise as the car shifts."

"Good plan."

The rifle cracks. A glass window explodes on the first SUV. The car alarm lets up a pulsating wail that rushes up and down the length of 101.

The reaction is instantaneous. Every zombie in site snaps around, pivoting toward the SUV.

Ben fires two more times, hitting the tires. Then he fires at the second SUV three car lengths down, just as we planned.

A nearby zombie raises its nose to the sky. It lets up a long keen. The sound dies away, but it continues to work its jaws. In my mind, I hear clicks rolling off its tongue. Based on the way other zombies gravitate toward it, I suspect it to be an alpha. Hopefully, the noise of the car alarms will be enough to distract them from us.

More zombies take up the keen, the sound traveling up and down the highway. They move, arms outstretched as they fumble their blind way forward. They crash into cars, trip over bodies and debris, but inexorably streamline toward the two wailing cars. I lose sight of the alpha in the churning horde.

Ben and I hustle back to the Dodge Gap. With the noise of the car alarms, we don't have to worry about the little bit of noise we make. The splash of the water is lost in the rest of the racket.

I squint into the late afternoon sun, relieved to see my kids hurrying toward the gap. The zombies have scattered, leaving a wide corridor for them to slip through.

Their opening won't last long, though. Another group of zombies from farther north lumbers in the direction of the car alarms; they'll reach the Dodge Gap in a matter of minutes. Carter and the others will have to move fast to get safely to the other side.

Reed and Carter carry the stretcher with Gary. The rest of the group fans around them, weapons raised as they inch onto the blacktop.

Then something happens. Everything is too far away for me to see, but a new sound erupts.

It's a third car alarm.

And it's sounding right where all my kids are.

"Fuck me," Ben growls. "A goddamn zom caught on the hood of that white Avenger."

My gaze shifts as we pick up speed. A zombie bangs on the front hood of the Avenger, its pant leg caught in the crumpled metal. The Avenger is no more than twenty yards from the Dodge Gap.

My heart rises into my throat as dozens of undead whip toward this new sound, drawn like flies to shit.

"Fuck-fuck-fuck!"

I break into a sprint, not caring that I make a shit ton of noise and splash water all the way up to my face. Ben races beside me.

My kids, realizing the sudden danger they're in, race into the gap between the Caravan and the Charger.

Carter is the first one through. The rest of the kids pour in after him. I lose sight of them as they charge into the narrow gauntlet.

Ben and I are 150 yards from the Dodge Gap. My breath burns, but I embrace it.

One-hundred yards. I run as hard as I ever have, desperate to reach my family and keep them safe.

Fifty yards and closing. We're almost there, almost there—

Over a dozen zombies find their way into the gap, clogging it with their rotting bodies and surging after my kids.

"No!" The cry rips from my throat, drowned out by the three wailing car alarms.

Ben doesn't hesitate. He brings his rifle up and starts firing into the mass, dropping them with headshots.

I've seen him shoot often enough during the last few months, but until this moment I didn't realize he's a *great* shot.

The mass of zombies is churning. He's fifty yards away and moving, yet hitting them like they're sitting still and he's five feet away. The sight of his cold precision sends a chill through me.

The zombies go down, their bodies piling up in the gap. I keep running as Ben shoots. Heads bob on the other side. I see Jenna's light hair, the gleam of Jesus's leather jacket, the dark flash of Ash's hair, and then a familiar, beloved face with shaggy hair. Carter.

He waves to me over the cars, gesturing for me to hurry. I watch in horror as he, too, draws a gun, clearly preparing to try and shoot an opening for me and Ben.

I shake my head and wave my arms, mouthing *NO* over and over even as I keep running. He needs to get the hell out of there, not waste precious seconds on me. Not risk himself by firing a weapon and drawing the attention of zombies.

To my relief, Carter seems to understand my message. He holsters the gun. Jenna latches onto him and they disappear from sight.

"Kate." Ben grabs my wrist, dragging me back. "Kate, we can't go that way."

He's right. More zombies have swarmed into the Dodge Gap, sealing off any hope we had of following the others.

Fucking would-be silencers that aren't really silent. On top of not being able to follow the Creekside crew, a small group of zoms is drawn by Ben's gunshots. They peel away from the road and head straight for us.

14

FIVE LEAF

KATE

"We gotta go." Ben grabs my forearm. "Move."

I home in on the ten zombies stumbling toward us. With nothing but open marshland between us, there isn't a lot to slow them down.

And one of them is keening and clicking, drawing the attention of its brethren. It's a plump woman in sweatpants and a visor.

The rest of the zombies cluster tight around the visor zom, heads turned toward it as they await instruction. More zombies peel away from the freeway, drawn by the call.

My first thought is to tell Ben to shoot the alpha, but there isn't a clear shot. There are too many zombies around the alpha with more coming. There isn't time—or bullets—to gun down the growing pack.

CarterReedJennaJesusCalebAsh. Their names flash through my brain.

"Kate." Ben's breath is warm against my ear, his voice urgent.

An ache in my throat, I turn and run. I can't care about the noise I make. Right now, it's more important to be fast than it is to be silent.

Ben races beside me. "We should head—"

He never finishes. His foot catches in the mud. Ben does a somersault, spinning in mid-air before landing hard on his back with a splash.

I spin around, weapons raised as the zombies surge toward us. The alpha keeps up a constant stream of clicks and keens, spreading out the pack in a wide line. It's a fucking zombie dragnet.

The group has swelled to at least twenty. I see two trip and fall but they get up just as quickly, hardly breaking stride in their desperation to reach us.

Ben, on the other hand, isn't getting up so quickly. He groans, levering himself up out of the water.

"Can you run?" I ask, not taking my eyes from the fast-approaching zombies. Fifty feet and closing. "What happened?"

"Cut myself on something," he grunts. "I'm fine. Let's go."

He's definitely not fine. Red seeps across his back, mixing with the mud and water. But his jaw is tense and eyes sharp with focus.

I know that look. I'd seen it in Frederico's eyes at ultras. Ben isn't going to quit. He might hurt, but he's not going down without a fight.

I match my pace to his, which has leveled off as a fast lope. It's not the sprint I want, but we're moving fast enough to pull ahead of the zombies.

The frontage road looms before us. The recycling center stares at us with its dead windows and chain-link fence. Ben and I exit the marshland, returning to the asphalt road. No longer hindered by uneven terrain and muddy water, we're able to pick up the pace.

Ben drips blood and water. It leaves a murky red line

behind us on the blacktop. His movements are stiff, telling me he's in pain. We need a place to hide.

Two blocks up, I spot a familiar building. Five Leaf Brewery. Carter and I came here many times for dinner and live music.

"The brewery." I hold up a finger and point to the red sign with a white maple leaf in the middle. Over the leaf in black letters are the words *Five Leaf Brewery*. "We're going there."

Ben grunts, which I take as a sign of agreement. We hustle toward it.

Behind us, the zombies sniff the air. The mud and wet on our clothing likely masks much of our scent, including that of Ben's blood. The commotion of the 101 drowns out most of our footsteps, making it difficult for them to track us now that we're not splashing through water. We pull farther away from them.

As we reach the brewery, Ben puts a hand on the side of the building to steady himself.

I try the door. Locked. *Fuck.*

I drop my pack and snatch off my shirt, leaving my torso exposed except for my sports bra. I wrap the shirt around a decorative river rock taken from a flower pot beside the door. Winding up my arm, I smash the shirt-covered rock through the glass.

Seconds later, we're inside the dark recess of the brewery. The familiar smell of hops washes through my nostrils, making it impossible for me not to think of Carter and Jenna.

They're safe, I tell myself. *They have each other. They're going to be all right.*

I can't let myself think anything else. Not if I want to keep the panic in my chest from taking over. Not if I want to keep myself alive and take care of Ben.

He and I fall shoulder to shoulder, stopping just inside Five Leaf. I close and lock the door behind us.

The inside of the brewery wasn't immune to the zombie apocalypse. Between the red vinyl booths are several decomposing bodies. Blood from the headshots that killed them has dried to a dull, uneven black.

Somewhere nearby comes a soft moan.

We freeze, listening.

It comes a second time.

Ben raises one finger. I nod in agreement. One zombie.

Just to be certain, I tap my foot on the floor.

The zombie responds with a growl.

It's coming from the back, near the bathroom. We advance through the dining room, bypassing the unmoving bodies near the center of the room. I avoid a small puddle of bullet casings on the floor. Several chairs and a table have been overturned, which we skirt.

We find the zombie clawing at the bathroom door, unable to get out. It's pushing at a door that will only open when pulled from the inside.

"We could just leave it there," Ben says. It's a sign of how bad he feels that he would even make this suggestion. The skin of his face has drained of color. Blood drips off the hem of his fatigues. "It can't get out."

I shake my head. "What if it calls others?" I tighten my grip on my knife and club. "You get the door. I'll get the zombie."

Face tight, he nods. "You're the boss, Mama Bear. I'll fall in line like all the others."

I give him a hollow grin, stepping up to the bathroom door. Ben places both hands on the wood and shoves. A *thunk* sounds, followed by a crash as the zombie knocks into something.

I charge through the door as Ben holds it open for me.

It's dark inside the bathroom, but a narrow window over the sink lets in enough filtered light for me to see. The zombie is sprawled on the floor next to a downed trash can.

It's a young woman in a Five Leaf polo and jeans. A black apron around her waist tells me she was a waitress in this place before she turned. Across both arms are long gashes and teeth marks, much of the skin torn free.

Her white eyes lock on me. Even though she can't see, her precision tracking has found me. Her lips pull back from teeth crusted with black blood.

I pounce, not giving her a chance to rise. My screwdriver punctures her eye socket.

The sudden silence is a welcome balm. It calms my nerves. Wiping my screwdriver clean on the waitress's apron, I turn back to Ben.

"Let's take a look at that wound."

15

WOUNDS

KATE

"I think you fell on glass," I pronounce a short time later. I hold up the muddy, bloody lump of his fatigue shirt, displaying the large jagged hole in the back for him to see. "Maybe a broken bottle."

Ben straddles a wooden chair. He twists around as I hold up the shirt, grimacing as he takes in the gash in the fabric.

"Does my back look as bad as the shirt?"

There's no way to sugar coat it. "Yeah." I drop the shirt onto the floor in a wad before reaching for my running pack. I always carry a small first aid kit with essentials. I make everyone carry it when we venture outside the safety of campus.

"Infection is our biggest worry." I dump out the contents of my small Ziploc with sterile wipes, bandages, and sewing kit. "There's no telling what was in that water."

"Better than a zom bite." Ben peers down at the assortment of supplies on the table. "Is that a sewing kit from the Marriott?"

"Yeah. We found a lot of hotel sewing kits when we cleared and inventoried Creekside."

Ben grunts and turns away. "Just get it done."

The sterile wipes come first. I clean the wound, taking in the hard muscles of his back. For an older guy, he's fit. Not I-bench-press-three-hundred-pounds fit, but fit from a lifetime of using his body.

Movement flashes in the corner of my eye. I look out the window and spot the zombie herd that followed us here from the freeway. The squat alpha in the visor stands in the middle of the road, nose lifted to the air. The car alarms have stopped, once again drenching the world in silence.

"The pack followed us here," I whisper. There's no way I can sew up Ben while looking over my shoulder at the zombies. I point to the far side of the dining room to a wooden staircase set against the back wall. "Over there. Come on."

I gather up my pack and the first aid supplies. Ben and I tiptoe up the stairs. He drips blood the whole way. I step around it as I follow him.

Upstairs, we are greeted by four closed doors.

"Dammit," I mutter. "I hate closed doors."

His face crinkles in amusement. "That makes two of us."

We stand still, listening. All is silent. That doesn't mean these doors don't have an undead surprise behind them.

The idea of checking each door and possibly battling multiple zombies while my companion bleeds out leaves me feeling tired. The puddle on the floor beneath his feet has grown six inches wide in the short time we've stood here. We need to take care of it, fast.

I cross to the first door and tap. No sound. I try a second time. Again, silence.

"Here goes nothing," I murmur, drawing my zom bat.

Ben takes the doorknob. He yanks it open and I leap inside.

A cluttered office greets us. A cluttered, blissfully empty

office. Other than a bit of smeared blood across the far wall, it's practically pristine.

"Thank God," Ben mutters, grabbing the ladder back desk chair and slumping down. "I wasn't in the mood to deal with more of those fuckers."

"Me, either." I cross to the window that overlooks the cluster on the street below. "They're still out there."

"They'll clear out soon," Ben replies.

I raise my gaze, looking to the expanse of 101 in the distance. Other than swarms of movement, I can't make out details. There's no way to know if Carter and the others made it to safety. Even if I used Ben's binoculars, there would be nothing to see.

"No sign of them, is there?" Ben asks.

I shake my head. "They made it. They must have. They're strong."

To my surprise, Ben says, "They are."

"You really think so?" I swallow against the anxiety forcing its way up my throat, turning my attention back to Ben.

"Most of the time I want to staple their mouths shut. But they're good kids. They function well as a unit."

I spread out the first aid supplies on the messy desk, shoving aside a computer and a large stack of papers to make room.

"You know, even when you say something nice, you always manage to say something rude at the same time." I pick up a restaurant towel from the desk and press against his back to staunch the bleeding.

"Ash did warn you that I was a grumpy fucker."

"Yeah, she did. Hold still, I have to improvise for a second." I press my knee against the towel, holding it in place against his back while I fumble with the Marriott first aid kit.

"This is the first time I've ever stitched anyone up," I warn as I thread the needle. "It probably won't be pretty."

"Good thing I'm not pretty."

For some reason, this statement makes me again take in the broad muscles of his back. My eyes trace the lines of tension that travel down his shoulders to arms covered in the sleeve tattoos. Some are faded and bleed along the edges, clearly older pieces of art. Others are new and vibrant.

Everything about him looks good. If I look like G.I. Jane—a statement that still stings, if I let it—he looks like G.I. Joe. Albeit a weathered, seasoned G.I. Joe.

The only thing that doesn't look good is the chafing around his waist. The pants have slipped down an inch, revealing a ring of red scabs marring his skin. Some are bright red, fresh and still raw. Others are covered with darker scabs, attempting to heal despite his insistence on wearing the fatigue pants.

I check a sigh, refraining from pointing out the chafe marks. There's no point in beating that dead horse.

I pull the towel away from the wound in his back. Though some of the bleeding has slowed, blood bubbles instantly to the surface as soon as I take the pressure away. This is going to be messy.

I use another wipe to sterilize my hands before getting to work. His chest heaves with an inhalation when my needle makes the first stab.

"I don't suppose you took Home Ec in school?" he asks.

"They didn't have Home Ec when I went to school. It wasn't cool for girls to learn how to sew and cook when I was a kid. Feminism and all that."

"You must be younger than you look."

His words are like a slap. "If you don't want this patchwork on your back to look like a Jack-O-Lantern, you'd better stop talking."

Tense silence follows this. I stab through his skin, not caring if the drag of the needle hurts.

I know there's a mere two millimeters between Ben's brain

and his mouth. He doesn't have a filter. Most of the time I ignore his comments. But this is the second time he's made a negative remark about my looks. First about my haircut, now about my age.

Maybe it's because I'm tired. Maybe it's because I don't know if Carter and the rest of my kids are safe. Hell, maybe it's because I'm trapped in a brewery surrounded by zombies and I'm scared. Whatever the case, his words upset me.

Why do I even care what he thinks? It's not like he said anything I don't already know. I look like a washed-up room mom.

I stab harder than necessary through his skin, rewarded with a grunt of discomfort.

Attempting to mop up the blood as I work makes the entire procedure even more awkward. In retrospect, I should have made him lie down on the desk. There's a reason surgeons have tables. Not that I'm a surgeon.

Thirty minutes later, Ben indeed has something resembling a crooked Jack-O-Lantern smile on the lower right side of his back. Serves him right. Not that I could have done a much better job even if I wasn't angry.

I tape a clean bandage over the whole thing, grab my pack, and leave the room. I head to the next door over and knock.

No answer from this one, either. I fling it open, letting out a long breath as my gaze sweeps across shelving full of supplies. One entire wall is lined with clean-pressed aprons, napkins, and dishtowels. The other side has a myriad of dining room supplies: salt and pepper refills, bottles and bottles of ketchup, mustard, and relish. Sugar packets for days.

I step into the room, turning in a slow circle. Not a bad haul. I'll have to bring my people back here on a supply run.

Thinking of my kids draws me to the window. It's dusk outside. If we were complete idiots, we could strike out and try to make our way back to campus. But with the flurry on 101 and the swarm we encountered in town, I know the safest thing to do is wait out the night. And Ben needs rest.

A soft step creaks a floorboard behind me. The exhaustion of the day hits me like a derailed train.

"Kate."

"What?" I don't turn around, staring out at Highway 101.

"That was a shitty thing I said back there."

I let out a long sigh. "Look, I know you don't mean half the shit you say. You're not a bad guy even though you seem hell bent on making everyone else believe that." I turn, closing the distance between us. "It's been a long day. It's too late for us to go back to Creekside now. I'm going to sleep."

Without waiting for a reply, I close the supply closet door in his face.

16

SURVIVOR'S REMORSE

BEN

He could not have made a bigger cluster fuck with Kate if he'd tried. God, why did he even try talking? He didn't mean to imply she looked old. But her hands had been all over his back. Between that and the pain, he hadn't been thinking straight.

He stretches out on the floor of the office, using an apron and a few dishtowels for pillows. His back hurts like a mother-fucker. Especially since he's lying on the hard wooden floor.

He should be sleeping. God knows he'll need his strength to get back to Creekside tomorrow.

He hardly sleeps when he has a bed and pillow. Attempting to fall asleep on the wood floor feels like an exercise in futility, but he tries anyway. If only to escape the disaster reel with Kate playing in his head on repeat.

He closes his eyes and huffs out a long breath, willing himself to sleep. When he does finally doze off, the nightmare starts.

This time, it's a mash-up of the College Creek massacre and Desert Storm. Ben finds himself in the desert under a black, smoky sky, shooting at Iraqi soldiers while yelling at college kids to take cover.

He wakes with a shout. Cold sweat bathes his skin. He gets to his feet and paces back and forth in the small room, trying to shake off the nightmare. It's an invisible presence sitting beside him in the dark.

His pacing takes him down the hallway to Kate's room. He can't stand things being off between them. He wants to make it right again.

Except it's the middle of the night. He has no business waking her up. Even if it is to apologize. Somehow he doubts a two a.m. apology will go over well.

As he turns away, he hears a sound through the closed door. It's a soft sound, ragged at the edges.

She's crying.

Before he realizes what he's doing, he's standing in the open doorway. Kate lies on a wad of towels and chef coats, curled tightly on her side. A faint shaft of moonlight illuminates a shiny track of tears across her cheek.

"Frederico, no," she murmurs. One leg thrashes.

The muscles across his back and shoulders go rigid. He knows what it's like to be caught in a bad dream. More precisely, he knows what it's like to be caught in a fucked-up memory masquerading as a dream.

"Frederico." The name comes out like a crippled cat.

He can't take it.

Ben crouches on the floor beside her and gives her arm a squeeze.

Kate flies into an upright position, the top of her head connecting with his chin. The soft crack of bone-on-bone reverberates in the tight confines of the room.

"Ben?" She blinks at him in confusion, the sleep haze leaving her eyes. "Has something happened?" The tendons in her neck stiffen.

He eases back from her, rubbing at his chin. "Sorry. You were having a bad dream."

"You woke me up because I was having a bad dream?"

He nods. As she stares at him, he feels like he needs a better explanation.

"I still have bad dreams. They're like, I don't know, movie reels you can't get out of. Hamster wheels where the bad stuff just keeps rolling out in front of you."

She continues to stare at him. He resists the urge to slink away in embarrassment.

If reincarnation is a real thing, he wants to come back as one of those fancy guys in suits who does public speaking for a living. Then, just maybe, he could talk to a woman. Maybe.

"You were calling for Frederico." It's his final attempt to get her to respond to him. He really will slink away if she just keeps staring at him.

Kate slumps, rubbing at her wet cheeks. "I miss him." Her words are soft and sad.

She's always so strong. It's one of the many things he admires about her. Seeing her hunched over and grieving makes something inside him crumple.

"You're right about the hamster wheel." Kate draws her knees up to her chest. "I just keep seeing that night when Frederico ran from me. He yelled and drew the zombies after him so I could get away." A fresh gush of tears rolls out of her eyes. She looks away from him. "He sacrificed everything so I could find Carter. If I can't keep him alive—if I can't protect him—" Her voice breaks off.

"You'll feel like Frederico's sacrifice will be for nothing."

She nods, resting her chin on her knees. "Yeah."

He thinks back to the brothers he lost over the years, both in the Sandbox and Somalia. So many. He can still list out names and ranks in his head.

"I still try to find reasons for the deaths of my brothers in the service." He lets out a long sigh. "I don't think you ever stop looking, Kate."

More fresh tears roll down her cheeks. "I just want to know that Carter and the others made it back to Creekside. Whatever else happens, I just want to know they're safe."

He has an urge to take her in his arms. Except he's not sure how that would go over. He's not exactly the strong cuddly type. Strong, sometimes. But not cuddly. A cactus has him beat on the cuddly scale.

He settles for sitting cross-legged in the moonlight next to her in what he hopes is easy companionship. At least she doesn't radiate anger anymore. That's an improvement. Now if only he can keep his mouth from saying something stupid.

She doesn't pull away, keeping her chin propped on her knees. He likes looking at her. Her profile is lean and strong. Her eyes focus on the small window in the room. A curtain of stars fills the rectangle of glass.

"I didn't realize you had so many tattoos." Kate is looking at his bare arms.

Part of the reason he keeps himself religiously encased in his fatigues are the tattoos. He has sleeves on both arms. He doesn't want to answer questions about the thirty years of art that cover him from wrist to shoulder.

Tonight, he's been stripped to the waist since Kate sewed up his back. He doesn't mind her seeing the tattoos. Maybe it's the darkness. It feels less exposed, less awkward.

"I enlisted when I was eighteen," he tells her. "I get a tattoo every year on the anniversary of my enlistment."

"That's neat." She squints, studying his arms. "What's that?" She points to Ben's right bicep.

Of course she would notice *that* one. It wouldn't be so bad if the fucking thing didn't have purple wings.

There was also the matter of the pink dress.

There's nothing to do but own it. "It's a fairy."

"Like, a tooth fairy? A small person with wings?"

"Yes."

Kate giggles. It's a nice sound. "What's the story behind the fairy?"

He starts talking, encouraged by her expression. "I got roaring drunk the night we graduated from boot camp. One of the guys was an amateur tattoo artist. Four of us got matching fairy tattoos that night in a public bathroom at a club." He chuckles at the memory. "The other guys all got cover-up art eventually."

"But not you?"

"Nah. I figure it's good to remember those times when you're a complete dumb shit. It helps you remember not to be a dumb shit again. Sometimes." He meets her eyes, willing for her to see how sorry he is for his earlier blunder. "Anyway, after that it became a tradition."

Her hand comes up, tracing the flames along his upper deltoid. He sits still, afraid the slightest movement will dislodge her.

"Flames of the oil fields of Iraq," he says. "From Operation Desert Storm. One flame for each of the friends I lost in battle."

"Nine," she says, counting them with her fingertips.

"Nine," he agrees. Encouraged by the feel of her fingers against his skin, he keeps talking.

He tells her the story of the art on his arms. The words *Got Him* on his left forearm represent the death of Osama bin Laden. The drone on his right wrist represents his tour in the War on Terror in Pakistan. The sunrise on his inner forearm is the sky the morning after he lost four men in Somalia during the Ethiopian invasion.

As he winds down, once again out of words, Kate lowers her hand and smiles at him. "That's beautiful, Ben."

Someday, if he ever finds a tattoo artist, he has another design in mind, this one for his left shoulder. The number sixteen in a puddle of blood. For the College Creek kids. They deserve to be remembered, even if only by him.

He doesn't say any of this to Kate. The shame is too heavy.

"Your skin is cold." Kate rises, crossing to the shelf of linens. She unfolds a starched chef's coat and shakes it out. "Here. You should wear something."

He takes the blazing white stiff shirt, unable to look away from her. He's pretty sure he's never seen a woman look so damn good.

"I meant it as a compliment," he blurts out. "What I said about G.I. Jane, I mean. I know it didn't come out like that."

She raises one eyebrow at him, not bothering to pretend. That's another thing he admires about her. She's real.

"And I didn't mean to say you looked old. Tonight, I mean. I just meant you look like a woman."

"Ben, do you even know what a compliment is?"

It's a fair question.

"In theory, yes. I'm just not very good in practice." He heaves an exasperated sigh. "G.I. Jane was played by Demi Moore, Kate. She's as hot as they come. How could that not be a compliment?"

Alarm bells go off in his head as the mood in the room shifts. Kate stiffens beside him, turning wide eyes at him. She doesn't look offended, thank God, but she does look off-balance.

Did he just call her hot? Yes, he did. Like a stupid teenager.

He doesn't know how to tell her she's so much more than that. She's smart. Strong. Decisive. Determined. Caring. Patient. So much more than a stupid actress in a movie he wishes he'd never mentioned.

Mouth dry, he refuses to make eye contact. He busies himself buttoning on the chef's coat, resolving not to speak until she does. It's safer that way.

"Thank you for the compliment," she says at last, a strange hitch in her voice.

Some of the tension leaks out of him.

They sit side by side on the floor, watching the sun come up in easy silence. It's the best night he's had in as long as he can remember.

17

HORDE

KATE

I don't know what to make of Ben's behavior. The only thing I know for sure is that underneath that gruff exterior is a man with substance. The more I talk to him, the more I like him.

Oddly enough, I remind him of Demi Moore. That seems a bit like comparing a three-legged mongrel from Puerto Vallarta to a New York show dog, but the sentiment isn't lost on me. He meant it as a compliment.

I decide not to overthink it. It makes me feel good inside. These days, there aren't a lot of things to make me feel good. Seems stupid to downplay the good moments when they come along.

"I never thanked you. I mean, for the coffee you've been leaving outside my bedroom."

"Do you like it?" He looks at her from the corner of his eye.

"Hell yes, I like it. Who doesn't like coffee for midnight watch?"

"I thought it would keep you warm."

The act of kindness keeps me warmer than any amount of steaming beverage could. Like the way he pulled me out of the nightmare tonight. I think of all the times Johnny has asked me to tell him the story of my journey to Arcata. Johnny doesn't understand how raw it all is.

Ben gets it. It feels good to be understood, even if my single loss pales in comparison to all he must have lost through the years. If the tattoos covering his arm are any indication, he's lost many.

It's hard to wrap my mind around his life spent in service to the military. Of losing so many friends. Of fighting in every major offensive our government has taken part in over the last thirty years. Including the current shit storm.

The window of the supply room is a pale square of orange. I rise, crossing to it. Ben joins me. Our shoulders almost touch.

"I've been thinking about our route home," I say.

"We need to go through town."

"My thoughts exactly. It's safer than trying to get across the freeway."

We watch in silence out the window. Highway 101 is relatively still, at least compared to what we'd seen yesterday. The swarming has died back to the regular milling we're used to.

I look for the alpha and the zombies who followed us last night from the freeway. They've moved down the street. Their heads loll as they stagger in small circles, blind eyes almost seeming to glow in the washed-out light of dawn. They stay in a loose cluster around the alpha as though waiting for a command.

"Do you hear that?" Ben frowns, pursing his lips as he leans closer to the glass.

"Yeah." It's a soft buzzing, like a fly, only louder. "What is it?"

Ben shakes his head. He retrieves his binoculars from the other room. He looks through them for several minutes, scanning the area.

"Fucking shit balls." Ben shoves the binos at me. "Do you see what I see?"

My heart rate spikes at the panic in his voice. I grab the binoculars. "Where do I look?"

"South. Toward Eureka."

I spin the binos south along 101, eyes flying over the wrecked cars, dead bodies, and zombies. Nothing looks out of the ordinary. Nothing different from what I saw yesterday. If anything, it's a good deal calmer than yesterday.

I continue to scan in a southward direction.

A dark spec comes into view. Then several more specs join the first. The distant buzzing grows louder.

My heart stops beating.

"Holy fuck."

"You see it, too, right?" Ben demands.

I can't peel my eyes away from the binoculars. I want to deny what I'm seeing.

Moving up the freeway is a cluster of people. People on motorcycles and in cars. That's the buzzing.

But that's not the worst of it. The people aren't alone.

Chasing them is a horde of zombies. An enormous, gigantic, big-as-fuck zombie herd. It's so huge I can't see where it ends.

There are hundreds of them. And they're being led by three alphas.

I can't see the alphas individually, but I do see three distinct whorls near the front of the horde. Each one is like an eye of the storm. The zoms nearest the alphas boil outward, carrying out the orders like worker bees.

Half a dozen questions pepper my mind. How are the alpha's orders dispersed through the herd? Are the three alphas working together or do they just happen to share a common goal at the moment? Do they share pack members, or is each zombie tied to a specific alpha?

Too many questions. Too much to work out and no time to spare.

The horde's pursuit of the small party of humans is relentless.

The mess is big enough to swallow a town whole. Or a college.

And it's coming straight for us.

"Oh, my God," I whisper.

Ben stomps out of the room. He returns moments later, rifle in hand.

"Open the window," he orders.

I stare at him stupidly. "What?"

"Open the window." Eyes hard, he brings the rifle up to his shoulder and racks a bullet into the chamber.

"We have to go," I argue. "That horde is heading straight toward campus—"

"Just open the damn window!"

I swallow my arguments and tackle the window. This might be my first apocalypse, but it's not Ben's.

The latch is stiff and encrusted with grime from months of disuse. The window squeals as I force it open.

The zombies that followed us here spin in our direction. The alpha keens and clicks.

Until I opened the window, their attention had been on the commotion of the road. Now, we're their focus.

"You'd better have a good plan." I back away from the window, wrestling with the need to get back to Creekside.

"I'm testing a theory." Ben slams his mud-covered orange running shoe into the screen, sending it tumbling to the ground below. He pokes the rifle through the open window and fires.

The head of the alpha zom explodes.

The pack moans in confusion. They turn in uneven circles, arms outstretched.

Then they separate from one another, dotting the road in an uneven, unorganized line. Half drift toward the brewery. The rest turn their attention back to the approaching motorcycles.

Ben slings his rifle over his shoulder. "I wanted to see what would happen when you take out the alpha. Looks like the pack reverts to following whatever sound draws it." His eyes narrow in concentration. "Let's get the fuck out of here. We have to stay ahead of that horde. We'll go out the back."

I don't have to be told twice. I snag my running pack and charge out of the room, leading the way downstairs.

18

YELLOW LIGHT

KATE

My arms pump, my legs churn, and my breath wheezes in and out of my lungs. Sweat flies from my temples like raindrops.

Ben labors beside me. The white chef coat he wears is an odd juxtaposition to his military fatigue pants and orange shoes.

We race through the streets of Arcata. A single word burns in my brain: *Creekside.*

I have to get back to Creekside. We have to warn Carter and the others. We have to keep them safe.

We have to protect the home we've worked so hard to build. No fucking way am I giving any of it up without a fight.

I mentally trace the off-ramps that lead to campus. The high ground location is natural defense, but it won't be enough to deter the massive horde. The swarm is too big, too wide. Some of them will naturally find their way to the off-ramps, to the roads that lead right to Humboldt University.

Cars. Maybe we can use cars to build a barrier.

I dismiss the idea. Cars won't be enough. We're going to have to think of something else. We—

"Kate!" Ben's frantic whisper claws at me. His hand latches onto my arm, dragging me to a stop.

The force of the stop is so abrupt I wheel backward. I swing my gaze around in a frantic arc, looking for danger.

A chorus of growls sends a chill across my shoulder blades. Coming straight for us is a pack of zombies two-dozen strong. If there's an alpha there, we're fucked.

"Which way?" Ben hisses.

"Cut through downtown."

With our northbound route blocked, I lead us northwest. My chest constricts from the hard running and near-crippling fear.

Keening fills the air. It seems to come from everywhere at once. From the freeway. From the city streets.

From right in front of us.

We skid to a halt as we near the Arcata Plaza. The fire I set six months ago burned half of it to the ground. Milling around in the charred remains is another thick clump of zombies.

They've been here ever since the fire. The crackling flames and the noise of the collapsing buildings drew them. With nothing else to occupy them, they've remained here.

Now, for the first time in months, they have something to stir them up. Near the center of the plaza is the same alpha we saw yesterday. The faded red baseball cap makes him easy to spot. A mass gathers in a tight knot around the alpha as it growls and clicks.

The calls of the swarm on the freeway shiver through the air, a faint yet distinct buzz. The alpha zom, seeming to hear the call of its brethren, lets up a long keen.

The zombies in the plaza react. En masse, with the alpha zom in their center, they begin a migration toward 101. They reach out with their arms, fumbling their blind way forward. Moaning gathers in a collective sound and grates at my gut.

Gooseflesh prickles down my arms. Everything is changing. Less than a month ago, we didn't have to worry about alpha zoms. A good pair of running shoes and a decent amount of stealth was enough to get by.

In a flash of clarity, I realize that won't be enough anymore.

We can't let the alpha zom leave this plaza. Its presence is too powerful. We don't need another alpha among the horde on 101. We don't need this group added to the hundreds already marching on us.

I turn to Ben. "We have to shoot the alpha. He can't leave the plaza."

Under normal circumstances, this comment from me would probably elicit a hearty *I told you so*, or at the very least, an *About fucking time*.

There isn't time for any of that. Ben gives me a single tight-lipped nod, his grip tightening on his rifle.

"Cover me," he says.

I drop into a crouch, maintaining surveillance of our street corner as Ben climbs onto a burned-out Hummer. The interior is charred black, but the exterior is still strong enough to hold his weight.

"Get ready to haul ass as soon as I fire." He raises his rifle to his shoulder and sights along the barrel.

My mouth is dry. The gunshot will bring every zombie in the plaza streaming in our direction. My eyes dart along the ruined storefronts and back down the way we came, searching for our safest retreat.

The rifle cracks two times. The red hat disappears. The zombies boil, a chorus of keens ripping through the air. They turn, lurching in our direction.

Ben leaps to the ground, slinging his rifle back over his

shoulder. His mouth is set in a grim line as he takes in the pack of zombies closing in on us.

Before the apocalypse, I considered myself a daredevil when I floored it through a yellow light. I'd dart through an intersection and scan my rearview mirror for any sign of a cop car. It drove Kyle, my late husband, crazy, and got me a lecture or an annoyed eye roll every single time.

What I attempt now makes my old-world, yellow-light-running ways look pathetic.

Doubling back will take too much time. Everything is riding on us making it to Creekside ahead of the swarm on 101.

The gap between the pack of zombies on the burned-out storefronts is only twenty feet wide and closing fast as they near us.

I squeeze Ben's hand in silent signal.

"Motherfucker," he growls, but he doesn't back down.

I tear straight down the narrow opening, danger be damned. Beside me, Ben never falters. He puts himself between me and the oncoming horde as we charge forward.

The gap narrows. Our feet are soft against the asphalt, but we are far from silent. Our clothing rustles. Our feet tap. Our running packs whisper against our backs.

The zombies hear us. I see it in the way every head turns in our direction.

Arms reach for us. Keening rises up among the pack. They pick up the pace, lumbering toward us. I grit my teeth and pour on a burst of speed.

This is for Carter. For Jenna. For Johnny. For Lila. For Eric. For Caleb. For Ash. For Jesus.

My kids. My family.

Ben smacks straight into the first of the undead who reaches us. He shoves the zombie so hard the thing is pitched ten feet across the ground. It careens into several of its fellows, knocking them all to the street.

Two more reach us, the others gaining speed behind them. There isn't time to fight. If we stop, we'll get swarmed.

I follow Ben's lead and body slam straight into the nearest one, knocking it to the ground. I leap over it just as Ben shoves another one away. We rip free of the gathering crowd and keep running.

By now, the entire pack is aware of our presence. We have to outrun them. It's our only chance. With the alpha out of the picture, we have a chance at losing them.

We sprint out of the plaza, the pack keening behind us as they follow. More keening goes up from nearby streets, making me sick with fear and anxiety. There's so many of them it's impossible to tell if there's an alpha among them.

I'm grateful for the many hours spent running up and down the bleacher steps. I'm grateful for the god-awful, two-hour sets of wind sprint I made everyone do. I'm glad for every drop of sweat I dropped on the track in the past six months. It's the only thing keeping us alive right now.

As we charge into an intersection, another milling pack of zombies stumbles in our direction. We hurtle past them.

One snags my sleeve as I race by. I yelp, spinning around to yank myself free.

Ben is there a flash, stabbing his knife through the monster's head. He rips me loose, pushing me away.

"Go!" he snaps.

Two zombies stumble into him, latching onto him with clawed hands.

No fucking way is this man going to die on my watch. I grab a weapon in each hand and leap into the fray.

One knife slams through the cheek of a young teenage girl. My zom bat finds the temple of the second zombie, a man in a tracksuit. Ben kicks a third zombie as it reaches us, his foot connecting with enough force to crumple its nose and face.

Our attack leaves three bodies on the ground. We jump

back as another four undead reach us. They trip on the bodies and go down.

It's the opening we need. Ben and I break free and keep running.

North and east. North and east. We zigzag through the streets, detouring when we must, but always pushing farther north and east, back to Creekside.

It feels like hours, but in truth, it can't be more than twenty minutes.

As last we reach the overpass that connects Humboldt University to the rest of Arcata.

"About fucking time," Ben wheezes. The side and back of his chef's coat are stained with blood. His close-cropped hair gleams with sweat. His face and neck bead with perspiration.

"Thank God," I gasp.

As we race onto the overpass, my stomach drops as I get a clear look at Highway 101 beneath us.

The wide earthen trench that houses the four-lane freeway is crammed with new zombies. The bodies we dropped over the side while clearing the campus, combined with the maze of abandoned cars and zombies already living there, has turned the road below us into a labyrinth.

The passage of the motorcycles and cars from Eureka has slowed to a near crawl due to the obstacles in the road. I see kids and families in the vehicles. My heart aches at the sight. They're going to be obliterated, pulverized between the horde behind them and the wreckage in front of them.

The zoms bear down inexorably, gaining on the poor people. The swath following them spreads east and west on either side of the freeway, the monsters stomping over and through whatever is in their path.

To my horror, several of the cars and motorcycles break away from the freeway. They veer east, taking the off-ramp that leads straight to Humboldt University. They roar past us and onto campus, punching the accelerators.

Two of the maelstroms remain focused on the vehicles struggling to make their way north on the freeway. But the third maelstrom shifts its trajectory. The zoms around the eastern-most alpha surge toward the off-ramp. There are hundreds upon hundreds of them.

They're headed straight for campus.

And that's not the worst of it. When I first saw the horde advancing from Eureka, I'd seen three distinct groups led by alphas. But now I see other small whorls of zombies, signifying smaller groups within the three main forces. Like platoons in a company

I freeze, mouth hanging open in horror as I take it all in. It's even worse than I imagined. The campus is going to drown in zombies.

"Explosives," Ben growls. "We need some goddamn C-4 and rocket launchers right fucking now."

We turn and keep running.

19

ARM

BEN

"We have to blow College Creek." He sucks in air, his rib cage aching from the exertion of their mad sprint through Arcata. "Those buildings already form a defensive perimeter at the front of the school. Blowing them will deflect the frontal assault."

Kate pants beside him as she hauls ass up Granite Avenue toward Creekside. Her cheeks are stained pink, her eyes wild.

"We need to take out the alphas."

"That won't be enough. Even if we can get to high ground to sniper the things, the rest of the horde will already be on campus."

"We still need to get rid of the alphas. We stand a better chance if the zoms aren't organized."

"You're right." Ben's mind races. "Eric. He's a crack shot. He can sight them from the rec center." That's near the College Creek dorms. From the top floor, he'll have a clear shot at the oncoming horde.

"Blowing College Creek won't keep them all out," Kate

huffs. It's one the few times Ben has heard her out of breath while running. "They'll be able to go around."

"Not if we blow it right. If we can block everything on the southwest, they'll walk right off the ledge and fall to the freeway below. They'll be drawn in that direction anyway. That's where all the noise will be once the dust settles." The east side was another problem altogether.

Kate voices his thoughts. "And the east side?" she demands. "What if some of them get through on that side?"

He hates not having answers. It's like being back in Somalia, when he and his guys found themselves ambushed. The fucking feeling of being trapped is almost enough to make him lose his shit. His fear of something happening to Kate helps him hold it together.

"We improvise," he says. "It's a shitty answer, but it's all I got."

"Okay." Her mouth is set in a determined line. "I don't have any better ideas. We go with your plan. You know it's crazy, right?"

The queen of crazy wanted to call him out? Half a dozen retorts came to mind, but he doesn't have any breath to voice them.

The stitch in his side has grown to epic proportions. His waist feels like a ring of fire from the chafing. The cut in his back hurts like a motherfucker. He ignores it all, nostrils flaring at the pain.

Somewhere behind them, he hears a car crash, followed by a scream. Seconds later is the sound of another crash.

That's two fuck heads down. Now if only there was a way to get rid of the rest of the fuckers who brought hell to their doorstep.

The door to Creekside is thrown open as they race up. Carter, Jenna, and Reed crowd the doorway. Ben and Kate barrel past them, both of them shouting as soon as they're inside Creekside.

"Explosives!" Kate calls.

"We need some grenades right fucking now!" Ben bellows.

Jenna, Carter, and Reed surge around Kate. They attempt to hug her and ask questions at the same time.

"Mom, are you okay?"

"We were so worried," Jenna adds. "What—"

"What do you mean we need grenades?" Reed asks.

Kate shouts over the talking, silencing them with her intensity. "Zombie horde," she snaps. "Coming our way. Alphas."

"We're under siege." Ben races for the stairwell, heading up to the armory on the second floor. He shouts as he runs, hoping his voice will carry and alert the rest. "Everyone arm!"

Kate, Carter, Jenna, and Reed tear up the stairs after them. They plunge into the dorm suite they converted into the armory.

"Under siege!" Ben shouts again, his gruff voice booming up and down the hall. "Everyone arm!"

The rest of the crew bursts into the armory. Everyone tries to ask questions. Johnny is there, ready to join the fight despite his injured Achilles. Even Susan is there, the young woman from the charter boat wanting to help.

Caleb and Ash take in the situation and begin arming themselves without question.

"We heard something from the rooftop," Ash says. "We didn't have any visuals."

"Zombie swarm from Eureka." Kate grabs a rocket launcher and swings it over one shoulder. "Coming right for us. Hundreds of them. Everyone, grab explosives."

This is all it takes to get the rest of the group to shut up. Within seconds, everyone is arming themselves.

Despite everything going on around them, Ben can't help

but admire Kate. Any drill sergeant would be impressed with the way she wrangles this group.

"Eric, grab a rifle," Kate says. "You're on sniper duty in the rec center. Everyone else, grab everything you can carry and haul ass downstairs to Skip. Ben will explain the plan while we drive. Carter, you're driving us to College Creek."

It's a testament to Kate's skills as a leader that she's made the decision to use a vehicle. For her, caution is always paramount. Moving silently and safely has, up until now, been more important than moving fast.

Ben sees that she is rapidly adjusting to the new paradigm of the alphas, dropping old rules and adopting new ones on the fly. Just like she had in Arcata when she made him shoot the alpha in the plaza. Flexible and adaptable. That's Kate.

She leads their group at a dead run back down the stairs. As they leave Creekside behind, Ben glances back. Framed in the doorway, her face wan with fear, is Lila. She watches them go, looking small and lost.

Her vulnerability makes something inside him harden. He has to protect her. He has to protect them all.

Skip is a beat-up Dodge Caravan that Carter and Jenna purchased before the apocalypse. Ben has a vague understanding of some beer company the two planned to start, though how a shitty van is tied to a brewing company is beyond him.

Except for the driver's and passenger's seats, all the others have been removed. This *should* make it easier for them to pile in. Except that no less than six beer kegs take up the right side of the van and there isn't time to take them out. Ben finds himself squashed against the back of the passenger's seat next to Caleb.

"Yo, did you guys ever play that game when you were teenagers to see how many friends you could cram in a car?"

Reed asks. "My brother and I fit eight people into a Volkswagon Bug."

"Thank God this isn't a Mini Coop," Ben growls. It's bad enough having Caleb's left ass cheek on his thigh.

"Everyone in?" Carter shouts as he leaps into the driver's seat. Jenna climbs in next to him.

"Go!" Kate tells him, slamming shut the side door.

Carter fires up the engine and throws the car into drive. Ben finds himself flung forward. He sprawls on top of Caleb as Skip makes a hard left. Johnny squawks as he lands on top of Ben.

"Ben, we need the details of the plan," Kate says.

"Four teams," Ben barks, attempting to right himself as Carter hauls ass around Creekside and out into the parking lot. "Eric, you're on sniper duty in the rec center. Jesus, you're with Eric. You watch his back while he takes out the alphas. It's imperative the alphas are taken down.

"Caleb, Ash, and I lead three teams to plant the C-4 while the rest of you cover us. Kate and Reed, you're with me."

Assigning Kate to his team is selfish, but he can't protect her if she isn't near. He might die today, but he's going to do his damnedest to make sure she lives.

"Susan and Johnny, you cover Ash," he continues. "Jenna, you're with Caleb. Caleb's team takes out the east building. Ash's team takes center. My team takes out the west building. Concentrate your explosives on the west side of the buildings. We bring them down and create a path that takes the zoms away from campus and down onto the freeway."

"What about me?" Carter asks.

"You stay with the van," Ben replies. "Keep it running and keep it away from the horde. If things go to shit, we fall back to Skip and try to outrun them."

The look Kate gives him is anguished. They both know that if they can't divert the swarm, their chance of survival is slim to none. It's slim to none now. The horde is too big, too all-encompassing. The noise of the van will bring them down like wild-fire. Attempting to run with so many hundreds out there will be equally disastrous.

They have one shot at this. They'll make their stand at College Creek. They'll either live, or die.

As Carter hits a curb and sends the van into a state of airborne, Ben experiences a moment of calm. Even with Caleb's ass currently in his ribcage, he has a clear view of Kate. Her eyes are fierce, her jaw set. She's drenched in sweat and grime and looks like she's ready to take on the entire swarm single-handedly. It's the most arresting sight he's ever seen.

If he dies today, he'll carry the memory of her ferocity into the afterlife.

20

STAND

KATE

The van tears past the Depot, the only place on campus that sold beer before the apocalypse. Steely determination sweeps through me. I take a good look at my apocalypse family, giving myself ten seconds to focus on how much I care about each and every one of them.

Carter. Jenna. Reed. Eric. Johnny. Jesus. Ash. Caleb. Ben. And Lila. These ten people are my reason for living.

"Listen up." I pitch my voice loud enough to fill the cramped interior. "We can do this. This isn't the hardest or the scariest thing we've come up against. It's just another obstacle to get past. When you see the swarm, just give them a big *fuck you* and blast them to hell. You got it?"

"Fuck you, zombies!" Reed shouts.

"Fuck the undead, Mamita!" Jesus adds.

Within seconds, everyone is yelling and fist pounding the air. Jenna turns back and gives me a wild-eyed grin before adding her scream to the mix. Carter beats his fist on the steering wheel even as he swerves around several undead that lumber toward the car. Ben wears a wild grimace as he bellows *fuck you* at the top of his lungs.

Carter whips the van around an abandoned car and skids to a halt outside College Creek.

My chest seizes.

We're too late.

The thought pings around my head as I gape out the window.

Dozens of undead spill forth around the dorms, hands outstretched as they beeline for the humming engine of the minivan. It's a beacon in their blindness.

And they just keep coming. Leading them is one of the alphas, a teenage girl with dark hair and a Victoria's Secret sweatshirt. Tight clumps of zombies cluster at the heels of the alpha.

"Everyone out!" Carter cries. "I'll lead them away."

There's no time to argue. No time to debate. There is only time for action.

In under sixty seconds, we've emptied out of the van. I fall into step beside Ben and Reed. Ben leads the way, charging toward the dorm buildings on the western-most side.

He hugs a box of C-4 to his chest. The giant rocket launcher —which I've never fired—bounces against my back. It feels strange to have a knife and a screwdriver in either hand with an enormous gun on my back.

Music blares, stinging my ears with its intensity. Carter blasts a loud rap song. Keens pepper the air. Every zombie stumbles toward him, white eyes reflecting the morning sun. I spot the teenage alpha with zombies frothing around her as she leads them toward Carter.

Everything inside me screams to go back to Carter, to protect him. This basic motherly instinct beats at me. I ignore it, knowing the best way to protect Carter is to stick with the plan. Reed and I have to cover Ben and take out the western-most building.

With one last look back in my son's direction, I turn to my task.

I run in a tight cluster with Ben and Reed. We dodge around a pack of zombies, bee-lining to our assigned building. With the music blaring from Skip, the zoms stumble past us without turning in our direction.

Ben crouches in the lee of an abandoned dorm with a piece of C-4 in hand. He smacks it in place and races to the next section of wall.

"Don't you need wires or a detonator?" I leap forward to block two zombies that stray in his direction. My screwdriver takes one through the ear. Reed slams his knife in the skull of the second.

"This shit will blow to high heaven when we shoot off the rocket launchers," Ben replies. "We just need to plant it."

More and more zombies pour around the sides of the building. I can't see Carter anymore, but music continues to pelt the air.

"Mama," Reed yells.

I spin around as three zombies reach us. One reaches for Ben, jagged fingernails pricking his scalp.

I tackle the thing to the ground. My screwdriver punches through his skull. I roll sideways as a second zombie swipes at me. It trips on the dead one and tumbles forward.

Reed is there. He stabs the creature and shoves it aside. I spring to my feet, wiping blood from my face with the back of my hand.

I freeze as a pack of five lumber by, following the sound of the rap music from Carter. I swallow my breath, struggling not to rasp. The zombies moan and growl, but continue past us without ever turning in our direction.

Stealth, I realize. That's our biggest asset. Our only asset.

We have to move quietly enough to avoid their attention and let Carter's distraction do the rest.

In theory, this is a great idea. In practice, it's difficult when there are so many zombies. More and more of them stagger into sight with each passing second.

Reed and I dodge through the melee with one another, sticking close to Ben as he slaps another stick of explosive to the wall. Half a dozen zombies are dangerously close to us. I have to draw them away from Ben and give him more time.

I scoop up a rock and hurl it as hard as I can at a first-floor dorm window. It cracks the glass, but doesn't shatter it.

Reed gives me a look of profound sympathy before hefting his own rock. His pitch shatters the glass.

The cluster of zombies veers away from us, heading for the broken window. Reed and I attack them from behind, dropping them with our knives, zom bats, and screwdrivers.

We rush back to Ben, putting our backs to him with our weapons raised as he works. Once finished with this area, we scurry across a breezeway to another part of the building. The crack of Eric's rifle fills the air. I can only hope he's successfully taking out the alphas.

As we pass the breezeway, I hear the rattle of iron. I glance at the tall wrought iron gate that separates College Creek from the large athletic field on the other side. Though many zombies have fallen during our target practice sessions, there are still a lot out there.

The rattle of the field gate draws the attention of another cluster of undead that fumble their way down the breezeway. They veer in the direction of the gate, moaning in response to the noise of their brethren on the other side. They reach the gate, latching onto the bars and rattling them. The wrought-iron fence begins to rock in its cement foundation.

As much as the scene worries me, at the moment it's not a threat. What is an immediate concern is a zombie woman with two broken legs who claws her way in our direction. Reed dispatches her with a blow to the head.

"Done," Ben says, dropping his empty box of explosives and turning to us. "Let's get the fuck out of here."

I couldn't agree more.

We turn, the three of us shoulder-to-shoulder—only to stop dead in our tracks. Between us and the way out is a massive wall of undead. At their forefront, leading the pack straight toward us, is the teenage alpha zombie in the Victoria's Secret sweatshirt.

21

NO WAY OUT

BEN

"Run," Ben says, turning to Kate and Reed. "I'll blow the buildings."

"Fuck that. We're not leaving you," Kate replies. Without another word, she lifts the rocket launcher onto her shoulder, taking aim at the mass descending on them.

Ben only has time to scream "*No!*" before she pulls the trigger.

The force of the rocket launcher throws her flat against the ground. The rocket shoots out at a wild angle, making a curlicue through the air before striking.

Her rocket flies into the flank of the undead closing in on them. The ground explodes, sending out a cloud of grit, smoke, and undead body parts.

The explosion sets off the zombies. They stampede straight for the noise, falling and tripping in their haste to reach the sound. Not even the teenage alpha zombie can rein them in.

A path opens up. Ben spins around to find Kate groaning on the ground. She rubs at the back of her head, her hand coming away sticky with fresh blood. The sight of it freezes his guts.

"Come on, Mama." Reed helps her up.

Ben pulls the rocket launcher from around her shoulder. "I'll take that," he growls. "You're going to bring a damn building down on us."

Kate's eyes are glazed from her fall, but Ben notes the stiffening of her jaw. She might hurt like hell, but she's still in this fight. Good.

The three of them make their way away from the dorms in a tight cluster, heading for the opening created by Kate's rocket. In the confusion, most of the zombies don't notice them. They take out any who get too close with a knife through the ear or eye.

A new explosion rocks the ground to the east. Following hard on the heels of the first explosion are three more in rapid succession. The dorm on the eastern-most edge of the cluster disintegrates in a reverse mushroom cloud.

The force of the blast throws Ben sideways. He smacks straight into several zombies.

A hand latches onto his arm. Another grabs his knee. Ben's nostrils flare in rage and fear as he tries to twist away.

Reed leaps into the fray, landing on the back of an undead just as it raises its mouth to bite down on Ben's thigh. A whip-quick strike across the back of the neck severs the brain stem and drops the monster.

Reed springs toward the next nearest zombie, executing the same lethal move. The kid is as fast with his knife as he is with his feet.

Ben kicks the rest of the way free and clambers to his feet, searching for Kate.

He finds her facing off against four undead, wielding her zombie club like a demon. Her face is painted in red blood, her eyes wild. He rushes toward her with Reed on his heels, the three of them dispatching the zombies.

He's about to tell them both to get the hell out of there

when another succession of explosions rips through the air. This time, it's the centerline dorm. Ben barely has time to register the impending collapse before a wave of soot and smoke rushes over them.

He reaches for Kate, throwing himself on top of her to shelter her from the blast. Reed dog piles in with them, the three of them going down.

The spray of debris is like acid across his skin, cutting through his clothes. A piece of shrapnel embeds itself into his shoulder, hurting like a motherfucker. He wipes grit out of his eyes, searching the cloudy landscape. His ears ring and his eyes burn.

Another building down. Another wall between the campus and the undead swarm.

The last building is on the west side—his building. He has to take it down. The C-4 is all in place, but fuck, they're too close to it.

His searches through the debris for an opening, but there are none. It's a seething mess of undead and rubble, and it's only getting worse.

How ironic. They might indeed save the campus if they manage to get this building down, but they might all die in the process.

"Reed." Kate's voice comes out in a gasp. She helps the slender boy sit up. A huge gash mars his forehead, spilling blood down his face and soaking his clothes.

"Get him out of here," Ben says. "Take cover. We can't wait any longer."

"What about you?" Her eyes are anguished as she looks to him.

"Move it!" he barks.

Kate loops her hands under Reed's arm and helps him to the protective shelter of a large fountain. He waits just long enough to see them hunker down on the far side.

Then he spins around, raises the rocket launcher, and fires.

The first missile strikes the side of the farthest building. Ben reloads and fires a second time, then a third, and then a fourth.

The backlash from the buildings is thunderous and absolute. A billowing wall of smoke and grit engulfs him, swallowing him whole.

The world goes dark.

22

IMPROVISE

KATE

The ringing in my ears is the only thing I hear. Something heavy sits on my back and shoulders. Reed's body is slack underneath me.

I attempt to open my eyes. My effort is rewarded by a blast of debris right in the face. I try to breathe, but all I get is a lungful of grit. Coughing bends me in half.

I try again. Pushing my nose into the sleeve of my shirt, I suck for air. I'm rewarded with a meager lungful. I suck a second time, getting more oxygen.

Bracing my knees against the hard stone beneath me, I shove. Something slides off my back with a sick wet sound. It's a zombie body. The head and the right arm are both missing, the orifices oozing black blood all over me.

Beneath me, Reed stirs. His eyes flutter open, then snap shut as he's assaulted by the same grime that hit me.

I crouch and press a hand to Reed's cheek in a silent question. He nods, mouth moving in answer, but I still can't hear. We help each other stand, holding onto one another. I wipe blood from the side of his eye. Or, I try to. All I manage to do is smear grit into the blood. Reed shakes his head back and forth, sending droplets of fresh red showering to the ground.

Absolute destruction surrounds us. The College Creek dorms lie in enormous piles of rubble. Whether by sheer dumb luck or precise calculation under pressure, Ben managed to place the explosives in just the right place on our building. The dorms on the west tipped the right way, completely barricading any entrance into the campus on this side.

I scrutinize the settling dust, alert for danger. Hands and feet move in the rubble. Only a few undead still stand nearby, moaning and turning in small circles of confusion. None are close enough to be an immediate threat.

To the east, the rest of the buildings have fallen. And emerging from the gritty air is the remaining zombie pack. They've reassembled around the teenage alpha zom, at least a hundred strong. She and her pack miraculously survived the explosions and are once again pushing into the campus.

The alpha clicks and keens a series of instructions. The pack spreads out on either side of her, sweeping straight for the heart of Humboldt University.

Where is everyone? Ash? Jesus? Carter? Johnny? Eric? Ben? I don't see anyone. I can't see my family.

I swallow against my dry, gritty throat. There has to be something I can do. Something to protect the campus. I don't know who's left alive, but hell if I'm going to roll over and let the swarm take Humboldt.

The buzzing in my ears recedes, allowing a new sound to make its way to my ears. Music. I hear music.

Carter.

A robin's egg blue Caravan charges through the ruined landscape, heading straight for us. Jenna hangs out the window, waving her arms at us. Carter leans over the wheel, eyes intent.

Tears of joy leak from the side of my eyes. Carter. Jenna. Reed. Three of my kids are still alive.

Movement in my periphery. Johnny staggers out from behind a pile of rubble. Ash, Jesus, and Eric are with him. Susan extracts herself from the bottom of a metal table that somehow survived the blasts.

We all converge on the minivan as it slams to a halt.

"Mom." Carter leaps out of the car and crushes me in a bear hug. I throw my arms around him, using the moment to dry my tears on his shoulder and gather myself. We're not out of the woods yet.

"I took out three alphas," Eric reports. "The fourth one had already moved past the library and was out of my line of sight when I got to the rec center. I'm sorry, I couldn't get her."

I give his shoulder a squeeze. "You did good, Eric." Three was better than one or none. That still leaves us with the problem of the last alpha, though. The teenage alpha.

I stare past the ruins, my eyes taking in the seething swarm that continues to boil onto the campus. If we stand here much longer, we'll be blotted from the face of the earth.

I have to do something.

"Ben is missing." Jenna scans the area, brow creased in worry.

I refuse to believe Ben is dead. He's too tough and too grumpy to die.

"Go find Ben for me." I kiss Carter's cheek. Not giving myself a second to reconsider the half-baked plan taking shape in my brain, I shoulder past him and jump into the driver's seat of Skip. It's time to improvise.

"Mom!" Carter spins around, but I slam the door.

"Take care of everyone," I say, throwing the car into reverse.

"Mom, stop!" Carter latches both hands onto the open window. "Mom!"

To my horror, he throws up a leg, hooking it through the window.

"Get down," I cry.

The look he gives me is fierce. He looks so much like his father my breath catches. In a maneuver that is part strength, part yoga ninja, Carter drags himself through the open window. He slides across my lap and scrambles into the passenger seat.

"What the hell, Mom?"

"I'm going to blow up the library. You need to get out, son."

"What do you mean, you're going to blow up the library?"

I jerk a thumb toward the back of the van. "The beer kegs. They're full of fermenting liquid. We have a bomb on wheels, sweetheart." I meet his gaze. "I'm going to blow the side of the library. If I'm lucky, it will be enough to bury most of those fuckers and solidify our barrier."

Carter stares at me, mouth agape. "Mom, there's a shit load of zombies between us and the library. We'll never make it."

He's right. In the last sixty seconds, the alpha and her pack have massed outside the library.

"I got this, *Mamita*."

I turn in surprise to see Jesus standing by the open driver's side window. The dents in his forehead stand out under the bright morning sun.

"I'll clear the way. You get the bomb to the library." His eyes are hard, focused. "Creekside crew! *¡Mi familia!*"

Before I can form a sentence, Jesus fist pumps the air and sprints away, shouting at the top of his lungs. He streaks in the direction of the rubble, firing his gun into the air.

A keen crescendos, mixed with howls and growls. Like a giant amoeba, the pack flexes and rotates, oozing in the direction of Jesus.

"Drive!" Carter shouts. His blue eyes flare, and he jumps into the back. "I'll get the kegs ready. It's a good thing Jenna and

I decided to age this ale or we wouldn't have a bomb right now."

There isn't time to argue. There isn't time to debate. There isn't time to pull Jesus back to safety. There isn't time to grab Carter by the scruff of his neck and heave him out of the van.

I do the only thing I can. I slam my foot on the accelerator and zoom toward the library.

"How are we going to detonate these?" Carter yells.

A glance over my shoulder reveals him packing lumps of C-4 around the base of the kegs. He has the kegs on their sides, the fermenting liquid leaking out all over the floor.

"Grenade." I tap my belt, touching the only grenade I have. In the confusion of the morning, I can't even recall how it ended up there.

"That'll work," Carter hollers. "The van has cruise control. We paid extra for it."

"You paid extra for cruise control?" I shout back, recalling the shitty state of the van when I first saw it. I can't imagine paying extra for any special feature on this rust bucket.

"Yeah, Jenna likes cruise control."

I zip past the tail end of the swarm, straight through the corridor Jesus made for us. A blur of rotting skin and dark blood fills my periphery. A look in the rearview mirror shows several dozen peeling off to pursue us, but most of them continue after their alpha. After Jesus.

"It's time for you to get out, son. I'll take it from here." I slow the van just enough so he can jump out.

"No way, Mom."

"I'll be fine. I'll put the van in cruise control and jump when I'm closer. I'll have a better chance of pulling this off if I don't have to worry about you."

Carter narrows his eyes at me. "Okay. But you have to promise to jump. No kamikaze stuff."

"I promise, sweetie. I don't plan on dying today. Who's going to take care of you guys if I'm not here?"

Carter flings open the passenger side door. The pavement whizzes past.

He turns for a bare second, our eyes meeting.

"I love you, baby."

"Love you, too, Mom. See you soon."

With that, he leaps. Even above the hum of the engine, I hear the impact of his body on the ground.

Carter.

I grip the steering wheel and zoom away, streaking toward the library. A glance to my right shows Jesus on top of a statue between the College Creek rubble and the library. He fires his gun into the air, doing his damnedest to draw the alpha and her pack.

I swerve around a group of stragglers. The library looms before me, a wide megalith of dark cement. All that *knowledge.* And I'm about to blow it all to hell.

Setting the accelerator to thirty, I punch the cruise control button. Then, I pull the pin, toss the grenade, and throw myself out of the van.

I have a brief glimpse of the grenade rolling across the floor of the van—then I crash headlong into a bush. Pain explodes as I tear through the plant and hit the ground on the other side. The grenade detonates, ripping through the air with an explosion.

The library leaps from its foundation. It seems to hang, suspended above the ground for several seconds.

The library crashes down as though in slow motion. It strikes the ground with a *boom* and ripples through earth and air. The rumble rolls outward, sending the building forth in every direction. A landslide of cinderblocks buries the left flank of the undead swarm. The rest are swallowed in an expulsion of flying debris—including the statue where Jesus is perched.

"Jesus!" I scream his name.

A cloud of grit and debris hurtles toward me. I curl into a ball and throw my hands over my head. The exposed parts of my skin burn as thousands of tiny particles scour over me like sand paper.

Then silence descends.

A few moans pepper the air. I raise my head, blinking through grime-encrusted lashes. The dust begins to settle, revealing a massive mound of misshapen debris all around.

There is no sign of the alpha, no sign of her pack. They are buried beneath the remains of the library.

"Jesus." I try to stand, but my legs give out on me. I hurt everywhere. My eyes scour the rubble as I search for some sign of him.

I notice several small branches embedded in my skin, probably from the bush I landed on. One protrudes from my bicep. Another is lodged just below my collarbone.

I pluck them out, barely feeling the sting. My eyes continue to rove, searching for Jesus.

I want to pass out. I want to disappear into the dark.

"Kate!"

I blink in confusion. I must have hit my head. I'm definitely hallucinating. Either that, or I'm dead. Because what I'm seeing right now makes no sense.

Out of the dust and smoke and confusion comes Lila. She has three automatic rifles across her back and a string of grenades across her chest. A Sig hangs from either hip. And she's riding a bicycle like a bat out of hell, coming straight for me. Grime and bits of blood spatter her face and clothing.

"Kate!" She leaps off the bike. It clatters to the ground as she rushes to my side. "Kate, are you okay?"

I stare at her. Maybe I'm not hallucinating. "Lila?"

"It's me." Her mouth tightens as she grips my hand. "I decided that if all you losers are going to die out here, I want to go down with you. It was really shitty of you guys to leave me to die with an unconscious man half-eaten by a shark. Can you sit up?"

My terrified Lila has finally pushed through. Hell of a time for a breakthrough, even if said breakthrough is taking its toll on her. Her eyes are a little too wide, her skin a little too clammy, and her hands a little too shaky for her to conceal her true feelings. She's terrified.

Terrified, but she's here all the same. Pride swells in my chest.

I once again try to stand. *Fuck.* It feels like a thousand needles are going into my skull at the same time. I groan without meaning to and plop back down.

"Kate?"

"I'm fine. We need to find Jesus. I—"

I break off as two zombies lope around a pile of concrete and smashed library computers. They've heard our voices and are coming straight for us.

"Look out!" I lunge to my feet—then trip on a chunk of concrete and go down. I sprawl forward, my hands scraping against the pavement.

Lila jumps in front of me, rocking back and forth in fear as she faces the zombies. Right before they reach her, she darts to the side.

"Over here, dick wads," she calls, leading them away from me.

The zombies moan, rotating in her direction. They scratch at the empty air in front of them, searching for Lila.

I scramble to my feet as Lila stabs the first zombie through the nose. She dances backward as the second one reaches for her. I come up behind it and cave in the back of its head with my knife.

Lila and I breathe hard in the sudden silence, the two dead zombies between us.

"Thanks." If Lila hadn't been here, I might very well be dead right now. It's a sobering thought. I wipe my cheek on my shirtsleeve, attempting to dislodge a clump of brain matter.

"I just saved Mama Bear." Lila gives me a shaky smile. "Now if I could just do that about twelve thousand times, we might be even."

"There's no score between us, Lila. We're family." I glance back in the direction of Carter. He's two hundred yards away, picking himself up out of some bushes with Jenna's help. Good. He's safe.

I turn my attention back to Lila. "Jesus is in there." I point. With the dust clearing, I can just see the top of the statue.

"In there?" Her mouth sags open.

I don't blame her. Protruding from beneath the building fragments are twitching body parts. The zoms might have been buried, but not all of them are dead.

"Come on. We have to find Jesus." I force my feet to move.

My equilibrium returns and I'm able to walk with Lila's help. I hurt everywhere, but I guess that's to be expected when you jump out of a moving car. At least nothing is broken.

I pause over a zombie. The body is pinned, but its jaw continues to gnash. I stab it through the eye. No reason to leave a potential ankle biter out there.

Lila moves a few feet past me, drawing her knife. She killed her fair share of zombies at the start of the outbreak, but it's been a while for her.

She pauses over another pinned zombie. Her chest heaves with an inhalation.

Her blade jabs down, punching through the zom's nose.

"You haven't lost your touch," I say.

Lila glances over her shoulder at me, shrugs, then continues to pick her way through the rubble. We're forced to climb over and around debris—broken furniture, shattered computers, and fragments of walls. Step by step, we inch across what had once been a large, peaceful quad for students.

Now, it's a death zone. Lila and I pause only long enough to kill any zombies that pose a threat before continuing on.

We reach the statue. My throat closes at the sight, tears stinging the back of my eyes. The base is covered in chunks of large cement slabs.

"Jesus!" I call his name. "Jesus!"

A groan sounds off to our left.

"Jesus?" I scramble over rubble and drop down on the far side of the statue. "Je—"

Words dry up in my mouth.

"Do you see him?" Lila clambers down beside me. "Is he— oh, shit."

23

RUBBLE

BEN

Silence.

Ben has never liked silence after battle. Silence after battle often means there's no one left to speak.

The quiet presses in around him like a black hole. The vast space threatens to swallow him. The silence is a physical sensation—a lack of movement.

The explosion. The ambush. His men. Where are they?

Ben feels his heart pound against his sternum, a frantic *thump-thump-thump.*

His men. The explosion. The blinding sear of orange flames that blew up the corner of the meat shop as they came around the corner—

He claws at the pile of mortar and crumpled stone in front of him. Out. He has to get out. He has to find his men. He has to find the fuckers who ambushed them.

A nail tears, breaking to the quick. Ben doesn't even feel the pain. His breath comes in short gasps as panic threatens to suffocate him. He shoves and claws, fighting to dig himself free of the hellhole he's been buried in.

Light hits his face.

Something is wrong.

The air on his face doesn't smell right. It's salty. And cool. It's not the bone-sucking heat of Somalia. It's—

A soft moan breaks through the ringing in his ears, followed by another. Somewhere distant, a high-pitched keening raises the hair all along the back of his neck.

The world around him recalculates, swinging wildly as he struggles to get his bearings. The dry heat of the African desert disappears from his mind, as do the shanty towns, shrub lands, and the familiar feel of being surrounded by comrades in arms.

Ben finds himself dropkicked from the streets of Somalia into the ruins of Humboldt University in Arcata, California. The force of the return is so strong his head swims.

Where is everyone?

Where is Kate?

His knees scrape painfully against the pavement as he drags himself the rest of the way free from the rubble. He feels his pants rip, feels the bite of rough stone against his skin.

Panting, he struggles to his feet. His legs sway, threatening to give way. His vision corkscrews. He blinks, waiting for it to clear.

The details fall in around him. The dorms are all down, piles of rubble that create a perfect barrier between them and the dead. Beyond the dorms, the library has also been leveled.

Ben has never been much of a reader. Books were fine for killing time, though he preferred a game of cards over a book any day of the week. Still, the sight of the collapsed library is like the loss of a good Hummer. They used that library. An excess of information was always at their fingertips. All gone now.

The library hadn't been part of the original plan, but it had been a damn good improvisation. The string of wrecked buildings has accomplished several things. Most zoms that breached the campus are buried. The collapsed library blocked the last large gap, leaving no egress for more zoms to enter campus. Even now, he sees large swaths of them tumbling down to the freeway on the west side as they follow the natural curve of the wreckage. It's far from perfect, but considering the situation, it's pretty fucking good. And effective. With any luck, they can weather the worst of this storm.

A figure comes his way. A tall, lanky boy with broad shoulders. His face is bloody, his body covered in a fine layer of gray grit that mingles with blood splatter. The figure raises a knife.

"Carter?"

The figure stops, knife poised. "Ben?" the boy whispers. His face collapses into a smile. "Ben!"

Before Ben can figure out what the kid is up to, he finds himself seized in a crushing hug. The act of affection is so foreign that it takes Ben aback. He pats Carter's shoulder, equal parts horror and appreciation over this open display of affection.

If Carter is at all put off by Ben's uncomfortable reaction, he doesn't let it show. "You're okay!" Carter pounds on his back and shoulder. "We were all worried. Come on, let's get back to the others."

"What's the sit rep?" Ben asks, following Carter through the rubble.

"The what?"

Ben grimaces, realizing again he's slipping back into a time and place that no longer exists. "What's the status of our people?"

Carter's face goes blank. "We don't know where my mom and Jesus are."

Colors swim in Ben's vision. "Where the fuck is Kate?"

"We drove Skip into the library," Carter explains. "Jesus led the alpha and the pack away to clear the way for us. Mom and I used the beer kegs and some C-4 for explosives. I jumped out of the van while Mom drove it the rest of the way and detonated the bomb.

Ben absorbs this. "Was that Kate's idea?" he says at last.

"Yeah."

Of course, it was. Only Kate would think of using beer kegs for bombs to blow up a library. Likely that was her definition of improvising. God, that woman. He isn't sure if he wants to yell at her or kiss her. Both, if he's ever lucky enough to get the chance.

"We have to find her." He marches in the direction of the library, marveling at the swath of destruction cut by the explosions. Any soldier could mistake this place for a Middle East war zone. Carter falls into step beside him while the rest of the group follows a few paces behind.

"I would have stayed with her," the young man says. "I tried to. She made me get out. You know how she is."

"You're a good kid." Ben has an overwhelming urge to tousle the young man's head, like he used to do with his own son. He deals with the urge by wrapping both hands around his knife hilts.

This isn't the first time he's had to remind himself that Carter isn't Sam. Sam, his son, is on the other side of the country. With a stepfather who was a much better father than Ben had ever been. He hopes they're all still alive.

"And yeah, I know how your mom is." The damn woman is like a starving, third world dog with a bone when she gets an idea. "Is everyone else alive and accounted for?"

"Yeah. Everyone is pretty scraped up, but we're alive."

It feels like a miracle. Not that Ben believes in miracles. But considering the fucking shit storm they'd entered less than an hour ago, it's surprising they didn't lose more. He's surprised to find himself relieved that even Caleb made it.

Someone off to their left waves arms in the air. Reed's afro sends out poofs of dust.

"He found something. Come on." Carter picks up speed. His long legs eat up the distance, forcing Ben to a jog to keep up with him.

The movement sends a spear of pain through his back. Dammit. He probably pulled some of Kate's stitches. He bites down on the pain and keeps pace with Carter.

As they near Reed, he spots the rest of their people. Susan looks to be in the best shape out of everyone. Other than blood splatter, she doesn't appear to have a wound anywhere.

The same can't be said for the rest of the crew. Caleb, Ash, Johnny, Eric, Reed, and Jenna all look like they've been dragged through a gauntlet by their hair. Every last one of them is bloody, bruised, gashed, cut, and limping.

"Look!" Reed points. "Over there in the old quad. By the statue."

Ben follows the line of his arm.

He spots Kate. Fresh blood runs down several wounds on her body. Her clothes are half torn from her body, revealing flesh that is badly abraded. She can't seem to walk upright and limps on one leg. She looks like she got run over by a car. Hell, knowing her, she probably jumped out of the minivan while it was still moving.

He pulls ahead of the group, scrambling over debris in his haste to reach her. He pauses only long enough to dispatch any living zombies he passes on his way.

When he's twenty yards away, he knows something's wrong. Her shoulders are slumped, her mouth drooping in a sad line.

"Kate?"

She turns, her eyes finding him as he scrambles over the last of the ruins that separates them. He drops down beside her.

He opens his mouth to speak. Before he can utter a word, Kate grabs him in an unexpected hug.

"I'm glad you're okay," she murmurs against his shoulder. "I knew you were too tough and grumpy to die."

He reflexively pulls her tight, overwhelmed by relief at finding her whole. "It sounds like you did your best to end up on the wrong side of the dirt."

"I did what had to be done."

Of course. Kate always lays it all on the line for her kids.

She peels herself free of his arms. He's reluctant to let her go, but drops his arms as she pushes away. The right side of her face has been scraped raw.

"Jesus is under here," she says, a hitch in her voice.

Ben had been so consumed with worry for Kate that he hadn't even noticed Jesus. Two-thirds of the man's body is buried under rubble and a slab of concrete the size of a bike. His eyes are closed, his face pasty, but he's still breathing.

That's when Ben notices another figure. Lithe and dark-haired, she crouches beside Jesus with a plastic bottle of water. She drizzles some of it across his forehead in an attempt to wipe his face clean.

Ben blinks, trying to make sense of what he's seeing. The girl looks like Lila, except she has three automatic rifles over her shoulder, a string of grenades across her chest, and a Sig on either hip. And she's *outside*.

"What the fuck?" He stares at her in shock.

Lila grimaces. "I know. About fucking time, right?"

The rest of the group arrives before Ben can form a proper response. Everyone is talking at once.

"Lila?" Eric gapes at her. "What are you doing here?"

"Where's Jesus? Did you guys find him?"

"Lila, no way!"

"You didn't mess around with explosives, Mama Bear."

"Anyone seen Jesus?"

"*Quiet.*" Kate's command cuts through the confusion. The grief in her eyes is thick, but she's holding it together. "Jesus is right here. Everyone, spread out. We need to get this concrete off him."

The mood sobers as the rest of the group finally sees Jesus. The grief hits them all at once, but Ben sees it hit Reed hardest of all. The young man's face crumples, his usual upbeat manner squashed by the sight of his friend buried in rubble.

Reed positions himself next the concrete slab. "Come on, guys," he barks. "On three. One, two, three—"

They heave. The giant piece of concrete is elevated on one side, revealing a body. Ben swallows at the sight of Jesus's crushed legs. The man groans in pain, his eyes closed.

"Keep pushing," Carter says.

They heave, tipping the chunk of cement. It thuds over, landing on yet more rubble.

"Mamita." The voice is weak.

Ben sees the way it hits Kate. The other man's voice goes through her like a spear, causing her body to jerk and her face to spasm.

"Jesus." She throws herself to the ground beside him. The rest of them cluster around while she picks up one of his bloody hands. Her other hand comes up to smooth away a chunk of bloody hair.

"You okay, Mamita?" Jesus coughs, pink spittle collecting at the corners of his mouth.

"We're all okay," she replies, voice catching. "You're going to be okay, Jesus. We're going to get you out of here. We're going to get you home. Ash is going to sew you up—"

"Mamita." Jesus raises his free hand.

Even through all the dirt, the bites along his left arm are visible. As Ben studies him, he sees more evidence of zombie bites. Parts of Jesus's torso bear marks, as well as the right arm Kate holds so fiercely.

"I got those fuckers," Jesus replies. "That's what matters."

Someone sniffles. Ash wipes her eyes. "*Eres un héroe,*" she whispers.

Jesus tries to smile, but ends up coughing instead. "*No te olvides de mí, bonita.*"

Ash sniffs again, refusing to look away. She kneels on Jesus's other side, clinging hard to his free hand.

"My legs hurt," Jesus says.

"I'm so sorry, man," Reed whispers, clustering close with Kate and Ash.

They stand around Jesus in a tight cluster. Ben forces himself to watch the life ebb out of the other man. He takes in the grief of those closest to Jesus.

Mostly, he watches Kate. This will be her first big loss, not counting Frederico. But that was different. That was a friend.

Kate's relationship with everyone in this group is different. She sees herself as their caretaker. Their adopted mother. Jesus may not be her flesh and blood, but for Kate, that won't lessen the grief.

Ben knows what it feels like to fail people. She's going to feel like she's been torn open by a meat grinder. He wants to shield her from the pain. He wishes he could take it all on himself. Instead, all he can do is watch the horror unfold.

"Take St. Roch, little brother." Jesus drags the bloody pendant from around his neck. "He'll look after you."

Reed reaches for the saint with trembling fingers. His hand briefly locks around Jesus's in a gesture of brotherhood before withdrawing with St. Roch.

"It's time, Mamita," Jesus whispers. "Will you do it? Before I turn? I don't want to be one of those fuckers. Not for a second. It would be an honor to have you do it."

Ash makes a soft wailing sound.

Kate's arms begin to tremble. Tears spill down her cheeks. Looking into Jesus's eyes, she nods.

Ben hates every second of this agonizing moment. He

knows exactly what it's going to do to Kate, but he's unable to protect her from it.

When Jesus draws his knife and hands it to Kate, Ben thinks he might be sick.

He steps forward. "I'll do it." Kate shouldn't have to say goodbye to Jesus this way. Damn that fucking bastard for asking it of her.

"No." Kate doesn't look at him. She only has eyes for the man dying beside her.

She licks her lips as she raises the tip of the knife and places it against Jesus's temple. Reed turns away, vomiting into the wreckage. Ash stays resolutely beside Jesus.

Kate smiles down at him, smoothing back his bloody hair with one hand. "Rest easy, Jesus."

"See you again someday, Mamita."

"See you again someday," Kate whispers.

Then she jams the knife into his skull.

Ben feels the killing blow all the way to his core. It punches him back to Iraq, to a day when the skies bled black from the burning oil fields. When he held a dead friend in his arms who hadn't looked all that different from Jesus.

He staggers, nearly crumpling under the weight of the memory.

The world flicks back to the present. Jesus, a knife sticking out from his temple, lies dead. His face is peaceful, the corners of his mouth turned up in a contented smile. He's gone.

The rest of them are alive, left to carry the weight of shit and devastation.

And then Lila starts to scream.

24

DOUBLE FEATURE

KATE

Reed sags to his knees next to me, head bowed and shoulders convulsing with loss. My hand still grips the knife in Jesus's head when the scream crashes over me.

I spin around to see a zombie latched onto the back of Lila's leg. The slimy fucker must have crawled free when we moved the concrete slab pinning Jesus.

Eric bellows, slashing with his knife. Caleb and Jenna crowd in, all three hacking with weapons.

Lila staggers free. There's blood everywhere. I don't how much is Lila's and how much belongs to the zom head that now rolls across debris.

"No fucking way," Eric cries, dragging Lila toward him. "No fucking way, Lila. Not you. Not you." He chokes on tears.

Lila sags into him, face pale. The back of her left calf is shredded, her blue jeans reduced to tatters.

"It's okay." Her hand comes up to stroke Eric's cheek. "It's okay, you asshole. Stop being a pussy."

"It's not fucking okay!" There's blood smudged on Eric's

glasses. He picks Lila up, cradling her against his chest as he plops onto an exposed wedge of concrete.

Lila. I didn't think there was anything left in me to break after euthanizing Jesus.

I was wrong.

I have no words. Or rather, I have too many of them. Sorrow closes off my throat, choking off all sound.

Jesus is gone. I lost him. I failed him. He came to me for protection and I failed him. Even worse, I failed Reed. Jesus was the closest thing he had to a brother.

And now I've failed Lila. And Eric, too.

I feel like I've been bombed from the inside out.

Zombies moan in the background. Distantly, I see a handful of them tottering around in the rubble. I see hands and legs protruding from underneath crushed concrete.

"It's okay." Lila continues to sooth Eric, stroking his cheek while he cradles her and sobs into her shoulder. "Seriously, Eric, pull your shit together."

From Lila's tone, you'd think they were bickering in Creekside, not facing death together in a zombie war zone.

"I can't," Eric sobs. "Lila, I can't ..."

"You can," she replies. "You have to." The compassion on her face as she gazes at Eric threatens to break me.

How is it that Lila—our frightened, agoraphobic Lila—has found her strength in the face of her own death? Here she is, a pillar of strength while the rest of us are falling apart.

Reed and Ash cry quietly over Jesus. There isn't a dry eye to be found among any of us.

A foot to my left, Ben stands like a statue. He's always harbored a fatherly affection for Lila. Now, his eyes are locked on her. I can tell from the cloudy look in his eyes that this new horror has triggered his PTSD. I grasp his hand and squeeze.

It's a selfish gesture. I want to bring him back to the present.

But more than that, I want his comfort. I think my legs would give out if I didn't have him to hold onto.

Lila kisses Eric's forehead and pushes free of his arms. She has to grab onto the slab of concrete to keep herself upright. Her good leg stands in a wide pool of her own blood.

"You're going to be okay, Eric." Lila's gaze sweeps over the rest of us. "You're all going to be okay. Honestly, I've been sick of all this shit for months. I'm ready to go."

She draws the Sig from her belt.

The act is like a lightning bolt slamming through Ben. He jerks free of me, lunging across our lopsided circle.

"Lila!" he bellows. He isn't fast enough.

The Sig fires.

Lila falls.

25

WAKE

KATE

Thirty-six hours after the alpha attack, music plays softly from an iPod in the Creekside kitchen. In the center of the living room is the small shrine Jesus had built for St. Roch. It's nothing more than a plastic storage tub spray painted red. Inside is a candle, a vase of plastic flowers, and a picture of St. Roch Jesus had drawn with colored pencils. It wasn't a work of art, but it wasn't bad.

In front of the shrine are two rocks Jenna painted. One bears Lila's name, the other Jesus's name. Both rocks are covered with pictures of flowers.

In front of the shrine are things that belonged to our lost friends.

Jesus's leather jacket. Lila's jar of cannabis salve. The gold St. Roch medallion. A picture of Lila and her family.

These are all we have left of our friends. We couldn't bring back their bodies. We'd buried them in the rubble at the foot of the statue in the quad.

Near the shrine to our lost friends is a cardboard box filled with a collection of beer and liquor I'd squirreled away. After losing Lila and Jesus, no one seems to care we're well on our way to blowing through half our stash in one night.

"I've never been much of a drinker." I finish this sentence by downing a shot of something brown. It tastes like shit and burns all the way down, but I don't care.

"Could have fooled me." Across the table, Ben takes a shot. His eyes are bloodshot.

"My husband was a recovering alcoholic." I reach for the bottle and pour myself another shot. "I never drank much, you know? To support him." As I throw back another shot, Kyle's face swims before me.

I said my goodbye to Kyle on my journey to Arcata. Most days, memories of him bring me happiness. Tonight, I wish he was here to hug me. I miss having someone to hold me.

Sometimes I wonder what it would be like if Kyle was here with me and Carter. Sometimes I'm glad he didn't live to see this fucked up world.

"You got married young," Ben says.

"What?" I blink at him, eyes watering from the shot. God, that stuff burns.

"You must have gotten married young."

"Why do you say that?" I grasp the bottle of amber liquid, weighing the wisdom of taking another shot.

"You don't look old enough to have a college student for a son."

Yes, I definitely need another shot. "I got pregnant in college. I was nineteen." I glance across the room to where Carter sits on the floor, Jenna between his legs. They share a bottle of warm beer between them. "Best thing that ever happened to me. I got Carter and Kyle in one fell swoop."

I throw back the next shot. My stomach roils. I close my eyes, hunching over the table as I struggle to steady myself against the nausea.

Beside me, a chair scrapes against the floor. Eric sits down next to me. His eyes are red and puffy. The smell of marijuana clings to him. He lets out a long exhalation.

The sight of him makes something inside me crumple. "Eric—" I break off, rendered speechless by the devastation on his face.

Eric leans sideways, head resting on my shoulder. He begins to cry. My heart breaks all over again. I put an arm around him and rest my cheek against his head.

"I'm so sorry," I whisper.

"Me, too," he whispers back. His speech is slurred, telling me just how stoned and drunk he is.

I can't hold back the tears. They gush from my eyes. I don't try to stop them.

Ben looks away and pours himself another shot. He looks as miserable as the rest of us.

"You know," Eric says, sniffling, "I'm pretty sure my parents and brother are dead. Even if they aren't dead, I'll never see them again. I know that. I've never once cried about it. I feel sad sometimes, but it's not the same. It's not the same as seeing someone—as seeing Lila—" He makes a choking sound.

I cinch my arm around him more tightly, wishing I could hug his pain away. Wishing I could turn back the clock and never tell Lila to go outside.

"I'm sorry," I say again. It's not enough, but it's all I have.

"I should have been paying attention," he replies. "It all happened so fast."

I suck in a breath, willing myself to tell him the truth. "It was my fault, Eric. I'd been encouraging her to go outside. If I had just kept my mouth shut—"

"It's not your fault, Kate," Ben says. "That was just plain bad luck. Nothing else."

Eric points a finger at Ben. "What the old guy says. He's right."

I close my eyes, touched by their words. Even when the

evidence says otherwise, they insist I'm blameless. Do they really believe that, or are they just being nice?

"Hey, guys." Jenna puts her arms around me and Eric. "Come on. We're all going to share a memory of Jesus and Lila."

My head swims as I push to my feet. Eric and I steady each other, leaning together. Ben appears on my other side. I get the feeling he's there in case I topple over.

"I'm not that drunk," I tell him.

"Okay," he replies, but he doesn't budge from my side.

"I have a rule," Eric tells me as we shuffle into the living room. "I never drink and smoke pot at the same time. I sort of broke that rule tonight."

"That's okay." I give him a squeeze. "I normally don't get drunk. Just seems stupid in the apocalypse, you know? Like I need to keep my guard up at all times. In case we all die. But tonight I think it's okay to break rules."

Ben gives me a look when I say this. I can't be certain, but if I wasn't drunk, I would say he looks sorrowful.

Eric and I lower ourselves into the lopsided circle on the stained carpet. Everyone else is there, all of us in various states of drunkenness.

Jenna makes her way into the center of our would-be circle, resting the tips of her fingers on the jar of cannabis salve Lila made.

"Lila," she says, "you were the best damned botanist I ever knew. Rest in peace."

I look down and realize I have a bottle of clear liquor in one hand. I didn't realize I'd carried it away from the table. I take a swig then pass the bottle to Eric.

"You were one crazy chick." Johnny raises a beer bottle in salute to the shrine. "I'll miss you stinking up the kitchen with your concoctions."

"I'll miss you telling us we're stupid for going to the track to run," I say. "Thanks for saving my life today."

"I'll miss your cooking," Reed says. When several people turn incredulous stares in his direction, he wrinkles his nose. "Okay, don't take this the wrong way, but you sort of sucked at cooking." This sends a ripple of laughter around the room. "But you were really good at heating up cans. And dammit, it was sweet of you to try and find protein sources for us." Reed's eyes water.

"I loved your cooking," Ben says. "You could have given any army cook a run for his money."

"She brought me a bag of clothes last night," Susan says. "And I know it might seem stupid that I would even care about clothes when my husband is unconscious from blood loss after a shark attack. But last night, it seemed like the nicest thing anyone had ever done for me."

"Lila never complained about sharing a room with me and Jenna at the start of the apocalypse," Carter says. "She always knew when we needed privacy and gave it to us."

We go around the room, all of us sharing memories of Lila. It feels good to remember happy times with Lila. But it also compounds her loss, sinking me deeper into sadness—and into the bottle in my hands.

After we share stories about Lila, Reed stands. A fresh joint is in his hand. "Jesus was my brother," he slurs. "We sold drugs together. We partied together. We stole shit from the mini mart together. We went through the Taco Bell drive-through every Thursday night to get seven-layer burritos with extra sour cream." He raises the joint in salute. In his other hand is a half-empty bottle of vodka. "I'll miss you, brother."

"He was a damn good shot," Ash says. "I never told him, but I admired him for that. And it was nice to speak Spanish with him."

Caleb, red-eyed and gloomy next to Ash, hunches his shoulders and tightens his knuckles around the clear bottle in his hand. His competition for Ash might be gone, but he's as miserable as the rest of us. Instead of adding a tribute to Jesus, he takes another long drink.

"He never complained," I say. "It didn't matter how long I made him run, or how much work we did. He just did whatever had to be done." My throat tightens. "He saved our lives today. He never hesitated. He saw the danger and acted. We all owe him our lives."

Ben speaks up next. "He wore that dent on his forehead like a fucking badge of honor. He was loyal. That's a rare quality."

A rare quality. Ben is right. Jesus had a lot of rare qualities. And now he's gone. Him and Lila.

Their loss hits me like a baseball bat. To keep myself from breaking down in front of everyone, I lock my lips around the bottle and take a long drink. The liquid burns all the way down.

"Woah there, Kate." Ben pries the bottle away from me.

Anger flashes through me. "Get your own bottle." I snatch it back.

His eyes weigh me. He doesn't try to take back the bottle. I feel two inches tall. I wish he would stop looking at me like he knows what I'm going through. I'm raw and wretched inside. I don't want anyone knowing how I feel right now.

I turn away from him and take another drink.

26

BEN

This isn't so different from that night in that shitty desert town in Iraq. Or that night in the dirty bar in Pakistan. Or in the med tent in Somalia.

Wakes are all the same.

Besides the two shots he took with Kate, Ben elects not to drink anymore. Kate isn't wrong about shit going sideways when everyone starts getting shitfaced. Someone needs to be sober. Gary doesn't count since he's still unconscious.

Besides that, if he's drunk, he won't be able to look after Kate. One look into her eyes tells him she's on the edge. She's taken on the burden of Lila and Jesus's deaths.

He knows what that feels like. He carries a long list of names in his head. People he's failed. People who have died because of him. He wishes Kate didn't have to carry that same burden. He wouldn't wish that on anyone, most especially her.

It's only a matter of time before people start getting sick. It's all a part of drowning pain.

Susan is the first to beeline into the bathroom and puke her guts out. Reed and Johnny aren't far behind her.

Ash has the grace to pass out on the sofa. Eric, stoned and drunk, curls up in the fetal position on the floor and also passes out.

"I—I think I need to lie down." Kate sways to her feet, blinking bloodshot eyes. One hand presses to her stomach.

"Mom, wait, I'll come with you." Carter sways to his feet.

"Yeah, I'm ready for bed," Jenna says. She and Carter cling to each other, keeping one another upright.

Ben rises to his feet without a word. He positions himself next to Kate. If she passes out, he'll be there to catch her. If she starts puking, he'll make sure she doesn't face plant in her own vomit. He's done that once or twice and it isn't pleasant.

"I don't need an escort," she growls at him. She takes one unsteady step toward the door.

He ignores her, keeping himself positioned next to her.

"Maybe we should turn tonight into sleep deprivation training," Caleb slurs from his slouch against the wall. "I mean, we're all up."

"Dude, half of us are passed out." Carter gestures to Ash and Eric.

"We could throw some water on them." Caleb punctuates this with another swig from his bottle of gin. The asshole has a stomach of iron.

"If anyone throws water on anyone else, you'll have me to answer to," Kate says.

She takes another unsteady step toward the door. Then walks right into the wall.

"Dammit." She smacks the wall with an open palm. She hits it a second time, then a third, until she's smacking the wall over and over with both palms. "Dammit!" she yells.

Ben is pretty sure any intervention on his part will not be welcome. He's grateful when Carter totters over to his mother and takes both her hands in his. She glares at him, trying to yank free. Carter is taller and stronger than Kate. He smothers her in a bear hug.

"It's okay, Mom," he whispers.

"It's not fucking okay!" She pounds her fists on his shoulders. Her sobs disappear into his chest.

Somehow, Carter gets her out the door. Jenna is on their heels, one hand on the wall for balance. Ben trails them, determined to see all three of them safely to their beds.

A few steps into their dorm room, Carter staggers. "Shit, sorry, Mom—" Hand covering his mouth, he rushes toward the bathroom. He doesn't even manage to close the door before he starts throwing up.

Jenna hurries after him as best she can. One look at her face and Ben is pretty sure she's not far behind in a round with the toilet.

Kate stares after them with red-rimmed, bleary eyes. She looks so wretched and lost Ben has to look away.

"Come on, Mama Bear." He takes her by one arm, intending to get her to her bedroom.

She stiffens and tries to shake him off. He ignores her efforts and remains by her side. He sees the battle raging in her features.

"Let me help you. Please." Before she falls and knocks out her front teeth, or something equally stupid. He resists her feeble effort to shove him away. He steers her toward the tiny dorm room where she sleeps.

She grunts then leans on him. It takes them a few minutes, but at last they enter the tiny rectangular bedroom with Grateful Dead posters all over the walls. He helps her onto the bed.

She tips sideways, moaning into the pillow.

Ben stares down at her. He hates feeling helpless. He knows what she's going through. How can he tell her that without sounding like a condescending ass?

"What did you do when you lost people?" Kate surprises him with the question. "You lost people, right?"

She reaches up and brushes her hand over his arm, which is covered by his customary fatigue shirt. He knows she's referring to the tattoos hidden beneath the fabric.

"Yeah, I lost people." A barrage of images tumbles through his head. Sand. Narrow, stinky alleyways of worlds far away from this one. A bloody courtyard filled with the bodies of college kids

He can never entirely shake free of those images. Cynthia came to haunt him last night. The lithe, blond-haired college girl made it her mission to crack jokes until she got Ben to laugh. He tries to remember her quick smile and sharp blue eyes, but overlying it are memories of her prone on the courtyard pavement of College Creek, her body shot up with bullets.

He sees all the kids. Ricky. Jim. KP. Suzy.

Pain blooms in his chest. All those dead kids. And now Lila is among them. Sharp-tongued, quick-witted Lila.

"Ben?" Kate blinks up at him from the pillow, curled into the fetal position. Her pale face makes him think she might be joining Carter and Jenna in the bathroom soon.

He sinks into the wooden desk chair, rubbing a hand over his face. "I think I need another drink," he mutters.

Kate moans, pressing a hand against her stomach. Ben registers the act. He has just enough time to snatch the wastebasket from under the desk before Kate heaves. She vomits several times into the trashcan before groaning and rolling back onto the bed.

A few bottles of water sit on the desk. He passes her one, moving the trashcan next to the door. He drapes a dirty shirt over the top to block the smell.

"I never drank when my husband died." Kate's scratchy voice fills the room. "I just ran. I've always preferred running to alcohol."

Ben returns to the desk chair. He searches for words in the darkness but doesn't find any.

"I know running can't solve everything," Kate whispers. "But dammit, it's times like this I really wish ... I wish I could lose myself on a trail and just *run*."

"Some days, I wish I could just lose *myself*." Ben isn't sure where the words come from. He stares around the room, as if expecting to find a third person there, even though he knows there's no one else.

"You've lost people, right?"

It's the second time she's asked him this question.

He feels like it takes a crowbar to pry his mouth open. "Yeah. I know how you feel." His voice is rough, the words dragged from his throat. Why is it so fucking hard for him to form words? "Cynthia ..."

Kate's face is half-buried in her pillow. There are no lights on in the room. Even so, Ben sees one eye staring at him in the darkness.

"Who's Cynthia?"

Maybe hearing his shitty story will help her forget her own. "One of the young college women I ... lost." He swallows back the emotion that tries to fight its way free. "Cynthia. Ricky. Jim. KP. Suzy. Tweedle Dumb and Tweedle Dumber. Shelby. Jen. Ditto. Erin. Jason. Scarlet. Andy. Ted. Ginger." The names fall from his lips, dropping into his lap like hundred-pound weights.

Kate's eye never wavers as he speaks. Bloodshot and grief-stricken, that single eye watches him from the pillow. "The kids from College Creek?" she asks.

He nods. "I need to find a tattoo artist." He rubs absently at the blank spot on his shoulder, the place that will some day bear a tattoo memorializing those poor kids. "I know what you're going through, Kate. It's shitty. I'd be a lying asshole if I told you it gets better. It doesn't. You just get better at dealing with it." Sort of. If insomnia is a clinical definition of dealing with it.

She rolls onto her back, staring up at the posters on the ceiling. "You would have been a shitty motivational speaker."

"Guess it's a good thing I signed up to carry a gun around for a living."

Her laugh catches him off-guard. It fades as quickly as it came.

"I feel like it's my fault," she whispers. "I feel like they're dead because of me."

"I know." Something inside him breaks at the pain in her voice. "Shit, Kate, the only thing that really makes it better is time. We both have to live long enough for time to work its magic." He stands. "You should sleep. Drink some more water if you can." He doesn't envy the hangover she's going to have in the morning.

"Don't leave."

He stands in the middle of the room, feeling awkward. More than anything, he wants to stay. He's never wanted to stay with a woman more than he wants to stay with Kate at that moment.

"Please don't leave," she says again. Tears leak out of her eyes.

Terrified he's going to wreck this perfect, fragile moment, he grabs a pillow off the bed and lays down on the floor.

He could lay on the bed. He's pretty sure that's what she meant when she asked him to stay. But he suspects this moment between them is because she's drunk and sad. She'll still be sad in the morning, but she won't be drunk. He can't stomach the idea of her waking up and recoiling from him. She can't recoil from him if he's on the floor.

"Here's a blanket." She pushes a quilt in his direction.

When he reaches up to take it, their fingertips brush. Kate grabs his hand.

"Thanks for not lying to me," she whispers.

He says the only thing that comes to mind. "You're welcome, Kate."

She laces her fingers with his. A few minutes later, her breath evens and the grip of her hand relaxes.

She's asleep. Kate is asleep, her hand laced with his.

For once in his life, his words hadn't completely fucked things up.

27

HANG OVER

KATE

I wake up with the worst hangover of my adult life.

I open my eyes. Psychedelic Grateful Dead posters hang on the ceiling above me, but all I see is Lila's face—the calm, determined set to her jaw when she raised the Sig to her temple.

Next, I see Jesus. His brave expression in the face of death. His earnest look when he asked me to put him down.

I close my eyes, trying to block out their faces. I still feel the jolt of the knife when it punched through Jesus's temple and into his skull. I still feel the way the air vibrated when Lila discharged the gun into her own head. I shrink back from the memories, wishing I could hide from them.

The only thing that really makes it better is time. Ben's gruff voice trickles in from my drunken memories of the night before.

That's when I notice my left arm hanging over the edge of the bed, the skin cold from being left uncovered. My fingers twitch, held in place by something.

I scrunch forward and find Ben on the floor, fully clothed. A thin throw blanket is draped over his torso, too small to cover his tall form. His eyes are open. He gives my hand a squeeze before releasing it.

I realize with a shock that he's been here with me all night. I'm equal parts grateful and embarrassed.

Our eyes meet. "When's the last time you had to hold back a girl's hair?" I ask.

"Technically, you don't have any hair to hold back."

I squint at him. "Did you just make a joke?"

His response is cautious. "Did you think it was funny?"

"I'll let you know later. When my head doesn't hurt so much."

The skin around his eyes crinkles. I think that might be his version of a smile. Another thing to ponder when my head doesn't feel like it's going to crack in half.

I reach out and find his hand. "Thanks for everything you did last night."

He squeezes my hand without speaking.

It's what Ben does that always touches me. It's the tattoos on his arms commemorating thirty years of life and loss in the army. It's the way he looked after me last night when I was no better than a drunk teenager. It's the warm coffee on a cold morning. It's the way he holds my hand in silence right now.

I remain prone on the bed. Eyes closed, I savor the feel of Ben's hand in mine. His palm is rough with callouses, his grip strong. I like the way it feels. I like *him* more and more every day.

My eyes snap open. "I forgot. I have a present for you."

"A what?" He frowns, as though convinced he didn't hear me correctly.

"A present. For you. Don't get too excited. It's not a Ferrari or anything."

I push myself into a sitting position with a groan. My stomach threatens to revolt. I lean back against the wall to let it settle.

Ben, watching the operation, wordlessly hands me a bottle of water. I down it with a grateful sigh.

"How are you feeling?" Ben ventures.

How am I feeling?

I want to stay in bed and let the world fade away. I don't want to wait out the agony of losing Lila and Jesus. I don't want to face the terror of losing more of my new family every morning when I get up. I want to run away from it all.

But after Federico died, I made myself a promise that I wouldn't run away from my problems. I owe it to him to stick it out. Hell, I owe it to all the kids.

I want to tell Ben all of this, but instead, I say, "I feel like any college kid feels after a night of binge drinking."

I groan again as I fumble at the top desk drawer. My brain feels like it wants to pound its way out of my skull.

"Here." I produce a stick of *Secret* deodorant hand it to Ben.

His brow furrows. He turns it over in his hands, frown deepening. "Are you trying to tell me something?"

My eyes widen. "That's not—I didn't mean it that way. We're all a little smelly. That's for your chafing."

He stares at me. "My *what*?"

"Your waist. The chafing from your fatigues."

"I thought runners used Vaseline for chafing."

"No." I shake my head, grimacing at the backlash of pain. "There's too much moisture in Vaseline. That just makes it worse. Antiperspirants work much better. They're designed to get rid of moisture. I use it under my sports bra."

At the mention of my sports bra, his eyes travel to my chest. I clear my throat, feeling embarrassed. I've never had much up top, even less with constant running chewing up my fat reserves.

"You're carrying a lot of heavy fabric around your waist," I say. "I don't know how well it will work, but it's worth a try."

He averts his gaze, suddenly absorbed in the blue

deodorant stick. He turns it over in his hands, face unreadable. After what seems like forever, he shakes his head and sticks it into his pocket. "Thank you. It's weird as shit, but I'll try it."

"It's the least I can do. You know, for holding up my non-existent hair while I puked like a high school kid on prom night."

His eyes soften. "Anytime." He hesitates before reaching across the short distance that separates us. He cups my hands between both of his, running his thumbs over my palms.

He's never looked at me the way he's looking at me now. I'm too hungover to grapple with the emotion squirming around in my chest. All I know is that I want to hang onto his hand. Hell, I want to do more than that. I want to hang onto *him*.

I don't do either.

I force myself to my feet, breaking away from him. I swallow against the sudden dryness in my throat.

"We should go check on the others." Realizing I'm being an asshole, I attempt to soften the abruptness. "None of them had a sober friend looking over them last night." I give him a soft smile, wishing I didn't feel like vomiting all over my bare feet.

The skin around his eyes crinkles again. I decide it's definitely his version of a smile. I've never seen Ben smile before today. It looks good on him.

"Let's go," he says to me. "We don't want to leave the little shitheads up to their own devices. No telling what they'll get up to unsupervised."

As we exit the room side by side, I lament my obscene intake of alcohol. I'm in no state to deal with whatever is manifesting between me and Ben. Somewhere in the last twenty-four hours, things between us have changed. I make a silent promise to think on it when my head stops hurting.

Right now, I have my kids to think about. I don't intend to fail them again.

I may have been drunk last night, but that doesn't mean my

brain wasn't working. At least, it was before my sixth or seventh shot of whatever that brown stuff was.

Our campus was almost overrun yesterday. The appearance of the alpha zombies has changed everything. We have to adapt to our new environment if we want to survive. I won't risk leaving us vulnerable again.

I have a plan.

28

FORTIFICATIONS

KATE

Surrounded by the Creekside crew on the rooftop of the dorm, I shade my eyes and survey the campus below. My brain feels like it's taking an axe to my skull, though I do my best to conceal the ill effects of my hangover.

"Dude." Beside me, Johnny squints. Based on his grimace, he's as hungover as the rest of us. "I wish you'd let us use some of that Tylenol."

"Nope." I keep my eyes on the ground below. "Resources are finite. Hangovers don't qualify for medication."

"Carter, your mom is a hard ass," Johnny mutters.

"I'm having a moment," Jenna says, who stands on my other side.

"What sort of moment?" Ash asks.

"One of those moments where you fall asleep drunk," Jenna replies. "Then you wake up and you're not drunk anymore, but the alcohol is still in your body and everything hurts like hell."

"I think we all had that moment, babe," Carter says.

"We *are* that moment," Reed adds.

I'm glad the mood is lighter today. Grief isn't something we can escape, but I hope Ben is right. I hope we'll scab over with time.

Standing with my Creekside family gives me strength. It's a good reminder not to let grief get the better of me. Last night was for loss and sadness, but now it's time to lock that grief away and get on with living. I can't take care of my living kids if I wallow in the ones I've lost.

"There are still a lot out there on campus." Caleb stands on the corner of the building, binoculars up to his face.

"They're in clumps of five to ten," Ben says, also with a pair of binoculars.

It's better than I had hoped. Even though there are a fair number of zombies on campus, their numbers are spread out. I have a plan to deal with them.

I turn to my companions. "Let's go back downstairs. I want to gather everyone for a Creekside meeting."

Once in the main dorm, I lean up against the wall beside the flat screen and Xbox. I take in the faces of all those who have entrusted me with their safekeeping.

Carter and Jenna, holding hands. Eric, looking lost and dazed without Lila. Reed, eyes puffy from missing Jesus. Caleb and Ash, always near one another but never in physical contact. Our newest companion, Susan, with her husband still unconscious in a dorm room.

And Ben. Sometimes I think he should be leading our small group. He knows more and has more experience than I could ever hope to have. Except even I'm not dumb enough to think he could hold our small family together. The kids count on me for that.

"First, we need to clear the university. We're going to split into two teams and kill every zombie on campus. I'll lead one team and sweep west. Carter, you lead the second team and sweep east." My son nods. "If you encounter any alphas, be sure to take them out first. The rest of the zoms will be confused when their alpha goes down. That will give you ample opportunity to take them out. That's Phase 1."

"What's Phase 2?" Jenna asks.

"We can't continue as we have. Humboldt University isn't safe." I sweep my eyes over them. "We have to fortify Creekside. That's Phase 2."

They shift and exchange looks. Susan raises a hand.

"Yes, Susan?"

"You don't expect us to blow up more buildings, do you?"

"Nothing that extreme. But you are right about one thing. Our home needs a wall."

"Like a Medieval village?" Jenna says.

"Exactly. We're going to start with Creekside and all the neighboring dorms that share our parking lot. We create a home base that is secure and self-sufficient. We can't run around blowing up buildings every time a horde comes. The way I see it, there could be a lot more. We don't know how prevalent this alpha phenomenon is."

"How do you plan to build the fortifications?" Ben asks.

"We dig up the fencing along the frontage road and bring it here," I reply. "I saw bags of cement in the maintenance shop a few weeks ago. We erect the fence here in the gaps between the dorm buildings. Then we get some cars. Put them in neutral, roll them in front of our perimeter and pop the tires. We scavenge rebar from the rubble of College Creek and jam them into the hoods and front grills of the cars. These will impale zombies that get too close." I make eye contact with everyone in the room. "It's not a sophisticated plan, but it will work with the resources and manpower we have." I push off from the wall. "We need to get started right away. I'm putting all endurance workouts on hold for a week. All our efforts need to be focused on campus clearance and fortifications."

"Did you come up with all this while you were drunk last night?" Reed asks.

"Yes?"

"Raise your hand if you think Mama Bear should drink more often." Reed sticks his arm in the air. His tone is light, but his usual big grin is dull. I can tell he's trying to rally. A few others also raise their hands, smiles rippling around the room.

"Let's get to work," I reply. "We're burning daylight. We have a home to fortify."

29

SHARK BAIT

KATE

I should be excited. After two days of hard clearance, we've managed to kill all the large packs of zombies on campus. After another four days of work, we've managed to relocate and install fencing between all the dorm buildings. And now, barely a week after we rescued him, Gary is conscious and well enough to meet all of us at Creekside.

And while I am happy about all these things, I'm too exhausted to feel real enthusiasm. Ever since the alpha attack, sleep has been even more elusive than usual.

I crunch on a few stale coffee beans, wishing for an intravenous injection of caffeine. A few people watch me critically as I pop the beans, particularly Ben and Carter, but no one says anything.

"Hey look," Reed says with forced cheer from his seat on the couch. "It's Shark Bait."

I look up as Susan and Ash enter the main sitting room. Susan pushes a wheelchair in front of her, which Eric and Reed had found inside of a janitor's closet a few days ago.

In the wheelchair is Gary. He's pale and gaunt, but his eyes are alert. From the smell of things, he's just had his first shower since getting attacked by a great white. His dark brown hair is still wet, sticking up at wild angles.

"Reed." Jenna frowns at him. "Don't call him that. Hey, Gary. Welcome to Creekside."

"Hey, guys." Gary grins at us, a good-natured smile landing on Reed. "It's cool. I like Shark Bait better than Shark Food."

"You're in an awfully good mood for someone who almost died," Ben remarks.

Gary is cheerfully unapologetic. "Thanks to all of you, my wife and I are alive. If that's not enough to put a man in a good mood, I don't know what is."

"I like this guy already," Jenna says.

"Yeah, I'm glad we risked our lives to save him," Caleb adds.

"I know I can't do much until my leg heals," Gary says, "but I want to help. Give me a job to do. Maybe I can cook?"

The sudden silence that descends is like a wet blanket. The good cheer Gary brought to the room is snuffed out. Ben's face darkens into a scowl.

No one has volunteered to cook since Lila died. Meals consist of someone picking out a bunch of canned goods from our supply room and heating them over the camp stove. My last meal consisted of warmed-up green beans.

Gary, sensing the shift, looks from us to Susan in confusion. "I said something. Whatever it was, I'm sorry."

It's not right to take out our collective sorrow on Gary. I throw back a few more coffee beans and cross the room to him.

"I'm Kate." I shake his hand. "We're glad you're finally awake." I make introductions, going around the room.

"Seriously, I owe you guys," Gary says. "Thanks for everything. Susan says Ash worked day and night to fight off infection and keep me alive."

Caleb flashes a proud smile at Ash. "She's good at what she does. We're all lucky to have her."

I can't tell if Caleb's compliment has a deeper meaning behind it. I haven't been able to figure out the extent of their relationship. As far as I can tell, things haven't changed between them since Jesus died. They share a dorm room, but even when they sleep the door is always open. They're never far from one another, but I have yet to see them touch.

"We are lucky to have Ash," I agree. "If you really want to step up and be in charge of the kitchen, the job is yours." No need to tell him we lost our previous chef to zombies. I don't think anyone is ready to talk about it, least of all me.

"I'm in," Gary says. "I was the cook for guests on our charter boat. I'm not a trained chef, but I can put stuff together that tastes good."

Eric and Reed start coughing. Small smiles pull at the lips of my people. Even Ben shakes his head as though amused by the comment. It's nice to feel the tension of the past week slacken.

"What did I say?" Gary asks.

"We don't eat much that tastes great," I say as diplomatically as I can.

"I'll do what I can to remedy that. Just show me where the supplies are."

WE LEAVE Gary with several boxes of food stores, placing them on the floor to make it easy for him to sort. Despite being confined to a wheelchair, he eagerly sets about going through them. The rest of us head outside, returning to the fortification of our home.

"For a man who almost died, he's in good spirits," I say to Susan as the two of us finish rolling a car into place in front of our fence. I'm so exhausted that all I want to do is sleep. Even Gary's recovery isn't enough to give me a boost of energy.

"He's always like this." A happy smile spreads across Susan's face. "It's one of the reasons I fell in love with him. He always got great tips from people on our boat." She taps her fingers on the hood of the car. "Do you think we should pop the tires now?"

"Let's wait until we're finished getting all the cars in place." We're two-thirds of the way finished with this phase of the fortifications. "Come on, let's go get the silver Mini Coop."

I plod beside Susan, steps heavy with fatigue. I have a few more coffee beans stashed in my pocket. I crunch on them as we walk a short way down Granite Avenue to the Mini Cooper.

"Are those good?" Susan points to the beans.

"Honestly? No. They're stale."

"So you're eating them because you're so tired you could fall asleep standing up?"

"Is it that obvious?"

Susan nods. "No one would be upset if you took the afternoon off and napped."

Like I could nap even if I tried. I shake my head. "My place is out here with everyone else, making sure our home is safe."

Susan gives me a sidelong look but doesn't say anything. We reach the Mini Coop. The doors are all locked, something we've run into more times than I can count. Susan pulls out a large rock wrapped in a T-shirt, which hangs from her belt; our official tool for our task of breaking into cars. She smashes the window and unlocks the doors.

A few minutes the later, the Mini Coop is in neutral and the two of us are pushing it up the road.

Three hundred yards away, a small pack of zombies stumble into view. Eric, Johnny, Caleb, and Ash stop what they're doing and fan out to eliminate the undead. From the haphazard resistance the zombies put up, it's clear none of them are alphas.

After our initial clearance of the campus right after the

attack, we haven't run into too many zoms. It's nice to know our destruction of the library and dorms wasn't for nothing.

"We owe you our lives," Susan says as she watches our people. "I've never properly thanked you for what you've done for me and Gary."

"Let's see," I say, attempting to make light of the situation. "When we met you, your husband was unconscious from a shark attack. The day after you arrive at Creekside, we're attacked by alpha zombie hordes and are forced to blow up some buildings." I make it a point not to mention the wake, or the burial of our friends in the rubble of College Creek. "Then I make everyone relocate fence panels and reinforce them with cars. Oh, and somewhere in between all that, your husband wakes up." I smile at her through the open car window as we continue to push the Mini Coop. "You've had a lot on your mind."

Susan shakes her head. "I could say thank you every day for the rest of my life and it still wouldn't be enough. Can you steer at little to the left?"

I adjust the steering wheel. The Mini Coop slides neatly into place between two cars.

Carter and Jenna roll up a few minutes later, pushing a beat-up Ford Mustang between them. Susan and I guide them into place.

The Mustang completes the section of the wall around the Juniper and Creekside dorm buildings. I survey the barrier, knowing I should feel satisfied. All I feel is exhausted.

"Good work," I say. "Let's try and finish this next section of the wall today." I gesture to the gap between Fern and Laurel dorms. "I saw more cars down in the parking lot of the Jolly." The Jolly is a big common area that used to be frequented by students.

"So you and Gary ran a commercial fishing boat?" Carter asks as the four of us walk together down the road.

"A charter boat. We took people out for fishing, whale watching, and kayaking. We were on our boat with two tourists from New York when the outbreak hit. One customer started eating his friend. Gary tried to separate them, but couldn't. At the time, we didn't know the guy was a zombie. We thought he was just some rich prick who bought some bad drugs.

"Anyway, Gary ended up hitting him in the head with a fire extinguisher. He only meant to stun him, but accidentally hit him too hard. The other guy, the one who was bitten, bled out on the deck of our boat.

"We were so scared. We thought we were facing manslaughter charges. We threw the bodies overboard. Our plan was to stay in the boat and sail down to Mexico before the authorities caught up to us." Susan lets out a long sigh. "We hadn't gone far when we heard about the outbreak on the radio and figured out what was really happening. No one was using the zombie word, but all the news reports talked about people going berserk and eating other people. We decided to stay put and live on the boat until everything blew over. You know how that worked out. And now here we are."

I try to imagine what it would be like to watch the world end from afar. It occurs to me that Susan and Gary haven't spent much time in the world of zombies. That makes me appreciate their willingness to help and be a part of our community even more.

I suppose there is some brightness in this fucked-up world.

30

FOOT SOLDIER

KATE

I hike toward the Creekside common room, glancing at my watch. It's time for a check-in call with Alvarez. We missed the last check-in due to the alpha attack, and he missed the check-in before that. I'm anxious to catch up with my young friend.

Upon reaching the main dorm, I find Carter and Jenna there. They collect their library books to make room for me at the kitchen table with the ham radio. Carter gives me a firm hug, something he's taken to doing every time he sees me. I hug him back, grateful for my son, then settle down in front of the ham radio.

"Mama Bear to Foot Soldier. Are you there? Over."

"Mama Bear, this is Foot Soldier. Good to hear your voice. You missed our last scheduled check-in. Over."

Alvarez. I sigh in relief at the sound of his voice, tossing a few coffee beans into my mouth. "I wasn't the only one to miss a check-in. You missed the one before that." I dispense with the official radio jargon.

"It couldn't be helped. A few of my people were nabbed by some bandits that came through the area." His voice turns harsh and brittle. "No way those assholes were going to get away with taking my people. I went back to the fort and pulled together a full platoon. We got them back."

"Is everyone okay?"

Silence drags through the ham radio for long moments. "We lost two. Two more were shot, but they're on the mend. On the bright side, we acquired a doctor. He was being held captive by the raiders."

"Maybe your doctor can talk to Ash, our medic. We have a man recovering from a shark attack."

"How did one of your people get attacked by a shark?"

"He wasn't one of mine when he was attacked. He and his wife own a charter boat. They were at sea when the shit hit the fan. Survived out there for months." I lay out the rest of the story, including our rescue of Gary and Susan.

"Shit. That's bad luck. Shark attack during the zombie apocalypse. Let's set up a time for our doctor to talk to your medic."

"Thanks, Foot Soldier. I owe you one."

"You can pay me back with another trip to the library. Can you find me a book on fish farming and fish management? One of the women in our group wants to start a fish hatchery. She used to work for fish and game and knows how to run one, but not how to build one."

I stare at the ham radio, not sure how to tell Alvarez that we lost the library. It hurts to think about all that knowledge buried in rubble. It doesn't help that it was my idea to blow it up.

"Mama Bear? You still there? Over."

"I'm here, Foot Soldier. I'm sorry to tell you this, but the library is gone."

"Gone? What do you mean, gone?"

"We had a ... situation up here. It's the reason I missed our last check-in call."

I relay an abridged version of the last week and a half. From the appearance of the alphas, to our battle to protect the university, and to our work on the new fortifications around the dorms.

Alvarez lets out a long whistle when I finish. "And I thought things were fucked up on my end."

"Have you guys seen any alphas in your area?" I ask.

"No. Not yet. I'll be sure to warn my people and let you know if we see anything." His voice sharpens. "Can you back up to the part where you guys blew up the library? That's a big loss for all of us."

"I know. We didn't have a choice. We created a barricade that buried half the horde and diverted the rest away from the campus."

"So you have a primary wall on the south end of campus? And you're building a secondary fortification around the dorms?"

"Yeah. We've been working from sun-up to sundown for the last week. We have another few days of hard work in front of us, but it's getting there."

"Damn, Mama Bear. Sounds like you're going to have your own fortress up there. Is everyone in your group okay?"

My throat tightens as I think of Jesus and Lila. All I can bring myself to say is, "I lost two of my people, too."

"I'm sorry to hear that. I know how hard that is. Are you sleeping?"

I snort. "Right."

His commiserative chuckle rolls out of the receiver. "I feel your pain, Mama Bear."

I close my eyes, comforted by his empathy. Like Ben, Alvarez knows how I feel. He's lost people, too.

It's one of the reasons I look forward to our ham radio chats every three days. Alvarez and I both lead our small communities; it's nice to have someone in my same position to talk to. He knows what it means to have people depending on him.

"Don't let the grief and the guilt distract you from your primary mission," Alvarez says. "Focus on the living."

"Is that how you get through the days?"

"Yeah. Sometimes, it's the only thing that gets me through."

I inhale deeply, flinching away from the memory of my knife as it slid through Jesus's skull. Of Lila's ruined head when her body hit the ground. I summon a mental image of my living family: Carter, Jenna, Johnny, Eric, Reed, Ash, Caleb, and Ben. I let their presence fill me, pushing back the darkness.

"Mama Bear?"

"I'm here."

"I'd take your alphas over my bandits. You know when I said they kidnapped a few of my people?"

A sick lump forms in my stomach. "Yeah?"

"The people they took were women, one of them just a teenager."

"Shit," I breathe.

"We found them, but not before they ... it was a long forty-eight hours, Kate. The worst part is that two of the fuckers got away. I'd feel better if they were all dead. Knowing they're still out there makes me uneasy."

I understand how he feels. I couldn't live with the threat of Johnson hanging over us. If these bandits hurt his people, Alvarez must be chomping at the bit to even the scales.

"Don't give up," I say. "Double up on watch. They might show themselves again, especially if they're short on supplies."

"I almost wish they would." Alvarez's laugh is hollow. "I'd like nothing more than to gut those fuckers with our fish hooks. Have I told you about those?"

Even though I can't see Alvarez's face, I can tell by his tone that he wants to change the subject. "You haven't mentioned the fish hooks."

"Big fucking things. Like, the size of a small baby. Apparently they're used for tuna fishing. We found some on a scavenging run. We're getting pretty good at fishing."

"My son and his girlfriend want to figure out a way to fish for oysters in Humboldt Bay."

"Oysters, huh? I wouldn't turn my nose up at that idea."

"Yeah, except there's no safe way to navigate downtown Arcata right now. We have no way of knowing how many alphas are out there."

"You'll figure something out, Mama Bear. You always do. If you could figure out how to run two hundred miles through a zombie apocalypse, you can figure this out."

Alvarez and I talk for another few minutes before Johnny shows up. He's been interviewing people from Fort Ross for one of the many books he's writing. I say my goodbye to Alvarez and pass the ham to Johnny.

As I exit the room, chewing on another few coffee beans, my gaze travels across the room to the shrine Jesus built to St. Roch. Reed hung his pendant inside. I stare at the pendant, something Alvarez said tickles the back of my mind.

If you could figure out how to run two hundred miles through a zombie apocalypse, you can figure this out.

I pause, my exhausted mind spinning. When running, how many times have I faced an unknown? Why should this situation be any different? All I have to do is break it into manageable chunks. That's what I always did with a long, hard race. Dissected them. Developed tactics for different terrains, weathers, and altitudes.

An idea takes shape in my mind. Alvarez is right. The alphas are a challenge to be overcome. I just need to develop a complex training plan to deal with them.

And I know just how to start.

31

IDEA

BEN

When he pads into his room a little after midnight, Ben has the shock of his life.

He flicks on his light and finds Kate curled up on his bottom dorm bunk, her head on his pillow. On the bed beside her is the collected works of Henry James. Her eyes flutter open at the rush of light.

He stands frozen. He'd be a lying sack of shit if he denied daydreaming about this very scene. Except he's pretty sure her reason for being in his bed doesn't match up with his fantasy. If that was the case, she wouldn't be wearing a thick jacket and blue jeans.

She looks like complete shit, though Ben is wise enough to keep this observation to himself. She's barely slept since Lila and Jesus died. She's working herself to the bone and popping coffee beans like they're candy.

He gets it. Sometimes, it's easier to be exhausted than alone with your own thoughts.

Kate sits up, awakened by the light. If Ben had known she

was sleeping in here, he wouldn't have gone near the light switch.

"I think I fell asleep." Kate rubs at her eyes. "I was waiting to talk to you."

He waits in silence, not trusting himself to speak. The last thing he wants to do is to provoke her into moving. He could stare at her in his bed for hours, even if she is dressed like she's ready to go outside.

That thought brings a frown. Why *is* she dressed like she's going outside? It's the middle of the night.

"I have an idea," Kate says.

Fuck. He should have known. "And you thought midnight was a good time to work out the details?"

"I don't want the others to know." She has the grace to look guilty, though not for long. "I need your help, Ben. I want to capture an alpha."

He closes the bedroom door so as not to wake anyone. "I don't think I heard you correctly." He narrows his eyes at her. "Did you just say you want to catch an alpha?"

She looks him straight in the eye. "Yes."

There is no response that properly conveys the lunacy of this conversation. Also, he's pretty sure he'll wake the entire fucking floor if he opens his mouth.

He does the only sensible thing he can think of. He turns his back on her, shrugs out of his coat, and tosses it across the back of a chair. Then he sits down in the same chair and begins unlacing his boots.

"Ben." Kate frowns at him. "Did you hear what I said?"

"I'm trying to *un*hear it, Kate."

She slips off the bed and comes to stand before him. "Hear me out."

"No." His belt comes off and he drapes it over the jacket on the chair back. His Sig and the holster go on top of the desk. The boots go under the desk.

Everything in its place. This brings some semblance of stability to the current situation.

He shoulders past Kate, grabbing the ladder to the top bunk. "I'm going to bed. You can keep the bottom bunk if you want."

Kate's arm snakes out, blocking him. "Will you listen to me?"

Two things happen. Her words fan a wildfire within him, heating his carefully tamped anger to an all-time high. Her proximity, coupled with the fact that she's in his bedroom with the door closed, sends a white-hot spear of arousal through him.

Both emotions are so intense he can't see straight. He wants to shout at Kate and kiss her at the same. Only his indecision on the matter keeps his feet welded to the floor and his mouth clenched shut.

She must see or sense something, because she drops her arm and steps back.

"I'm sorry, I need to explain. I've been thinking about the alpha zoms. They're a puzzle we need to solve. There are so many things we don't know about them, but the most important fact is their language. They communicate, Ben. They speak and they organize. We need to learn their language."

"And how, exactly, do you plan to learn their language?" he demands. "How is capturing one those fucking things going to help with that?"

"I don't know!" Kate throws up her hands. "I don't know, okay?"

"Because it's impossible," he snarls. "If we bring a dog to Creekside, we're not going to miraculously learn how to boss it around by barking."

"But people across time have learned how to communicate with animals. Why should this be any different?"

He's going to blow a gasket. It's that simple. He can't hold it back any longer. The mental image of Kate risking her life to catch an alpha, then subsequently putting herself at risk *every fucking day* by trying to figure out how to communicate with it, makes him want to break something.

He opens his mouth, anger-fueled words gathering in his throat.

Kate, seeing his face, presses a hand over his mouth. The contact is enough to distract him, giving Kate her opening.

"Before you go ape shit, hear me out. We have to adapt. Three months ago I wouldn't have dreamed of letting any of you snipe zombies. Now, it has to be done anytime there's an alpha sighting. We need to learn everything we can about the alphas if Creekside if going to survive." Her mouth tightens.

God dammit, he knows that look. It's her *the-devil-and-all-the-armies-of-hell-can't-stop-me* look.

The worst part of all this is that she isn't wrong. They *do* need to adapt.

He's known it for a while. But he was thinking more along the lines of extending the perimeter of the dorms to include other parts of campus. Not capturing an alpha and bringing it home like a rabid pet.

"I know it's a crazy plan," Kate says. "A lot of my plans are crazy. But I need your help. I trust you to have my back. If I have to do something stupid, I want you by my side."

Her words take his breath away. His anger is snuffed out in a millisecond, replaced with something else. Unable to digest the sudden onslaught of feelings, he turns away.

"You couldn't have said all that before I took my boots off?" he grumbles.

"Does that mean you'll come?"

"Yes." He grabs his belt, Sig, and jacket, settling them back into place. "No way in hell I'd let you go out there alone. You know that."

"Thank you, Ben." The smile she gives him is so bright he has to look away.

"To be honest, I was hoping you'd give up and take the bottom bunk." He shoves his feet back into his boots.

"You didn't really think I would, did you?"

"No." He frowns down at her. "That's not your style." He pushes past her, grabbing his headlamp on the way out. The moon is almost full, but having extra light won't hurt.

The ache in his crotch doesn't subside until he's all the way downstairs and has some fresh air in his face. The woman is going to be the death of him in more ways than one.

She, too, dons a headlamp and flicks it on as they head outside. They're halfway across the compound, heading toward the gate, when a voice stops them.

"Where are you guys going?"

Kate and Ben freeze like two teenagers caught sneaking out of the house at—Ben glances at his watch—12:16 at night.

Eric comes out from the front door of Laurel dorm, a roll of packing tape in one hand.

"What are you doing?" Kate asks.

"Inventorying food in Laurel. I did another sweep and found a bunch more edibles."

"In the middle of the night?"

Eric shrugs. Apparently insomnia is rampant in this compound.

"So what are *you* guys doing?" Eric asks again.

Ben doesn't even bother trying to answer. This is all Kate's idea. She can decide what she wants to tell Eric.

"We're running an errand," she replies. "We'll be back in a few hours."

"An *errand*?" Eric raises a skeptical eyebrow.

"We'll be back soon." Kate attempts to march past him.

Eric isn't so easily brushed off. "You're leaving the

compound?" he asks, incredulous. "You're going *outside* in the middle of the night?"

Ben grunts. This is going about how he'd expected. And Eric isn't about to be deterred.

"I'm coming with you. Whatever you're planning, I'll help."

"You don't even know what we're doing," Kate replies.

Eric eyes them. "As long as you're helping Creekside, I'm in. Unless ..." he frowns at them. "You guys aren't, you know, going out for a romantic stroll or something?"

Once again, Ben decides to let Kate field the question. There's nothing he can say that won't make him look like an idiot. Not the least of which is the fact he'd actually consider a stroll outside these walls in the middle of the night if it were with Kate.

"No," Kate says quickly. "We're going to catch an alpha zom. We're going to bring it back and study it." She delivers these two sentences like a threat, as though they'll kick some common sense into Eric.

Common sense that Kate herself doesn't have. Unfortunately, these kids are almost as crazy as their surrogate mother. Eric actually perks up at the idea.

"Good idea," he says. "I have some extra rope in Laurel. Be right back."

"Grab the dolly, too," Kate calls after him. To Ben, she says, "Might as well make use of him if he insists on coming."

"Dolly? For the alpha transport?" Ben asks.

"Yeah."

It's a good idea. Better than him carrying an undead fucker over his shoulder, which is what he assumed he'd be doing until now.

Three minutes later, he, Kate, and Eric exit the compound together with the dolly.

"Where are we going?" Eric asks as they close and lock the gate.

Kate doesn't answer right away. This puts Ben's hackles up. "You know where one is, don't you?" he asks.

She looks at him. "Yes. I found it a few days ago when I was digging up fencing."

"Where is it?" From the look on Kate's face, he isn't going to like the answer

"It's down on the freeway. Sandwiched between a few cars and a whole lot of zombies."

"How do you know it's an alpha?" Eric asks.

"The way the others react to it. It's trying to give orders to make the horde move, but they're in a logjam with all the abandoned cars and bodies."

"And your plan to get the alpha?" Ben has no doubt Kate has something up her sleeve. Her large backpack has not escaped his notice.

"I have some rope," Kate says. "I think we can drop the rope around its neck and pull it up."

32

CARNIVAL GAME

KATE

Ben is such a skeptic. If he weren't so capable, I wouldn't have bothered to ask him along.

Or at least, this is what I tell myself. The truth is that I feel safe when he's around. Trusting Ben feels like vulnerability. I don't like it, yet I can't seem to separate myself from it.

"It will work," I tell Ben and Eric.

They hit me with cloned expressions of incredulity.

"You want to drop a rope around an alpha's neck and pull it up from the freeway?" Eric echoes.

At least my plan was clear. "Yes." I look at Ben. "If you don't like it, you have between now and the time we arrive at the overpass to come up with something better."

He scowls at me. I turn away and keep walking, knowing he'll follow.

We've done a good job of clearing the campus. The university isn't leak proof yet, but I have ideas how to make it a true safe zone. Just as soon as we bag an alpha and start studying it.

Tonight, the sidewalks and roads are quiet, deserted. I walk with Ben and Eric on either side of me down Granite Avenue. Eric pushes a dolly.

This road has changed so much. No longer littered with bodies of murdered students and subsequently cleared of zombies, it almost looks like it did before the apocalypse. If you can ignore the shattered windows, broken doors, abandoned cars, and a complete lack of ambient light.

The milling horde down on the freeway fills the air with a gentle hum. The farther we walk, the louder it becomes.

When we reach the end of Granite Avenue, I pad up to the chain-link fence that lines the twenty-foot drop to the freeway. The beam of my headlamp casts light on the scene. I take in the tight pack of zombies crammed below. There are several hundred, all of them remnants of the monster horde that came here from Eureka.

For the moment, we're safe from them. The walls of the freeway keep them penned off.

Even so, they aren't a problem I plan to ignore. I've been thinking of ways to get rid of them. The best idea I've come up with so far is to dump some gasoline from the overpass and drop a few matches. The problem with that plan is there's no guarantee the fire will remain contained. The last time I set something on fire, half of the Arcata Plaza was incinerated.

I'll figure something out. For now, I need to focus on the task at hand: catching an alpha.

"It's over there?" Eric points to a red pick-up truck beneath the overpass. A tight cluster of zoms swirls around a center point.

"Yeah. The alpha is there." If it weren't dark, they'd be able to see the gray-haired woman in the navy blue sweat shirt.

Ten minutes later, we reach the overpass. Ben has a knife in each hand, eyes flicking up and down the road. It's clear for the moment, but there are zombies not too far away in downtown Arcata.

I drop my pack to the ground and pull out a coil of rope and a Boy Scout handbook.

"Polishing up your knot-tying skills?" Ben frowns at the Boy Scout book.

"Yeah." I loosen the noose I've tied, creating a large loop to drop over the alpha's neck.

"What if we accidentally pull off its head when we drag it up here?" Eric asks.

I shrug. "Maybe the head will still work."

Ben and Eric exchange tight looks. In that single exchange, I can see how much the two of them dislike this whole idea. Well, I don't like it much, either. If my gut didn't tell me it was the right thing to do, I wouldn't even be out here trying it.

"Ben, you keep watch on the overpass. Make sure no zombies sneak up on us. Eric, help me with the alpha."

Ben takes up position in the center of the overpass. Eric watches me as I pick up the rope. I spread my stance and press my hips against the cement barrier for balance, peering into the mass of zombies below.

I shine the light on the alpha. The woman's gray hair is a dim smudge beneath the starlight, the navy blue sweatshirt invisible in the dark. The alpha is like the dark center of a flower, the rest of the zoms are like swirling petals of gore around it.

I lower the rope over the side. Unfortunately, the alpha is five feet north of the overpass. Dropping it neatly over its head isn't an option.

As soon as the rope is fifteen feet down, I begin swinging it. Forward and back, forward and back. I gather slack in my other hand.

The rope sails out, gliding right over the alpha. I release the slack.

My timing is off. The rope misses and swings back, thumping against several zombies as it does. They moan and spin in small circles, arms swiping at the open air in search of whatever it was that brushed past them.

I try three more times and miss.

"This feels like a sick carnival game," I grumble.

"You mean the ones that are rigged so you never have a chance to win?" Eric asks.

"Exactly."

Behind me, I hear a moan, followed by the now-familiar sound of a skull being crushed.

"Is Ben okay?" I don't take my eyes from the rope as I swing.

"He's fine," Eric replies. "Just took down a straggler. Have you thought about making the noose bigger?"

I decide to try it. Otherwise, we could be out here half the night trying to catch the alpha.

I try four more times with the enlarged noose. On the fifth try, the noose sails neatly over the head of the alpha—and the zombie right next to it.

"Dammit," I growl. "I was afraid that would happen." Now I have two zombies.

"Screw it," Eric says. "Let's pull them both up."

I nod in agreement, pulling the noose tight. The alpha and the other zom mash into each other. The alpha immediately starts to hiss and click, sending all nearby zombies into a frenzy. They push and shove in an outward circle, almost as if they're forming a defensive perimeter around the alpha. Eric and I strain against the rope as our two captives struggle against us.

"Ben," I call softly. "We need your help."

He swears when he sees we've accidentally lassoed two of the undead. "Fuck me," he says. "Come on, let's get this over with."

He and Eric plant themselves on either side of me, both of them grasping the rope.

"On the count of three," I say. "One, two, three—"

As a unit, we heave. The zombies rise a foot off the ground.

The regular zombie hisses and moans, swiping futilely at the air around it. The alpha lets loose another complicated series of clicks and keens.

The zombies around the alpha double their efforts, pushing outward in a lopsided circle as they attempt to protect their alpha. Several of the cars groan and creak as the zombies slam into them, sliding a few inches across the pavement.

"One, two, three!" I hiss. "One, two, three!"

We throw all we've got into pulling the rope upward. The alpha's commands pick up momentum, its sounds coming faster and more urgently. The monster is halfway up to the overpass, dangling in mid-air above the horde. The zombies below us grow more and more frenzied.

The rope swings chaotically as the two zombies struggle against the bonds. It makes it harder for us to reel in. Sweat beads my temples and drips down my back.

"One, two, three," I say. "One, two, three—"

Something scrapes against the pavement behind us. I glance over my shoulder and swear.

Three zombies have drifted onto the overpass, no doubt called by the urgency of the alpha.

"You go," Ben says. "We'll get the fuckers up here."

I don't argue. I break away, leaving them to wrangle the zoms.

I pull out the short metal zom bat from Jesus, holding it in my right hand. In my left hand is a knife.

The zombies lurch across the overpass, drawn to the call of the alpha. Shit, they're moving fast.

I advance on the closest of them, putting myself between it and my people. I move on tiptoe, striking before it even realizes I'm there. My zom bat caves in its frontal lobe and drops the monster.

In the thirty seconds this takes me, the other two zoms have closed in behind Eric and Ben. They're no more than five feet away from my two friends.

I spring back in their direction. I bury my knife in the nearest of them. I don't have time to yank the blade free. I release it and throw myself at the last of them when it's a mere foot from Eric.

We hit the pavement, me landing on top. The smell of rot and death rush up my nose and down my throat as it hisses at me. I drive the zom bat down. The nose and cheekbones collapse under the force, splattering blood in every direction.

I roll to my feet just as Ben and Eric drag the two struggling zombies onto the overpass. Ben knifes the regular zombie while Eric says, "We've got to shut this thing up!"

He's right. Below, the mass of zombies has started keening. The high-pitched sound crescendos up and down like a knife lacerating the sky. The alpha continues to click and keen.

I grab a handful of rope and shove it into the clacking jaws. A hiss comes out of the thing's mouth, the teeth bearing down on the rope. I lean with all my weight, forcing the wad of rope all the way to the back of its throat. Ben wraps a length around the face.

"We have more company." Eric darts toward two more zombies that have reached the overpass.

The alpha writhes and flops like a dying fish. I sit on its torso, attempting to pin it in place while Ben ties off the rope around its head.

The alpha bucks, twisting and struggling to break free. Shit. This is a lot more trouble than the time I captured a few zombies with Carter and Jenna. Those undead hadn't been smart enough to even know they'd been captured.

I throw all my weight against the alpha, my feet digging into the concrete as I push the writhing form down.

"Done," Ben says, yanking the knot tight over the face.

"Thank God." I wipe sweat from my eyes. "I'll grab the feet. You get the arms."

As soon as I remove my weight, the alpha bucks and almost manages to trip me. I dance to the side, then lunge for its feet. One tennis shoe clocks me in the stomach. I grunt and secure my grip around both ankles.

Eric has dispatched the two zombies, but more are drifting up from downtown Arcata. Shit.

Ben and I hustle over to the dolly while Eric heads off another zombie that reaches the overpass. At least a dozen more are coming our way. And the zombies down on the freeway sound like they're ready to riot.

At least we've managed to silence the alpha. I can only hope it will be enough to calm the horde.

Ben and I set the alpha on the dolly. It wriggles like a snake, but I once again sit on top of it while Ben straps it in place. It's secured in under two minutes.

"Eric," I whisper-shout.

He's poised on the far side of the overpass, waiting as another three zombies approach. I gesture to him with both hands. He backs warily away from the zombies before running toward us.

The keening has begun to fade. Without the alpha to stir them up, the zombies are already forgetting what it is they were supposed to be doing.

Good. With any luck, the dozen making their way toward the overpass will also get distracted and wander off.

We jog away, pushing the dolly before us with our prize.

33

LANGUAGE DEPARTMENT

KATE

I hadn't expected every inhabitant to be awake and anxiously awaiting our return. Apparently Jenna, who had been on watch when we slipped out, woke everyone when she saw us leave. Everyone is standing just inside the gate when we arrive.

"Mom, what the hell?" Carter says. "If you hadn't left with Ben I'd be out there right now looking for you!"

"We were worried," Reed puts in. "I could hardly believe Mama Bear and her old man just waltzed out of here with Eric like it wasn't the apocalypse."

"I had an errand," I reply. Then I wheel the alpha into the compound.

Silence greets the introduction of the zombie strapped to the dolly. Then everyone starts talking at once.

Susan is incredulous. "You're jeopardizing Creekside and bringing that thing in here?"

"Mama, are you sick?" Reed puts a hand to my forehead.

"'Bout damn time we caught one of these!" Johnny says. "We need to study it."

"Are you stupid?" Ash says. "We need to kill it, not study it."

I hold up my hands to quiet everyone. "We'll discuss my actions just as soon as we secure the alpha zom."

"An *alpha*?" Susan gapes. "God, this just gets worse!"

"How did you catch an alpha?" Reed looks impressed. "Man, I wish I could have seen that."

"Creekside common room," I bark. "Everyone go inside and wait there. Ben, Eric, and I will be there shortly."

"Do you need an extra hand?" Johnny steps forward, eyes thoughtful as he studies the alpha. "I can help."

"I'll help, too," Carter says.

"Me, too," Jenna adds.

"We have it covered, thank you." I make my voice firm to let them know I can't be wheedled. "Creekside common room. We'll be there in fifteen minutes."

They're not happy, but they disperse.

"Well, it wasn't a full-scale riot," Ben mutters beside me. "That went over better than I expected."

I frown at him. "Ash called me stupid and Susan accused me of putting our entire compound at risk."

Ben shrugs. "They aren't wrong."

I'm too tired to argue. He, Eric, and I deposit the alpha zom in the second floor of Juniper, one of the unused and uninhabited dorms in our compound. We leave the thing strapped to the dolly and lock the door.

As we return to Creekside, Eric draws up beside me. His expression is somber. "I agree with you on this. We need to adapt. We need to face this alpha threat and get ahead of it."

"Thanks, Eric. That means a lot."

Ben grunts, scowling at nothing in particular. "You know I always have your back. No matter what."

I give him a grateful smile. "I know, Ben. Thanks."

This mollifies him. His expression softens and he gives me a curt nod.

Now it's time to face my people and explain my plan for this monster I've brought into our home.

———————

"HOW MANY OF you saw the movie *Gorillas in the Mist*?"

Everyone under the age of thirty gives me a blank stare. Which means no one except Ben has any idea what I'm talking about.

"*Gorillas in the Mist* is the story of a naturalist who went to Africa to study gorillas," I explain. "She lived with them and learned how to communicate with them."

"You're not saying you want us to immerse ourselves with that—that *thing*?" Ash says.

"Don't forget about the part where Sigourney Weaver goes on a crusade to protect the gorillas from poachers," Ben adds.

Thank you, Ben.

"That's not the part of the movie I'm talking about. I'm referring to the part where Sigourney Weaver studies the gorillas and learns how they communicate with each other. Then she learns how to communicate with them. The alphas are communicating with the other zombies. We need to learn their language."

Johnny and Gary lean forward. Jenna straightens, waiting intently. Reed's eyebrows fly up and he cocks his head at me in consideration. Ben's expression is grumpy as always, but he's resigned himself to my plan.

Everyone else looks at me like I've left the plantation. Carter gapes at me like I've lost my mind. Susan and Caleb look at me like I've brought a great white into the room. Ash looks like she wants to relocate.

I have to sell them on this. I have to make them see what I see. All of them.

"Survival of the fittest," I say. "You're either in front of the train or you're getting run over by it. We can sit on our hands while the alphas evolve and organize around us. Or we can get the jump on them and figure out how to defend ourselves against them. We can't just keep blowing shit up every time they come around."

"No offense, Kate, but I think we should do just that," Caleb says. "The only good alpha is a dead one."

"We've already had to evolve. Think about it. Would we have been using guns in the open to snipe zoms two month ago? When Ben and I ran through Arcata ahead of the Eureka horde we had to shoot an alpha to get through. What I'm staying is that we've already had to evolve. The alphas are forcing our hand. We can't rely on old tactics. We need to study them and adapt our defensives accordingly."

"We're talking about monsters inside our home!" Carter says.

I rest a hand on his arm. "I understand your concern. It's valid. Letting zombies inside our compound is dangerous. We'll board up the doors and windows on the second floor of Juniper and reinforce the stairwell entrance." I look to Ash and the other skeptics. "Our safety is the priority. That's why we have to do this. This is the long game. I agree it's uncomfortable, but think of it like an insurance policy."

"You mean it's a bitch to pay but nice to have when your ass gets rear-ended?" Reed asks.

"She means it's like those laps we do at the track. They suck balls but we're all grateful we're not overweight pigs when we run from zoms."

Ben. Ever the eloquent one.

"We evolve," I agree. "It's the only way to thrive. The minute we stop evolving, we die. It's that simple."

Silence. I can see my argument having an effect. Comprehension is dawning on those who, only a few minutes before, opposed my plan.

Ben breaks the silence. "Get over yourselves. You all know she's right."

If my argument swayed the naysayers, Ben's words are a punch to the gut. Maybe it's because he's usually the first to condemn anything remotely risky. It's fortunate I've had the last few hours to sell him on the idea.

I see the moment when Ash, Susan, Caleb, and Carter come to my side.

"Why does mom always have to be right?" Carter grumbles.

Ben raises an eyebrow. "It's her super power. You should know that better than any of us."

"The alpha will be under lock and key at all times," I say. "It won't escape. Neither will the two regular zombies we're going to lock up in there with it."

"What?" Eric's chin snaps up. "You want to bring in *more*?"

"We need to watch an alpha with its pack. We have to give it a pack to command if we want to learn how it's done."

"Carter and I know how to catch regular zombies." Jenna gives me a tentative smile. "We helped you do that before."

I nod. A few pillowcases and some string did the trick that time. Those zombies had been a walk in the park compared to the alpha.

"How do you plan to observe them when you have them locked up?" Gary asks.

"We'll cut a hole in the ceiling on the third floor. All observations will happen from above."

Johnny's hand shoots up. "I want to lead the research team." He cracks his knuckles. I haven't seen him look this jazzed since he started work on his *How to Thrive in the Apocalypse* book. "I'll decipher their language."

"What makes you an expert?" Ash asks. "Do you even speak more than one language?"

Johnny gives her an incredulous look. "I'm a writer.

Language is my *thing.*" He glances at me. "Words are *my* super power."

"The job is yours, Johnny."

"I volunteer to be his assistant." Gary's hand shoots up in to the air. "I want to help. When I'm not cooking, I can be observing."

"Dude." Johnny slaps him high-five. "We're the language department of the apocalypse."

"Undead Language Department," Reed declares. "We need to make you guys a door plaque. Are you going to keep office hours?"

"What's your qualification?" Ash asks Gary.

"My fucked-up leg." Gary says this with what I have come to regard as a perpetual well of cheeriness. "It's perfect for sitting in the same place for hours on end."

"Excuse me." Susan raises her hand. "Sweetheart, not to be a downer, but how do you propose to get down the stairs, across the parking lot, and up to the third floor of Juniper?"

Everyone contemplates his wheelchair in silence. Gary's brows knit together.

"We don't have to overthink this," Johnny says. "I'll just grab some two-by-fours and make a portable ramp. We have that pile we grabbed from the woodshop. It'll be good exercise for me to push Gary up and down the stairs since I've been out with tendonitis."

"What he said." Gary points at Johnny.

"Just until you can get yourself on a pair of crutches," Johnny adds. "And so long as you know there are no in-and-out privileges. Once you're in Juniper, you're there 'til it's time for you to make dinner."

"Deal." Gary grins. "When do we get started?"

"I need a video recorder," Johnny says. "And a portable voice recorder of some kind."

"Time to scavenge." Reed rubs his hands together with a grin. "I love going through other people's shit. I broke my favorite bong last week. Maybe I'll find a decent replacement."

34

COMPANY

KATE

"Mom." Carter pounds twice on my bedroom door before barging in. "Mom, get up."

The urgency in his voice has me bolting upright. "What is it?"

"There are people outside."

Alarm spikes through me. "What kind of people?" I jam my feet into my shoes. The last time people found us, they stole our food and threatened to kill us.

"Families."

The word stops me cold. "Families?"

Carter's lips are tight. "Yeah."

I snag my jacket off the floor and pull it on over my T-shirt. Jenna is waiting for us in the hall.

"Caleb was on watch and spotted them," she says. "They got here just before sunrise. Caleb has his rifle trained on them."

We hustle into the stairwell, up to the third floor, and then climb the ladder to the roof.

We've been busy the past few days, having completed our ring of cars around the compound as an extra line of defense.

The only thing we have left to do is place the rebar poles to impale zombies, and there's a pile in the parking lot waiting for us.

Caleb, Ben, and Ash are all crouched on the edge of Creekside, rifles to their shoulders. The sky is a murky blue, the rising sun staining the horizon a blotchy yellow.

I hurry to the edge of the roof, following the line of the rifles to a spot on the ground.

Between securing our compound and capturing the alpha zom, I've been feeling like we're on top of the madness the world has thrown at us. That feeling goes out the window as I peer between Laurel and Fern dorms.

Standing just beyond the cars and fencing is a man, hands raised above his head.

"How many?" I take the binoculars Jenna passes to me.

"I counted seven," Caleb replies. "Five adults and two kids. Though there could be others out of eye sight."

"Have you spoken to him?"

"Other than to tell them to halt or risk being shot, no," Caleb replies.

"They need to turn their asses around and leave," Ben growls.

I focus the binoculars on a man with a scraggly beard and a scuffed brown leather jacket who stands at the forefront of the group. Even in the half-light, I see the gaunt hollows of his cheeks and neck. I recognize the desperate look in his ragged eyes.

I shift the binoculars to the cluster of people behind the lead guy. They look as gaunt and desperate as the man. I see the forms of the kids, but they're hidden between the adults and I can't make out their faces.

"Did they say what they want?" I lower the binoculars, passing them to Carter. The rest of the group has arrived on the rooftop, all of us surveying the newcomers.

"He asked for help," Caleb replies grimly, never taking his eyes off the people at the far end of his rifle.

Help. They look like they need help.

"I'll talk to them." I turn, heading for the ladder.

"Mom, no." Carter grabs my arm. "It might not be safe. You remember what happened with Johnson and his crew."

How can I forget? Even so, I can't write off the newcomers without meeting them first.

"Human beings are few and far between. We can use friends more than we can use enemies," I reply, repeating something Alvarez once said to me. "I'm going to give them the benefit of the doubt."

"I'll go with you." Ben steps up to my side, eyes narrowed and lips compressed.

"But—" Carter begins.

"We have three options," I reply. "We can shoot them. We can tell them to go away. Or I can talk to them." The sun has crept up over the last few minutes, making it easier for me to see the ragged group of people on the other side of our car barrier. "I'm going to talk to them."

No one tries to stop me as I make my way to the ladder. Ben is on my heels.

I want to believe there are good survivors out there, like us. People who don't see the apocalypse as an excuse to indulge the darker side of human nature. Ash, Caleb, and Ben are all examples of that. Susan and Gary, too. We're a stronger group since they joined us.

Before we exit Creekside, Ben puts a hand on my arm. "We need a way to signal each other if something goes wrong."

I frown. "Like a code word?"

"Exactly."

I think for a moment. "How about Five Leaf?" That was the name of the brewery we holed up in the night we rescued Susan and Gary. I think of that night more often than I should.

Ben nods, mouth set in a firm line. "Five Leaf. I'll stay two steps to the right of your five at all times. You do the talking. You see anything off—and I mean *anything*, Kate—say the word."

Taking a deep breath, I head toward the perimeter fencing. The morning is crisp, the asphalt damp from last night's rain. The air smells fresh, cleansed of the dust and debris that's hung in the air ever since we blew up College Creek and the library.

Ben keeps his rifle raised, barely making a sound as he dogs my footsteps. I stop when I'm ten feet away from the newly erected fence, grateful to have it between me and the strangers.

The man in the battered leather jacket stares at me, hands still raised. I don't have to turn around to know Caleb and Ash still have rifles trained on him from the rooftop.

"My name is Kate." I raise my voice to carry over the line of cars that separates us. I've become so accustomed to the quiet —of being quiet—that raising my voice automatically makes me glance around for zombies.

"I'm Leo." The bushy man's eyes dart from Ben to my people on the roof. "This—I—we saw the explosions. We—we came from—" He swallows. Even from twenty feet away, I sense the grief roiling off him.

My breath catches in my throat. I suddenly know exactly where this ratty band is from. Cold sweat beads my spine.

"You came from Eureka."

He flinches, as though I've ferreted out a truth he was trying to hide. "Yes."

A low growl of fury rumbles up from Ben.

"You led that horde straight to us." Fury washes through me, making it difficult to breathe. I see my knife blade as it slams through Jesus's temple. I see Lila fall.

I have a very strong urge to wrap my hands around Leo and strangle him.

"We didn't mean to," Leo whispers. "We were desperate.

We've been living in in a condo complex in Eureka ever since the outbreak. We've been surviving, but we weren't prepared for—for the zombies getting smart." His voice is strained. "There were forty-seven people in our community before they hit us. We had no choice but to try and outrun them."

Forty-seven.

Only seven people stand outside our home.

The thought makes me sick. A pang goes through my heart. It's an effort to keep my face impassive. "We've seen it, too. The zombies are evolving."

"They've become goddamn hunting packs." Leo's voice twists with agony.

"You were in cars. You painted a big target on your backs with all that noise. Hell, we heard you from miles away."

"They were everywhere," Leo replies. "Our complex was overrun. The vehicles were our only options."

"You got some of our people killed," Ben snarls. "When you roared past campus, you brought them right down on us."

Leo's face ripples with anguish. "We didn't do it on purpose. We didn't know what else to do."

"That doesn't change the outcome." Ben's lips are pressed into a tight line.

What would I have done, had I been in Leo's position? Zombies behind us, an impassible car maze in front ... I close my eyes and shake my head. Leo took the only road open to him. I would have done the same thing had I been in his position.

I stare at the other man, meeting his gaze. He licks his lips, looking back at me with hope.

"We saw the explosions and hoped to find other survivors on campus," Leo continues. "It took us over a week to figure how to get here after we ran out of gas ... zombies are everywhere." This last part trails off in a whisper. I have no doubt he lost people after they ran out of gas.

"What is it you want?" I need to hear him spell it out.

Leo stares at me. Seconds tick by.

"We want to live," he says finally. "We came here looking for other people. We've lost everything ..."

He looks so lost and so tired it makes my heart ache. I know that look. There have been times when I've felt just how he looks. No one can fake that.

I can't turn my back on it. Even if these people did inadvertently bring about the deaths of Jesus and Lila. Or maybe it's because of their loss that I find myself wanting to help. As if doing the right thing can bring us all redemption.

I glance at Ben, my mind made up. He gives me a tight look.

"No one comes in without first getting checked for bites," he says in a voice pitched loud enough for only me to hear. "And they surrender all their weapons."

I nod, turning back to Leo. "We'll be having breakfast soon. You can come in and share a meal with us if you agree to a few conditions."

I don't know what I expected his response to be. A smile of relief, maybe. A heartfelt thanks.

What I don't expect is for Leo's shoulders to slump, as if a giant weight has just slid off them. He puts a hand over his eyes, a quiver running through his body.

Ben stiffens, bringing the rifle up.

"Don't." I put out a hand, pressing on his shoulder. "Don't. It's okay."

A single sob breaks out of Leo's throat. It's a sound of mingled sorrow and relief. He wipes his eyes and turns, beckoning to his tiny group of fellow survivors.

"Name your terms," he says in a quavering voice.

"Everyone surrenders their weapons and agrees to a full inspection for bites. No one comes in here with a bite."

"Or anything that looks like a bite," Ben mutters.

"Or anything that looks like a bite," I amend.

Leo is nodding before I even finish. "Yes, okay. Whatever you say."

I don't even think he's listening to me. I could probably ask for his right foot and he'd hand it over.

"Come on," Leo calls to his people. "It's all right. They're going to help us."

His people creep forward. They're filthy and hollow-eyed. They look like they've barely eaten. Their clothing is torn and caked with grime.

When they look at me, my throat tightens. I may have failed Jesus, and I may have failed Lila. Hell, in some ways, I even failed Frederico.

Maybe, just maybe, I can begin to make up for it by helping these people. There's room in Creekside for new family members.

35

NEWCOMERS

BEN

He watches the newcomers devour their food like starved dogs. They smell like death. They don't look much better.

Ben is trying to sort out which he dislikes more: having an alpha zombie and two regular zoms locked up in Juniper for observation, or having strangers in Creekside. He's still undecided.

He personally made the men strip down and let him check them for bites. They had their fair share of bruises and scrapes and cuts, but he'd found no bites.

"We don't hang onto the bitten," Leo told Ben when he inspected the man. "We're not stupid."

Ben didn't ask him to elaborate on those statements. He tried not to look too long at the sunken ribcage and clear signs of hunger that clung to the members of the group. Besides a few small backpacks with bottles of water and some candy bars, they appeared to have nothing other than the clothes on their backs.

Even so, Ben keeps his guard up. It could all be a ruse. He prefers to err on the side of paranoia.

They had few weapons, mostly knives. A few had short spears of rebar. No firearms of any kind. They surrendered everything without argument.

The seven newcomers now sat in a tight cluster on the floor, eating spaghetti that Gary made for breakfast.

Ben wants to blame them for Lila and Jesus's deaths. It would be easy. But he's been in enough battles to know shit happens. It's not their fault.

There are two kids in the group. They scarf their food down like ravenous animals, not even bothering to use their silverware. Ben hasn't see kids like this since he served in Africa. The sight grinds away at his intrinsic hostility to strangers.

Kate tries to keep an impassive expression, but she's no good at it. Or maybe it's just because Ben watches her so often he's become good at reading her. The plight of these people picks at her heartstrings.

She's going to let them stay. He sees it in her eyes. These half starved, half dead strangers will fill the part of her that's been empty since Lila and Jesus died. They could not have picked a better place to come calling.

"We have some spare rooms you can use," Kate tells them when they finish eating. "You can freshen up and get some rest. We have running water. It's cloudy today so it probably won't be warm, but you can at least wash up. We'll get everyone new clothes."

"Will you let us stay?" asks a woman with gray-blond hair. Her name is Stacy.

"We can talk about that tomorrow," Kate replies. "If you stay, you have to pull your weight."

"We can work." Leo sets down his empty bowl. "We can help. We can help with whatever you need. I worked on a farm before all hell broke loose."

"What kind of farm?" Carter asks.

"Marijuana farm." Leo shifts, unease suddenly in his eyes.

"It was a legal one for medicinal cannabis. I managed the grow beds. I saw your indoor garden downstairs. I can help with that. Expand it."

They could use an indoor gardening expert. Especially after the loss of the library. They could use anyone who knows anything about growing things.

"We'll talk later," Kate says. "First, we'll take you to a spare dorm suite. You can freshen up and rest."

Ben takes up a rearguard position with Caleb as the newcomers file into the hall after Kate. The two of them exchange glances. For once, Ben feels no animosity toward the other man. From the look on his face, Caleb is as wary of the newcomers as Ben is. Good. That means he'll be vigilant. They need vigilance with so many strangers in their home.

Kate doesn't take them to any of the empty suits on the second floor. Instead, she leads them up to the third floor. Ben approves of this. All the food and weapons are stored on the second floor. He knows Kate wants to give these people the benefit of the doubt, but at least she's being sensible.

The small group of survivors enters the empty suite with a look of awe and appreciation. The plain kitchen and living room with its band posters must feel like a safe haven after the hell they've endured.

"Did you clear out this place yourselves?" Leo asks.

"Yes," Kate says. "This is our home. It's called Creekside."

"Thank you for your hospitality," he replies, clearly not missing the way Kate leaned on the words *our home*.

Jenna and Carter bring in two black garbage bags stuffed with clothes we've gathered from the dorm rooms.

"Hope there's something in here for everyone," Carter says. "If there's a size missing we can take a look in some of the other rooms."

"It's perfect. Thank you." Leo wads a dirty hat in his hands. "Look, I'll be honest. There's nothing left for us outside these walls. If you guys throw us out, my people are as good as dead. I know we're on probation. We don't want to waste any time trying to prove ourselves. Put us to work now. We know you guys are working on fortifications. Let us help."

Kate shakes a head. "You guys are exhausted. Take a day to sleep and restore yourselves. We can talk tonight."

"We don' t need to wait. Let us help with the fortifications and prove ourselves. Believe me, every last one of us knows there are worse things than being tired." Leo raises his eyes to Kate's.

Ben sees a man close to breaking from the pains of the world. He knows what that feels like. Something in him eases as he watches Leo. The man's people gather behind him in a tight knot, every last one of them looking to Kate with hope in their eyes.

Slowly, Kate nods. "Okay. If you insist."

THEY TROOP OUTSIDE. Even the little kids come, stoically refusing to leave the side of the woman—Margie—with her silver hair in a bun. Ben follows at the rear where he can keep an eye on everyone.

Clouds cover the sun. It smells like more rain is coming. A dozen zombies have gathered outside the north side of the wall. No matter how many they kill, there are always more that replace them.

"We can take care of those for you." Leo gestures to the milling undead.

"Thank you." Kate smiles at Leo. "That would be very helpful. What do you need to get it done?"

Leo shrugs, eyes flinty. "Just about anything will do the trick." He walks over to the pile of rebar from the ruins of

College Creek. Leo extracts a piece and hefts it in his hand like a spear.

The others join him, even the two kids, all of them grabbing weapons. Rocks. Chunks of concrete. More rebar. Judging by the way they look at the zombies on the other side of the cars, Ben can tell they've done their fair share of killing.

As Leo leads his people out of the compound, Carter pulls out the screwdriver and hammer he always wears at his belt. Jenna and Susan are right behind him, also drawing weapons.

Kate, of course, has to join them. Ben edges up behind her, staying vigilant.

"What do you think of them?" she whispers to him.

He recalls the broken look he'd seen on Leo's face. "I think they're good people." He takes half a dozen steps with her, watching the back of Leo's head. "But you shouldn't take my word for it. I'm not the best judge of character." He'd misjudged Johnson, after all. "One slip out here and people die."

Even though she'd been drunk, he wonders if she remembers the things he told her about College Creek. About the kids he'd failed to keep alive.

"I don't want this to be one of those times when I make a mistake." Kate draws in a long breath, her gaze taking in the dorm buildings that surround them. "But I want to help them."

This is one of the things Ben admires most about Kate: she gives a shit. She gives a shit about perfect strangers she hears calling for help from a charter boat in Humboldt Bay. She cares about strangers who show up hunted and half starved on her doorstep. Shit, there isn't anyone she doesn't care about.

"Trust your instincts," he says. "The rest of us will back you up."

"Thanks, Ben." She gives him a small smile before jogging away to join Carter, Jenna, and Susan. They slip through the front gate after Leo and his people. Ben follows, keeping watch as he promised.

Twenty feet in front of them are Leo and his group. The two little kids are armed with big rocks. Something about the sight of their small hands wrapped around weapons makes his stomach clench.

He'd seen child soldiers in Somalia and Uganda. It was no less disturbing in Africa than it is now. Still, in the zombie apocalypse, the defenseless person is the dead person. Arming these kids wasn't the wrong thing to do.

The group of zombies outside the compound has grown to eight. With Leo's people, we number eleven. Maybe the kids won't have to fight.

Leo wields a piece of rebar in one hand, a rock in the other. He sprints forward, breaking away from the group.

He's fast and silent. He reaches the foremost of the zombies as they begin to rotate in our direction. He drops it with a swift strike of the rebar. As a second zombie closes in, he leaps toward it and smashes it with the rock.

The rest of his people rush forward, each of them silent and vicious in their attack. The little kids dart after them. Ben watches in fascination as the kids bring their rocks down on the skulls of any zombie that hits the ground, making sure the dead stay dead. Kate sprints into the battle, leading Ben and the others.

It takes their combined force no less than two minutes to bring down the eight undead.

Spattered with blood and surrounded by bodies, Leo's people survey one another, checking for wounds and bites. The little kids compare blood splatter.

Ben sees the moment when the Creekside crew adds seven new members to the ranks. It's when Kate looks at the kids. She takes in their little hands and the blood flecked all up and down their arms. It's all over after that.

Ben doesn't blame her for a second. It's over for him, too.

"Your people are skilled zombie hunters," Kate says.

Leo looks like he might collapse from exhaustion, but he straightens his spine. "We've had enough practice for a lifetime."

Kate nods. She and Leo exchange a long, silent look. Leo radiates earnestness. Kate is helpless to turn away from it, though she pretends to weigh it.

"There are a few things all new members of our group have to agree to," she says.

"Name your terms."

She draws in a breath and launches into the same speech she gave Ben when he joined her. "Cars are no longer a safe mode of transport. Even bikes are questionable. Anything that draws the attention of zombies is dangerous."

Leo and his people nod. None of them speak, so Kate continues.

"My people rely on endurance for survival. Anyone who joins our community agrees to six days a week of endurance training."

"What's endurance training?" Leo asks.

"Running," Carter explains. "We train at the track."

"Every member of our group can run for four hours at a time," Kate says. "It's an essential survival tactic."

"That training has saved my ass," Ben pipes in. "When the alpha swarm hit Arcata, Kate and I had to run like rabbits to get away."

"You guys run?" Another man in Leo's group, a pale-haired fellow, looks intrigued. "I am—was—a PE teacher. And I ran track in high school."

"Me, too," Jenna says. "Which events?"

"Four-hundred and eight-hundred-meter sprints," the man replies.

"I did hurdles." Jenna smiles. "Kate's workouts aren't anything like regular track workouts, but they're fun."

"I can't promise it will be easy," Kate says, "but I will get you strong. We have an ex-military member who teaches us how to shoot. On top of training, there's the other essential survival chores that have to happen. We work hard and train hard. Everyone pulls their weight."

"I'm in." The younger man steps forward. "My name is Christian."

"Me, too," says Stacy. She looks closer to Kate's age, with ash blond hair. "I don't like running, but I don't like the idea of being dead, either. Or undead. I'll work hard and train hard."

"We're all in." Leo extends a hand in an offering.

Kate doesn't take his outstretched hand. "You haven't heard it all yet."

"There's more?" Leo's expression wavers.

"We have three zombies locked up for observation. We're studying the alpha zombies and learning what we can about them."

The silence to this declaration is absolute.

"We're a package deal," Kate says steadily. "We want to help you, but you have to accept the parameters of our community."

Leo swallows, looking from his people and back to Kate. "I take it the zombies are secure?"

"They're on the second floor of an abandoned building. The windows of the room they're in have been boarded up. So has the door. All observations happen through a hole cut into the ceiling on the third floor."

Leo swallows again. "Okay. We accept your rules."

This time, when he extends his hand, Kate shakes it with a kind smile.

"Thank you," Leo says. "I'm not exaggerating when I say you've just saved our lives. You won't regret it."

36

CHECK IN

KATE

"And that," I tell Alvarez, "is how we ended up doubling the number of Creekside. We are now sixteen people." I don't mention the alarming rate we're going through food. I prefer to focus on the positive things. "Leo and his nephew Todd both worked in the"—I pause to clear my throat—"*cannabis* industry. They know a lot about farming. They're in the process of expanding our indoor gardens."

"I sure could use their expertise," Alvarez replies. "We're having shitty luck with our garden. I think it's too cold here. Or maybe the soil is bad. Hell if I know. We're having a hard time growing food."

"At least you have seagulls to fall back on."

Alvarez groans. "Don't remind me, Mama Bear. I know I shouldn't complain, but I'm sick of eating those filthy things. Can you believe two guys in my camp are trying to domesticate some? I keep telling them we need to focus on chickens. If we can ever find any."

"We have our first kids," I tell Alvarez. "Their names are Kristy and Evan. They're eight and ten. You should see them kill zombies. They scurry in after the adults and bash any downed zombies over the head with rocks to make sure they're really dead." I grimace into the ham. "Ben calls them our child soldiers."

"That's ... I don't know what to say to that."

"I didn't know what to think at first, either. But now I think it's a good thing. They can defend themselves. You never know when that might come in handy. They train every day with the adults, too. Their workouts aren't as intense, but I make sure they get the exercise they need to make them stronger. The lady who looks after them, Margie, is a retired kindergarten teacher. Let me tell you, those kids get an education with her."

"Oh? What do you mean by that?"

"Math is taught in the supply rooms and usually involves inventorying newly scavenged supplies. Reading involves survival stories. Margie went through every dorm room in Creekside to round up suitable books. Basically, she's combining survival skills with general education. She was something of a prepper before all this happened."

"A prepper? Doesn't sound like that worked out too well for her if she ended up on your doorstep."

"It started out okay, but she lived in a condo. She had a two-bedroom place stocked full of supplies. She banded with a big group of people. Her supplies were used up pretty quick. The good news is that she knows how to can food and preserve meats. She's been talking non-stop about finding some chickens."

"If you guys manage to find any that aren't dead, save a few for us, will you?" Alvarez asks.

"I'll FedEx you some eggs. You can hatch them and start your own chicken coop."

He chuckles. "That's a deal, Mama Bear. How are the newcomers taking to your running regime?"

I think back to these past two weeks with Leo's people. I

don't know the details of what they endured before they made it to Creekside, but whatever it was left them desperate enough that no one complained when I took them to the track the first time. They looked at me like I was nuts when I laid out their workouts, but no one complained.

"They're coming along," I say. "I'm taking it slow to help them build up their strength."

"You sound good, Mama Bear. Best I've heard you sound since that alpha attack."

I consider this. Things *have* lightened up since Leo's group joined us. "They're good people. We all have baggage, but we're working together for a common goal. How are your people doing? Any more sign of those bandits?"

The silence on the other end of the ham is heavy. "None."

"And the alphas?"

"It's a good thing you gave me a heads up. It saved us the first time we ran into one."

"Have you seen a lot of them?"

"Only two. There are no large groups of zoms out here, except maybe in Braggs, but that's a good ninety miles from here. Speaking of alphas, how's the science experiment going? Have you guys learned anything useful about alphas yet?"

"Not yet."

It's certainly not for lack of effort. Gary and Johnny have thrown themselves into the job with complete dedication. They spend most nights together after dinner going over alpha recordings taken during the day and trying to find patterns in them.

"I'm sure there will be a breakthrough eventually," Alvarez says.

"Yo. Mama Bear." Johnny, who sits on the other side of the table, taps his watch. "Time is up. Like, thirty minutes ago." He grins at me, though he makes it a point to flip open his notebook and uncap his pen.

I chuckle. "Hey, Foot Soldier, I gotta go. Wandering Writer is chomping at the bit. Who's the girl he's talking to?"

Johnny makes a face at me.

"Bella. She's right here tapping her watch at me."

"Funny, Johnny is doing the same thing to me."

"Is she really tapping her watch?" Johnny asks.

I roll my eyes and ignore the question. "Check back in three days from now, Foot Soldier?"

"Three days, Mama Bear."

37

INFRASOUND

KATE

I climb to the third floor of Fern where Johnny and Gary have set up their observation room. I like to check in on the boys once a day. We've had the alpha for a little over two weeks now. While we haven't had any breakthroughs, they've done a remarkable job at breaking down and recording individual sounds made by the alpha.

Our people have cobbled together enough two-by-fours and pieces of plywood that we now have a ramp system for Gary in both Creekside and Juniper. As far as I know, Johnny has only tipped over the wheelchair once. I would have excused Gary from this assignment altogether if he hadn't been so excited by it. Between cooking for all of us and observing the alpha, Gary has managed to be as busy as the rest of us.

Gary and Johnny's voices drift down the stairwell to me. It's clear they're having a spirited debate about something.

"I'm telling you, there's something else going on that we can't replicate with our human vocal cords," Johhny is saying.

"That doesn't make sense," Gary argues. "They have the

same vocal cords that we have. We should be able to make any sound they make."

"They're not the same. They're undead, remember?"

"I know, man, but *biologically* their vocal cords are the same."

"Maybe they changed. I mean, the rest of their bodies changed. Now they're blind, mindless cannibals. Have you ever heard of infrasound?"

I enter the room. "Infra what?" I ask.

Both young men turn their attention to me. "Hey, Kate," they say in unison.

The room looks like a cheap flea market stand. Notebooks, pens, books, VHS tape recorders, and cassette players are all over the floor and furniture. I don't know how they get from one side to the other without tripping on something.

Without a steady source of electricity, we've had to fall back on more primitive recording methods. Luckily the town of Arcata, with its population of outliers and anti-establishment folks, has a fair amount of pre-Internet tech. A string of homes just on the other side of the freeway produced no less than two hand-held recorders, five tape players, and two shoe boxes worth of cassette tapes.

"Gary and I were just talking about infrasound," Johnny says. "Those are sounds below the human range of hearing. Elephants make them. They use it to communicate over long-range distances. Maybe the alphas are doing something like that."

"You have the weirdest shit catalogued in your brain." Gary looks torn between annoyance and admiration.

"It's the job of a writer to be interested in weird shit."

I approach the hole we've cut into the floor of this room. We've covered the two-foot square opening with a section of chain-link fence to make sure no one falls through on accident.

In the room below, the alpha paces back and forth. It grunts and clicks. The two regular zombies we've captured follow the alpha. Back and forth, back and forth they go across the room. The oozing wounds on their bodies have seeped onto the carpet, leaving a reddish-brown smear to mark their trail. The smell is akin to ripened road kill on steroids.

"Tell me why you guys are talking about infrasound," I say.

"Watch this." Johnny leans over the hole and makes a complex string of clicks and keens with his mouth. It sounds so like the language of the alpha zom that I shiver. But despite the resemblance of sound, the zombies below don't react.

"Same happens when I do it. Watch." Gary repeats the same complex string of sound. Again, nothing happens.

"Now, watch this." Johnny picks up one of the tape recorders. It looks like a boom box from the nineties. We had to scavenge in five houses to find enough batteries to power it, but Johnny insisted on having it due to its size.

He positions the boom box next to the hole, turns up the volume, and hits play.

The exact same series of clicks and keens roll out of the big black speakers.

The reactions below are instantaneous.

The two regular zombies rush to the farthest corner of the room. When they hit the walls, they scratch at the dry wall. They grunt and moan, bumping against the wall as though trying to walk through to the other side.

The alpha, on the other hand, does no such thing. The old woman alpha advances on the opening above, lips peeled back in snarl. It hisses and grunts, the sounds coming out of its mouth in rapid fire.

"We think she's defending her property," Gary says. "She thinks another alpha is trying to take her pack out from under her."

"Notice how neither Gary nor I could replicate this same reaction when we mimicked the sounds," Johnny says.

"Man, I'm telling you, that's not it," Gary argues. "Did you know that in Mandarin, the same word has multiple meanings depending on voice inflection? We must be missing something. We're not making the sounds the right way."

"No, man." Johnny shakes his head. "We're replicating exactly what we hear. There's something else at play. I'm telling you, it could be infrasound. We need some sort of machine to help us detect undetectable sounds." He taps the end of his pen against his temple, grimacing. "Think we can find something like that in one of labs on campus?"

Gary snorts. "Even if we could, none of us would know how to use it."

"You guys are missing the most important discovery." I frown at them quizzically. "Did either of you realize this series of sounds drove the regular zombies *away*?" I point to the two creatures that continue to scratch and dig at the far wall of their prison. "Do you realize what we might be able to do with this?"

They look at me as if I've just hit them both over the head with a frying pan.

"Woah." Johnny goggles at me. "Dude, Kate, I'm sorry for being an idiot."

"We missed the forest through the trees. We're fucking idiots, man." Gary elbows Johnny in the ribs.

"*You're* the idiot," Johnny shoots back with an easy smile. "You're the one who keeps going on and on about Mandarin inflections."

"I'm telling you—"

"Guys, shut up for a second." My mind snaps into overdrive as an idea rushes in. "We need to test this out. We need a megaphone to see if we can use the recording to repel zombies from Creekside." The idea makes my insides tingle. This could be the very thing we need to protect our home from alphas.

"Megaphones. Yeah, good idea." Johnny nods. "We should get the ones at the track."

Gary makes a face. "Dude, those are, like, fifty feet up in the air. How do you propose getting them down?"

38

SECURITY SYSTEM

KATE

"I think you're violating every OSHA law ever written." Ben comes to stand next to me. He shades his eyes as he looks up.

Reed currently hangs from a metal beam in the covered section of the university bleachers, held in place by a rope harness crafted by Todd and Caleb. In his hands are a screwdriver and wire clipper. He works to remove the megaphone mounted to the top of a ceiling support while Todd and Caleb hold him up by the rope.

"What's OSHA?" I ask.

"Occupational Safety Health Administration. A bureaucracy dedicated to keeping people from dying or getting maimed on the job. I think the entire administration would be apoplectic if they had to keep track of you."

I frown in surprise. "Did you just ... make another joke?"

He continues to shade his eyes and watch Reed's operation. "Maybe."

"That's two jokes in the six months I've known you."

"Yep."

"Keep that up and you might be funny four times in an entire year."

"Yep."

I can't help it. A laugh bubbles up. Ben gives me his eye-crinkle smile.

My stomach flutters. Other than our mission to retrieve the alpha zom, we haven't spent much time together. I haven't forgotten our shared moment the morning of my hangover. Or that moment in his bedroom when I thought I might end up in the bottom bunk with him.

"How many of those things do you plan to retrieve today?" Ben asks. "The kid might really break his head open, you know."

This comment is followed by shouting between Reed, Caleb, and Todd.

"Dudes!" Reed calls down. "Hold still, will you?"

"We *are* holding still," Todd shoots back. "You keep swinging around."

"There's wind up here. Not my fault."

"Just hurry up and get the damn megaphone," Caleb shouts. "Your ass is heavy."

"We'll start with one megaphone," I say to Ben. "No reason to risk Reed's head if my idea doesn't work."

Several hours later, everyone except Gary is gathered on the rooftop of Creekside. Johnny holds the megaphone in one hand. With a pair of trimmed headphone wires and a soldering gun, he connected the megaphone to the boom box with the alpha recording.

"Good thing I grabbed those electrical wiring books before Mama Bear blew up the library," Johnny says.

"I hope you guys grabbed an *Anarchist's Cookbook*," Todd says. "We might need one of those someday."

"Shhh." I wave a hand at the guys to shut them up. "Everyone, pay attention."

On the ground below, Carter and Jenn stand on the western side of the compound. They each hold a metal pot and spoon.

"This feels counterintuitive," Susan says. "Since when do we call zombies to us?"

"It's gonna be okay, babe," Gary calls up from the hallway below. He might not be able to get up the ladder, but he still wants to be close to the action. "Don't worry. This is going to work."

"I'm just saying," Susan mutters.

She isn't wrong. We've gone to great lengths to secure our home and keep zombies out of our living space. Banging on metal pots to draw some toward us *is* counterintuitive. Not to mention dangerous if my plan doesn't work.

I peer over the edge of the building at Carter and Jenna and wave my arms over my head. At my signal, the two of them beat on the pots with their spoons. Everyone on the rooftop cringes at the noise.

It doesn't take long for the zombies to arrive. A dozen make their way toward Creekside, shuffling along with their arms outstretched.

I let Jenna and Carter pound away for another sixty seconds. Then I wave my arms again, signaling them to stop.

We wait for the zombies to bump up against our barrier. Then I turn to Johnny.

"You're on," I tell him.

Johnny positions himself at the corner of the rooftop, aims the megaphone in the direction of the zoms, and hits play on the boom box.

The recorded sequence of clicks and keens bounds through the quiet. A shiver runs across my skin at the unearthly sound.

The reaction of the zoms below is instantaneous. With a collective moan, they fall back from our perimeter. On the ground below, Carter flashes me a thumbs-up.

"Is it working?" Gary calls. "Is it driving them away? Somebody tell me what's happening!"

"It's working," Susan cries. "The zoms are retreating!"

"Ladies and gentlemen," Johnny says grandly, "what we have here is a bona fide zombie apocalypse security system. Hold your applause. Just leave a tip in the jar and we'll call it good."

This sets off a string of eye rolls and groans.

"It was Kate's idea," Margie, the former kindergarten teacher, says. "She's the one who should get the tip."

"You're forgetting one thing," Ash says. "The radio runs on batteries. We're going to need to scavenge a ton of them to keep this thing operational."

"Nah, I just need to figure out how to wire the radio to the solar panels." Satisfied with the zombie retreat, Johnny sets down the megaphone.

"Guess this means I have to let these idiots dangle me from a rope again." Reed jerks a thumb at Todd and Caleb.

In response, the other two young men deliver simultaneous middle fingers. Reed doubles over laughing.

"What we need," I say, breaking up the revelry, "is an extensive library of alpha commands. Gary and Johnny, you've done good work. Now you just need to do more." My mind spins with the possibilities. If I have anything to say about this, we're going to have a full dictionary of alpha zom words at our disposal.

39

RECIPES

KATE

"I can't wait to get these pieces moved downstairs. I want to get the seeds planted within the week."

I glance up from where I lie on the floor, twirling a tiny Allen wrench between my fingers as I disassemble a bed leg. On the opposite side of the bed, Leo and his nephew, Todd, dismantle the other legs.

Leo has drawn up plans to convert several floors of the Laurel dorm building into an indoor garden. Right now we're dismantling dorm room furniture to convert into growing beds.

"Marge wants to go on a scavenging mission back into downtown Arcata to hit up the hardware store for canning supplies," I say.

"We don't have to rush. We won't have any food to can for eight to twelve weeks," Leo replies.

"Marge just likes canning," Todd adds. "She wants to start teaching the kids how to do it."

Not for the first time, I find myself grateful for the new additions to Creekside. "You know, the indoor garden was only a vague idea before you guys stepped up to spearhead the project."

"It's the least we could do. You took me and my people in when we had nothing. After losing so many back at the condo complex, you gave us a fresh start." Leo glances at me from beneath the mattress. "Was there a Mr. Kate? Before the apocalypse, I mean?"

I sigh. "Yes. But he died a few years before the apocalypse."

"I had a fiancé. A step-son." Leo doesn't look at me as he finishes his side of the bed. "I tried to get to them. When I heard reports of what was going on, I rushed home from work. By the time I got there ... You know the story. It's not unique."

"Doesn't mean it hurts any less." I recall the day I arrived home to find my husband dead.

"I just mean I'm not special or unique in my pain. We've all lost people."

"I lost both my parents," Todd puts in. "My sister was off at college in Washington. If she is alive, I'll never see her again."

I think of my College Creek kids, all of them stranded in Arcata with their families lost and scattered. "We have to make new families. It's the way of things."

"That's what Christian says. It's a good way to look at things now," Todd says.

"Hey, guys." Eric strolls in. "Kate, I need you to come look at something."

A distant part of my brain wonders what he's doing here. Eric is on scavenging duty with Caleb and Ash. The three of them are supposed to be looking for seeds we can plant in the garden.

"You need me right now?" It's pretty obvious I'm in the middle of something.

"Yeah, now." Eric shoves his hands into his pockets.

The young man hasn't asked anything of me since Lila died.

Miraculously, he doesn't even seem to harbor any ill will toward me. He does, unfortunately, smoke more pot than ever before.

"I found something," he tells me.

I glance over at Leo and Todd with an apologetic shrug.

Leo waves me off. "The furniture will be waiting for you when you get back." Then, oddly, he winks at Eric.

I'm not sure what that's all about. Eric is already slinking out of the room, hands in his pockets. I sigh and pad after him. Time is valuable, especially as the days are getting shorter as we head into fall.

I follow Eric out of Fern dorm and back in the direction of Creekside. We pass Margie and the two kids as they return from a trip to the nearby creek to gather water. With them are Reed and Stacy. The adults all lug giant five-gallon buckets. The kids carry gallon jugs, one in each hand. They strain under the weight, but neither of them complains.

"You're going to make them do fractions?" Reed asks. "With buckets of water?"

"Let me guess," Margie says dryly. "You weren't much of a math fan when you were in school."

"I'm not a math fan *out* of school."

"There's no better way to teach fractions than with water and various container sizes," Margie says. "It's the best way to get kids to visualize the concept. Granted, I used to use measuring cups and water from the tap, but buckets and jugs and creek water will function the same."

Eric and I leave them behind and head into Creekside. Once upstairs, Eric leads me to the dorm room he used to share with Lila.

I pause just inside the door. Lila's pink-and-yellow flowered blanket has been straightened, the decorator pillows in place.

Eric makes it a point to make the bed every day. It was something Lila did before she died. Seeing the neat blanket tightens my chest.

"Look what I found." Eric lays a hand on a pile of spiral-bound notebooks spread across the bed.

"What are those?" I move to the foot of the bed, taking in the many monoblocks of color.

"They're Lila's notebooks. All of them. She never threw anything away. Here, sit down." He drags a desk chair up for me and closes the door.

I don't want to sit. I want to get back to dismantling beds with Todd and Leo. I suppress an impatient sigh. If Eric needs my attention, I'll give it to him. I sit.

"These are all her recipes for her cannabis salves and tinctures." He pushes one of the notebooks into my hand. "Take a look."

I flip it open. Lila's neat handwriting marches across page after page.

Emotion blooms in my chest. I remember seeing Lila with these, bent over the kitchen counter as she meticulously measured, mixed, pounded, and stirred her ingredients. There are notes with all her recipes. Many of them are crossed out and rewritten with slightly different measurements of the various ingredients.

I miss her. I miss her scared eyes and her acerbic tongue.

"Lila." I close the notebook and press it to my chest.

When I look at Eric, I see the same emotion in his eyes. They're misty with sadness, though a tender smile pulls at the corners of his mouth.

"All her work and experiments of the past few years." Eric picks up another notebook, flipping through it. "We can recreate her medications and salves."

Before the world ended, Lila had a dream of starting her own medicinal cannabis company. Everyone liked to poke fun at her, mostly when she, Reed, and Eric quarreled over the dwindling supply of buds.

"Her muscle salve worked." I rub absently at the ankle I

rolled on my journey to Arcata, thinking about how well her salve had helped me heal.

"Johnny and Carter have both been using it. Now we can make more." Eyes brightening, Eric pulls open a drawer and pulls out a Zip Lock with two buds. "Look at this. It's shitty bud full of seeds."

From my time spent with the kids, I've gathered that shitty weed has seeds. The more expensive, premium buds don't have seeds.

"Now that we have seeds," Eric says, "Do you think Leo and Todd could get them to grow?"

My eyes narrow. "You want to use our indoor garden to grow marijuana?"

"Pharmacies are going to dry up. We've looted our fair share, but the supply is going to run out. It's in our best interest to develop other medicinals."

If his face wasn't so earnest, I'd think this was a ploy to restock his pot supply. Eric spends more time stoned than not, but at the moment, there is no hint of fuzz in his eyes. He's stone sober and he means every word he says.

"I have to think on it," I say. "Let me go over Leo's plan for the garden and see if there's a corner we can set aside for a plant or two. Your job is to go through these books and make a compilation of all the final recipes. Make a combined list of all the ingredients. There's no use to put in a pot plant to make medicinals if we don't have any of the other components."

"Okay." Eric takes the notebook back from me and returns it to the stack, spending more time than necessary straightening the already neat pile. "You're really going to consider it?"

"Yeah." I put an arm around his shoulders and squeeze. "We owe it to Lila, don't you think?"

He nods, sniffing once. "Yeah."

As I head to the door, Eric says, "Wait—Kate. I—uh, want to talk to you about something else."

"What is it, Eric?"

"I was—uh—thinking about the cemetery." He shifts, not quite meeting my eye.

"We don't have a cemetery."

"The rubble where we buried Lila and Jesus," he amends. "We need to mark it. Set it apart from everything else. Maybe find some fencing to put around it."

It's not a bad idea. The problem is that it would take half our people and at least two days to find fencing and transport it to the site. It's not the best use of our resources. I don't say any of this to Eric, though.

"Just think about it? Please?" Eric asks.

"Okay. I'll think about it."

"Wait. Kate?"

Once again, he stops me when I try to leave. "Yes, Eric?"

"Thanks. For being here. For all of us, I mean. You hold us together."

I give his shoulder a last squeeze. Before he can delay me any longer, I push out the door and into the hall—

—and right into a sitting room decorated with streamers and a big, homemade banner with the words *Happy Birthday Kate* written in big bubble letters. Every member of Creekside is there, big smiles filling the room.

"Surprise!"

40

SURPRISE

KATE

"Surprise!"

The word washes over me. I stare, dumbfounded.

"Happy birthday, Mom!" Carter, arm draped around Jenna's shoulder, grins at me.

"My mama is officially old." Reed emerges from the crowd and crushes me in a bruising hug, lifting my feet off the ground. He twirls me in a half circle and plops me next to the kitchen table.

In the center of it is a large chocolate cake. A paper plaque sits on top, the words *Over the Hill* written in black marker. Beneath the words is the number *40*.

"Guess who made the cake?" Jenna jerks a thumb at Reed.

"Hey." Reed puts his hands on his hips. "I had to make the cake when Mama Bear was sleeping. I dare any of your asses to make a cake on a barbeque with a headlamp for light."

"I was talking about the decoration on the cake," Jenna replies.

"Oh." Reed cocks his head at the paper plaque that looks like it was drawn by a third-grader. "I'm pretty much the next fucking Picasso. Ya'll better save that. It will be worth millions someday. Do you like it, Mama?"

"I—" I sputter, trying to find words. "How?"

"How did we know it was your birthday, or how did we pull off the surprise?" Johnny asks.

"Both."

"It *is* your birthday, right?" Caleb frowns.

"Of course, it's her birthday," Carter says. "You didn't think I'd forget, did you, Mom?"

I shake my head, still in shock over the surprise. I turn on Eric. "*You* were a distraction."

He shoves his hands into his pockets with a grin, not bothering to deny it. "How'd I do?"

"You've officially tipped your hand. I now know you're a grade-A bullshitter."

Everyone chuckles, crowding forward to hug me or clap me on the back. I catch sight of Ben at the back of the gathered crowd. He wears his general gruff expression, arms folded over his chest, but he gives me a wink when our eyes meet.

"I hope I'm in good shape like you when I'm old," Evan, the little boy, tells me.

"Hell, I'm already old," Margie says. "If Kate doesn't give me a heart attack during training, I might get in shape one day."

"Heart attacks are half the fun," Johnny tells her.

"Says the punk who's on a recovery cycle," Margie grouses.

"I'll be passing you in another week. Just you wait, old lady."

"Gary made a special casserole," Susan tells me. "He's been working on the recipe for days."

"We had to break into the student store to get powdered potato cups," says Christian.

Since arriving, the former PE teacher has helped me add new strength training routines to our workouts. He's shaved off his beard, revealing the face of a man in his early thirties.

Christian wasn't exaggerating when he said he ran the 400 and 800 meter sprints. Reed is still our fastest runner, but Christian chases his heels anytime I make them race.

Gary and Susan bring out his casserole, which turns out to be the apocalypse version of shepherd's pie. The top is covered with the powdered mashed potatoes. The bottom is a gooey mixture that bears a loose resemblance to cream of mushroom soup with caramelized onions and peas. I may have turned my nose up at it prior to the zombie apocalypse, but tonight, on my birthday, it's the best thing I ever tasted.

It turns out Gary has a sense for seasoning. He's made some pretty interesting and delicious canned food casseroles on the barbeque. In comparison to Lila, he's practically a gourmet chef, though I would never disrespect Lila's memory by saying that aloud.

After dinner, Reed prepares to cut the cake. "Someone get a candle or something," he yells. "Anything flammable. Oh, and make sure there's forty of them for our Mama Bear."

Jenna produces a potpourri candle with three wicks. "This is as good as it's going to get."

"Peppermint scent?" Reed makes a face.

Jenna shrugs, lighting the candle with a book of matches.

"One more person wants to sing you happy birthday." Johnny holds up the ham radio. "Foot Soldier, are you there? Over."

"Wandering Writer, this is Foot Soldier, over. Where's Mama Bear?"

"She's right here, Foot Soldier," Johnny replies. "Get ready to bust out the birthday melody!"

"On three," Carter calls, plunking the peppermint the candle in front of me. "One-two-three—"

The entire room bursts into song. My gaze passes over each and every one of my companions. Carter. Jenna. Reed. Johnny. Eric. Ben. Caleb. Ash. Susan. Gary. Leo. Christian. Todd.

Margie. Stacy. Little Evan and Kristy. And Alvarez, two hundred miles away. Everyone here, for me. My heart swells with love.

I blow out the candle, sending a silent wish out in the world. *Protect my people. Keep them safe.*

After everyone has cake, Carter taps a spoon against a glass. "Alright, everyone, time for Mom's birthday present."

"Presents?" I ask. "On top of food and cake?"

"One more," Carter says. "This one took a lot of planning. Jenna and I may have gone on a super-secret mission with Ben back to a certain brewery."

My mouth falls open. "You *what*?"

"Don't worry." Ben holds up his hands in self-defense. "I took enough grenades to take down a large village in China. They were perfectly safe."

I narrow my eyes in mock scowl. "No more super-secret missions."

"Don't say that until you see what we have." The crowd parts as Carter lugs a box in his arms. Glass clinks inside.

He plunks the box in front of me. It's wrapped in Hannakuh paper.

"I found that!" Kristy jumps up and down, beaming. "I was playing hide-and-seek with Evan and found it under a bed!"

"It is the most beautiful paper *ever*," I tell her, tearing into the gift.

The lid to a cardboard box pops open as the wrapping paper falls away. Brown bottles with beer caps fill the interior. I lift one out, my body going still as I take it in.

On the front of the bottle is a hand-drawn label in the shape of a half-ellipsoid. A green mountain fills the upper curve, bisected by what is clearly a trail. On the trail is the silhouette of a runner. Over the top of the mountain are the words *Over the Hill.*

Carter can't contain himself any longer. "Jenna designed a beer label for you!" He beams at his girlfriend.

"And Carter made a special brew for you," Jenna says. "It's a lager."

I pop the top of the bottle. The glass is cool in my hands. Not ice cold like the good old days when we had refrigerators, but cool like it's been stored in a dark closet.

The first sip washes over my tongue. I close my eyes, letting the taste carry me back to a different time. To a time when Kyle and Frederico were still alive. To a time when my free time was spent training for ultramarathons and researching races to see where my next adventure would take me. To a time when running wasn't something I did for self-preservation.

To a time when the world wasn't overrun with the dead.

"It tastes like a finish line." My voice is rough with emotion.

Carter and Jenna gather me in for a hug. I squeeze the two of them, holding them close. My love for them threatens to explode out of my chest.

This is, by far, the best birthday I've ever had.

———

HOURS LATER, I leave the party and make my way back to my room. I have a slight buzz from the beer. Everyone else had one bottle, but I got three—on top of a couple of shots of moonshine that Reed and Johnny have been brewing. I feel happy from the inside out.

To top everything off, I don't have watch tonight. Leo took my shift as a birthday present. I might have insomnia, but at least I'll be warm and comfortable in my own bed.

Flinging open the door, I switch on the light—and freeze.

Gone are the Grateful Dead postures, the baskets of stinky boy laundry I never got around to moving, and the cluttered desk of a college kid.

Every surface area is spotless. The window is open, letting

in fresh air. And did someone spray pine air freshener? Where did someone even find pine air freshener?

Even the stained bedspread is gone, replaced with a graphic quilt. It depicts the silhouette of a howling wolf with a full moon hanging overhead.

But the part that really takes my breath away is the walls. Covering every square inch—the ceiling, the walls, and even the bulletin board on the back of the desk—are pictures of nature. Trees. Rivers. Waterfalls. Deserts. Hillsides. Wildflowers. Oceans.

For the first time in months, I feel like I'm back on the trail. Like I'm surrounded by the beauty and serenity I've missed so much. A piece of my old life gifted to me.

Another birthday gift. And I know who it's from.

41

ROOFTOP

BEN

When Ben hears steps on the ladder, he doesn't turn around. He secretly hopes it's Kate, though he promised himself not to hold his breath. She's busy with her party; it's too much to hope she'd have time to find him up here. Besides, it's not like he left a card.

"Hey."

Her voice washes over him. He closes his eyes, savoring it.

He turns and finds her standing there, outlined by the starlight.

"Did you do that?" she asks. "The pictures? My room?"

"You told me you missed the trails."

She tilts her head at him. He can tell by the way she stands that she's drunk. Maybe not shitfaced like she'd been at the wake, but there's a looseness to her limbs and posture that gives it away.

"When did I tell you that?"

He wishes he could see her expression, but it's dark and she's too far away.

"The night of the wake. You said you missed the trails." He sucks in a breath, trying to work up the words he really wants to say. He blurts them out before he has time to second-guess himself. "If there was a way to give you a real trail, I would. Honestly, I thought about it. But I figured I might get myself killed trying to secure a section of the woods for you." Now he sounds like an idiot. "I'm still useful around this place for a few things so I decided not to risk it."

She takes half a dozen steps in his direction, coming close enough that he can now see her face.

"It's one of the nicest things anyone has ever done for me. Thank you, Ben."

"You deserve it."

The five paces separating them evaporates. Before he can fully comprehend the disappearance, she stands on her tiptoes and kisses him.

He's barely let himself dream of this moment. Kate is so far out of his league it's not even funny. Not to mention that he can be an asshole.

But here she is, standing under the starlight, kissing him. And even though he knows he's not good enough for her, he seizes the moment.

He pulls her close and kisses her back. She feels as good in his arms as he'd imagined. His blood heats as she leans into him, running her hands up his back.

The words come out all by themselves. "You taste like a bar."

The perfect moment fizzles. Kate steps out of the circle of his arms.

"Really?" She wrinkles her nose at him. "You lead with all that stuff about wanting to build me a trail, then close with *You taste like a bar*?"

Give him a gun to point at some bad guys, and Ben knows just what to do. Give him a grenade to lob, and he's a pretty good shot. Hell, throw some undead at him and he's more than up to the task of dispatching them.

Giving him a woman he wants is like to scrambling his brain with a fork. Giving him a woman he's crazy about is like scrambling his brain with two forks.

"You did have a few drinks, didn't you?" he asks.

"A few, yeah. So did everyone else. You taste like Reed's cake, by the way."

Five steps once again separates them. Ben searches frantically for a way to regain his footing, to overcome the gap that always seems to hang between them.

His brain completely fails him.

Kate's shoulders sag. She presses her face into her hands.

"I shouldn't have come up here. I might be drunk, but I'm not that drunk. Whatever this weirdness is between us, it's a mistake."

"I like the weirdness." Fuck. Could anything more asinine have come out of his mouth? "I like you, Kate."

"I like you, too, Ben. I don't know why, but I do." She shakes her head. "But we're not stupid teenagers. We're both adults. We're both smart enough to know this won't go anywhere. We're too different to ever be a real couple."

Then she's gone.

The rooftop is empty, deserted. He wishes he could rewind it all and try again.

Ben stares at the space where she stood. The emptiness sucks him in.

Before he realizes what's happening, he's standing in the courtyard of College Creek surrounded by the helpless kids gunned down by Johnson and his lackeys. The scene swirls, spitting him out in the baking heat of Pakistan, where he kneels beside the cot of a dying comrade.

And, finally, he finds himself at the bedside of his newborn son, Sam. Signing over full custody to the woman he'd had a fling with for a few weeks while on leave. The remembered pain of that day staggers him.

More than anything, he'd wanted to be a part of his little boy's life. And he had been, in a way, for a few weeks every year whenever he was on leave. But Sam's stepfather had been much more of a father than Ben had ever been. It had all been for the best. Ben wasn't cut out to be a husband any more than he was cut out to be a father.

He reels, heart pounding as he yanks himself free of the flashbacks. Leaning over his knees, he takes in big gulps of air.

Tonight was all for the best, he tells himself. He'd have messed things up with Kate sooner or later. Better sooner and just get it over with.

He doesn't regret the gift for her. Not for a second. He wanted to do it for her. And it feels good to know his feelings for her aren't one-sided. That's tonight's consolation prize, his takeaway from the disaster.

He tries to be okay with it. He tries really, really hard.

42

MISSED CALL

BEN

Ben paces on the rooftop, scanning the university campus with his binoculars. It's been exactly one week since he fucked things up with Kate. His insomnia is at an all-time high.

He and Kate co-exist like they always have. They seem to have mutually agreed to pretend the kiss never happened. Except Ben can't pretend it didn't happen. It's all he can think about. He wants to ask for a do-over, but hasn't the first clue how to go about doing that.

"What are you looking for?" Johnny asks. It's his turn on watch, meaning he has to stick around even if Ben is feeling paranoid and decided to join him.

"I don't know," Ben replies.

He's been fighting the itch for days. It has nothing to do with Kate. It's not the normal kind of itching from a mosquito bite, either. It's a buzzing in his gut, a sense that something in the world isn't right.

A lifetime in the army has honed his instincts. He's had enough bad luck to recognize when it's looming around the corner.

What pisses him off is that even when he knows shit is about to go down, it often doesn't do him a damn bit of good.

"What do you mean, you don't know?" Johnny asks. He has his notebook open on his lap. How the kid can watch anything while he scribbles away in that thing is beyond Ben.

"I have a feeling." Ben pauses, watching a group of eight zombies stumble their way through campus. He makes a mental note to tell Kate. A team should go out to dispatch them later today.

"Like, a bad feeling?" Johnny asks. "Like, a sixth sense?"

Ben lowers the binos with an exasperated grumble. "Exactly." He resents the kid for his eloquence.

Johnny scribbles something in his notebook. "Tell me what it feels like."

"No." Ben returns the binos to his face, sweeping the fortifications around Creekside.

"Come on," Johnny wheedles. "This is for posterity. You know I'm recording our life here at Creekside. Tell me what premonition feels like."

Ben rounds on him. "It feels like shit is going to hit the fan and I don't know how to stop it." He glares. "It sucks balls, kid."

Johnny grins at him. "I'm going to quote you on that."

Letting out another huff of disgust, Ben tosses aside the binoculars and heads down the ladder. He knows better than to open his mouth around that kid.

"Bring up some dinner for me," Johnny calls after him. "I hate cold food."

Ben ignores him even as he makes a mental note to get food for Johnny. He stomps into the common room. It's bustling with eighteen bodies, two of which happen to be kids who decided this crowded room was a great place to play tag.

Ben stands in the doorway, mouth twisting with distaste. It's time to knock down some walls and make this dorm suite a genuine gathering space. It's getting too damned cramped for his taste these days. He'll talk to Kate and see about putting together a team to execute the remodel. It will be a good excuse to talk to her.

He finds Kate sitting at the kitchen table, chewing at her bottom lip as she fiddles with the receiver of the ham. At the look on her face, Ben feels his hackles rise.

Things might have regressed to a strictly professional level with them, but hell if he's going to stand by and say nothing if she looks worried about something. Besides, the anxiety in his gut is expanding, making him even more edgy.

"What's going on?" he barks, coming to stand beside the table. A few people glance up at his sharp tone. Ben realizes he's switched into his military voice. "I didn't mean to talk like a drill sergeant," he says, attempting with moderate success to modify his tone.

Kate looks up with a wrinkled brow. "It's Alvarez. He missed our regular check-in three days ago. He was supposed to check in this morning ..." Her voice trails off. "I'm just worried. That's two missed check-ins."

"It's not the first time he's missed a call," Carter points out, pulling out a chair to sit beside his mother. "Stuff happens. I'm sure he'll be in touch as soon as he can."

Kate continues to worry at her bottom lip. "I just have a bad feeling, you know?"

"That makes two of us," Ben mutters, turning away. His voice is lost in the general hum around them as Gary comes in off the balcony with a fresh pot of spaghetti, the sauce made from the first harvest of Lila's tomatoes in the garden.

That night, sleep is impossible. His room feels cramped and stuffy. Between the itchy foreboding gnawing at him from the inside and endless thoughts of Kate, his head might explode.

He goes to the common room to get some water. Not that water will help him sleep, but he could use the distraction. He's just grabbed a cup when the ham radio crackles with sound.

"Mama Bear, this is Foot Soldier. Fort Ross to Humboldt. Is anyone there? Over?"

Ben jerks, knocking the ham receiver to the floor in his haste. Fumbling it into his hand, he answers.

"Fort Ross, this is Humboldt. Where the hell have you guys been? You have Mama Bear worried sick. Over."

A beat of silence. "Who is this?"

Ben wracks his brain for a call sign. He's never spoken to Alvarez on the ham before. He says the first name that comes to mind. "This is Word Smith. I live with Mama Bear and Wandering Writer."

Word Smith? Where the fuck did that name come from? He's the last person who should be using that call sign.

"We've been waiting for your call," he says.

"Good to hear your voice, Word Smith. Shit has gone sideways at Fort Ross. We're under siege."

"What's the sit rep?" Kate mentioned Alvarez had a military background.

"Word Smith, are you military? Over."

"That's affirmative. Thirty years of service. Over."

"Thank fucking god. Maybe you can help us. Can you get Mama Bear? I don't want to tell this story twice. Over."

"Affirmative. Back in three. Over."

43

SIEGE

BEN

As he rushes away to get Kate, his premonition kicks into high gear. This is the shoe drop he's been expecting. Whatever Alvarez is about to tell them, it's not going to be good.

A short time later, the entire Creekside crew, minus the children, is gathered around the ham radio. It had taken only minutes to wake everyone.

"Foot Soldier, this is Word Smith. Over."

Several heads swivel in his direction, Kate's the first among them. Ben feels his face heat and keeps his eyes locked on the ham. Why the fuck had that handle popped into his head?

"Word Smith, this is Foot Soldier. Everyone there?"

Kate takes the receiver from Ben. "Foot Soldier? This is Mama Bear. We're all here. What's your status? Over."

"Not good, Mama Bear. We're fucked. Over."

"That is not a detailed report of the situation," Kate grinds out. "Details, Foot Soldier. Right now. Over."

"Remember those bandits I told you about? The ones who kidnapped our people?"

"Yes."

"They're back, only there's more of them. It started with raids on the perimeter of our land. The livestock. The horses. The orchard. The fish we left out to dry. Then a few of our people disappeared."

Ben feels his temper start to boil. He grips the edge of the table, fighting against the flashback that tries to force itself to the forefront.

"We formed search parties. More of our people disappeared," Alvarez says. "Then over two dozen people on bicycles were spotted north of Fort Ross on Highway One. They were heavily armed and heading straight for us. We secured the fort just before the bandits arrived."

Kate's knuckles are white around the receiver. "What's your situation now?" she asks.

"Mr. Rosario, the bandit leader, wants Fort Ross."

At the mention of the name Mr. Rosario, Kate's entire body stills. Ben's hackles go up at the sudden rage that paints her face. He doesn't know who this Mr. Rosario is, but Kate's reaction is enough to make him want to start shooting something.

"It gets worse," Alvarez says. "Rosario has seven of my people. She's given us twenty-four hours to surrender. After that, she'll execute one of them every day she has to wait."

Seconds tick by. Kate visibly wrestles with her anger, jaw clenched so hard Ben can hear her teeth grind.

"Twenty-four hours?" Kate barks. "When did the clock start ticking?"

"Twenty-seven minutes ago."

Kate leans over the table, her face a set mask of determination. "I'm coming, Foot Soldier. Hold on. I'll be there. Over and out." She slams the receiver down on the table, glaring at everyone and nothing. "Will someone please tell me why that crazy bitch is named Mr. Rosario?" she shouts, lifting her eyes to the ceiling as though the answer might drop from the sky.

The room stills, everyone frozen by this uncharacteristic display of anger.

Reed tentatively raises a hand in the air. "Mama?"

"What?" Kate snaps.

"I know the story of Mr. Rosario."

"Tell me." She attempts to rein in her fury and completely fails.

"Mr. Rosario was the original drug lord of northern California. When his wife caught him cheating, she cut off his balls and locked him in a shed in the woods and left him there until he starved to death. His wife took on his name and took over his business. The story is that she set up a compound around the shed where he died. She runs all her operations from there."

Hands on her hips, Kate glares. Not at Reed, but past him, like she's seeing a memory she'd rather forget. Ben can relate to that.

Then she stalks out of the room, leaving everyone sitting there in stunned silence.

Ben is the first one to move. Kate isn't going anywhere without him. He charges out the door after her, Carter and Jenna right on his heels.

Kate is inside her room, shoving supplies into a running pack.

"Mom?" Carter pokes his head around the doorframe. Ben and Jenna hang back behind him. "You can't do this."

"My friend is in trouble," she replies, not looking up. "I'm going to help him."

"Did you hear the part about Fort Ross being surrounded and outgunned by a band of raiders?" Carter says. "You can't go."

Kate spins on him. "You know what that bitch did to me and Frederico. She captured us. She chained a collar of bells around our necks and pushed us out into a forest infested with zombies. We almost died trying to get away. She did it for her own entertainment."

Ben sees red. The mental image of Kate with a collar of bells around her neck makes him want to strangle something.

"I'm going with you," he says.

Kate flicks a glance at him, nods, then goes back to shoving supplies into her pack. "This will be a volunteer mission only."

"Um, Fort Ross is two hundred miles away," Jenna says. "It's not safe to drive. You saw what happened when Leo and his people tried to drive."

"You're a badass, Mom, but even you can't run that far in twenty-four hours."

Kate straightens, flinging her pack over her shoulders and snapping it into place. "I'm not going to run. I'm taking the boat." She marches past them and into the bathroom, filling her pack bladder with boiled water kept in jugs on the floor.

"What boat?" Carter demands.

"Susan's boat."

"You don't know how to drive a boat," Jenna argues.

"I'll have Susan show me."

Carter turns to Ben. "Will you talk some sense into her?"

"We just need to take enough firepower to blow those fuckers to the moon and back," Ben says. "That will take care of them. We can figure out the boat."

Kate spins toward him, jabbing a finger into his chest. "That's what I'm talking about. You're in charge of pulling together everything you think we'll need. I'll get the alpha zom recordings." Her mouth sets. "I'll sic an entire horde of zombies on that bitch if I have to."

"Mom!" Carter shouts. "This is a suicide mission!"

Kate blinks, briefly coming down from her state of focused rage. She grabs Carter in a fierce hug. "I can't lose Alvarez, baby," she says. "I just can't. I already lost Lila and Jesus. I can't lose anyone else."

"Those were accidents," Jenna says. "We all miss them, but it's no one's fault they're gone. Don't throw yourself away trying to fix something that can't be fixed."

"We can do this." Ben steps forward. "A small guerilla team. Me. Caleb. Ash. Reed for his speed and Eric for his sniper skills. We boat down the coast. It won't take more than seven or eight hours. Those assholes will never know what hit them. Like you said, we'll take the alpha recording. If we can't out-gun them, we'll turn the zoms on them."

Face contorted, Carter glares at Ben. "Just because you're in love with my mom doesn't mean you have the right to encourage her suicide mission!"

The room goes silent. Kate's face turns red.

Ben considers crawling under a table. He stomps out of the room instead. "I'll go get the guns."

He slams the door behind him. Maybe sometime in the next twenty-four hours, he'll regain some of his self-respect.

44

APOCALYPTIC BOUNCE HOUSE

KATE

"There's only one problem with your plan," says Susan after I lay out the bullet points to the assembled group. "My boat is almost out of fuel. It's the reason Gary was in the water when he was attacked by the shark. He was siphoning gas."

I pace, chewing at my bottom lip as I sort through options. "Can boats use regular gas?" There are enough abandoned cars around.

Susan shakes her head. "No. They use MDO. Marine diesel oil. The closest marina is in Eureka, but there are too many zoms there. Our best option is to try the communities on the west side of the bay. Lots of homes there have docks and boats. We can siphon from them. I think we have enough gas to make it across the bay."

"Then that's what we do." I nod, mind racing. "This is a volunteer-only mission. You all know the risks. No one is obligated to help."

"You're not taking my boat unless I drive it," Susan says. "Besides, you saved Gary's life. This is the least I can do to repay the favor."

"I'm going." Leo folds his arms over his chest. "Rosario raided our lab and stole some of the proprietary hybrids we developed. Butchered them and sold them on the illegal market. I've been wanting to get back at that bitch for years."

"Great." I nod to Susan and Leo, grateful for the help. "We need to be packed and ready to leave by sunrise." That's a little less than two hours. "Are there any other volunteers?"

To my surprise, nearly everyone volunteers. Even Carter and Jenna, despite the fact they think this is a kamikaze mission. I chose the four people Ben named to round out the team: Caleb, Ash, Reed, and Eric.

Carter is pissed I'm leaving. My son doesn't get mad very often. But when he's mad, he stays mad. For a long time. I can only hope to earn his forgiveness.

"You and Jenna are in charge while I'm gone," I tell them. "Keep up the workouts. Focus the rest of your days on scavenging and installation of new solar panels for the indoor gardens."

Carter is so furious he can't make eye contact with me. Jenna gives me a hug. "Be safe, Kate."

"I'll be back before you know it." I kiss Carter on the cheek, pretending he isn't giving me the cold shoulder. If I die on this mission, he'll remember that I love him.

I find Ben in the armory organizing firearms. I feel awkward after the thing Carter said. I decide to use the same tactic I've been using ever since our awkward kiss. When I enter the armory, I pretend like nothing happened.

"Think we have what we need to take down Rosario?" I ask.

Ben doesn't look up. "Long-range weapons and explosives," he says. "Those will be our best line of defense to take these fuckers down. We also have a handful of compact travel rifles that fold in half and fit into a pack."

I take in the two large backpacks filled with weapons and explosives. "Ben, you don't have to come. This is my fight."

He gives me a flat, what-the-fuck look. "This woman chained bells to your neck and set zombies after you, Kate. She deserves to be strung up by her entrails. That's exactly what I'm going to do if I get my hands on her first." He goes back to sorting weapons.

"Everyone you named agreed to come with us."

He snorts. "Of course they did. There isn't a person in this place who wouldn't follow you into hell, Mama Bear."

"Susan and Leo are coming, too. Susan to pilot the boat. Leo to get revenge on Rosario."

"Good. We can use their help. Don't forget the alpha recordings. Wish those kids had time to get more than that single command." Ben slaps some extra magazines into a backpack. "Do you mind grabbing my bug-out pack and running shoes from my room? I'll meet you downstairs with the rest of the ammo."

"Sure, Ben," I say, grateful to have his help on this mission. "See you downstairs."

———

"SHIT. THIS SUCKS." Susan runs a hand over her face, pursing her lips as she stares at her boat.

We stand ankle-deep in the swampy waters of Humboldt Bay. *Fairhaven*, the charter ship, has been left to its own devices for weeks. It's become wedged in the soil and lists to one side.

"She's going to be a bitch to get out of that mud," Susan continues. "It's going to take some time."

Alvarez doesn't have time. Lives are depending on us. We've wasted enough time just getting here.

Crossing the highway hadn't been any easier this time. We had the trick of setting off car alarms to draw the zombies away, but Eric still managed to get himself grabbed by a zombie with broken legs that was stuck under a car. Only Reed's quick reflexes had saved him.

"Let's not stand around with our thumbs up our asses," Ben growls, sloshing through the water to the boat. "Let's get our gear loaded and get this girl out to sea."

We have two large backpacks crammed with munitions. To me, it looks like enough to resupply a small army. For the first time, I'm glad I know how to fire a gun. I won't hesitate to shoot Rosario if I have the chance.

Caleb and Eric climb into the boat while the rest of us pass gear up to them.

"See if you can find a tarp or something to put over the weapons in case it rains," Ben says.

"Aye-aye, captain," Caleb says with a mock salute.

The look Ben gives Caleb has enough rancor to level a city block. The tension between the two men is electric.

"I haven't figured out why those two don't like one another," Leo whispers.

"Neither of them talk about it," I whisper back. "

Once we get our gear loaded, I turn to Susan. "Now what?"

"The good news is that the tide is in. A captain is never without her tide chart." Susan taps her jacket pocket. "I checked before we headed out. Good thing I have one that goes through the end of the year."

"What's the bad news?" Ben asks.

"Hold up," Susan replies. "There's more good news. The bow of the boat isn't stuck in the mud. Only the stern."

"But that's where the propeller is," Caleb says with a frown. "We sort of need the propeller."

"Are you ready for the last piece of good news?" Susan says.

"You have a secret M&M stash downstairs?" Reed asks.

"Not quite, but it's almost as good as that. There are seven of us, which means we have at least a thousand pounds between us."

"That's good news?" Leo asks. "Won't we just grind the boat farther into the mud?"

"Not if we're all standing in the bow. Come on." Susan leads the way, herding us all toward the front of the boat. "The theory is simple. We stand on the bow together and jump up and down until we get the stern out of the mud."

We all stare at her.

"Like an apocalyptic bounce house?" Reed asks.

Susan grins. "Exactly."

Under Susan's direction, we pile around the bow, all of us standing on the lip and gripping the railing. If Susan wasn't adamant that this was a tried and true method of freeing a boat that had run aground, I'd think she was delusional.

"We need to synchronize our jumps," Susan says. "Everyone, squat down."

We obey, dropping onto the balls of our feet and using the railing for balance.

"On the count of three, everyone needs to push up in a jumping motion. Make sure you don't let go of the railing or you could end up in the mud. Ready? One, two, three!"

We shove. To my amazement, the entire back end of the boat shifts upward. Not a lot, but enough for my skepticism to morph into hope.

"Let's do it again," Susan says. "One, two, three!"

For a second time, we crouch down and jump. The stern of the boat shifts again.

"We need to get a rhythm going," Susan says. "No more long pauses between each jump. Ready? On my count. One, two, three! One, two, three!"

We push in time to her count, rocking the boat up and down. With each jump, the back of the boat lifts a few inches higher.

"Who needs a tow truck when you have an apocalyptic bounce house?" Reed asks with a laugh. "This is kind of fun."

"Focus," Susan tells him. "We're almost there. One, two, three! One, two, three!"

The back end of the boat abruptly lifts free. At the same time, the front of the boat tips forward at a dangerous angle. Ash slides off the bow and lands in the muddy water below.

"Shit," she snarls, getting to her feet and shaking off the muck. "I didn't bring a change of pants."

None of us had room for much in our running packs. The whole point of them is to pack light so we can move fast if necessary.

"On the bright side," Susan calls down to her, "we got the propeller out."

"It's not your ass that's muddy and wet," Ash replies.

The *Fairhaven* bobs in the shallow water, rocking in the gentle current. Ash climbs onto the deck and Susan hands her a dry shirt.

"It's the best I can do." She gives an apologetic shrug. "I used all the towels on Gary's leg."

"We have to tell Johnny about this," Eric says. "This needs to go in his book."

"Which one?" Caleb asks. "That guy has a lot of different notebooks."

"*How to Thrive in the Apocalypse*, for sure," Reed replies. "Everyone needs to know about the apocalyptic bounce house method. It's brilliant."

"It's standard protocol for a grounded boat," Susan replies.

"That doesn't make it any less brilliant."

I look down at my watch, which I set to zero just after my conversation with Alvarez. It's already been five hours since we spoke to him. The first prisoner of Mr. Rosario will be executed in nineteen hours unless we stop her.

"Everyone grab a seat," Susan says. "Time to sail out of shallow waters and find some gas."

45

OUT OF GAS

BEN

The *Fairhaven* trundles along. It's not a fast boat by any stretch of the imagination, but after traveling exclusively on foot for over six months, it feels like they're moving at warp speed.

"There." Susan raises a hand and points. "Manila. That's where we'll look for gas."

"That wouldn't happen to be the marina where Gary got attacked, would it?" Eric asks.

Susan's cheerful expression evaporates. "No. The shark attack was several miles south. Sharks don't usually come this far up in the bay. I'm hoping the waters will be clear of zombies and sharks."

Ben squints. The microscopic town is a brownish smudge on the horizon. It doesn't look promising in his opinion, but he keeps his mouth shut. They're fucked if there's no fuel. They're double fucked if there are zombies and sharks in the water.

As though on cue, the *Fairhaven* sputters and lurches in the water.

"Dammit." Susan pushes the throttle. "Come on, baby," she murmurs, urging her boat forward. "Get mama to the shore."

Ben lets out a breath as the boat motors on, once again pushing through the water.

"What happened?" Leo asks from where he stands at the bow.

"I told you we were low on fuel," Susan replies. "I think it is now safe to say we are dangerously low."

"What's the difference between low and dangerously low?" Reed asks.

Ben snorts. It's impossible for him to hold back his words. "It's the difference between driving to Manila and swimming to Manila."

Kate frowns at him. Fuck it. He gives her a non-apologetic shrug. He's an asshole. Everyone knows it.

"Ben isn't wrong." Susan watches the growing smudge of Manila. She rubs a loving hand across the dash of the boat. "Come on, baby. Mama doesn't want to go for a swim today."

Ash mutters something cross in Spanish.

"I second whatever you just said," Ben tells her. "It sounded cranky."

"I didn't bring a swimsuit," she replies.

This brings a few chuckles. Ben just feels grim. He's pretty sure no one packed a swimming suit. That means if someone goes into the water, they're either going in fully clothed or in their underwear.

The *Fairhaven* gives another lurch, stalling in the bay. Ben watches Kate and measures the mounting anxiety on her face. She starts looking this way when she's contemplating something particularly nuts.

It's her concern for Alvarez. He understands it, even if Alvarez isn't a personal friend.

The *Fairhaven* coughs and spits in protest, then keeps going.

Ben lets out a breath. He focuses on the approaching landmass, willing it to come closer, closer ...

The charter boat gives one last sputter. Then another.

Then the engine clicks off.

Silence fills the air, so loud his eardrums feel the pressure. In the distance comes the cry of seagulls.

"Damn." Susan's voice is the only sound beside that of the gulls.

Kate's face is pinched, her jaw set as she gazes at the shoreline of Manila. The hamlet is a solid quarter mile away. Ben already knows what she's thinking.

He heads her off at the pass. No way is he going to let her risk her life.

"I'll go." He stands, unbuttoning the shirt of his fatigues.

Caleb turns sharp eyes on him. "Me, too. I completed in a few triathlons. I'm a good open water swimmer."

Of course he is. "Fucking golden boy," Ben mutters.

"You guys sure about this?" Leo says as he comes around from the bow.

"It's not safe," Kate says.

"Tell me you weren't planning to jump into the water thirty seconds ago," Ben says to her.

She doesn't respond.

He snorts and tosses his shirt aside, next going for his shoes.

"We'll find some gas," Caleb says. "Then we'll find a boat or a kayak or something and come back."

"I'll go, too," Ash says, rising. "Safety in numbers."

"No." Kate stops her. "I don't want our group fractioned any more than it already is." Her attention turns to Ben and Caleb. "You get gas and get back here as fast as you can. In one piece. Understand?"

Caleb gives her a somber salute as he hands his shirt to

Ash. "Yes, ma'am." There is no mock or teasing on his face this time.

Susan studies the coastline through the binoculars. "The waters look clear," she reports. "Zombies sink when they fall into the water. Be careful as you get closer to shore."

"No shark fins?" Caleb asks.

"No shark fins."

"Eric, rooftop," Ben says. "Get the rifle ready. You see a shark fin, you shoot."

"Got it." Eric grabs a rifle, scrambling onto the rooftop of the *Fairhaven*.

Ben removes his belt from the loops of his pants and refastens it above his waist, double checking the strap on his knife to make sure the blade won't slip free in the water. Then he hands both of his guns to Reed. "Hold onto these until I get back."

"Be careful out there." Reed takes his gun. Then he removes his knife and zom bat from his belt. "Take these. Mama Bear always tells us to have a Plan B and Plan C whenever possible.

"Thanks, kid."

Ash also exchanges her spare weapons for Caleb's firearms.

"I'm taking notes," Eric says, even though he doesn't have a pen or a notebook in hand. "You both better come back. Johnny will expect precise details for his book."

"I meant it when I said you better come back in one piece." Kate puts her hands on her hips as she faces Ben.

"Only way I could possibly come back," Ben replies. All the drama is making him edgy. Not giving himself time to think too hard on what needs to happen next, he sheds his pants.

Ben's never paid too much attention to his body. It's always served him well enough and gotten the job done. And hell, he's pushing fifty. Though he's lean and fit, his muscles aren't what they once were. He's scarred and tattooed and has an uneven tan.

One thing he's never paid much mind to is his underwear.

He always bought whatever was cheapest at Walmart, or whatever the military gave him if he was overseas. His tighty whities aren't exactly white anymore. There may even be a few holes in them.

He feels like a dumpy old man next to Caleb. The young man is nothing but miles of smooth dark skin and hard muscle. He wears dark red boxer briefs, which make him look like an Olympic swimmer. Fucker.

"Dude." Eric blinks at Ben from behind his glasses. "Those are some bad ass tattoo sleeves."

"Is that a fairy on your arm?" Susan asks.

Ben doesn't stick around any longer. Checking his belt and weapons one more time, he dives off the boat and into the frigid waters of Humboldt Bay.

46

MANILA

BEN

Caleb hits the water seconds later. The younger man shifts into a perfect freestyle, long arms pulling at the water as he swims away.

Ben took a few swim lessons as a kid. He spent long summer days at the Y staying cool at the pool with his buddies.

As an adult, he used to take his son, Sam, fishing at Lake Barry in the summers. The two of them had often gone out for swims in the afternoon when it got hot.

This sums up Ben's experience in the water.

Not wanting to look like an ass, Ben takes off after Caleb, attempting to mimic the form of the younger man.

He tries to recall his childhood swim lessons. He can't even recall the name of his teacher, let alone anything she taught him. When he and Sam swam in the lake during their fishing expeditions, they had foam noodles or some sort of floatie to rely on.

It doesn't take long for him to realize swimming in the bay is vastly different from swimming anywhere else. Not only is the water cold as fuck, but the current wants to push him south, away from Manila. Already his muscles are burning. He takes in a mouthful of saltwater with every other stroke.

And he thought running sucked ass. Barely five minutes in the water, and he has no illusion as to which is the more difficult of the two.

"Ben." He pretends not to hear the voice calling after him from the boat.

"Ben!"

He keeps paddling, settling for a pathetic dog paddle in lieu of the freestyle stroke he can't do anyway. Caleb is already fifty yards ahead of him.

A minute later, something round and white is thrown in his direction. It splashes ten feet to his right.

A life preserver.

It's a knife to his pride, but fuck it. He doesn't want to drown out here while golden boy takes all the credit for saving Kate and the others.

He paddles over to the life preserver and grabs it. Latching onto it, he starts kicking.

Now, this is more like it. He can almost imagine he's back at Lake Barry with Sam. He misses the kid. He misses him a lot.

He's spent his whole life missing Sam. It started the minute he exited the hospital, leaving his newborn and all the rights to him in the hands of his mother.

He never should have done it. He thought it had been the right thing for Sam, but he remembers how sick he felt when he signed the custody papers. He wanted to tell Sam's mother that he'd resign his commission and move nearby to help raise their son.

The sentences tried to force their way past his lips. But even back then, words had failed him.

He was lucky Shelia never tried to keep Sam from him. She let him visit when he was on leave. She made sure Sam got all the letters Ben wrote. She even made sure the kid sent him a birthday card once a year and let Ben take him on trips during the summer.

Ben pushes away thoughts of Sam. He knows without a doubt he'll never see his son again. If the boy is even alive, he's on the other side of the country.

He shifts his focus to Caleb, who's now a hundred yards in front of him. Gritting his teeth, Ben kicks in a vain attempt to keep up with him. He periodically dunks his head into the water to check for zoms. The salt water stings his eyes, but he'll take stinging eyes over a zom bite anyday.

Caleb is already out of the water by the time Ben reaches the shoreline. He stands there like a young Greek god. Ben never looked that good, not even when he was young and in the best shape of his life after boot camp.

"Ben!" Caleb waves his arms to get his attention, his soft voice nearly swallowed by the lapping water. "Move! There are zoms in the water."

Ben pours on speed, kicking as hard as he can. He opens his eyes underwater. Everything is murky, but he spots two pale white forms below him in the water.

Fuck and double fuck.

He's exhausted from the long paddle from the *Fairhaven*. His legs feel like jelly and his breath is raw fire in his throat. He kicks harder, trying to get ahead of the zombies.

As he reaches the shoreline, he feels something tickle against his leg. He kicks harder.

The rocks of the shore bite into his knees. He pulls his feet beneath him and starts to stand.

Something grabs his leg.

Before he can act, Caleb is there, knife in hand. He pounces, knife slashing through the water. The fingers around Ben's ankle release. As Ben hurries the rest of the way to shore, he sees a zom float to the surface of the water.

"I saw it as I swam in," Caleb says. "It was walking along the bottom of the bay. It followed the sounds of my kicks all the way to shore."

Ben grunts, exhausted from the swim and pissed off that he owes one to Caleb. He sits down on a boulder to catch his breath.

"Why did you volunteer for this mission if you can't swim?" Caleb asks.

"I can swim."

Caleb gives him an exasperated look. "You know what I mean."

"Not a lot of water in the Sandbox."

"*Ben.*"

He spits out a mouthful of salty saliva, scowling up at the young man. "Because Kate was getting ready to do it, okay?"

"And you wanted to protect her."

Caleb is prodding him. Fuck that. "We can't afford to lose her," Ben snaps. "She holds everything together. We'd all be zombie snacks if not for her."

Caleb tilts his head, studying Ben in a way that makes him want to sock the other man. "That's why I did it. Well, that and the fact that I'm a good swimmer."

"You can brag about it when we get back to the boat." Ben stands, wincing as rocks cut into his bare feet. Fuck.

Looking down, he realizes how badly he is in need of new underwear. There's a tear in one side he hadn't noticed before. Could this day get any worse? He hopes Kate didn't notice. He looks like a crazy old man from an asylum.

Caleb smirks at him. "Dude, we'll find you some better drawers before we go back. Can't let your woman see you looking scruffy."

Ben feels his face heat. He flips Caleb the bird and stalks off. His destination is a dock with two small motorboats lashed in place. The boats have taken on water and are half-submerged on the shore. No one said they needed working boats, just boats with gas.

He changes course mid-stream. Finding the boats is all well and good, but they need something to put the gas in.

He angles away from the water. The house nearest the dock had been an elegant mansion in the 70s. The wood is peeling and worn from the saltwater. The windows are all leaking, the glass fogged from the inside. The roof looks like it endured its own private apocalypse long before the actual apocalypse.

Off to his right, the water of Humboldt Bay laps at the shore. The coastal breeze rustles the wind-bent pine trees and thick clumps of calla lilies growing near the shore.

He bypasses the house, heading instead for the shipping container on the south side of the house. No doubt the owners stored all sorts of shit inside. That's just the sort of place he'll find a gas can.

He pulls out a knife and zom bat, keeping an eye out for undead. He's grateful as he steps onto un-mowed lawn. Much better than moving on sharp gravel.

Sensing movement behind him, he looks back to see Caleb following. Little fucker. Anger crawls up his spine, indignant at the other man's simple existence.

Focus, dumb ass, he tells himself. Getting distracted is going to get him killed.

Reaching the container, he pauses outside to survey it. The outside has been spray-painted with graffiti. Someone went to the trouble to place baskets of fake flowers on either side of the doors, along with a doormat that says *WELCOME*.

Maybe this was someone's man cave. Or a woman's cave. Whatever.

He taps a hand on the shed. To his dismay, a growl comes from inside. Damn. He'd been hoping to get lucky.

"You sure we need to go in there?" Caleb licks his lips, tightening his grip on his weapons.

"Where else are we going to find a gas can? The master bedroom? Get ready. On three."

Caleb's answering glare brings satisfaction. It's short-lived. Turning back to the shed, Ben prepares to face whatever is on the other side.

He grips the door latch. It lets loose an awful metallic squeal as he lifts it, rusted from exposure of the sea air. It's like a foghorn going off.

Two reeking zombies jerk into the sunlight. They're dressed all in camouflage, bandoliers slung across their chests.

Caleb and Ben raise their weapons, bracing for combat.

But the zombies don't advance on them. They dance in the doorway of the container, moaning and swiping at the air.

"What the fuck?" Caleb frowns.

Ben follows the younger man's gaze. That's when he notices the blue dog leashes wrapped around each zombie's neck, holding them in place. The leashes are suspended from the ceiling just inside the container.

"They must have hung themselves," Caleb says.

"I don't think so. Their feet touch the ground." Ben scans the area, the skin between his shoulder blades crawling. "I think someone strung them up inside to protect their assets."

He pulls a small battery-operated flashlight off his belt. It's no longer than his palm, but the beam is bright.

"Where did you get that?" Caleb asks.

"Found it in a dorm room." He always carries it on his belt, just for times like this. Good thing it still works after being dunked in saltwater.

He shines the beam into the container. His jaw drops open.

"Do you see what I see?" Caleb whispers. "It's a prepper's wet dream in there."

The younger man isn't exaggerating. Inside the container are enough supplies to rival a WalMart.

"Holy fuck," Caleb breathes. "We've hit the jackpot, old man."

"Maybe." Ben can't shake the unease that crawls between his shoulder blades. "We can't assume this place is abandoned. These zoms look like guard dogs to me." Guard dogs Ben intends to eliminate.

He brings the zom bat down into the forehead of the first zom. Then he whips the bat sideways and takes out the second. The undead dangle from their leashes, brain matter dripping onto the ground.

"Come on. Let's find a gas can and get what we came for." Before whoever strung up the guard zoms comes back.

Ben shoulders his way past the corpses, Caleb on his heels. He scans the interior, trying not to get caught up in the sight of all that canned food. He's here for a gas can, not refried beans.

"Old man, we seriously need to get you new underwear. Especially if you're going to walk around looking like that." Caleb hurls a small plastic package at him.

Ben catches the package. "Looking like what?"

"Like *that*." Caleb gestures to him. "Like a lovesick puppy. Except you're too grumpy to be a puppy. A lovesick alligator."

Does *everyone* know how he feels about Kate? Hell, he can barely put words to it. No one else seems to have that problem.

"I'm not lovesick."

"Whatever. Are those your size?"

Ben looks down at the plastic package in his hands. It contains brand new boxer briefs similar to the ones Caleb wears. They're all black.

"You know what?" Caleb asks. "It doesn't matter if they're your size. Anything is better than those rags you have on. Your ball sack is hanging out."

Scandalized, Ben takes a minute to survey himself. "It is not," he snaps.

"Whatever. It's about to hang out. Just change, old man.

You're hurting my eyes." Caleb takes the flashlight from him and ventures deeper into the container.

Ben changes, kicking the old underwear into a corner. Good riddance.

"For what it's worth, I think she likes you, too," Caleb says from the back of the container. "She's too good for you, by the way."

That's one thing they both agree on.

"Man, they have a decent amount of weapons. We need to bring the boat back here and load up."

"That's a terrible fucking idea." Just thinking about it makes Ben's shoulders itch even worse. "Someone left those zoms here to guard their shit. What if they come back and we're here?"

"I'm telling you, those guys are the owners and they hung themselves. Don't tell me you wouldn't love to have extra weapons for the attack on Rosario's people."

Of *course* he wants more weapons. What an asinine thing to say. "It's too risky."

"This place is abandoned and ripe for the picking," Caleb replies. "You're just being paranoid. Everything is going to be fine."

"Is that what you told yourself when you teamed up with Johnson?"

Caleb stops cold, giving Ben a scathing look. "Are you ever going to let that go?"

"Can *you* let it go?" Ben counters. "You have sixteen deaths on your shoulders."

"They're as much on my shoulders as they are yours."

Ben narrows his eyes. "I tried to save them. You just stood there."

Caleb's mouth tightens. "I'm not going to argue with you. It's pointless." He stalks out of the container.

Ben marches after him, anger pounding in his temples the way it always does when he thinks of the murdered College

Creek kids. Just because Caleb eventually found the balls to kill Johnson doesn't clear his name. Far from it.

Ben can count the number of hours he's slept in the last two days. Six. Six fucking hours. Every time he tries to close his eyes, he sees those poor kids. He sees Cynthia. That sweet girl deserved a chance at life. Caleb stood by while Johnson stole it from her.

Ben wants to punch a hole in something.

Caleb heads to the dock. As he crunches over the ground on his bare feet, Ben hears a succinct *snick*. Too late, he registers the long line of catfish wire strung across the ground.

"Get down!" he screams at Caleb.

He dives for the younger man. The two of them roll across the ground as a loud *pop* echoes in the air.

A flare whistles upward, leaving a long trail of orange smoke above Manila. Ben missed the tripwire only because he'd walked on the grass to spare his feet. The wire was clearly put up to snare anyone walking toward the container—or away, in Caleb's case.

"Fuck!" Ben *knew* they weren't alone. Now they've just alerted the owner of that shipping container. "Move! Get to the gas."

He and Caleb haul ass to the dock with their gas cans. Caleb siphons the gas while Ben scans the area for hostiles.

Dammit, he needs a gun. When the owner of that container shows up, they're fucked.

Nothing moves in or around the house. The silence makes Ben even edgier.

"Almost done?" he snaps.

"Almost. Let me fill this second can. Get the paddleboard ready."

"The what?"

"The paddleboard." Caleb gestures with his chin at a giant,

bright-red oblong object. "How old are you, man? Haven't you ever seen a stand-up paddleboard?"

"Spend thirty years of your military career in the Sandbox and see how much you know about shit like that."

He stomps over to the paddleboard. Using some bungee cords they found in the bunker, he straps the first gas can into place. He keeps up a constant surveillance of their surroundings, ready for the attack.

It doesn't come. Seconds tick by as Caleb fills the second gas can. Ben's palms are sweaty with anticipation.

They should have been here by now. Whoever set up that alarm system should be back here to defend their possessions. Where are they?

"Maybe whoever stockpiled the container is dead." Caleb scurries over with the second gas can. "Maybe I was right about those two zoms."

Ben wants to believe that, but he can't shake the feeling shit is about to go sideways. "Let's get the fuck out of here." He won't be able to relax until they're back at the *Fairhaven*.

SPEEDBOATS

KATE

Ben and Caleb are halfway back to the *Fairhaven*, rowing a paddleboard across the water. The rest of us stand alert, rifles raised and pointed toward the shoreline. Just because I've never fired one doesn't mean I'll hesitate. Whoever set that flare gun trap obviously wants to know if someone trespasses on their space. I don't intend to let anyone hurt Ben or Caleb.

"Do you hear that?" Reed tilts his head to one side, frowning. "It's a buzzing sound."

Shit. Worry spiders over my skin. The last time we heard a distant buzzing sound, it was an alpha army on the march.

"Which direction?" I ask.

"South, toward Eureka," Reed says.

I grab the binoculars and scan the horizon. Two dots bob on the water, getting larger with each passing second. I hear the distinct rumble of engines.

"Fuck." I push the binos at Reed. "Do you see what I see?"

Reed grabs the binoculars from me. "Boats," he says grimly. "Two of them. They're coming right for us."

"Dammit." Fear pounds through me. I have no doubt

these are the people who set up the flare gun. I don't know what's in Manila, but it's obvious they want to protect it.

"Ben! Caleb!" I wave my arms to get their attention, not bothering to lower my voice. "We have company!" I point in the direction of the oncoming boats.

A flurry of curses carries across the water. The two men haul ass back toward the *Fairhaven* on their paddleboard, arguing the whole way.

"I told you the owners were coming back," Ben says.

"How was I supposed to know they'd come by water?" Caleb snaps.

"Shut up and paddle!"

Fear and irritation pound in my temples. I can't listen to them anymore.

"How long before those boats reach us?" I ask Susan.

Her lips press into a thin line. "Three minutes, tops. Leo, I need your help." Susan passes him a funnel. "I need you to start pouring the gas in as soon as Caleb and Ben get here. I'm going to fire up the Fairhaven."

Leo positions the funnel in the gas opening just as the paddleboard bumps up against the side of the boat. Caleb lobs the first gas canister over the side. Reed passes it to Leo, who immediately begins pouring it into the funnel.

"There's a bunker on shore," Caleb says in a rush as he clambers on board. "Enough stuff to stock Creekside for a month. We think those guys are the owners." He jerks a thumb at the oncoming boats.

"And dipshit here set off their tripwire." Ben jumps onto the deck, face flushed with fury. He marches over to the weapons pack, pulling out ammo clips and his rifle. It's a really bad time to notice how good he looks mostly naked, or that fact that he found a new pair of underwear.

"Hope you're ready to shoot that thing." Ben hands me an

extra clip of ammo. His face is set, eyes focused. "Get ready to defend the *Fairhaven*."

The boats are no longer dots on the horizon. They're close enough for me to see that they're two speedboats. A look through the binoculars shows me three men on each boat, all of them armed. They're closing in on us.

"We have to go," I shout. "Leo, close the fuel tank. Susan, fire up the *Fairhaven*. We're out of time."

The *Fairhaven* sputters to life, the charter boat coughing as fuel races back through its engine. Susan leans into the accelerator.

"Come on, girl," she murmurs. "Get us the hell out of here."

"We can't outrun those boats." Ben raises his rifle, sighting down the scope. His lean muscles are taut, the tattoos tense along both arms as he takes aim.

Before he can fire, gunshots crack from our pursuers. Bullets pierce the water on either side of us. One bullet hits the back of the *Fairhaven*.

"Motherfuckers," Susan screams.

Ben fires. A spray of glass goes up from the closest of the speedboats.

Almost as soon as Ben starts shooting, the speedboats fall back. They slow enough to stay out of range, but close enough to tail us.

"Fuckers," Ben growls, lowering his gun.

The *Fairhaven* gains speed as Susan aims the boat in a southward direction. Directly in front of us looms Indian Island, a small chunk of land that sits in the middle of Humboldt Bay. Susan aims her boat toward a narrow channel on the east side of the island. The speedboats continue to follow us.

"What do you think they want?" I ask.

"That bunker is where they store their supplies," Ben says. "Most likely they want to protect it."

"But we've left. We didn't steal anything besides gas from sunk boats."

"They don't know that."

"You think they want to risk a shootout over some stuff even after we've left?"

He shakes his head. "I don't know what they want. But they're following us, which isn't a good sign." He stalks away and grabs his fatigues, climbing back into them.

"Leo," I say, "any idea who these guys are? Did you have any run-ins with them when you lived in Eureka?"

"No," Leo replies. "We occasionally spotted other groups when we were out scavenging, but mostly we avoided one another."

The speedboats maintain a safe distance behind us, but always stay within eyesight. I edge over to Ben, who is once again fully clothed.

"Do you think they're herding us into an ambush?"

"The thought did cross my mind." His gaze flicks to the speedboats and back to me. "We need people on the bow and stern."

I nod. "Eric, Caleb, Reed, come with me," I call. "We're keeping watch on the bow. Ben, Ash, and Leo, you guys patrol the stern."

As I lead my team onto the bow, the *Fairhaven* leaves Indian Island behind. We return to the wider part of the bay. To our right is a narrow peninsula dotted with homes and rolling sand dunes. On our left is the city of Eureka.

I haven't seen Eureka since I first journeyed to Arcata to find Carter. At that time, I'd been able to navigate the city and avoid zombies by being quiet.

That wouldn't be possible now. The waterfront streets I once moved through on foot are now packed with zombies. They turn in our direction as we approach, many of them walking right into the water as they attempt to follow our sound.

"Oh, my God," Reed says. "It's a Costco! Anyone want to try and load up on samples before we go to Fort Ross?" He points to the giant wholesale store that backs up to the bay.

"Pay attention," Ben snaps at him.

Costco. It's surrounded by the undead. I can't help but wonder what might be inside. Maybe when Johnny and Gary learn more of the alpha language, we'll be able to drive the zombies back and get inside the store. But these are thoughts for another day.

I turn my attention back to the water. It's a clear path between here and Hookton Channel, the waterway that leads from Humboldt Bay to the open waters of the Pacific Ocean.

The speedboats are still tailing us. My unease ratchets up several notches. Everything is looking too easy.

I edge around the boat in Susan's direction. She's the only one of us that's seen this waterway semi-recently. "Do you recall anything about this area those guys might use against us?"

Susan's expression is tight. "That's the town of Samos." She points to a tiny town on the peninsula to our right. It's little more than a scattering of homes and rolling sand dunes. "That's where Gary was attacked by the great white. There's a lot of zoms in the water. This area is dangerous. If those pricks on the speedboats make a move, it's going to be in here."

"Kate, there's something in the water," Eric calls from the bow. "Grab the binoculars."

I hurry back to the bow, binos in hand. I study the area of water indicated by Eric. The water is dotted with pale white objects.

"Are those … ?" I frown, leaning closer for a better look. What I see chills me to my core. "Holy fuck. We're in trouble."

All across the bay are zombies. Hundreds and hundreds of

zombies, all of them thrashing around in the water. There's no clear path through them.

"What is it?" Ben hustles over to us. His nostrils flare when he sees the zombies. "Motherfuckers. It's a trap."

"What's happening?" Susan demands.

There's no time to sugarcoat our situation. "The bay is clogged with zombies."

"How? They should be sinking?" Susan's voice is pitched with panic. "They always sink unless they're really dead."

All I can do is stare at the hundreds of undead in the water. As we get closer, I see ropes around the zombie necks, holding them in place. Someone captured all these zombies and strung them across this section of the bay.

"We are so fucked if any of those body parts get stuck in the propeller," Susan cries. "We have to do something!"

"Those assholes drove us right into their dragnet," Ben growls. "Fucking pirates."

A look over my shoulder confirms Ben's suspicion. The two speedboats are edging closer to us. If we accelerate to get away, we risk our boat getting tangled in the zombies.

"God damn assholes," Ben snarls. "If those fuckers want an old-fashioned shoot-out, I'll give them one."

48

DEAD WATERS

BEN

His attention narrows on the two speedboats. Ben can practically feel the smug bastards gloating. No way are these fuckers getting the best of them.

"Eric, Ash, Caleb," he barks. "Rifles up! We're going to take out those bastards. The goal is to kill them before they get close enough to kill us."

"I'm a good shot." Leo shoulders up with his rifle. "I've been hunting since I was a kid."

Ben nods. "Line up, soldier." He, Caleb, Ash, Eric, and Leo spread out in a line along the stern.

"I need everyone else up here," Kate calls. "We're going to shoot through the ropes. The zoms will sink if the rope isn't holding them up. Susan, keep the boat moving. We'll clear the way for you."

Kate wastes no time getting to work. The sound of gunfire is the best music Ben has heard since they started this insane mission. He can't help feel a burst of pride as he watches Kate take aim from the bow.

He turns his attention back to the assholes in the speedboat. Ben raises his rifle and sights down the scope, looking for the first bastard who's going to die.

He exhales and taps the trigger. His shot goes wide, splitting the windshield. Fuck. He's a decent shot, but hitting a moving target at two hundred yards while standing on the back of a charter boat is a tall order.

The rifles crack on either side of him as his companions open fire. One man on a speedboat goes down.

"Hell, yeah," Eric mutters. "Take that, asshole."

As Ben sights through the scope again, he sees his next target raise his own rifle. Fuck. These guys really need to die.

Bullets pierce the water all around them, a few even hitting the *Fairhaven*. The rest of his companions crouch low for cover, but Ben maintains an upright position. He shoots three more times, finally dropping his target. He edges the rifle to the right, sighting on the next target.

Kate's voice carries to him. "We're through! The zoms are sinking. Gun it, Susan!"

Ben shifts his weight, anticipating the momentum of increased speed. The slight movement saves his life. A bullet whizzes just past his ear and hits the driver's console.

"Shit!" Susan cries. "Will someone please get rid of those fuckers before they kill me?"

The charter boat picks up speed. They're fully in the zombie dragnet now, the tethered dead thrashing as their bodies are dragged down by their own weight.

Ben once again takes aim, this time focusing his crosshairs on the driver of the closest boat. The man is hunched over the wheel while his companions fire on the *Fairhaven*. All Ben can see are his eyes and the top of his head.

It will have to be enough. He squeezes the trigger three times in rapid succession. The top of the driver's head explodes in a shower of blood and windshield glass.

Then he hears the hollow *thunk-thunk-thunk* of bullets

hitting flesh. He turns in time to see Leo. The man had propped himself up on one knee to fire at their pursuers. Red blooms across the front of his shirt. The rifle falls from his hands.

"Dammit!" Ben catches Leo as he falls. "Man down! Susan, get us the fuck out of here."

The *Fairhaven* rumbles forward through the churning waters. Zombie hands scratch at the side of the boat. Susan ducks down, steering as best she can while gunshots ring behind us. Ash, Caleb, and Eric remain crouched down behind the stern and continue to fire.

"Leo!" Kate skitters across the desk, hunched over to avoid the bullets. "Ash, I need you over here!"

Even before Kate reaches Leo, Ben knows the other man is dead. He's seen enough men die to know all the signs. The slack muscles. The unhinged jaw. The blank, staring eyes. And the blood. Too much fucking blood.

"Leo." Kate presses her hands over the open wounds as blood fountains up between her fingers. "Ash!" she yells again.

Ash drops to all fours and crawls over to them.

"Leo!" Kate is near hysteria.

"He's gone." Ash, face crumpled with grief, presses her fingers against the side of Leo's neck. "He's gone, Kate."

"No," Kate snaps. "There must be something you can do."

Ash stares, eyes moving between Kate and Leo. "I'm sorry, Kate."

"No, no, no!" Kate pounds her fists on the deck. "Not another one!" Tears of anger and frustration pour from her eyes.

Ben watches the grief take her again. The guilt. It would be easier to have someone peel the skin from his body.

"We're past the dragnet," Susan calls. "I'm taking us into the ocean." The hum of the *Fairhaven's* engine increases as the boat picks up speed in the open water.

"They're not following," Caleb calls. "They're slowing down!"

Probably because they don't want to waste the gas it would require to pursue them out into open water, Ben thinks grimly. The fuckers put their zombie dragnet here for a reason.

Ben shifts, wanting to comfort Kate, but Reed and Eric beat him to it. They kneel on either side, each putting their arms around her. He watches her draw comfort from them. The tension inside him eases, even though the desire to go to her doesn't subside.

He always thinks of Reed, Eric, Carter, Jenna, Johnny, and Lila as the "original" Creekside members. Even though the core group has opened their arms to new members—himself included—there's a closeness between them that doesn't include anyone else. Ben has never been much of a joiner, but there are times when he's envious of them. Times like now.

"What the hell just happened?" Kate demands of no one in particular. She wipes at her eyes as Ash drapes a tarp over Leo's body.

"Trap," Ben says. "We triggered their alert back in Manila when we stumbled into their stockpile. They drove us neatly into a trap they set up to catch other boats." At least his team had taken out a few of the assholes.

He doesn't even want to think about how they're going to get back to Arcata when the time comes. This area of the bay has definitely been taken over by a hostile group. It will be a problem they'll have to deal with at some point.

No one speaks. They stand in a lopsided circle around Leo's shrouded body. Poor bastard. Blood seeps out from under the tarp. The whine of the speedboats is gone, their pursuers no longer behind them

"Put Leo's body over the side," Kate says, voice hollow.

49

OPEN WATER

KATE

I look at my watch. Six hours and twenty-three minutes. That's how much time has passed since I last spoke to Alvarez.

We sail through Hookton's Channel and enter the wide waters of the Pacific Ocean. The sea is frothy with slate-gray waves.

I sit apart from the others, turning out to face the ocean.

A man died because of me today. A good man. And it's all my fault.

The ocean spray hits me in the face. I close my eyes, trying to soak in the serenity of the open waves.

It doesn't work.

For some reason, I don't see Leo's face behind my closed lids. I see his chest where the bullets struck him. I see red that blooms like a Rorschach test before my eyes.

The land blurs by on my left, the pale dun-colored beach and the taller dark brown rock cliffs. To my right, the ocean is unending miles of slate blue.

Time fades into the background. I can't escape the Rorschach blotch. I see it in the variegated patterns of the ocean cliffs. I see it in the ebbing shadows of the ocean. I see it behind my eyelids when the sun hits them.

I don't turn when I feel a weight on the seat next to me. I don't want to talk to anyone.

"I volunteered to try and convince you to eat dinner." Ben's gruff voice washes over me. "But I know you don't want to eat."

"You're right. I don't." I keep my eyes closed, not ready to face a living human right now.

"You're blaming yourself for Leo's death. I get that."

Relief washes over me. I'm glad he doesn't try to tell me it's not my fault. "The worst part is that I broke up a family. Todd doesn't have anyone now. Leo was his uncle, his flesh and blood. Real biological families are a rarity these days."

"Todd has us. Families in this new world are made from the scraps of the old. You know that better than anyone."

I finally turn toward him. "When the hell did you become a poet?"

He grimaces. "Every once in a while, my brain decides it's okay to connect with my mouth. It's not going to be an everyday thing so don't get too excited."

Our eyes lock. I study his gray irises. I see more in his eyes than I want to.

I let my gaze wander, taking in the handsome seams around his eyes, the ones that carry the sorrow he wears on his arms. The white shadow of stubble across his jaw accentuates the strong angle of his face.

If he'd remained silent, what would things have been like the night we kissed?

"I'd be in trouble if you were like this all the time," I murmur.

"No chance of that happening." His breath whooshes out of his lungs. "Not that I need to tell you that. I'm not a nice guy."

"That's not true. You're one of the most selfless people I know. You just chose to let the asshole take the lead most days."

Another long look passes between us. The yearning I feel in my chest threatens to crack me open. I'm the first to look away.

"Nothing will bring Leo back," I say.

"No. Nothing." Ben sighs. It's a heavy, weighted sound. "If I bring you some food, will you eat? It will put everyone else on the boat at ease. It won't fix things for you, I get that. But is it so bad to fix things for the ones you love?" He gestures with his chin to the far side of the boat.

Eric and Reed sit side by side, each of them eating out of a can of chili. They stare at me, concern plain on their faces.

My heart swells at the sight of them. Ben is right. I do love them. They're as much mine as Carter and Jenna.

"You'd do anything else for them," Ben says. "What's a little food in comparison to running through Arcata with alpha zoms after us?"

Reed lifts the can in my direction, head cocked in question. "Food, Mama?" he calls.

"What about it, Mama Bear?" Ben raises a gray eyebrow at me. "After that, we can get you a tattoo."

"Wh—what?"

He shoves up one sleeve of his fatigue shirt to display the tattoos that cover his forearm. "You can wear the pain."

"Does it help?"

"Not really. But it beats throwing myself off a twenty-story building. Same rule should apply to you."

"Is this the part where your mouth and your brain aren't connected?" I ask.

"Maybe."

"Remind me to pick up a roll of duct tape the next time we go scavenging. It might help keep the asshole at bay if I put a piece over your mouth."

"I doubt it." The eye crinkle he gives me is genuine. The way he looks at me takes my breath away. I think of what Carter had said before we left Arcata.

He leaves my side as Reed and Eric approach, one with a spoon and the other with a can of chili.

"It's not warm, but it still tastes good," Eric says.

I take it from him, even though my stomach is in knots and food is the last thing on my list. Ben's voice plays in my head. *Is it so bad to fix things for the ones you love?*

"Thanks, guys." I take the food.

They sit on either side of me, keeping me company with their silence as I eat. I soak in their presence, grateful for my apocalypse family.

My eyes drift to Ben. He stands beside Susan, the two of them bent over a map.

He glances up, our eyes meeting across the deck of the *Fairhaven*. He gives me a knowing nod as he watches me eat with my boys. I smile back in silent thanks. Even though I can't make sense of all that lies between us, I'm glad he's a part of my apocalypse family, too.

50

DEAD IN THE WATER

BEN

They've been boating southward along the coast for two hours. Ben paces up and down the deck, unable to relax. Not even the clean, cold air of the Pacific Ocean can calm his nerves. He wants to be at Fort Ross already. The calm before the upcoming battle is making him edgy.

He decides it would be a good time to go through the weapon packs and reconfirm their inventory. It will be helpful to have an exact count on their munitions when they get to the fort—

Ka-thunk. Ka-thunk.

This sound is followed by an awful groan from the *Fairhaven.*

"Oh, shit," Susan says.

"What the fuck was that?" Ben snaps.

"*¡Que mierda!*" Ash's voice carries from the bow. "You guys better come see this."

The *Fairhaven* gives another groan, the engine coughing and sending up a plume of black smoke.

Ben rushes to the bow where Ash stands. Blood and body parts bubble up from beneath the boat.

"Dammit," he growls. "I think some zoms got hung up on the bottom of the *Fairhaven*. They're breaking loose now."

"I can't steer," Susan shouts. "I think there's a body part in the propeller!"

As if to confirm her statement, the *Fairhaven* lets loose several loud thuds, followed by a distinct snapping sound. The charter boat instantly decelerates. More zombie body parts float free.

"The steering is shot." Panic lights Susan's voice. "She's dead in the water!"

The *Fairhaven* lurches sideways. A huge wave picks up the boat, driving it toward the coastline. In less than thirty seconds, the half mile between them and the land is reduced by half.

"*¡Hijo de puta!*" Ash cries. "Guys, we have another problem! We're headed straight for those rocks."

Kate and everyone else rushes to the bow, including Susan.

"What can we do?" Kate asks. "Can someone go under the boat?"

"Not with these waves," Susan says. As if to emphasize her point, the current gives the boat another shove, driving it toward the coastline. "Even if the water were calm, I don't have the right gear. The tide is high and this part of the coast is littered with rock. We are in big trouble."

Kate stares, taking in Susan's white face and the waves that push them inexorably closer to the shore.

"Can anything be done to salvage the boat?" Kate asks. "Anything at all? I'm open to any idea, even if it sounds crazy."

"There's no way for us to repair the propeller out here." Susan swallows, face pained. "We're dead in the water. This coast will rip the *Fairhaven* into kindling."

Ben studies the shoreline. There are rocks for as far as he can see. Big, boat-killing rocks. They're everywhere. And the current seems intent on driving the *Fairhaven* right into them. He knows what has to be done, but he waits for Kate to say it.

Kate shades her eyes, studying the coastline. Her jaw is tense, but she isn't panicked.

"Is there anything at all you can do to steer the ship?" Kate asks. "We need to get as close to the shoreline as we can."

"The *Fairhaven* doesn't have sails. There's no way to steer it," Susan says.

"What about an anchor?"

Susan's face spasms. "Gary and I ... lost it." She doesn't elaborate.

Kate lets out a long exhale. "Okay. Everyone, gather your things. Pack as much food as you can. Prepare to abandon ship."

Susan lets up a wail, but doesn't contradict Kate. In fact, she's the first one to scurry across the deck in search of her running pack.

"Take off your shoes," Kate orders. "They'll weigh you down if you try to swim with them. Tie your shoes to your packs so they aren't lost in the water."

Ben beelines to the weapon packs he collected for their mission. They can't save Alvarez and Fort Ross with running shoes. Next, he strips off his shoes and socks, securing them to the outside of his pack.

He packed everything into two large backpacks, which he and Caleb had carried to the *Fairhaven*. They each weigh at least fifty pounds, if not more.

He pulls on his backpack of gear. If he's going down, he's going down fully armed. They can't go up against Rosario's people without firearms.

The deck of *Fairhaven* is quiet. Everyone is quiet as they gather their things. Kate's muscles are taut, her eyes fierce as she pulls on her running pack.

This is the woman who has him in knots. She's always at

her best when her people are threatened. Nothing gets that woman out of a funk like a threat to her family.

Minutes tick by. They're caught in a waiting game, stuck in limbo as they wait for the current to carry them as close as possible to the shore.

"Shit," Susan screams. "Everyone, hold on!"

Ben grabs the closest railing as the *Fairhaven* lurches sideways, grinding against several large rocks. The stern whips around, pushed by the tide. Ben grabs onto the railing to keep from pitching over the side.

"Drop the packs if they're too heavy," Kate tells him and Caleb. "You are both more important than anything in them."

Ben doesn't bother telling her there won't be anything to use against Rosario if they lose the artillery bags. He plans to do his damnedest to get them to shore. If only because he can't stand the thought of what will happen to Kate if they fail to rescue Alvarez.

The wait is agonizing. The waves continue to drive the boat closer to the shore—and subsequently closer to the rocks. The tide beats at it with relentless fists, once again spinning the boat around. The *Fairhaven* surges, driven straight into two boulders. The boat groans, becoming lodged between the two rocks.

This is as close are they're going to get to shore. They're two hundred yards from land. That's going to be one hell of a swim with these waves and rocks. It's going to make Humboldt Bay look like a cakewalk.

Then comes a sound even worse than the sound of the rudder snapping. The hull groans and squeals. Ben can feel the pressure building—building—

The hull snaps. Ben can't see it, but he feels the vibration up through his hands as he grips the railing.

Susan cries out. "No!"

"Will the weapons still work if they get wet?" Kate asks him.

"Yes. So long as we dry them out and clean them well."

Her attention is on the shoreline. He doesn't have to ask what she's looking at. The rocks. They dot the coastline like zits, some of them as large as the *Fairhaven*.

Swimming through that maze will be a bitch. Doing it with the pack full of weapons might be suicide.

"Drop the artillery bags," Kate orders. She picks up a length of rope. "Tie the packs to one end." She looks at Ben. "Are you okay tying the other end around your waist?"

"So we can fish them out of the water once we're on shore?"

"Yeah. That way you can cut it away if you need to. Do you think it will work?"

He has a better chance of surviving if all he has to contend with is the rope. He can cut through it pretty easily if things get hairy. "It's worth a shot."

"Okay. Let's try it. Don't drown on me out there." She squeezes his wrist.

"Back at you," he replies. Ben decides not to dwell on the wrist squeeze. Right now, he has to focus on not dying.

"Everyone, get ready to swim," Kate calls.

Fuck. Twice in one day in the water. Ben is not looking forward to this. His only consolation is that this time he doesn't have to do it in his underwear.

His body begins to secrete adrenaline, just like it used to do before he went on a mission or into battle. It makes his heart pound and his limbs jittery. He shifts closer to the portside railing, ready to jump when Kate says the word.

A screech of metal goes up from the *Fairhaven*. The entire ship shudders. Susan's shout is drowned out in the noise.

The shoreline seems a thousand miles away, a maze of jagged rocks standing between them and safety. It will be a miracle if they all make it.

"We go in groups," Kate calls. "We look out for one another. Everyone makes it to shore. Understand?" At everyone's nod, she assigns groups. "Ash and Caleb. Eric and Reed. Susan and Ben."

"You're with us, Mama," Reed calls.

Kate nods, grouping herself with Eric and Reed. Ben is relieved. Those two will give their all to get Kate to safety.

"I don't want to leave." Susan wraps her arms around her chest. "The *Fairhaven* is all Gary and I have. We lost everything in the outbreak."

Ben grabs her arm, propelling her to the side of the sinking charter boat. "Your husband survived a fucking great white shark. Are you going to let a swim in the Pacific get the better of you? Man up!"

His words have the desired effect. Susan's face hardens, the agony over the loss of the *Fairhaven* momentarily buried.

"Stay with me," Ben tells her. He has no intention of failing Kate. She told him to get Susan to safety and he plans to do just that.

51

SWIM

KATE

I've never been much of a swimmer. Sure, my parents made sure I was drown-proofed as a kid. Basically, if someone threw me into a swimming pool, I could swim to the edge and get myself out.

Which is a far cry from jumping into the rock-riddled waters of the Pacific Ocean coastline.

The only alternative is going down with a sinking charter boat. Not an option.

I can't let my fear show. Everyone is looking to me to get them out of this. Reed and Eric are glued to either side of me, waiting for the command to jump. Caleb and Ash keep glancing in my direction, watching my face. Ben always keeps track of me, even when we're not on a boat about to sink into the ocean. The only one not paying any attention to me is Susan; she's too busy fretting over the loss of her boat.

Time is running out. If I delay any longer, someone is going to drown. Someone might drown anyway.

Don't think like that, I chastise myself. We're all going to make it. Even if I have to drag one of my companions by the hair, I'm going to make sure every one of us gets safely to the shore.

"We should be happy it's not raining," Eric says. "That would really suck."

"Dude, way to see the glass half full on a boat sinking into the ocean." Reed and Eric exchange high fives.

"Can we save the high fives for the beach?" Caleb growls.

"We might not all have hands to high-five with by the time we get to shore," Reed argues. Despite his light tone, the whites show all the way around his eyes. He's as terrified as the rest of us. "Eric and I were just seizing the moment. Carpe diem and all that."

Time to put a stop to the pointless banter before someone ends up with a fist in his face. Judging by the tension knotting Caleb's shoulders, that could be any second now.

"Everyone makes it to shore alive." I make my voice firm, giving everyone my mother-knows-best confident look. "We take care of one another, and we all survive. We jump on the count of three. Ready? One, two, three!"

I grab the railing with one hand and fling myself over the side. I scream all the way down. Which isn't very far.

There are a lot of warm oceans in the world. Florida, Hawaii, Mexico, and Southern California to name a few.

Northern California doesn't make the list. Not by a long shot, and not at any time of the year.

The current hits me like a fist, frigid water closing over my head in a burst. Cold shoots all the way to my core, numbing me almost instantly.

The ocean soaks my running pack, seawater saturating the light fabric and everything inside. The pack pulls at my shoulders, creating resistance as I kick upward.

My head breaks the surface, bare feet and arms churning to keep me afloat. Salt stings my eyes. I turn in a quick circle, making a scan for all my people.

Reed and Eric are with me in the water. Ash and Caleb are ten feet in front of us, the two of them already swimming toward the shore with long, sure strokes.

Ben and Susan are nowhere in sight.

I spin around, looking back up to the boat. Ben is at the railing, yelling for Susan to hurry. She appears seconds later, red hair blowing in every direction.

Big bubbles push to the surface of the water, air pockets from the boat as it sinks from the tear in the hull.

"Jump," I shout to them.

Susan turns, moving away from the railing. Ben grabs her, scooping her up. She yells and struggles. Ben drops her over the edge and leaps into the water after her.

"Go," I say to Reed and Eric, not waiting to see Susan and Ben surface. They're both in the water; I have to trust they'll help each other to shore. "Swim!"

The two of them break into an awkward simulation of the freestyle. It looks more like a glorified dog paddle. My own movements are no better.

Waves knock me in every direction; sometimes forward, sometimes backward, sometimes sideways. My eyes sting from the saltwater. It's so cold I can hardly breathe.

At one point, a pair of waves smashes me and Eric into one another. I grunt, the impact with Eric shoving me under. I kick back to the surface later, fighting my way forward.

"Rock," Reed screams. "Rock!"

I turn my head just in time to see an angular black form. It's right in front of me.

My heart pounds. I jerk, swimming as hard as I can to the right, trying to cut around the rock. Water surges. My shoulder and rib cage connect painfully with the stone.

My bare feet scrape against the rock. Pain spiders through me. I use the contact to push free, shoving myself out and away from the rock. Another swell lifts me, threating to suck me backwards into the rock. I kick with my legs and pull with my arms, straining to break free.

I burst past the swell just in time. It bursts against the rock. The rebound force pushes me forward, another five feet closer to the shore.

I keep swimming, flicking my eyes in search of Eric and Reed. They're five feet in front of me, both pushing hard for the shore. Reed's head swivels as he searches for me.

"Right behind you!" My shout swirls away in the crashing waves. I'm not sure if Reed heard me until I see him turn his attention back to the shoreline.

My legs and arms burn from the exertion. My eyes sting from the assault of saltwater. I cough and splutter each time a wave hits me in the face, choking on the briny water that inevitably creeps into my mouth and down my throat.

My running pack drags on me, weighing me down. I grit my teeth, refusing to cast it aside. Losing it could mean dying.

One hundred yards, I tell myself. That's how far it is to the shoreline. What's one hundred yards compared to a one-hundred-mile race?

Piece of cake. I've got this.

Another wave crashes over my head, pushing me down.

One hundred yards. So what if I feel like a drowned rat? I've trained for this my entire life, albeit on land instead of in water. I can do this. Pain and physical discomfort is nothing but an inconvenience. It can't stop me.

Something scrapes against my feet. A swell flings me forward. I sprawl onto my stomach, the water pushing my body over a jumble of fist-sized rocks.

A yowl bursts from my lungs. Water crashes over my head, causing me to choke on another mouthful of seawater. It shoves me hard against the rocks. They scrape against my ribs and knees.

Someone grabs my left arm. Someone else grabs my right.

I sputter, spitting out water as Eric and Reed haul me to my feet. The side of Reed's face is bloody, blood running out of his nose and along the side of his face from a bad scrape. Half of Eric's shirt is torn, blood staining the edges of the fabric.

I latch onto my boys, letting them help me over the rocks. The three of us huddle together against the sheer cliff face that borders the beach.

I suck in great gulps of air, wiping water that drips into my eyes. "You guys okay?"

Even as I ask the question, I scan the shoreline. Nearby, Caleb and Ash climb out of the water, holding onto one another as though the wind might whip them apart. They wrestle with the rope attached to Caleb's belt, hauling in the weapons pack. Ash sports gashes on both knees.

Ben. Susan. They aren't here yet.

I pick my way back toward the waves, large rocks stabbing at the bare soles of my feet. Every step hurts. It feels like the stones are trying to punch through my skin.

Ben. My chest seizes. Where is he?

I rotate my head to the left and right, scanning the waves.

There. I see them. They paddle beside one another, pushing hard for the shore.

The pain in my feet becomes inconsequential. I shed my pack and rush forward, splashing up to my knees in the surf.

Susan and Ben ride the waves. A swell picks them up, hurling both straight toward the shore.

I jump toward Ben, latching onto his arm as he surges by. Caleb appears out of nowhere, grabbing Susan. The two of us hold onto our friends, keeping them from doing a face plant into the rocky shore.

Ben manages to get his legs underneath him, locking wobbly knees as the tide rushes back out.

He coughs up water. Leaning on his knees, he vomits up

what seems like half the ocean. His chest heaves as he straightens.

"I've never been much of a swimmer," he gasps.

I give his arm an encouraging squeeze. "Join the club. Come on, let's get the weapons in."

Together, we haul on the rope still tied to his belt. The pack catches a few times on the rocks, but with a little patience, the ebb of the tide eventually brings it to us.

My teeth chatter as I stand there in sopping wet clothes. Ben shivers beside me.

"If I was good with words, I'd find a subtle way to put my arm around you," he says, teeth chattering. "We both know how well that would go so I'm just gonna lay it out straight. I'm freezing my balls off. Can I put my arm around you?"

I can't help it. I bark a laugh. Ben does that eye-crinkle thing again, swinging the sopping weapons pack onto his back.

"Is that a yes?"

"Only because you're freezing your balls off. If it was any other appendage you'd be out of luck."

"Look at that," Caleb says. "One of your moves finally paid off, old man."

I'd forgotten he was standing here, but I'm too cold to care. Ben flips him the bird and puts his arm around my shoulders, pulling me tight against his side.

Truth be told, it doesn't help. I'm still freezing. But it feels good to have him touch me.

I haven't been touched—really touched—since Kyle died. It's been almost three years. It makes me realize how lonely I've been. I relax against Ben as we join the rest of the group against the face of the cliff, enjoying this odd moment between us.

The rest of the group is huddled together. The beach is strewn with debris. Driftwood, lumps of seaweed, and even the bodies of unfortunate sea creatures. A half-decayed bird carcass is tangled in a clump of seaweed. Dead starfish and purple sea urchins dot the rocks. I even spot the scattered bones of long-dead animals.

Past the crashing waves, I see the angles of the sinking ship. Susan watches in stony silence. I can't tell if it's tears or seawater streaking her cheeks.

"The *Fairhaven* was everything to us," she says to no one in particular, voice dull. "All our savings. Our home. Our livelihood."

No one says anything. I search for the right words. In some ways, it feels like another fatality. I know it's only a boat, but to Susan, it's so much more than that. Hell, to all of us it's more than just a boat. It was our way to Alvarez.

It was our way *back* to Arcata.

Another fatality on my shoulders. If I hadn't insisted on trying to help Alvarez, Leo would still be alive. The *Fairhaven* would still be in one piece.

"It was a total bitch to get to the boat from Creekside anyway," Reed says after a few moments of extended, glum silence. "If I had to cross Samoa Highway one more time, I was gonna go postal."

This breaks up the tension. It also, unfortunately, brings up the next question.

"Now what?" Caleb asks.

Everyone looks at me.

Yeah, now what, Mama Bear? I think bitterly. Here I thought I'd be a knight in shining armor rescuing Alvarez and the residents of Fort Ross. All I've managed to do is get some of my people killed and strand the rest on a deserted beach.

I look at my watch. Nine hours have passed. The first of Alvarez's people will be executed in fifteen hours. There's not a damn thing I can do about it.

I don't know where we are, but we must be at least a hundred miles away from Fort Ross, probably farther. My people could make the journey, but at what cost? How many others will I lose?

"This isn't what you guys signed up for," I say. "We've had nothing but disaster since we set out from Creekside. Everything has been complete shit and we haven't even gone very far. And now we're beached like dead whales who-knows-where." Anger creeps into my voice, frustration over our situation. "I have no idea how to get home. I have no idea how to get to Fort Ross."

I sweep my gaze over each face. Susan stares at her sinking boat. I think half her heart is still on the *Fairhaven*. Reed and Eric watch me with blind loyalty. I have no doubt they'll follow wherever I lead. Their devotion is a heavy weight to bear.

Ash and Caleb aren't much different. When they look at me, they see their leader.

And then there's Ben. I may not know how to handle the attraction between us, but I have no doubt he'll go wherever I lead.

I can't do this. I can't drag them into more danger. The price has already been too high.

"Home." The word is dragged from my throat. "We need to figure out a way home."

I expect sighs of relief. I expect a few them to be happy the crazy train is turning around.

"That's not what you really want to do," Ben says. "Don't lie to us."

I shake my head. "I can't drag you guys on foot all the way to Fort Ross. It's—Susan, how far is it?"

She shrugs, turning away from the water. "Hundred miles, give or take." Rummaging around in her pack, she pulls out the sodden tide book and a crinkled map. "Let me figure out where we are."

"You don't know?" Ben asks her. "Weren't you paying attention?"

"Getting shot at and driving through a zombie drag net may have fucked up on my concentration," Susan shoots back.

Surprise registers on Ben's face; the idiot is no doubt just realizing he was being an ass. I step between them in an effort to spare them both.

"It's not fair for me to drag you guys a hundred miles into a war that might be lost by the time we get there," I say.

"It probably won't be lost." Ben surprises me with his optimism.

"You—you don't think so?"

He shrugs. "There will just be a bigger shit hole to dig them out of."

Now there's the cynicism I've come to expect.

"Leo wanted Rosario taken down," Ash says. "If we turn back now, he'll have died for nothing."

"If we turn back now, I sacrificed the *Fairhaven* for nothing." Susan's jaw is set in a hard line as she grips the edges of her soggy map. "I know everyone here has lost a home. I shouldn't be such a baby about it. But dammit, I loved—*love*—that boat. If I have to face Gary and tell him it's gone, I want it to be for a good reason."

"They need us," Reed says. "Alvarez is our friend. You said he saved your life."

"He did, but—"

"Foot Soldier saved my mama. Life for a life. Let's go get his sorry ass and kill those fuckers who want to steal his house."

"Fort," Eric corrects. "It's a frontier fort, Reed, from—"

"Dude, you know what I mean!"

"Don't quit on us now," Ash says. "You're our Mama Bear. Mama Bear doesn't quit when things are hard and scary. Hell, you went unarmed into the frat house and delivered that bottle of brandy laced with acid. This is practically a cakewalk compared to that. Tell me I'm wrong." Her eyes narrow at me in challenge.

My throat tightens. Emotion presses against the back of my eyes. I try one more time. "This has been nothing but a shit show since we left Creekside—"

"And it's going to be a shit show no matter what direction we go." Eric leans forward. "You've trained us for this, Kate. We're ready to make this journey. We can get to Fort Ross in, what? A day if we push hard? Maybe two?"

"Two at most," Reed agrees. "I'm pretty sure Alvarez would rather us be fashionably late than not show up at all."

I draw in a long, slow breath. When I cast my eyes around the circle, I see six people ready to walk into hell. Or run into hell, if I'm being accurate.

"Okay. Okay, let's do this."

People slap one another on the back and grin. Reed wraps me in a bear hug.

So much for trying to do the right thing.

"If there are survivors at Fort Ross, we save them," Ben says. "And if there are no survivors, we eliminate every last one of Rosario's people."

"Even if we have to burn down Fort Ross to do it," I add.

This time, Caleb gives me a bear hug. "That's the Mama Bear we know and love. Did you bring any acid?"

I punch him lightly on the shoulder as everyone laughs.

"We build a fire and take a one-hour break to dry and get warm," I say. "Then we get moving. We need to cover as much ground as we can before the sun goes down."

We break into small groups. I stray away by myself to gather driftwood and dry seaweed, needing to think. Our journey is not going to be easy. I need to—

"Guys!" It's Reed. "Look what I found."

Reed holds a long piece of driftwood in one hand, holding it over a small exposed section of sand about twenty feet away.

Approaching him, I spot the biggest footprint I've ever seen.

It's round, four inches across the widest part with five giant toes.

A chill crawls up my spine that has nothing to do with my damp clothing or the coastal breeze.

"I was just taking a piss when I noticed it," Reed explains, using his free hand to gesture with excitement. "I mean, what are the chances I'd find it? There's hardly any exposed sand out here. Do you think—?"

"Oh, shit." Susan's words crackle.

I stiffen, turning sharply in her direction. "What?"

"Motherfucker." She stares at the map in horror. "We're in one of the impassable zones of the Lost Coast."

"*What?*" My stomach flip-flops. "What makes you say that?"

Susan spreads the sodden map out on the ground, weighing the corners down with rocks. The rest of us gather around for a closer look.

"See here and here?" Susan taps two curves of the coastline on the map. "That the spit of land you see there"—she points to a jetting cliff just north of us—"is this point. And that point to the south of us is right here." Again, she shows us a place on the map. "We're in the southern impassable zone of the Lost Coast."

"Are you sure?" I ask. "Is there any chance you could be mistaken?"

"Even without the map, the signs are all here," Susan replies. "That footprint Reed found belongs to a black bear. Bears live on the Lost Coast. Plus there are all the dead animals on the beach." Her eyes are anguished as she gestures to the dead bird, the many animal bones, and the dried up sea urchins and starfish. "The impassable zone is infamous for killing *everything*. I'm so sorry. I should have been paying better attention. Now the tide is coming in ..."

I momentarily stop breathing. She's right. The tide has been creeping in ever since we arrived. I don't need a tide chart to see the strip of land between the cliffs and the water is narrowing.

This is bad. Very, very bad.

"Fuck," I breathe.

The Lost Coast is legendary in the ultrarunning world. Frederico and I had spent our fair share of time dreaming about it and poring over its details on the Internet. We'd talked on and off over the years about running here, but never got organized enough to do it.

The complete trail is a little over fifty miles. Experienced backpackers will take six to eight days to complete the route. Ballsy ultrarunners will do it in one day, but not without meticulous planning around the tide.

The Lost Coast is famous for its rocky beaches, remote tranquility, and wildlife. Most specifically, it's known for its impassable tidal zones, areas of the trail that get completely covered with waves and riptides at high tide.

And we're standing in one.

52

TIDE

KATE

"Will someone please explain what the fuck is going on?" Ben demands.

"What the hell is an impassable zone?" Eric asks.

"I'll tell you as we go." I turn to the group. "Everyone, grab your shit and get your shoes on. You have three minutes. Go."

"Shit-shit-shit!" Susan yells. "We're going to die out here."

"We're not going to die," I snap. "Get your shoes on, Susan."

I hurry to pull sodden socks out of my pack and shove my feet into equally sodden running shoes.

Ben and Caleb fasten on the large bags laden with weapons. Damn. I wish there was time to rearrange all the gear so they didn't have the lion's share of the burden.

"Everyone, fall into line single file behind me," I say. "Reed, you're my strongest runner. You bring up the rear. It's your job to make sure no one falls behind. Can you do that?"

"Yes, Mama." Reed takes his place at the back of the pack, solemn in his assignment. He might be a goofball much of the time, but he knows when it's time to drop the act and put on his game face.

"Everyone listen to me very closely," I continue. "We are in a very dangerous section of Northern California. It's called the Lost Coast. It's so rugged that when they built Highway 1, the authorities decided it was too treacherous and that it was just easier to divert inland. And those guys had dynamite and heavy equipment.

"There are several sections of the Lost Coast trail that are impassable at high tide. People have died out here. The tide is rising. This section of the beach will soon be completely covered in seawater. If you don't drown in the high waters, the rip tides will suck you out to sea."

"How long is this section?" Caleb asks.

From everything I had read on the Lost Coast, the two impassable sections are each about four miles long. I turn to Susan for verification. "Four miles?"

"Thereabout." She's once again gripping her red hair in her hands.

"We have to run," I say. "The rocks are going to make this hard. This is nothing like running on the track, or even around the streets with zombies. Keep your eyes on the ground. Always track one to two steps ahead to make sure you don't fall or roll an ankle. Whatever you do, haul ass. Susan, how much time do we have before the tide is fully in?"

"An hour?" Susan looks at us helplessly. "Not much more than that."

"Got that?" I sweep my eyes over my people. "One hour. It will be a hard hour. Run hard. Remember, keep your eyes one to two steps ahead of where you plan to step. Let's move."

To the average person, running fifteen-minute miles might sound like a piece of cake. Hell, even at a fast stroll a person should be able to walk a mile in fifteen minutes.

But we're on a beach. There is no beach in the world where a runner will be as fast as he is on pavement.

This particular beach, with its jumble of sea-tossed rocks, is even worse.

Even though I told the group we have to run, true running isn't possible. There's no way to establish an even gait with the uneven terrain. It's more like loping strides as we leap among the rocks.

We haven't gone more than fifty feet before someone behind me goes down with a yell.

It's Susan.

"I'm fine." She staggers to her feet, favoring one ankle. "Twisted my foot on a rock."

I give her my best Mama Bear look. "You have to ignore the pain," I tell her. "Don't focus on it. Focus on getting the fuck off this stretch of land and into the safe zone. You got it?"

I don't wait for her to respond. There is no time to baby anyone out here. If I let up, we could all die.

The water edges inexorably closer as we run. I try not to look at the patch of giant boulders that approaches ahead of us, all of them hugging the tall cliffs. As the water creeps closer, it will force us onto those large rocks.

Fear pounds in my temples. I push as hard as I dare, slowed by the rocks underfoot. Breath saws in and out of my lungs, partly from exertion, partly from fear.

A shout goes up behind me. I turn in time to see Ash go down. A wave drenches her. Eric and Caleb haul her to her feet. She splutters, wiping salt spray out of her eyes.

"I'm fine," she gasps, face set with determination. "I just slipped." There is blood on her hands where she caught herself on the rocks, but otherwise she looks okay.

I nod and plow onward, focusing on the terrain right in front of me.

How are Ben and Caleb faring with the weapon packs? A glance over my shoulder shows them keeping pace, but how long can they keep it up? The weapons won't mean a thing if we drown out here trying to hang onto them. We can find other weapons. We can *make* other weapons. And I still have the alpha zom recording.

I open my mouth, ready to tell Ben and Caleb to ditch the bags. Just as I do, a giant wave looms up, foamy fingers reaching for me.

It crashes down over my head, sucking my feet out from under me. Water gushes down my throat and nose. I tumble sightlessly through the waves.

Rocks scrape against my back. A scream tries to force its way out of my mouth. All I get is another lungful of water.

My eyes sting from the saltwater. All around me is cold and blackness.

53

SPRINT

BEN

It's a stop-action horror movie unfolding right before his eyes.

Ben sees the wave coming. He sees Kate standing in its path.

He opens his mouth, but there's no time to shout a warning.

One second Kate is standing there. The next second, she's gone.

His entire world stops spinning. *No.* She can't be gone.

"Kate!" Caleb drops his artillery pack to the ground.

"Caleb!" Ash screams, but he's already leaped into the water.

"Fuck this." Ben drops his pack. He doesn't give a shit if he drowns. If he loses Kate, there's no reason to keep going.

As he splashes into the ocean, he finds Reed by his side. The boy's mouth is set, eyes narrowed in concentration.

"We are not losing Mama," he states.

"Fucking right we're not losing her," Ben snarls.

A wave rushes them. He and Reed grab onto one another. Ben bends his knees and braces himself.

The cold descends, sucking the breath from his lungs. It

yanks at him, trying to haul him out to sea. Ben digs his nails into Reed's arms and leans back, fighting the pull of the water.

The wave is gone almost as quickly as it arrives. He and Reed sputter in the surf, still hanging onto one another like lifelines.

Ben searches the waves. There. He sees Kate's cropped hair. It disappears, sucked under by a wave. A second later he sees the sleeve of her pink shirt

Caleb cuts through the waves, snagging the flash of pink. Kate's head appears as Caleb drags her upright. The younger man battles the waves, trying to drag them both to shore.

"Come on!" Reed cries. Caleb and Kate are no more than ten feet away, struggling toward them.

Ben and Reed fight their way through the surf to Kate and Caleb. Kate's face is set, the fight in every muscle. Caleb looks like a spawn of Poseidon rising out of the surf, one hand still tangled in Kate's shirt as saltwater streams down his face. Reed and Ben each grab one of Kate's arms, freeing Caleb to steady himself.

The four of them fight their way through the waves that suck at their feet and legs. Kate heaves, throwing up water even as she forces her feet to carry her back to the shore.

As soon as they exit the water, she croaks out a single word: "Move!"

Everyone stares at her as she vomits up more seawater. "Move!" she snaps. "Reed, lead them."

"But—"

"Go!" she screams.

Reed takes off, leading the pack. Ben takes up the rear with Kate, shouldering the pack of weapons.

"Leave it," she wheezes beside him. "Too heavy."

"No."

She coughs, taking a few staggering steps forward. She should be wrapped in a blanket by a fire with something warm to drink, not trying to run down this godforsaken stretch of beach.

"You're not dying for that shit," she tells him.

"I'm not dying. Move, Kate."

She glares at him, though not with any heat. He watches her set her jaw and plow forward. He glues himself to her side, matching her pace.

Now, finally, he has a true understanding of what she's been training them for. Why she talked about the importance of relegating pain to a distant part of the mind and pushing on. Why she insisted they all be able to run for four hours straight without being tired or sore the next day. Why she made them run up and down the bleacher stairs. Why she made them sprint around the track.

It was all for this. So that when the day came, they could keep themselves alive.

The terrain is complete shit. It wasn't made for running. Kate makes it look easy, springing along beside him. She might look like a drowned cat, but she moves like a gazelle.

Ben lumbers along, lungs burning. The pack drags on his shoulders. He refuses to let it slow him down. He's hauled packs every bit as heavy as this before. Granted, he wasn't running for his life from the goddamn ocean, but he's logged lots of hours with heavy gear packs. They're getting out of this place with their guns, no matter what.

Water splashes around his feet. Dammit. The tide has crept up even farther, pushing them up against the cliffs. He grits his teeth, moving several inches away from the water. They can't afford to play chicken with the surf. It cost them precious minutes to save Kate. They might not be so lucky a second time.

The bleached remains of an enormous tree looms before them, ejected from the ocean on the Lost Coast. It sits perpendicular to the shore, blocking their path. The trunk is three feet in some places. Those in front of them clamber over before disappearing down the far side.

He and Kate tackle the tree, the two of them grappling with the smooth bark. Kate flings one leg sideways and slides over. Ben follows suit. They land on the other side and keep running, catching up with the rest of the group.

"See that spit of land?" Susan points, never slowing her pace. She limps on her twisted ankle, but manages to keep up with the rest of the group. "Just on the other side of those boulders. We'll be safe there."

"That's at least a mile away," Eric says.

No one has a reply to that. The water pushes them closer and closer toward the cliff. Motherfucker.

He grits his teeth and throws all his concentration into running. Left foot, right foot, watch that rock, left foot, sidestep that chunk of driftwood, right foot. His legs burn. His chest burns. His shoulders ache. He's wet. He's cold.

But he's alive. He intends to stay that way. The pain and discomfort of trying to sprint down a rocky beach can go fuck itself.

Eric trips on a rock and sprawls. Ben grabs him by the back of his pack, hauling him up. The side of his cheek has a gash. The front of his shirt is torn.

"Don't stop" Kate huffs. "Shake it off, Eric."

He nods, pushes up his glasses, and keeps running.

Kate has conditioned the shit out of these kids. He doesn't know any other barely-twenty idiot who could push hard like this without complaint.

Who would have thought that running for his life along a beach in the middle of nowhere would make him admire Kate even more than he already does? Life can be fucked up like that.

"Push!" Kate screams. "Run with everything you've got." She follows her own order, picking up her pace.

Ben struggles to keep up. It's obvious why she's ratcheting up the tension.

The last five hundred yards is a field of massive boulders. Once they hit those rocks, it will be a full-out scramble.

And most of them are already covered with water.

54

IMPASSABLE ZONE

KATE

I'm wet. I'm cold. I'm terrified.

Worries scroll through my brain. *What if someone falls and breaks something? What if another sneaker wave comes? What if the weapon packs are too heavy? What if we can't cross the boulders in time? Whatif-whatif-whatif ...*

I feel like I'm running in Jell-O. I know what my body is capable of, but the terrain holds me back. And every millisecond of delay brings the tide closer to us.

I drop back behind Ben, determined to see every last one of my people out of the impassable zone.

"Stay next to me," Ben snaps, wheezing as he sucks in air. "I can't see you—"

"It's too narrow," I snap back, maintaining my position behind him. Running side by side will mean one of us will be in the water, which is too dangerous. "I'll be fine. Keep moving."

He grinds to a halt. "I need to be able to see you—"

"Move, god dammit," I scream at him.

He gives me a solid glare before turning his back on me and resuming his run.

Our stretch of beach abruptly disappears, depositing us at the foot of the boulder field. Ben scrambles onto them, pausing only long enough to make sure I'm still behind him.

I leap up after him, legs bent and arms stretched forward for balance. I move like a giant crab, leaping from rock to rock. Each time I land, I crouch only long enough to secure my balance with my hands. Then I leap for the next stone.

"I'm too old for this shit," Ben gasps. Despite his complaining, he moves with the same dexterity as the younger men. Even with the giant pack on his back, his balance is solid. His active life in the military has kept him in great shape.

I scramble and leap along with him. The ocean pounds the rocks directly to our right, sending up spray and gouts of water. Our path narrows as the water reaches steadily for us.

Ahead of us, a huge wave rears over the shore. It looms directly over Ash and Caleb. The rest of the crew is only a short distance ahead of them.

"Look out!" I shriek.

Their reflexes are whip-quick. Ash drops down between two large rocks and wedges herself between them. Caleb throws his arms around a boulder. Reed, Eric, and Susan dash forward, cranking hard to get ahead of the water.

Caleb and Ash are lost in a crash of gray water and white flecks of sea foam. I freeze where I am, crouched on a giant black boulder beside Ben. I hold my breath, waiting for the tide to recede.

The water rolls back. I let out a cry of relief when Ash and Caleb pop up from the rocks and continue their frantic scramble. We catch up to them, the four of us spidering together over the rocks. The others have reached the safe zone.

Ben slips. He tips sideways with a shout.

"Got you!" I grab his arm, counterbalancing him with my own weight.

"Thanks." He shoves a neighboring boulder with his foot, righting himself.

I leap for the next rock right as another wave rears up. "Get back," I cry, lunging closer to the cliff wall. Ben, Caleb, and Ash all do the same.

I reach out and latch onto Ben's hand just as the wave hits us. The water pulls at his body. Digging my nails into his flesh, I hang on, refusing to let go. I wedge my feet between two rocks, bending my knees for leverage.

Shivering and terrified, I shake my head to clear water from my eyes as the wave recedes. Ash crouches beside me. Ben is draped on the rocks by my feet, both of my arms wrapped around his forearm.

"Caleb!" Ash scrambles to where he lays on his back in the valley between several rocks. "Caleb!"

Keeping one eye on the water, I join Ash. Ben is right behind me. We reach Caleb as he picks himself up. A nasty, jagged cut gushes blood across his thigh.

"You're okay," I tell him, looping an arm under one armpit to lever him up. Ash grabs his other arm while Ben grabs the back of his pack. "You're okay, Caleb."

I have no idea if he really is okay. I only know that he has to be okay enough to make it another two hundred and fifty yards to the end of the impassable zone. Reed, Susan, and Eric have all made it. They wave their arms and yell as us from a safe spot well away from the water.

"Incoming!" Reed bellows.

I look up just as another wave hits us. I throw my arms around Caleb, clinging to him. I have a brief flash of Ben and Ash doing the same thing.

The four of us hang on for dear life as another wave closes over our heads. We're pushed sideways toward the cliff. Stone presses into my side. Water rushes over my face. I refuse to let go.

As soon as the water clears, we hurry to right ourselves. Caleb sits up, lifting himself off me. Ben picks himself up off the rocks. Ash removes herself from the top of Caleb's bad leg where she fell.

"You're okay," I murmur to Caleb. "Two hundred and fifty yards. You've got this."

"I've got this," he growls in agreement, jaw set with determination. He lifts himself up, springing forward with more agility than I would have thought possible considering his wound.

By this time, we're forced to hug the side of the cliff, scrambling over the boulders as fast as we can as waves collide into the rocks at our feet. My back aches from the constant crouch. My quads burn from the squatting. I ignore the pain, throwing all my focus at safety.

Safety. It's no more than two hundred yards away.

A surge of water rises around us, soaking us up to our ankles. The world beneath our feet becomes inky black. We're forced to halt and wait for the water to recede so we can see where to step.

"Don't stop!" Eric yells. "Hurry!"

I grind my teeth, resisting the urge to shout back. As soon as the water clears, we're off again. Ash leads the way, springing from rock to rock like a gymnast. She doesn't even have to lean forward to balance with her hands like the rest of us.

One-hundred-fifty yards. We're almost there.

Another surge of water gushes forward, this time rushing all the way up to our knees. I grab onto the side of the cliff for balance as the tide sucks back out, leaning and fighting for balance.

One-hundred yards.

Caleb stumbles on his injured leg. Ben catches him, keeping him upright. Seeing the two men work together gives me a surge of pride.

The feeling is short-lived as water once again gushes forward. This time, it comes up to our thighs.

This time, it doesn't recede.

"Shit," I snarl. To my people, I bark, "Move! The tide is in. Swim!"

Ash, still in the lead, is the first to splash down into the surf. The tide pulls at her. She fights to stay on course for the safe zone on the far side of the rocks.

Fifty yards. That's all that lies between us and safety.

"Drop the packs," I order. "Now."

Caleb doesn't hesitate. He slings off his weapons pack and chucks it as hard as he can in the surf. With any luck, it will wash up onto shore. Honestly, I don't care what happens to the weapons so long as Caleb is okay. He jumps after Ash, long, sure strokes cutting through the water.

Ben hesitates.

There is no time for arguing. I summon every ounce of Mama Bear authority.

"Drop it, Ben. Right now!"

Cursing, he flings the pack into the water. He crouches against the cliff, fear plain on his face. I recall he's not a strong swimmer.

"Hang onto me," I order, grabbing his hand. "Don't let go."

I drag him forward into the surf. The tide is unyielding. First, it sucks us out toward the ocean, only seconds later to shove us back toward the cliff.

I do my best to stay upright, kicking off the rocks beneath my feet. I paddle with my free hand, gripping Ben's hand in the other. Together, the two of us fight our way forward.

Twenty-five yards.

It's the longest sprint of my life. Half running, half swimming through water, I hang onto my friend as the ocean tosses us back and forth like pieces of driftwood.

"Let go of me," Ben gasps, sputtering as a wave douses him in the face.

"Not an option," I grind out in response.

A wave rushes toward us. I coil my legs in readiness. Right before the breaker hits us, I push off, dragging Ben after me.

The water picks us up, hurling us toward the shore—

—and right into the waiting arms of Eric and Reed.

"We got you," Eric yells, grabbing Ben by the neckline of his shirt.

"Come on, Mama." Reed wraps both arms around me, dragging me toward safety.

Another wave hits us. The four of us tumble backward. A searing pain rips across my right hip as I'm sucked over a rock.

Reed and I tumble free of the surf, rolling onto a rocky shoreline. A heartbeat later, Eric and Ben wash up beside us.

Susan, Ash, and Caleb are all there. They help us to our feet.

Half staggering, half running, we rush away from the water. I nearly sob with relief when my feet hit sand. Granted, it's not the fine sand you find at a tropical beach. It's a thick-grained sand made up of hundreds of tiny pebbles. But it's still sand.

As soon as there's a hundred yards between us and the surf, we collapse in a heap. Wet, injured, and exhausted, we lay in a silent, gasping heap.

And just when I think we've finally earned a reprieve, it starts to rain.

55

INVENTORY

KATE

TINY BLACK PEBBLES PRESS INTO MY CHEEK AS THE FIRST raindrops hit me.

My chest heaves. My body shivers with the cold. The arrival of the rain almost makes me sob. I swallow back the despair that presses at my gut. My people need me. I can't let them know how scared and worried I am.

And just because I can't resist torturing myself, I look at my watch arm. It reads twelve hours. It's been twelve hours since the clock started ticking on Fort Ross.

Even though we technically just traveled four miles closer to Alvarez and his people, I don't feel any further along. In fact, knowing more miles of the Lost Coast lie before us makes me feel like crying all over again.

Keep it together, I scold myself. *Lives depend on you.*

Sometime during our frantic flight across the impassable zone, fog has boiled up. Sea spray and rain clouds turn the sky to dull gray.

At least we'll have daylight to travel the remainder of the Lost Coast. It's the only positive thing I can find right now. It will have to be enough.

I sit up, brushing sand off my soggy clothes. "Inventory." My voice comes out as a croak. "Inventory."

"What?" Ash blinks up at me from where she's sprawled on the sand. Even wet and covered with bits of seaweed from our near-death experience, she still looks like a CrossFit model.

"Inventory," I say again. "I need everyone's inventory."

When everyone stares at me in confused silence, I realize I've slipped into running jargon.

"I mean, I need everyone to take stock of their bodies and report. Ash, you first."

The list isn't pretty. There isn't a single one of us without some sort of wound.

Ash has a bad scrape on one arm and a tender ankle.

Susan's ankle is already swollen from her fall on the rocks.

The gash on Caleb's thigh oozes blood.

Eric has gashes on his face and hands.

Reed took a header with a rock. Blood covers half his face.

Ben's clothes are ripped in several places, blood seeping through.

I have a scrape on my right hip, the jagged, bloody skin showing through.

It could be worse, I tell myself, ignoring the despair that threatens to suck me under. *There are no broken bones. None of us got swept out to sea. We're all alive.*

"Hey, look!" Caleb points. "One of the weapon packs!"

Sure enough, one of the weapon packs has washed onto shore. Ben limps up to the edge of the surf to retrieve it.

"Everything is better when you have firepower." He drops the pack into the sand and drops down beside it.

"Ash," I say, "do you still have your first aid kit?"

"Affirmative." She pulls off her sodden running pack. "I don't know how much use everything inside will be."

"Disinfectant on all the wounds," I say. Seawater carries a lot of bacteria. We could each use our own personal bottle of disinfectant and a lifetime supply of bandages, but we'll have to make do with what we have. "If anyone needs stitches, see to it they get them. Susan, I'll wrap your ankle." I glance down the beach, at the black sand the Lost Coast is known for. "We move out in thirty minutes."

"What?" Susan stares at me aghast. "We can't move out. None of us are in any shape to move."

"None of us are in any shape to stay here," I reply. "We have no shelter and little food. We're wet and cold and we can't build a fire in this rain. Any one of us could get an infection from our cuts and scrapes. Our best hope at surviving is to get the hell off the Lost Coast."

"But my ankle—" Susan begins.

I cut her off, knowing how crucial it is to keep everyone in a suck-it-up mindset. "I'll wrap it. The natural swelling will create a sheath to splint it. It's possible to run on it."

"*Run?*" Susan's voice is a shriek.

"Mama ran almost a hundred miles on a messed-up ankle," Reed puts in. "You should have seen her when she arrived in Arcata. Her bad ankle was twice the size of her good one."

Susan's face turns incredulous.

Sympathy softens me, but I don't let it show. "Pain isn't relevant, Susan. I know you hurt. I know you'll hurt more in the coming miles. But giving in to pain will get you killed. You can't stay out here. Your only option is to keep moving."

A mix of frustration and fear flushes the angles of her face. I remind myself she's new to the running world. Until a few weeks ago, she didn't even know what ultrarunning was. I put a gentle hand on her arm.

"Trust me, please. I'll get you out of here if you let me."

She nods, lips compressed. I open my pack and pull out a soggy shirt. Using my knife, which miraculously is still attached to my belt, I cut off several strips and set about wrapping Susan's foot.

Reed and Caleb both receive stitches from Ash. There aren't enough sterile wipes to go around, so I make sure those with the deepest wounds get them. I also wrap Ash's ankle with the remains of my shirt, grateful hers doesn't look as purple and swollen as Susan's.

During this time, I mentally plot out our next steps. The Lost Coast trail is about fifty miles from north to south. According to Susan, we just exited the southern impassable zone.

Judging on what I know of the route, I estimate we have about thirty miles left to travel. Due to the time of year, we'll have light for the next two or three hours. I hope everyone packed a headlamp.

From what I recall reading about this next part of the trail, we will have a shit ton of climbing. I need to make sure I pace everyone accordingly. We have to move fast enough to get off the trail by sunset, but not so fast I blow everyone up by mile twelve.

With all of us wet and cold, hypothermia is a real threat. The rain is only a light drizzle, but there's no telling how long it will last or if it will get worse. At least if we're moving, we have a chance at keeping our bodies warm.

Once we're off the trail, we can find a house, a car, or some kind of shelter. We can scavenge food and medical supplies. We can regroup and figure out our next steps.

I check my pack for the small tape recorder Johnny gave me with the alpha command. It's in a one-gallon Ziploc and appears to be intact. I don't dare take it out in this rain to check it.

The recorder could possibly be the most valuable thing I have. I wrap it and the Ziploc in a pair of shorts, hoping to give it a little extra protection, then return it to my pack.

"I'm going to distribute the weapons," Ben says. "That way

we don't risk losing everything in another disaster like we just had."

Caleb nods in approval as Ash puts the finishing touch on his stitches. Ben distributes the various guns, rifles, explosives, and ammo. The rifles he brought are collapsible. It fits easily in my pack with the tape recorder and water bladder.

Who would have thought I'd ever run down a trail with a rifle in my pack? I wish Frederico were here to see this.

"Everyone, pull out any food you have," I say. "I need to know exactly what we have so I can ration. That includes water." Neither Ben nor Caleb have water or running packs, which means the rest of us will have to share. I don't want to risk drinking from streams unless we have no other choice.

Two minutes later, I stare at the pathetic pile of food at my feet. Two cans of black beans. Seven granola bars. A bag of M&Ms. Two sticks of beef jerky. Ten litres of water to share among five people over thirty miles.

This is not good.

"We eat the beans now. Ration the rest for today's journey. We eat every two hours. Small bites only."

"How are we supposed to go thirty miles on *that*?" Susan gestures to the pathetic pile of food.

I share her sentiments, but I don't let it show. No one can know how worried I really am.

"It will have to be enough," I tell her. "It's all we have."

"We've trained for this," Eric says. "We can do this."

"*You've* trained for this," Susan snaps. "I've only been running with you guys for seven weeks."

"Couch potato to ultramarathon," I reply, trying to make my voice light. "I knew people who specialized in that sort of training."

"Couch potato training?" Ash asks. "What does that mean?"

"It means they don't train enough. Sometimes because they're lazy, but usually because life got in the way."

"So these couch potatoes still showed up to run on race day?" Reed asks.

I nod. "It wasn't always pretty, but people can gut out just about anything if they put their mind to it. Besides," I add to Susan, "you're in better shape than you give yourself credit for. You and Gary survived for months on the *Fairhaven*. You can't tell me ship life was easy."

Susan weighs my words. "It is hard work," she says after a moment.

"There you go. Just think of it as cross training for the Lost Coast."

She closes her eyes, a small smile wrinkling her mouth. "You are the strangest woman I've ever met. I can't believe I actually feel inspired by what you just said. No one cross trains on a charter boat for ultramarathons."

"They do now." I refuse to back away from the sliver of optimism I've managed to instill in her. "You can start a new fad."

"Johnny will write about it in his book," Eric adds. "Couch potato charter woman to ultramarathon runner." Everyone looks at him. "Yeah, that sounded weird, didn't it?"

"Um, I think I just found another bear print." Reed stands in the sand, staring at something directly at his feet.

I head toward him, my heart sinking at the large animal print filling up with rainwater. Leading away from Reed into a narrow canyon is a line of identical tracks. It's even larger than the last one we saw, these easily five inches across.

"Black bear," Susan confirms, voice flat. "I forgot to mention no one is allowed to backpack on the Lost Coast without a bear canister for food. Bears can smell food up to two miles away."

No one speaks. Every single one of us is thinking of the various edible items stashed in our packs. The two granola bars in my pack make me feel like a bear magnet. Zombies, I can handle. Bears? No, thank you.

"We could eat everything now," Ash ventures.

I hesitate then shake my head. "We're moving away from the bear tracks." I hope. "We need to conserve the food. We'll need a constant source of fuel to keep us going throughout the day."

We wolf down the two cans of beans, passing them around in pensive silence as the rain patters down on us. I toss the cans to the ground when we finish. It felt weird to toss garbage on the ground at the beginning of the apocalypse. Now, none of us is phased by it.

"Lace up," I say. "We've got an ultramarathon to run."

56

PACER

KATE

There's a time-honored tradition in the ultramarathon world known as pacing. Simply put, pacing is accompanying a racer on part of his or her race. I used to pace Frederico for as far as fifty or sixty miles when he ran hundred milers.

On a granular level, pacing isn't as simple as just running with another person. It's studying the route ahead of time and watching for flags so your runner doesn't get lost. It's monitoring the food and beverage intake over the long miles to make sure your runner keeps himself fed and hydrated. It's helping him through rough spots—when he's bonking, raging, or puking his guts out on the trail. It's keeping an eye on the clock to make sure your runner doesn't miss any important cutoffs.

On top of that, a pacer has to monitor his own food and drink intake. You can't pace a person if you're laid out on the side of the trail.

As I usher my group down the beach, I realize this will be the toughest pacing job of my life. Not only do we have to contend with Mother Nature and all she throws at us, I have myself and *six* people to monitor. We're starting out wet, cold, and injured with limited resources.

There are no aid stations waiting for us at regular intervals. There is no option to drop from the run if things get hard. There are no gear bags waiting for us with dry clothes and clean socks.

As we jog down the beach, black pebbles slowing our journey, I fall into step beside Susan. Her jaw is set. I have no doubt she's in pain from her rolled ankle, but it's good to see her sucking it up. She'll need that grit to make it out of here.

"Have you hiked the Lost Coast before?" It would be helpful to have someone with knowledge of the trails.

She shakes her head, panting as she jogs. "Hike, no. Gary and I boated down here plenty of times for the fishing. I grew up with stories of the Lost Coast." Her brow wrinkles. "Mostly of people getting washed away by the tide, or just lost. Or having a close encounter with a bear."

Well, there goes that idea. Susan knows about as much as I do about the Lost Coast, which is just enough to leave me terrified.

I pull ahead, leading the pack down the black beach. Reed brings up the rear. My sweeper. Every race has sweepers, people who bring up the back of the pack to make sure no one gets left behind.

We enter a stretch of beach that is true sand, the fine grains glistening black beneath my running shoes. I shift a little closer to the water where the surface is firmer for running. The cliffs to our left are tall, tan, and vertical.

"Black Sands Beach," Susan calls.

"No shit," Ben grumbles.

"I mean, that's the name of this beach," Susan says. "The end of the beach marks the midway point of the Lost Coast Trail."

"How much farther after that?" Eric asks.

"About twenty-five miles." I let that sink in. No one says anything.

The rain continues to peter down. Even though I'm running, I'm cold. The wind from the coast, combined with the rain and clothes already soaking wet, are a bad combination. A glance down my line of runners shows me everyone in the same condition.

I mentally run through the list of hypothermia symptoms. Shivering. Slurred speech. Shallow breathing. Slow pulse. Clumsiness. Confusion. Drowsiness. And worst of all, unconsciousness.

These are very real dangers.

I grit my teeth. I'm getting everyone out of here if it kills me. I've survived zombies. I've survived loss. I've survived way too much other shit to lose to the trail.

After running a little over an hour down the sand, I spot the end of Black Sands Beach. A pale line of dirt zigzags its way up the cliff. From that point on, the trail follows the contours of the land as it meanders down the coast. Which means no more risky run-ins with the tide. It also means the end of the beach running, thank god. I'm ready for good old-fashioned dirt beneath my feet.

"This way," I call, gesturing to the trail.

As I jog toward it, I feel something stir in my chest. I haven't had a real trail run since the start of the apocalypse. My feet move faster of their own accord, carrying me toward what feels like an old friend.

There have been so many times in my life when I turned to the trail for comfort. Having that cut out of my every day existence hasn't been easy. Ben understands that. It's the reason he covered my room with pictures of nature on my birthday.

I glance in his direction. He looks back at me, nodding in understanding. Somehow, he knows what this means to me. It's baffling how well he understands me.

I climb a short way onto the trailhead and pause, waiting for the others to catch up. Fennel and thistles line both sides of the hard-packed dirt. Farther ahead are gnarled cypress trees, bowed sideways from the constant battering of the elements. I inhale, pulling a lost world into my lungs.

"If we weren't all at risk of dying, I'd say the world has just delivered a gift to you." Ben is the first to reach me. The two of us are momentarily shielded from sight by the tall shrubs growing along the trail.

"It suits you out here." His voice is gruff as always, but his eyes are soft as he takes me in, framed by the trailhead. "It's like seeing you in your natural habitat."

His words create a warming sensation in my body. Regret flickers through me. I wish I'd ignored what he said to me the night we kissed.

"Kate?"

"Yeah?"

"I'm sorry for what I said. That night of your birthday, I mean." The words rush out of him. "On the roof. I shouldn't have said what I said. What I wanted to say that night was that I'd been wanting to kiss you for months."

I stare at him, tongue glued to the roof of my mouth. Of all the times to pick for an apology, Ben would decide to do it when we're sopping wet and stranded on one of the most dangerous trails of Northern California, our only privacy a tall scrub brush.

Ben hunches his shoulders, like he's trying to disappear into his own body. "Words aren't my thing, Kate. I'm sorry. Really sorry. I just want you to know that. You know. In case we die out here. I want you to know."

He looks so contrite and miserable. I find myself releasing the mortification I've been dragging around like dirty socks for weeks, letting myself bask in the knowledge that he wanted to kiss me as much as I wanted to kiss him.

But I can't help but compare Ben to Kyle. The comparison is a chain around my neck as real as the one Rosario once put there. Ben could not be any more different from the man I was married to for almost twenty years. The fact that we're attracted to each other doesn't change the fact that we might not be compatible in the long run.

"Thanks for telling me the truth. It means a lot," I say instead.

"Can I—can I try again?" he asks.

I stop breathing. I can't look away. There is nothing that I want more than to kiss this man. It makes no sense, but there it is.

It occurs to me that I might be in love with Ben.

Anxiety mounts within me, a rising tide that scrambles my brain. Kyle's easy smile flashes before me. Easygoing Kyle with his kind smile.

Ben doesn't even know how to smile.

"I—I don't think that's a good idea." My whisper is husky. I force myself to step back. "This thing between us, whatever it is, I'm not sure it's a good idea."

He draws in an uneven breath, breaking eye contact. I'm both disappointed and relieved when he doesn't make any argument.

"Creekside is a small community," I continue, trying to rationalize everything in my own mind. "It's tightknit. If we end up not liking each other as much as we think we do, it could disrupt everything. I ... I need your friendship, Ben. I don't want to risk losing that by doing something stupid."

"Okay." It's his turn to take a step back.

Something inside me crumples. I consider the wisdom of throwing my arms around his neck when a shout goes up.

"Mama Bear! Wait up!"

Our moment evaporates—as does our privacy—as Caleb hikes up onto the trail, the others following behind him.

I'm thankful for the distraction. Ben turns aside as though studying the plants growing along the path.

"This is the end of the beach trail," I tell the group. "From here on out, we won't have any sand or riptides to deal with."

"*Gracias a Dios*," Ash mutters.

"This is a true trail run," I continue. "There are some climbs ahead of us. We'll walk the up hills and try to run everything else. We'll pass through a few primitive campsites only accessible by foot. It's isolated out here, but there's always a risk of running into zombies in the campgrounds. We need to proceed cautiously."

"Don't forget the bears," Eric says. "That was one big ass track back there on the beach."

"Bears." I nod. "There are bears and rattlesnakes."

Caleb taps his gun. "I can take care of any rattlesnakes."

Ben snorts. "You ever try to kill a snake with a gun? You have to be one hell of a shot."

"If we see a rattlesnake," I say, "give it wide berth. It's more afraid of us than we are of it. Besides, there's little chance of running into rattlesnakes out here today. It's too cold. Just don't be stupid if we do happen to run into one. What we are likely to run into is poison oak. I know we're all limited on clothing right now, but if anyone has long sleeves or long pants, now is the time to put them on. Make sure you know where your headlamps are. Oh, and be on the lookout for ticks."

"Ticks?" Ash looks horrified. "Ticks, as in the little fuckers that carry Lyme Disease?"

Lyme Disease is a bacterial infection caused by the bite of a tick. Initial symptoms are flu-like, but if untreated with antibiotics, a person can have lasting inflammation and neurological conditions.

"Yes. You can usually feel them bite you. If you feel a bite, stop and check." Frederico and I picked countless ticks off ourselves and one another over the years. "A very small percentage of ticks carry Lyme Disease. Even if they do, they have to be embedded in your skin thirty-six to forty-eight hours to transmit the bacteria. Just make sure you get them off as soon as you feel them bite and you should be fine."

Six sets of eyes stare at me in horror.

"I'm not sure what's worse," Reed says. "Getting bitten by a tick or getting bitten a zombie."

"Tick," Caleb says. "At least with the zombie it's over quick."

Reed opens his mouth to respond, but I cut him off.

"Stay alert. Keep your eyes on the trail. I estimate we've traveled anywhere from seven to eight miles today already. We have another twenty-five miles to go. Today, you guys are going to finish your first ultramarathon. We stay together. We look out for one another. We get the hell off the Lost Coast and survive. Everyone understand?"

I wait to see everyone nod. "All right. Let's go."

I drop gears into a power hike, leading the group at a brisk walk up hill. Even though every part of me yearns to run—to fly up the hill and soak in the beauty like I used to—I force myself to moderate my pace. There will be plenty of time for running. The last thing I need to do is burn everyone out at the beginning of our journey.

I'm the first to reach the short summit up from Black Sands Beach. Everyone has their heads bowed as they march up hill. No one is paying any attention to me, not even Ben.

I take advantage of the momentary privacy to exhale, letting fear out of my chest. It washes over me in a hot wave so potent it almost has me on my knees.

Frederico. I wish he were here. I wish we had done this trail together.

Help me, Frederico, I say silently. *Help me get everyone out of here alive. We've trained, but not for the Lost Coast.*

His reply comes clear as a bell in my head. *You're never*

completely ready for any race, no matter how hard you train. There's always a surprise or two on race day.

How many times had he said something similar to me when he was alive? More times than I can count.

Then, as though from a great distance, I hear him again. *You got this, Jackalope.* I'm not sure if it's Frederico's voice or just the crash of the ocean.

Tears prick the back of my eyes. It feels like he's here. Maybe a part of him is.

A strong hand grips my shoulder.

I squeeze my eyes. I want it to be Frederico. I miss my friend so much.

But it's not Frederico.

"You got this, Mama Bear," Ben murmurs.

Footsteps sound on the trail behind us. Ben shifts. To anyone coming up on us, it looks like he's falling in line behind me on the single-track trail.

But I know better. Ben is shielding me with his body, giving me a few precious seconds to gather my fear and stuff it back down a deep dark hole. He's giving me a moment to find Mama Bear. After what I just did to him, he's still looking out for me.

I'm an idiot for turning him down. I want to kiss him. I want to kiss him almost as badly as I want to get off the Lost Coast. And I squandered my chance like a coward.

There's nothing I can do about it now. I take off, jogging down the slope to the open trail beyond. It winds through a grassy meadow, the greenery bending under the weight of the pattering rain.

The group follows in my wake. Everyone is silent, our foot-steps and breathing the only sounds of humanity.

Something happens over the next few miles. Tension sloughs off me. Anxiety recedes to a distant part of my mind. It's just me and the trail. My old friend. Everything is better when I can run.

God, how I've missed the wilderness. How I've missed running for hours on end through the trees with nothing but my thoughts and labored breath for company. Being here on the trail is like returning to a long-lost home.

I breathe in deep. I can almost see Frederico running ahead of me, gray ponytail bouncing with every step.

I draw to a halt after an hour. It's still raining and the mist from the ocean hangs low in the air, decreasing our visibility to only a few hundred feet.

"Five minute break," I say. "Time for food and water."

I take out two of the granola bars. I break them into small pieces and hand them out as everyone arrives. After everyone eats their small bite, I make them drink.

We're going to run out of water at some point. This is a fact I can't change. We can move on very little food, but dehydration is riskier for us than a water-borne illness.

Well, I drank river water on my way to Arcata and didn't die. There's a good possibility the water out here is clean. It's remote enough that the risks should be low.

Should be.

"Bathroom break," I call. "Girls on the right side of the trail. Boys on the left. Stay within eyesight of each other."

As I drop into the grass with Susan and Ash, the dark-haired woman turns to me.

"I have to go number two," she grumbles.

"Oh, my god," Susan says on my other side. "I don't think I'm going to be able to stand back up. My legs are already killing me."

"Just squat and let it out," I say to Ash. To Susan, I say, "I'll help you up, don't worry."

"I think my muscles are frozen in place," she replies.

"I'll get you up," I reassure her, not for a second letting her see sympathy or worry. I'm her pacer. I need to convey confidence if I want her to feel confident.

"I can't poo in front of people," Ash says. "I have poo anxiety. Seriously, when I traveled with my girlfriends to Las Vegas and shared a hotel room with them, I didn't go all weekend."

"Just relax and let it out. Trust me when I say you don't want to be carrying any extra weight with you."

"How did you go at Creekside?" Susan asks. "We're all crammed in with one another."

"I go when everyone is either asleep or out during the day. My butt cheeks won't relax unless I'm alone."

I purse my lips. "Ash, you have to go."

"It's no use. It won't come out." Ash pulls up her shorts and stands.

I frown, trying to think of what to do for her. "Just call out if you need me to stop."

"*No puedo creer esto,*" Ash grumbles, moving back to the trail.

I help Susan to her feet, making it a point not to ask her about her ankle. She needs to focus on being strong, not on the pain.

"Motherfucker," Susan groans. "Oh, my god. I thought I was sore after that first week of running with you guys."

I chuckle knowingly. "Yeah. Trail and beach running will beat you up in ways a track never can."

"I have muscles here." Susan prods her ribcage. "I didn't know it was possible for ribs to hurt from running."

"Just think of the story you'll have for Gary when we get back," I reply. "He may have survived a shark attack, but you're surviving a run down the Lost Coast."

Susan frowns "I haven't survived yet."

I tap her gently on the temple. "Survival is up here, Susan. If you can survive for months on a boat, you can survive a day on a trail. They're not all that different. Besides, the hardest part is behind us. There are no more impassable zones."

She opens her mouth—no doubt to argue—but the boys return to the trail and cut off whatever she was going to say.

"Mama Bear, you should have told us to pack toilet paper," Eric complains.

"We should have practiced shitting in the bushes," Caleb says. "It's hard to wipe with grass."

"You should have gathered stuff from the forest and had us practice wiping," Reed adds.

"You all went number two?" Ash demands.

"Hell, yeah," Caleb says. "It's not like I could drop my pants when we were running for our lives from the ocean. I've had to go for a while."

"*Animales*," Ash says under her breath.

"Try shitting in the desert and wiping your ass with sand," Ben says. "You haven't lived until you've wiped your ass with sand that's a hundred degrees."

"Yeah, yeah, old man," Caleb says. "Always have to one-up us, don't you?"

"You wouldn't complain about wet grass if you'd ever wiped your ass with sand," Ben retorts. "It's like comparing Charmin to sandpaper."

Everyone bursts out laughing. Even I join in, embracing the brief moment of mirth with the trails stretching out on either side of us.

Then a chill travels across my body, reminding me that I'm cold and wet.

"Let's keep moving. We have to get off this trail by sunset."

57

CHAFING

BEN

He doesn't know how long they've been at it. Two hours? Three? It feels like a thousand.

The beam of his headlamp illuminates the land around him. The southern trail of the Lost Coast is beautiful. Giant Douglas fir trees march up and down the undulating terrain, breaking apart every now and then to give them a glimpse of the ocean far below. Ben might actually enjoy being out here if he didn't feel like shit.

His body screams with every step he takes. How the fuck does Kate find joy in this shit? He's pretty sure it would be less painful to be trampled by horses.

"Mama, wait—" Reed staggers a few steps off the trail and dry heaves into the dirt at his feet.

This is the fourth time they've had to stop for Reed. He has a reputation for a weak running stomach for a reason.

Ben doesn't complain about the momentary break, though he doesn't miss the covert glance Kate steals at her watch. She can't stop worrying about Alvarez.

"Water." Kate holds out the straw of her hydration bag.

He drinks, mindful not to take more than a few mouthfuls. There isn't much left and he doesn't want to think about what they're going to drink once it runs out. He's had dysentery and giardia, one in Somalia and the other in Afghanistan. It hadn't been pretty. And that was with first world medicine at his fingertips.

"Think we could find some berries or something to eat?" Eric asks.

"Are you kidding?" Reed straightens up, wiping his mouth with the back of his hand. "Don't you remember the part about bears being out here? Bears eat berries."

"Humans eat berries," Eric replies. "I'm fucking hungry, man."

"Let's all keep our eyes out for berries." Kate steps between the two boys, who glare at each other.

Ben doesn't recall ever seeing the two friends quarrel before. It's a sign of how fatigued everyone is.

"There might be other edible plants. Let's just keep our eyes out." Kate doesn't say what they should look for. Ben has a sneaking suspicion she knows as much about edible plants as the rest of them. But she won't ever let herself crack in front of her kids.

"We have to keep moving," she says. "Come on."

A few people groan, but everyone falls in line. Ben grits his teeth and focuses on the trail at his feet. His thighs are on fire, chafed from the stupid boxer briefs Caleb found him back in that bunker. This is what he gets for being vain and worrying about what Kate thought. Hell, he couldn't even talk her into a kiss. Why the fuck was he worrying about his underwear?

With hours of silent running, he's had ample time to process the rejection. It chafes almost as much as the underwear. Even though Kate is too good for him, and even though he can't list one compelling reason why she might want to be with him, it still smarts.

Partly because it took him days to work up the courage to apologize to her, but mostly because his infatuation with her is reaching epic proportions. Never in his life has he been so crazy about a woman. Not even when he was a horny teenager. For fuck's sake, she turned him down right to his face—twice—and he still can't move on.

The searing pain around his thighs is almost unbearable. Should he ditch the underwear altogether? That will get him ridiculed, but he's beyond giving a shit.

The only thing that stops him is the fatigue pants. He doesn't want to imagine his balls bouncing against the thick fabric. The last thing he needs is a chafed ball sack.

His waist also itches and burns from the chafe marks that have accumulated over the weeks. He's added quite a few new ones today. In some areas, bits of his skin have thickened like calluses from the constant abuse.

He should have brought the stick of *Secret* deodorant. He hasn't touched it since the day Kate gave it to him. It sits on the small nightstand next to his bed, a token from Kate that fills him with a weird sort of pleasure.

"Where's a stick of deodorant when you need it?"

Someone next to him barks out a laugh. It takes him a beat to realize he's spoken aloud.

"My bodily odor is the least of my worries," Ash says.

"Not for that. Kate gave me a stick of deodorant. She said to use it as an anti-chafe."

"Then I could definitely use some, too," Ash says. "My toes are killing me. I can feel blisters forming."

The light, misting rain covers Ash with a thin layer of sheen. Her skin is pale.

"You alright?"

"I'm freezing my tits off, but yeah, I'm okay."

The trail has widened, letting them run two abreast. Ben alternates between monitoring the trail and scrutinizing Ash.

"You look like shit," he pronounces.

"Back at you, old man."

"You're shivering."

"I got dunked in the ocean and have been running in the rain ever since. What do you expect?"

Ben searches for the right words. They all look like shit. Hell, they all *feel* like shit.

But Ash is looking worse than shitty. She's looking like shit to the power of three.

"I just want to make sure you're okay," he says at last.

She gives him a sidelong look. "I think that's the nicest thing you've ever said to me."

"Nice isn't my go-to."

"I don't know why. You're a good person." She coughs, hunching over as she runs. "I remind myself of that every time I want to tell you to go fuck yourself."

"That happens a lot?"

She coughs again. "What?"

"That you want to tell me to go fuck myself?"

She chuckles. "Not as much since you started chasing Kate around. She brings out your nice side."

He decides not to comment on that. Apparently everyone in Creekside knows about his infatuation. He has no doubt they'll all soon know the color of his underwear, too. If they ever make it back.

"So where are you chafing?" Ash asks.

He grunts, deciding not to comment on that, either.

"Thought so," she replies with a knowing look. "If it makes you feel better, I have chafing down there, too. The inside seam of the shorts. And I think the skin under my sports bra is rubbed raw."

"The saltwater stings like a son-of-bitch." The crusty white deposits all over his clothing make everything worse.

"Gives a whole new meaning to rubbing salt in a wound,

huh?" Another shiver runs over Ash's body. "You know, as shitty as I feel, I actually like it out here. No zombies."

"No zombies *yet*," Ben corrects. "Kate said there are some campgrounds farther down the trail."

"You know what I mean. There are no piles of dead bodies. No stink. We don't have to whisper and look over our shoulders for fear of drawing zombies."

"We just have to watch the tide so we don't get swept out to sea."

"I'll take the tide over zombies any day." She glances over at him. "Would you rather drown to death or get eaten by a zombie?"

He considers his answer. Honestly, he doesn't really care how he goes. When it's his time, it's his time. "I just want my death to mean something when it happens."

"You don't want to die of natural causes as an old man?"

"I'm not sure any of us are slated for death by old age."

"That's negative thinking. I'd rather drown in the ocean than get eaten by a zom. I don't ever want to be one of those things."

"Would you rather get bitten by a zombie, or by a shark, like Gary?"

"That's a fucked-up question, Ben."

He'd been *trying* to be sociable. He doesn't see how his question is any worse than her question. This is what he gets for trying to make civil conversation. Every response that comes to his head isn't pleasant, so he keeps his mouth shut.

Ash gives him another sidelong look. "I'd rather get eaten by a shark. At least my death would nourish another living creature. Anything is better than feeding the undead."

They lapse into silence after that. Ben stays near her, doing his best to keep an eye on her without being obvious. She's sucking it up, but she still looks like shit. And she keeps coughing.

The ground beneath their feet is becoming muddier by the minute. Ben has mud splashed up to his knees. His clothes are damp and encrusted with salt. The salt makes his clothing rough.

The chafing gets worse by the minute. He also feels it starting to burn on the inside of his upper arms, too. He steels himself against his discomfort when he sees Ash shivering.

"We should stop," he says. "Build you a fire."

She shakes her head. "It's still raining."

"We can still build a fire."

"We both know I need more than a wet fire."

Ben doesn't reply. He doesn't know what to say. It's obvious Ash has hypothermia. He's known it for the past few miles but doesn't know what to do about it.

"Even if we do stop, we barely have any food," she continues. "We can't afford to stop."

"I don't know if you can afford *not* to stop." Ben looks farther up the trail. Kate plows up another rise in the land.

Ash follows his gaze. "I can hold on. Please don't say anything. I don't want anyone to suffer or die because of me." She puts her chin down and keeps running.

Ben doesn't want Ash to die. He scans the landscape, looking for any place that might offer enough shelter for them to build a fire and get warm. Hell, he wouldn't mind a fire right about now. Or a break.

"You should tell her how you feel," Ash says.

Ben grunts. He wants to pretend he doesn't know what Ash is talking about, but what's the point? "She knows."

Ash looks at him. Her lips are pale, her cheeks a fleshy white. "You should tell her again." Her teeth chatter. "If we die out here, you don't want the words to go unsaid."

Ben has nothing to say to that.

58

PAIN CAVE

KATE

I don't let them stop. Even though fatigue is in every line of their faces. Even though their shoulders droop and their steps are sluggish. Even though Reed can't get his stomach under control and staggers along like an animated doll, barely able to keep water down.

Things are only going to get worse. Our only hope is to get the hell off this trail. Off this trail, and into a house where we can get everyone warm and dry.

My people stretch out in a line behind me, laboring up a long climb as rain drizzles down. I shine my headlamp down the trail behind me, conducting a quick count to confirm I haven't lost anyone. My gaze flicks over Ben as he power hikes with Ash at the back of the pack.

Worry for our situation helps me ignore how conflicted I feel about Ben. I don't know if turning him down was the smartest or dumbest thing I've ever done. It's easier not to think about it.

Caleb is the nearest to me. His shoulders are hunched, his face set in a grimace of discomfort as he pushes up a hill.

I drop back to check on him. "Hey, Caleb."

"Hey." Caleb braces his hands against his thighs, using them to help leverage himself up the long climb. "I can't believe you did this shit for fun. It sucks ass."

Sweat drips down his temples, mingling with the rain. His breathing is labored, fogging against the cold air. The hair on his legs is stuck full of trail flotsam: burrs, foxtails, cuts from the thistles, and ... damn.

"Hold up, Caleb. There's a tick on your leg." The tiny black bug is nestled right above his sock. I crouch down and pick it off, squishing it between my fingers.

His grimace deepens. "You look like you've done that before."

"A few times, yeah. I've already picked two off myself." I give the rest of his legs a quick check. "All clear. I don't see any more."

He continues to labor up the trail. "Does this fucking thing have a top?" he demands. "I think my legs are going to fall off."

I recognize his state. It happens to everyone in an ultra. He's in the pain cave, a place of mental and physical misery. So much of ultrarunning is a head game. I need to figure out a way to pull him out of his funk.

"I didn't tell you guys the truth about the southern half of the Lost Coast," I say.

"What's that?"

"It has over ten thousand feet of vertical climbing."

"Is that a lot?"

I chuckle. "Oh, yeah. On a scale of one to five, one being easy and five being difficult, the southern half of the Lost Coast is a six. That's good news for you."

He snorts. "How so?"

"It means you'll have major bragging rights when we finish. Like, pound-your-fist-on-your-chest kind of bragging rights."

All that gets is a grunt. We plow up the hill side by side. I wrack my brain, trying to think of something else to distract him.

"If you could eat one thing right now, what would it be?" I ask.

"Medium-rare prime rib with a mountain of horseradish," he replies without hesitation. "I haven't had decent beef since the start of the apocalypse."

We haven't had any fresh meat in months. "I think I'd have chicken," I say. "One of those rotisserie ones stuffed with rosemary, lemon, and garlic. Now that we have a wall at Creekside, we should find some chickens."

"I'd rather have a cow or two."

"Okay. Let's see what we can figure out."

"Can I tell you something?" His voice comes out with a wheeze. "I'm pissed off at you for not making us run more stairs. Like, really pissed."

"Really?" I wipe rain out of my eyes. "That can be arranged when we get back to Arcata."

That gets a small smile out of him. "I hate stair repeats. Can I tell you something else?"

"What?"

"I'm so fucking hungry that I'm considering eating some of these plants. I'm trying to imagine the ferns are miniature green cows."

I understand the feeling. Hunger grates at me as well. "We'll have an M&M stop soon."

"Sorry if the idea of five M&Ms doesn't excite me all that much. Can I tell you something else?"

"Sure."

"You know the only reason Ben swam to shore to get gas for the *Fairhaven* is because he was afraid you'd do it? The man can barely dog paddle. He had no business swimming in Humboldt Bay."

The switch in conversation catches me by surprise. It feels

weird to talk about Ben, but it's worth it to keep Caleb's mind off his misery. "It's not a good idea. Me and Ben, I mean."

"He likes you. You like him. What more do you need?"

"Sanity."

Caleb chuckles, his face relaxing with mirth. "Well, I'm probably not the only one who thinks he's not good enough for you, but I know he'd die for you. Probably with a smile on his face. Hell, he stripped down into holey underwear for you. From a man's perspective, that's worse than taking a bullet for someone. He's got it bad for you, Kate."

I'd hardly noticed his underwear. I'd been too busy trying not to notice how good the rest of him looked.

More rainwater drips into my eyes. Flicking it away, I think of my tiny dorm room, every inch of wall and ceiling covered with pictures of nature. Regret and longing once again flicker through me.

"Why are you telling me all this? You and Ben don't even like each other."

Caleb's face goes stony. "I like him just fine. He's the one who doesn't like me." An anguished look flashes across his features. "He has good reason. I fucked up and people died. I figure that maybe if I put in a good word for him, maybe he'll forgive me someday."

I don't know what to say to that. Caleb looks even more morose and miserable than he did when I first joined him. I need to change the subject and find a way to perk him up. The Lost Coast will eat him for lunch if I can't help him shift his mindset.

"What about you and Ash? She cares about you, you know."

That brings Caleb to a standstill in the middle of the trail. He looks from me to Ash, who labors away behind us with Ben at her side.

"How do you know that? Did she say something to you?"

"No. But I see the way she looks at you when you're not glued to her side."

Caleb resumes his power hike. "I messed things up with her."

"How so?"

"Johnson sent me on an errand. Turns out it was just an excuse to get me away from Ash. By the time I got back, he'd cornered her in a bedroom of the frat house ... Ash was fighting back, but it wasn't pretty. Johnson laughed the whole thing off when I showed up. Ash ... things were never the same with her after that."

"Is that why you guys sleep with your bedroom door open every night?"

He nods. "I don't ever want her to feel cornered." The agonized look he gives me has nothing to do with the pain of the trail. "You know I'd do anything for her, right? I'm not asking for anything in return."

The pieces snap together. The restrained closeness between Ash and Caleb finally makes sense. The way they're always together, yet never touching.

"Not that I'm a relationship expert, but I'd say sooner or later you're going to have to let go of that guilt."

"Maybe." Caleb looks back again at Ash. "You really think she has feelings for me?"

"I'd bet on it. But you won't know for sure until you talk to her."

"Let's make a pact. You agree to talk to Ben, and I'll agree to talk to Ash."

"No."

"No? Come on! You just said—"

"This isn't a negotiation, Caleb. I can't go there."

"Whatever, Mama Bear. You—hey, look!" He plants his hands on his hips, staring past the waist-high shrubs that grow along this part of the trail. "We made it to the top."

Sure enough, our feet have carried us to the top of the long incline. The foggy coastline snakes along below us, illuminated by the moon and stars. The water is a frothy gray.

I take in Caleb's posture. The hunch of pain is gone. The twisted expression has been replaced with a smile. I give his shoulder a squeeze.

"Nice work."

"Thanks, Mama Bear."

I leave Caleb to run the forthcoming downhill on his own, dropping farther back down the trail to check on Eric. He's near the top, slogging his way up with gritty determination. His arms are covered with scrapes from the thistle bushes. If possible, his leg hairs have even more burrs and foxtails than Caleb's.

"Hey." I fall into step beside him. I give him a once over to check for ticks. "How's it going?" No visible signs of ticks.

"I keep reminding myself that it sucked to be fat," Eric replies. "Even if this hill sucks, at least it's keeping me skinny. Oh, and the fact that we have, like, half a granola bar to split among seven people."

"Don't forget the M&Ms. And there's still one stick of beef jerky left."

"You probably shouldn't have told me that. I'm considering mugging you right now."

Eric's sense of humor is enough to tell me he's in a good headspace. "Think you can take me?"

"You are pretty skinny."

"But I'm faster than you."

"True." Eric chuckles. "How far do you think we've gone?"

I glance at my watch. We left the beach four hours ago. We've had to stop at least seven times for Reed. I try to pick up the pace on the flat sections, but my people are chilled by the rain. Their muscles are stiff with the new demands the trail puts on them. I doubt we've even gone fifteen miles. Which means we have ten to twelve miles to go.

"Maybe thirteen or fourteen miles," I reply.

Eric perks up. His glasses are spotted with rain, but he doesn't bother trying to wipe them dry. "That means I've done my first half marathon. That's thirteen miles, right?"

"Thirteen-point-one miles."

"Hey, that's cool. I always wanted to run a half marathon." His face sobers. "Lila used to ridicule me for that. Back before the world ended, we'd hang out in the hallway and trade insults. Well, it wasn't exactly hanging out, but you know what I mean."

For the first time in a long while, thinking of Lila makes me smile. "I can imagine it. It took me a while to realize you both enjoyed bickering."

"She used to tell me to lay off the crack pipe and lose some weight if I ever wanted to run more than ten feet." Eric taps his now-flat stomach. "I wish she was here. I mean, not *here*. She'd hate it out here. The forest would definitely not be her happy place. Not like it is for you."

"Is it that obvious?" I know how miserable it is for all of them out here. Hell, it's not like I'm comfortable, but my discomfort is overridden by my love for the trail and my long time away from it.

"You're keeping it under wraps, but I know you, Mama Bear." Eric winks. "Happiness is practically oozing out of you. Well, maybe not happiness. You're just in your element. That's all I mean. Even more so than when we're on the track or running for our lives through Arcata."

A soft laugh bubbles out of me. "I'm glad I don't look like I'm having my own personal party." I sober. "Eric, I'm sorry."

"For what? For wanting to rescue Alvarez?" He shrugs. "You didn't force any of us to come. He's our friend, too."

"Not that. I mean Lila. It's my fault she went outside that day. If I hadn't been pushing her to leave Creekside—"

"Stop, Kate." Eric holds up a hand. "It's not your fault." He looks down at his feet as he splashes through a puddle. "We both know Lila wasn't cut out for the apocalypse. It was only a matter of time."

"We don't know that—"

"I do." Eric looks at me, but all I can see is the water smearing his glasses. "I cared about Lila. A lot. But I always knew she wouldn't make it for the long haul."

Hearing him say that makes me wish for a big, giant do-over. There must have been something I could have done differently to help Lila. I refuse to believe her fate was predetermined.

Our feet splash in the wetness pooling on the trail.

"I miss her," Eric says. "Finding her recipe book was like ..." He makes a choking sound.

I wait in silence. The ocean pounds away in the background, ever present.

Eric recovers himself. "I'm going to keep part of her alive. When I get back to Creekside, I'm going to start making her recipes." He draws in a deep breath that has nothing to do with physical exertion. "My mom was a recipe blogger. Did I ever tell you that?"

"No, you didn't."

"Yeah. She specialized in recipes you could cook in under thirty minutes. She used a lot of processed food. Which I didn't realize was scary until I moved to Humboldt and got assaulted with propaganda on organic whole foods. I think Mom had five different casseroles you could make with a can of Campbell's Cream of Mushroom soup." He chuckles. "Anyway, I feel like I can pay tribute to both of them in my own way if I keep Lila's recipes alive. Although Mom wouldn't like it if she knew about the pot. Even if it is for medicinal purposes. Did I ever tell you about my first night of the apocalypse?"

I shake my head. I've made it a point not to ask people

about that. If I don't want to talk about my experience, why would I think anyone else wants to?

"I was so stoned," Eric says. "Like, majorly stoned. I got my hands on a new hybrid ... never mind. Anyway, I thought it would be fun to take mushrooms while I was stoned. I had just finished three batches of brownies to trade for three term papers and wanted to celebrate." He grins to himself, lost in a happy memory. "I thought these two zombies were hot chicks. They had on low-cut tanks tops and super short skirts. They looked scary but I thought that was just the combination of mushrooms and pot. I was trying to work up the nerve to hit on them. Then they started eating this guy and I thought my mushrooms were totally taking the wheel. Then Carter and Reed found me."

Despite the fact that I'm freezing my ass off, wet from head to toe, and hungry enough to eat raw seaweed, I laugh. I laugh so hard I double over.

It's not funny. Not really. People died. A lot of people. But somehow Eric's description makes me laugh.

He grins at me. "Who would have thought that being a chicken shit with girls would save my life? If you think that story is funny, I could tell you so many more."

Eric rattles on, spinning a long story about a high school crush, a botched attempt to get a prom date, and a faulty soda machine. I escape into the conversation, grateful to have my own distraction from the cold, wet, relentless trail.

59

CONFESSION

BEN

"There's something I want to tell you." Ash's voice rattles out through her chattering teeth. Ben wishes he had a jacket or a blanket or anything warm to put over her shoulders.

"We can talk later," he says. "Don't waste your energy."

"No." Ash shakes her head. The ocean crashes, a constant hum in the background as they run. "I should have told you a long time ago."

"It's waited this long."

"Stop arguing with me, *anaciano casacarrabias*."

He has no idea what she just said, but he can hazard a guess. Ash often flips into Spanish when she insults someone.

"Do you remember that day when Carrie and Melissa went missing?"

"Yeah." How could he forget it? Those two girls snuck out of College Creek while everyone slept. Their note said they were going to the dorms on the north side of campus to see if they could find food.

Ben knew it was a lie. They'd been afraid of Johnson. They'd run away.

Johnson had known it, too. He had a thing for Melissa. The way he'd looked at her left no doubt in Ben's mind what he intended, and it wasn't flowers and a romantic stroll.

"I looked for them," he tells Ash. "After the massacre. When I went my own way. I scoured the north side of campus for any sign of them." That was how he'd found Kate and the others at Creekside, though he hadn't revealed himself to them at the time. He'd been hell bent on tracking down Johnson and killing him. "Ash, I don't know what happened to them, but if they made it to the north side of campus, I never found them."

He'd even looked for their bodies among the undead. The girls weren't cut out to survive. They were scared of everything and didn't know the first thing about taking care of themselves. Hell, Carrie admitted to having never done her own laundry until moving away to college, and half the time she just took everything to the dry cleaner and paid to have it washed.

"They never made it to the north side of campus," Ash whispers. "They tried to sneak away. I was keeping watch at the time. Johnson caught them."

Ben grinds his teeth. He wants to plug his ears, but there's no escape.

"Johnson and Ryan." Ash swallows. "They caught Carrie and Melissa as they tried to sneak away. I—" She stops, a cough wracking her body.

"I asked you," Ben says. "The next morning when we realized they were missing. I asked you if you saw anything."

"I lied." Ash doesn't look at him. "I'm sorry, Ben. I was so fucking scared of Johnson. The only reason he didn't try to touch me in the beginning is because he knew I could defend myself. But it was only a matter of time."

"What happened to Carrie and Melissa?" Ben demands.

Ash dissolves into another round of coughs. She looks worse than ever, though this time Ben doesn't think it has anything to do with the hypothermia.

"I have never been so scared as when I was living in that *maldita* frat house with all those boys. I'd face a hundred zombies before I'd put myself through that again. Caleb did his best to shield me." Her face crumples. "But he couldn't be with me every second of the day. Johnson made sure of that."

Ben wants to hit something. "What did that fucker do?"

"Not as much as he wanted to do. But a lot more than I wanted." Her face is wet with rain, but Ben doesn't miss the tears snaking down her cheeks. "Johnson and Ryan killed Carrie and Melissa. They caught the girls and dragged them to the library. I—I found their bodies. They'd been raped before Johnson and Ryan killed them." She chokes on a sob. "I didn't do anything to stop them. I could have told you. I could have intervened, but I was a coward."

Something inside Ben cracks open.

God dammit. He'd known. In his gut, he'd known Johnson and Ryan had done something to those girls. The tally in his head goes up. Instead of sixteen kids on his conscious, he now has eighteen.

"Why are you telling me this?" His voice comes down like a hammer. He couldn't hold his anger back even if he tried.

"I'm sorry I lied to you that day," Ash whispers. "If I'd told you the truth—if I hadn't been a coward—I could have saved the rest of the students. If I'd told you the truth, you could have gotten the rest of them away. You could have taken them to Creekside, to Kate—" Her voice breaks. She stops in the middle of the trail, body convulsing with shivers. "It's my fault all those students died," she gasps.

Ben has no words. He'd failed Ash. That was the simple truth. He'd seen the fear in her eyes when he questioned her about the disappearance of Melissa and Carrie. He'd suspected she knew more than she let on.

Yet he had done nothing.

Every day he'd stood by and done nothing. He'd been in

denial as to how dangerous Johnson was. He'd stood by with his thumb up his ass and all those kids had been slaughtered.

Anger and self-loathing boil up within him. He can't speak. He doesn't know how to tell Ash how very, very sorry he is.

"Ben," Ash murmurs. "I just wanted you to know the truth. Don't hate Caleb for something I did."

Her knees buckle. Ben catches her as she falls.

60

OLD FRIEND

KATE

"Kate!" Ben's bellow grinds me to a halt in the middle of the trail.

I spin around and find him running toward me, Ash clutched to his chest. She's unconscious, her body flopping with his cadence. Caleb tears down the trail back in their direction.

Hypothermia. The word flashes through my mind. The wet. The cold. The exhaustion. It's gotten the better of Ash.

"We need a fire," Ben shouts. "Right fucking now."

I spin on my heel, taking in the soaking trees, the soaking trail, and the soaking ferns. Rain continues to patter down from the sky. The fog sits low against the land, compounding the dampness.

Caleb takes Ash's limp body. Ben sprints toward me. "Fire," he shouts again. "We're going to lose her if we don't get fire."

"There's nothing to burn," Eric whispers, face riveted on Ash and Caleb. "Everything's wet."

Something in me hardens. No way am I going to let Ash die.

"We burn a tree down if we have to," I snap. So what if our

world is drenched in water? So what if we have no food and are on the brink of running out of water? "Whatever it takes. We get a fire started."

Eric wipes at the water on his glasses, eyes wide. "Come on, Reed," he cries, bolting off the trail and into the greenery. "We need to find a place to start a fire!"

Thirty minutes later, our party crouches inside a tight ring of Douglas firs a quarter mile off the trail. The ground beneath the trees is the only piece of relatively dry land we've found since emerging from the ocean.

Our fire is pathetic. Finding dry wood has been a joke. The only thing we've been able to burn are pine needles.

"Come on, girl," Caleb murmurs, his face twisted in anguish. "You've survived worse. A little cold isn't gonna get the best of you."

He's stripped out of his wet shirt, his bare chest pressed to Ash's back. She's been stripped to the waist, in nothing but her sports bra. The sight of the chafe marks under her armpits and along the bottom of her sports bra makes me wince. The salt in the clothing has been brutal on all of us, but somehow it all looks worse on Ash. Her arms and legs are covered with tiny cuts from the thistle patches we pushed through.

"Shit." Ben leaps to his feet, stalking out of our shelter. He marches up to a young pine tree, running his hands over the wood. "Fuck me. I can't believe I didn't see these earlier."

"What is it?" I join him at the tree.

He pulls out his knife and begins prying out a section of bark. "See these?" He points to a few dried white streaks on the outside of the bark.

"Bird poop?"

"No. Dried sap. See these bumps in the bark? They're filled with sap. My old man showed me how to make fires with bark like this when he took me camping as a kid."

Realization dawns. Tree sap. It's flammable. With sudden

hope filling me, I yank out my knife and also begin prying up a section of bark.

In less than two minutes, we have two large handfuls of bark. We rush back to the shelter.

"Everyone, get back," Ben orders. He begins snapping the bark into smaller pieces, revealing small, gooey pockets of sap.

I've never seen Ben so focused. He crouches before the small pile of burning pine needles, holding a raw edge of bark over the flames. Within several seconds, the sap ignites.

"No way! How did you do that?" Reed gapes.

"Tree sap," I explain. "Ben's idea. Go find some more bark like this." I hand Reed a sample from my harvest with Ben.

He wordlessly takes the bark. With a nod at Eric and Susan, the three of them hurry into the rain to find more bark.

Ben stares at the fire with fixed intensity, steadily feeding it larger pieces of sap-infused bark. He also throws handfuls of pine needles onto it, sending up huge puffs of smoke and steam every time he does. Eric, Reed, and Susan return with another armload of bark.

I kneel on one side of Ash, working my hands up and down her bare arms in an attempt to warm them. Caleb rubs her stomach, trying to do the same. Every part of her is damp and chill, her skin sickly white.

Susan, Reed, and Eric all strip out of their running shirts and have pulled extras out of their packs. They hold the pieces of clothing over our fire, trying to dry them so Ash and Caleb can use them as blankets. Ben curses under his breath, worried eyes constantly flicking to Ash.

If this had been a real ultra, Ash would be in a medic tent right now. That's what happened to me at the JFK fifty-miler when I got hypothermia. A thunderstorm had shown up at the start of that race and decided to stick around for the duration.

By the time I staggered to the finish line, I hadn't been in much better shape than Ash. The race director put the medal around my neck and hustled me off to the medic tent, where I spent the next five hours. They packed hot water bottles around me, layered me with blankets ...

Wait. Water bottles.

I snatch my pack off the ground and stare at the water bladder inside.

"Does anyone have a pot or something we can heat water in?" I ask.

"I have a collapsible metal bowl in my pack." Reed dives into his pack, rummaging inside. He produces the bowl and pops it open.

"Figure out a way to hold it over the fire," I tell him. "We're going to heat water." I stand, grabbing the running packs dumped in a pile on the ground. The bladders inside all need to be filled.

Ben looks at me sharply. "Where are you going?"

"Water. We need to heat water and put it in our bladders and pack them around Ash. Maybe get some hot water into her."

"You can't go out there alone," he says with a scowl.

I scowl right back. "There are no zombies out here. Hell, there are no *people* out here. You need to focus on the fire. Get it nice and hot. The rest of you, keep drying out clothing. And figure out a way to suspend that bowl over the fire."

I turn my back on Ben, ending the conversation. I march out from beneath the trees before anyone else can argue with me.

In my head, I retrace the route we'd taken to get here. About a half-mile back, we crossed a swollen creek that came up to my knees. That's where I'm going to get water.

I take off at a run, charging through the water-laden grasses that grow close to the coast. I dodge around trees and clumps of thistles, making a mental note to check everyone for ticks again when I get back.

What's wrong with me? Why am I worried about ticks when Ash's life is on the line?

I shake my head, struggling to get my emotions in order. I can't slip now. My kids need me.

I burst through a clump of fennel and clear a mess of cobwebs out of my face. The trail looms in front of me, a muddy track stretching to the left and right.

"Finally." I leap onto the dirt path and take off at a sprint, my headlamp illuminating my way.

It's the fastest I've moved since first setting foot on this trail. It doesn't take long before I realize just how depleted I am. Between the near-miss with the ocean, the stress of all the events leading up to the shipwreck, and the short supply of food and water, I'm wasted. My body is sluggish, refusing to move as fast as I know it can move.

Ash. Ash. I say her name over and over in my head. I charge through puddles. Mud and water fly up, soaking me all the way to the waist. *Ash.*

I hear the creek before I see it. I tear around a corner and drop to my knees at the bank. My cold, wet fingers fumble with the first bladder. The plastic opening keeps slipping in my grasp. My fingers are too numb to grip properly.

"Dammit!" I hurl the bladder to the ground in frustration, breath rasping.

Ash.

Tears sting my eyes. I got her into this mess. I can't fail her.

I snatch up a bladder and flip it upside down, pinching the seal between my knees. This time, when I pull at the plastic, the opening slides free.

I push the first bladder into the water. The creek is flowing so fast it almost rips it out of my hands.

Crouched there on the side of the bank, alone in the rain, it all comes crashing down on me.

The helplessness of our situation. The fact that I have six

green runners in my care and that I'm trying to keep them alive on one of the toughest trails on the west coast. The odds are stacked against us, and no matter what I do, things just keep getting worse.

My breath quickens. I swallow back tears. Now is not the time for self-pity.

Something moves on the far side of the bank. I blink, trying to clear water out of my eyes. The world is blurry from all the rain, which seems to be coming down harder than ever before. Just great.

I fill the rest of the bags, wondering if there's a way to warm the water inside without melting the plastic. Reed's bowl won't fill more than one liter of water at a time. That's not fast enough. It—

I see movement a second time. My chin jerks up.

An animal materializes on the other side of the bank, staring at me. He stands about a foot and a half high—if you don't count the antlers. The elegant set of antlers sits like a crown on his furry brown head.

"Hola, chica." The jackalope cocks his head at me, watching as I fill the water bladder.

I lick dry lips, queasy at the sight of him. The fact that my old nemesis is here tells me exactly how stressed and exhausted I am. The last time I saw him, I'd run over a hundred miles and lost my best friend. I haven't even gone twenty-five miles, yet here he is.

Hallucinations aren't unusual on an ultra. Now that I think about it, I have been up for nearly twenty-four hours. I've been shot at. Shipwrecked. Nearly drowned. Then forced to grind away on a trail for hours in the rain without proper food and water. No wonder I'm seeing things.

I finish filling the water bladder, all the while ignoring him. When I finish, I get to my feet and turn my back on the hallucination.

"Don't rip off my antlers," the jackalope says, then leaps over the creek and lands beside me. I flinch away from him, running back down the trail.

There's no way to drop a hallucination. He hops along beside me, not even breaking a sweat. The little fucker isn't even wet.

Of course, he's not wet. He's not even here. He's a figment of my imagination.

"Go away," I snarl.

"You need me," the jackalope says.

"I don't need you."

"Do you remember that time you worked the aid station at Bryce Canyon and a thunderstorm hit?"

"I don't have time for this!" I scream, clutching the bladders to my chest.

I spin on my heel and keep running, retracing my steps back toward our camp.

"Fine. Whatever," he shouts after me. "Just don't forget what happened to your canopy."

My mind races back to a time when the world was normal, when the most I had to worry about was getting injured on a training run or making sure Carter did his homework.

My memory hurtles me back to the reddish-brown landscape of Bryce Canyon, a national park in the state of Utah. The towering cliffs and sweeping vistas of that place were nothing short of magical.

I was supposed to run the hundred-miler with Frederico, but a bad fall on the trail a few weeks before had left me with a broken wrist. Rather than stay home and sulk, I volunteered to work one of the aid stations. Little did I know one of the biggest storms of the season was headed straight for us.

The late spring storm had been brutal. Rain. Hail. More rain. I spent the day ladling out soup to soaked, muddy runners with chattering teeth. The worst part had been at two in the morning when our aid station canopy, laden with water from the storms, had tipped over—

I grind to a halt, mind racing.

Yes. The canopy. Water had collected in the canvas. It created a giant bowl.

"That's it," I breathe. I snap my head around, searching.

The jackalope is gone. All I see is the rain and trees.

It doesn't matter. I know what to do. I know how to save Ash.

61

HOT WATER

BEN

He alternates between swearing at the fire, worrying about Ash, scanning the area for signs of Kate's return, then swearing some more.

"I think this shirt is finally dry." Eric moves around the fire and drapes it over Ash and Caleb.

"More wood," Ben says. "We need more wood."

Eric turns without a word, leaving their makeshift shelter to search for more logs. With the help of the sap-filled bark, they have a decent fire going. They can feed it regular logs now so long as they aren't too sodden.

"Come on, girl," Caleb murmurs, rocking Ash in his arms. "You're too strong to give up now. You didn't make it through hell to die like a deer in the woods."

Ben feeds another log to the fire. It's wet. Not soaking, but wet enough that it sizzles and sends up a gush of steam as soon as it hits the flames.

The interior of the fire is burning steadily. What he needs now is a poker to break apart the logs and expose the coals within. That's the best place to put the new logs.

He casts about the dark shelter of the trees, searching for a branch that can be used as a poker.

There's nothing. Everything serviceable has already been fed to the fire.

He spots a Douglas fir tree twenty yards east. Eric crouches beneath the boughs, picking up pieces of wood.

"Be right back," Ben says.

Reed and Susan glance at him. Caleb never looks up, continuing to rock Ash back and forth.

"I need a long branch," Ben tells Eric as he arrives at the Douglas fir. "Something that can be used as a poker."

"Like this?" Eric extracts a branch from the stack in his arms. It's a sturdy piece of wood two inches thick and three feet long, the length covered with green lichen.

"That'll work. Give me what you've collected so far."

"It's kind of dry," Eric says, passing the bundle of wood to Ben.

"Good work. Find more."

Back at the fire, he uses the branch to stoke the fire. The larger logs break apart, exposing orange-yellow coals. The newest log catches fire, long tongues of flame licking upward.

Perfect. Ben moves around the fire, adding more logs to all sides. Within fifteen minutes, the fire has doubled in size. Heat roils off it in steaming puffs.

"Nice work." Reed fans steam and smoke out of his eyes. He fiddles with the bowl, attempting to tie a fresh sapling around it to create a holder.

It'll never work, but Ben doesn't say this. From the look of anguish on Reed's face, it's better if the kid has something to preoccupy his thoughts.

At least Susan is doing something productive. She stands next to the fire, a shirt in each hand as she dries them over the flames. It's slow work, but Ash already has two other shirts draped over her.

Where the hell is Kate? He peers into the drizzly gloom. There's no sign of her anywhere.

He does his best to ignore the knot of anxiety forming in his chest. Kate is more than capable of taking care of herself. Hell, she made it all the way to Arcata without his help and she'd been alone for much of the time.

None of this makes him feel any better. He should have gone with her. How long has it been? At least thirty minutes, probably more. How long does it take to get water?

The wait is killing him. He straightens, intending to go search for her. There's nothing else he can do with the fire right now. Besides, maybe he can find some more dry wood while he's looking for Kate. Anything is better than standing around watching Ash struggle. It's more than he can take.

Just as he turns to exit the shelter, Kate bursts into view. She runs hard through the brush, juggling five hydration bladders in her arms.

"Take off your shirt," she yells as soon as she sees him.

"What?"

"The shirt. Your shirt. Take it off," she orders.

He doesn't ask questions. He would have added it to the blanket efforts if it wasn't so thick and would take too long to dry. From the urgency in Kate's face, he knows she has a plan. Hell if he's going to get in the way of that.

He peels off his damp fatigue shirt as Kate dashes into the shelter. She sees the blazing fire and nods in approval.

"Where's Eric?" she asks.

"I'm here." Eric hurries into the shelter, cradling an armload of wood.

"You three." She points a finger at Ben, Reed, and Eric. "I want you each to grab a corner of Ben's shirt. Hold it over the fire." She sets her pile of bladders on the ground, pausing only long enough to press a hand to Ash's forehead. "Hang on, girl," she murmurs.

Caleb lifts anguished eyes to her. Kate gives his shoulder a squeeze. "Keep doing what you're doing."

As she grabs one water bladder and approaches the fire, Ben suddenly understands what her plan is.

Kate empties the full bladder of water onto the shirt. The camouflage fabric bows downward, creating a bowl above the flames. A few droplets sizzle down into the flames, but the majority of the liquid remains trapped in the tight weave of the shirt.

"Fucking brilliant." Admiration washes through him.

Kate flashes him a quick smile before turning a worried frown back in Ash's direction. "It hasn't worked yet."

No one says anything. They all stare at the water in the center of Ben's shirt.

"A watched pot never boils," Eric says, breaking the silence.

"This isn't a pot," Ben says, right as Kate says, "We don't want it to boil. We just need to warm it up enough so we can fill the bladders back up and put them next to Ash's skin."

"The fire is helping," Caleb says. "Her stomach is finally starting to warm up." He runs a hand up one of her arms. "Her arms too."

Twenty minutes later, Kate holds the first bladder of warm water out to Caleb. He sandwiches it between his chest and Ash's back, never loosening his desperate grip on the young woman in his arms.

Kate grabs the next bladder and empties it into the shirt. "One down," she murmurs.

"How did you think of this?" Reed asks.

"You wouldn't believe me if I told you."

"Oh, now you have to tell us," Eric says. "You can't get cryptic on us."

Kate stares into the flames, not answering.

"Mama," Reed wheedles.

She gives him a small smile. "My imaginary friend helped me out."

Ben can't keep his mouth shut any longer. "Your *what?*"

"My imaginary friend. He visited me while I was filling the water bladders and told me how I could heat the water."

If her face wasn't dead serious, and if Ben didn't know her as well as he did, he would say she was full of shit. But Kate doesn't spin fancy stories. She doesn't lie, either.

"Do you guys know what a jackalope is?"

Ben listens in astonishment as she tells them about a rabbit with antlers that appears to her in times of great physical stress. She tells them about the time she ran some crazy race in Death Valley in the middle of the summer. That was the first time the jackalope appeared.

Then she tells them about her thirty-mile journey through the Avenue of the Giants. It's the first time Ben has ever heard her share details of her two-hundred-mile trek from her hometown to Arcata. Johnny would be out of his fucking mind right now if he was here.

She shares a story of ripping off the antlers of her imaginary jackalope and drop-kicking the little beast into the woods. Eric's eyes bug behind his glasses when she tells this part. Ben is pretty sure his eyes might be bugging a little, too.

At some point on her trek through the Avenue of the Giants, she and the little creature had made up. The jackalope helped Kate say goodbye to her husband and her best friend. She stares into the fire as she speaks, not bothering to wipe away the few tears that leak down her cheeks.

Ben feels fissures crack open inside him as Kate talks. He feels her pain. It echoes so much of what he carries around.

"That," Reed proclaims when Kate finishes talking, "is the weirdest fucking thing I've ever heard."

Kate shrugs. "I hate that little fucker. But he's been there when I needed him. He's helping us save Ash."

"Is he still here?" Ben frowns out into the darkness, as though he might find a horned rabbit staring back at him.

"No. He left right after he delivered his message."

"Does he have a name?" Eric asks.

"No. He's just the jackalope. That was Frederico's nickname for me for years."

No one says anything. They all know about Frederico. She's talked about him more in the last ten minutes than she has in all the months Ben has known her.

"Eric is right," Caleb says. "We need to name him. I think he may have saved Ash's life. Her skin is really warming up now."

Kate sticks her finger into the water balancing over the fire. "This batch is almost ready. We can keep rotating the bladders and make sure they stay warm."

"We're naming the jackalope," Reed declares. "How about Randy?"

"*Randy?*" Ben furrows his brow.

"I don't know. It just came into my head."

"That's a stupid-ass name," Eric says. "How about Hopper?"

"*Hopper?*" Ben scowls across the fire. He hadn't realized it could get any worse than Randy, but it just did.

"Creekside?"

Every head in the clearing jerks around. Ash's eyes are slits as she blinks blearily.

"You're awake." Kate kneels next to her, running a hand over the younger woman's forehead and arm. "You're warmer."

"I want to name your jackalope," Ash murmurs, voice slurred. "He saved my life."

As Kate gazes down at Ash, every line of her body says just how much she cares about her people. The curve of her cheek as she smiles. The gentle hand on Ash's forearm. The line of her back as she leans in to kiss Ash's forehead.

Ben can't take his eyes off her. He never knew it was possible for one person to care so much about others. It radiates off Kate in waves. It's the most beautiful fucking thing he's ever seen.

Kate sits back, smiling at Ash. "I'll give you the privilege of naming my imaginary friend."

"Creekside," Ash whispers. "His name is Creekside. He got you to us in Arcata. He's our guardian spirit."

"Creekside," Caleb echoes. "That's a great name."

Kate stiffens, her eyes traveling past Ash and Caleb. Ben's hand flies to the gun holstered at his side. He flips up the safety strap and slides it out.

He stares past Kate, trying to see whatever it is that she sees. He scans the clump of lupine bushes that sag in the rain, purple flowers bowed under the unending barrage. He scans the knee-high brush and the tight knot of trees that shelters them.

Then Kate does something unusual. Mouth twisting into a grimace, she extends one middle finger into the air.

Everyone stares at her in shock.

Then Reed bursts out laughing. "He's here, isn't he?"

"Yes." Kate turns her back on the empty space of air she just flipped off.

"Creekside?" Eric says. "Really?" He squints at the empty space behind Ash and Caleb.

"Yep." Kate's expression is a mixture of a grimace and a chagrined smile. "He wants you all to know he likes his name. Oh, and he wants me to make sure you all know how awesome he is. He may have even thumped his chest. Two times."

The bizarre conversation finally catches up with Ben.

A jackalope. A horned *bunny*, for Christ's sake. It talks to Kate, and she tells him to fuck off with her middle finger.

He feels something rise in his chest, a pressure worming its way upward.

Before he realizes what's happening, a chuckle slips past his lips. Five sets of eyes turn to him in surprise.

Another chuckle bubbles up. Then another, until he's bent over roaring with laughter.

"I'm sorry," he wheezes between guffaws. "It's just nice to know I'm not the only one out of my goddamn mind."

Kate bursts out laughing. It's the first genuine smile she's given him since that disastrous birthday kiss. Their eyes lock.

And even though he's soaking wet in the middle of the woods with nothing on but a pair of pants, Ben is suddenly warm from head to toe.

62

DEAL WITH IT

BEN

The fire continues to blaze. Ben sits with his back against a Douglas fir, staring into the flames.

Everyone is curled up on their sides, asleep. The rain has finally stopped. His clothes have mostly dried out.

He likes watching Kate sleep. She looks good when she isn't worried all the time. She lies on the ground next to Ash, one hand entwined in the younger woman's.

It's well past time for Ben to pass his watch shift to Reed. He doesn't bother. It's not like he can sleep anyway, and Reed snores blissfully on the ground. At least someone out here should benefit from a good night sleep. And the quiet time has given him a chance to clean the weapons still in their possession.

Something moves. Ben shifts, then relaxes as Caleb gets to his feet. The young man moves gingerly, not wanting to disturb Ash. He walks to the edge of the firelight and turns his back to take a piss.

"I've been holding that for hours," Caleb says to no one in particular, letting out a long sigh of relief.

"It's the last good piss you're going to have for a while," Ben replies. "We're all out of potable water."

Caleb pulls his shorts back into place and turns. "I should probably care about that, but I don't. I'll drink out of the creeks and streams." The younger man stretches his arms, eyeing Ben from across the fire.

When Ben looks at Caleb, he realizes he doesn't feel hatred and loathing anymore. For the first time, he sees Caleb for what he really is: a young man no more than twenty-two or twenty-three years old. A young man with a good heart who hadn't chosen his friends as wisely as he should.

Fuck. When do young men ever do anything wise? Ben had more than his share of loser friends throughout his life. More than his fair share of bad decisions, too. And not just when he was a young man.

"Why are you looking at me like that?" Caleb asks.

"Like what?"

"Like you don't think I'm the first-born of Satan."

The darkness moves behind Caleb.

Ben blinks, realizing how exhausted he is. How long has he been awake? Twenty-four hours, at least, if not longer. Maybe he's starting to hallucinate like Kate.

The darkness continues to move. A rancid smell wafts through camp.

"What's the smell?" Caleb asks, wrinkling his nose.

The smell hits Ben full in the face. It's like walking past a dumpster in a dark alley. No way in hell a hallucination can smell like death.

"God, it smells like a garbage dump," Caleb says. "Where's it coming from?" He turns, peering in the direction of the stench.

Ben shifts into a crouch, drawing his gun. In his fatigued state, he'd left his knife on the other side of the fire where he'd used it to strip wet bark from logs.

Since they arrived at the Lost Coast, they've been without

the constant stink of the undead hanging in the air. Apparently, their reprieve is over. A zombie—or zombies—has found them.

The darkness behind Caleb solidifies.

Except it's not a zombie.

Outlined in the firelight is a creature that easily weighs six hundred pounds. It rears up, rising seven feet into the air. A roar rips free from its mouth, vibrating Ben down to his core.

The world narrows to a split second. All Ben's time at College Creek blurs by in his mind's eye. He sees a new version of Caleb in the replay.

Caleb was always the voice of reason in Johnson's ear. Anytime the other boy let his brutal streak show, Caleb was there, attempting to talk him down. Most of the time it worked.

Then Johnson started putting distance between himself and Caleb. He'd go out scavenging with Ryan and some of the crueler boys. He always had an excuse and a buddy-buddy fist bump for Caleb when he returned, but the truth was that he shied away from the moral compass of his friend.

Caleb had been there on the day of the College Creek massacre. He'd been the one screaming at Johnson.

Stop! Don't do this! Johnson, stop!

Ben finally realizes the truth.

Caleb is one more person Ben has failed. He's another College Creek casualty. He failed Caleb as surely as he failed all the kids who are dead and gone.

Caleb was right. Ben had done nothing. He'd had plenty of chances to kill Johnson. He'd failed.

He'd failed them all.

Most of them are gone. He'd never have a chance to make up his failure.

But Caleb is still here. Ben still has a chance at redemption.

He isn't going to fail Caleb a second time.

With a shout, he flings himself toward the younger man. He crashes into him, sending Caleb flying into the brush.

The bear drops to all fours, another roar ripping through the camp.

Ben's world narrows to a singular focus.

The bear. The smell. The enormous paws that could shred him open with one swipe. The teeth that could tear off his arms.

Ben hits the ground, skidding across dirt and pine needles on his back. Pure instinct takes over.

The gun in his hand comes up.

The bear charges.

Ben fires, emptying his magazine. His shout is lost in the roar of challenge that issues from the great animal.

The bear crashes to the ground, body skidding into the firelight. Its face is a mash of red from the bullets. Blood pours out of the ruined muzzle, staining the ground.

Ben's breath rasps in and out of his lungs. Adrenaline beats in his ears. His legs tremble as he gets to his feet.

Caleb crouches in the brush just outside of their shelter, slack-jawed in shock and horror.

Moving on shaky legs, Ben crosses the clearing. He holds out a hand to the other man.

"I'm sorry." His voice is hoarse. There is so much more to say, but it's the best he can do. The intensity of the adrenaline makes his arm tremble.

Caleb rises and lets out a long breath, eyes still wide. He grasps Ben's hand. A beat passes. Then he yanks Ben into a hug.

It's not an embrace by any means. More of a shoulder bump and some slapping on the back. Ben returns the back slaps with awkwardness.

The anger he's carried around since the day of the College Creek massacre dissipates, puffing away like smoke in a breeze. Caleb grins at him, face still crazed with fear from his near-death encounter with the black bear. Ben returns the grin, feeling feral.

"Ben?" Someone grabs him by the shoulder and whips him around.

The entire camp is awake, everyone on their feet as they gawk at the dead black bear.

Kate stands in front of him, eyes wild as she scans his body. "Are you okay? Did the bear get you anywhere?"

Adrenaline still pounds through him. Bloods roars in his ears. He can't form words.

"Ben?"

He grabs her by the arms, squashing her against him. She squawks in surprise.

Ben silences her with a fierce kiss on the lips. He drinks in the taste of her, savoring the glory of being alive. Of not hating Caleb.

God dammit, he never hated Caleb. He hated himself.

The roaring in his ears subsides. He becomes aware of applause.

The kids are clapping, hooting, and catcalling.

"About time!" someone shouts. It might be Reed.

"Way to grow a pair," someone else says. That might be Caleb, the little shit.

Ben disengages, putting an arm's length between himself and Kate as a semblance of sanity returns to him. She made it clear she didn't want him to kiss her.

He decides he doesn't give a shit. "Deal with it," he says to her.

She gapes at him. Someone hoots with laughter.

He stares down at her, still half feral from the encounter with the bear. His chest heaves. It takes all his will power not to drag her back into his arms and kiss her again.

Is she angry? He can't tell.

This thought is followed by the formation of words, which flow out of his mouth.

"I'm not sorry," he tells her. "Deal with it."

She blinks, her face still painted with shock and surprise. Then she grabs him by the front of the shirt, knotting her fist in the fabric. "You deal with it," she snaps, dragging him forward. She rises up onto her toes to kiss him.

This kiss is longer, deeper. It would be perfect, if not for the fucking peanut gallery ringing the two of them.

"You owe me a night shift," Ash says. Her voice is a croak, but the glee is unmistakable. "I told you he'd make a move before we got to Fort Ross."

"Dammit, old man," Caleb says, "you screwed me. You weren't supposed to grow a pair until we got back home."

"I get Eric's pair of Nikes," Reed crows.

"And I get Eric's alien socks," Susan adds.

"Fuck both of you," Eric replies. His voice is jovial, not an ounce of rancor there despite his words. "Joke's on you. The Nikes have mold on the inside and the alien socks have a hole in the toe."

"Don't be a sore loser," Susan says. "It doesn't suit you."

"Hell, Ben had to swim in holey underwear, survive pirates and a shipwreck, escape the impassible zone, and kill a bear to work up the nerve to make a move," Eric replies. "Up until ten seconds ago, I thought I had this in the bag."

Ben wants to hold Kate in his arms and kiss her for the next twenty years, but he can't take it anymore.

"Do you little shits have to talk all the time?" he demands. "Sixty seconds of silence. Is that so much to ask for?"

Everyone bursts out laughing. He feels his face grow hot. He sneaks a look at Kate. Her brow is furrowed in consternation, but she hasn't retreated. She leans into him, her shoulder pressed into his bicep.

He decides to go big. Why not? He just killed a goddamn black bear.

He puts both arms around her shoulders, pulling her close against his chest. Kate doesn't resist or protest. She turns a shy smile up at him before resting her head against him.

Ben decides this might be the best night of his life.

"Hey, guys." Reed is the first to recover from the fit of laughter. "I think we have the food problem sorted out." He gestures to the dead bear.

"Dude." Caleb takes in the massive proportions of the dead animal. "That thing must weight six hundred pounds. Do you know how to butcher an animal?"

"I do."

Everyone turns to Eric in surprise. He shrugs.

"My dad used to take me deer hunting as a kid. A bear can't be all that different."

Four hundred and fifty pounds different, but Ben doesn't bother to point this out. Even if it's hard to imagine the stoner-electrician knowing how to butcher a bear.

Hell, it was impossible to imagine Kate resting her head on his chest, but here she is. Anything is possible.

Ben makes a silent promise to himself: this will not be the first and only time he holds Kate. By some miracle, he's managed to get past both their bullshit, if only by a hair. Now that the door's been cracked open, he doesn't intend to stop until she's all his.

He squeezes her one last time before releasing her. Retrieving his knife from the fireside, he turns to Eric. "Let's get to work, kid."

"I'll get sticks," Reed volunteers. "This will be like a real camping trip, only with bear instead of marshmallows."

"I knew I should have packed salt." Ash forces herself into a sitting position. "Only savages eat wild bear without salt."

Ben, standing over the carcass with Eric, looks up to find Kate watching him. The banter of the kids fades to a distant hum as their eyes meet. When she smiles at him, his whole body sings.

63

CANDELABRAS

KATE

Stomach full of bear, I lead the group away from our camp-site in the dead of night. I did a tick check on everyone before we set out and removed seven of them in total. I can already see patches of poison oak flaring up on several of us. There's a patch on my arm that itches like crazy.

Each of us still wears a headlamp, the beams cutting through the dark. We lost six hours with our stop. Even though the group needed the rest—and it was mandatory for Ash—it was still six lost hours of trail time. We should have been off the trail and on the road by now, well on our way to Alvarez and Fort Ross.

It's been over twenty hours since I last spoke to Alvarez. His deadline with Rosario is almost up. As I power hike down the muddy trail, I try not to let worry for my friend take over.

My group is in rough shape today. Everyone is stiff and sore, myself included. The hard hours of travel combined with bad weather—not to mention a night sleeping on the ground—has left us all depleted.

There won't be a lot of running today. Even if everyone

weren't exhausted, sore, and cold, the trail is choked with more thistles and poison oak. Some of it grows as high as my chest. My hope is to keep everyone moving at a fast power hike.

The rain has stopped. And we have cooked bear meat to keep us fueled for the journey. The ocean pounds against the coastline in a constant hum. The air smells fresh and clean. Things are looking better today than they had yesterday, even if the group is sore and exhausted.

My thoughts stray to Ben. He's in the middle of the pack, keeping an eye on Ash. He's taken it upon himself to be her watchman. Caleb, too. I don't know what happened before the bear attack, but the two men appear to be on good terms now.

My mind keeps straying to our kiss. Kisses. I do my best to ignore the equal parts of thrill and terror that thunder through me. It's my job to get my people off the Lost Coast. I can't do that if I'm mooning over Ben like a high school idiot.

"Maybe we should ditch Arcata and move out here," Susan says. "At least we know there are bears to eat."

She hikes behind me, her gait uneven with her swollen ankle. She seems to have found a rhythm she can maintain. The fact that she's upbeat enough to talk is a good sign.

"We can live in tents," I reply.

"Tree houses," Susan replies. "I'm not living on the ground where things can eat me. I can't wait to tell Gary I ate bear."

We pass a primitive campground overlooking the ocean. There are a few pieces of driftwood for benches and fire rings that haven't seen a fire in months. There is no sign of people, no tents or backpacks of supplies for us to scavenge. We continue by without slowing.

The next campground we see will be Usal Beach at the southern terminus of the Lost Coast. That's where we need to reach. I estimate we have ten to twelve miles before us. If I can keep everyone moving at a brisk pace, we should be able to make the journey in three to four hours.

The group falls silent as we hike, everyone focused on the job of moving. I monitor them, making sure to take regular breaks for food and water. We've been forced to fill our water bladders from the streams. The Lost Coast is remote enough that I'm not too worried about water-borne illnesses. Even so, I lament the lack of purification tablets and a proper means to boil water.

Three-and-a-half hours later, the group grinds to an abrupt halt. The sun has just started to rise, filling the Lost Coast with soft gray light. It's just enough for us to fully see the magical sight before us.

We stand in awed silence as the trail opens up to reveal an ancient grove of giant redwood trees. Verdant green moss and ferns crawl across the ground and up the trunks of the most amazing trees I've ever seen. They have wide, squat trunks, each one adorned with a dozen or more crowns that pierce the sky like giant forks.

The trees stand in silent witness to our presence. All we can hear is our own breathing. Not a single leaf or animal rustles. The lack of sound presses in on all sides. It feels like the gentlest, softest, baby's blanket.

"What is this place?" Reed asks in a hushed voice.

"The candelabra grove." My heart lifts. In all my years of trail running, I've never seen a sight like this. In the panic and craziness of the last twenty-four hours, I'd forgotten all about the legendary candelabra grove. It's part of the reason the Lost Coast was on my bucket list.

Frederico, I think, *wherever you are, I hope you can see this.*

"This is a redwood grove, but it's the only one of its kind in the world," I explain. "These trees were formed by the coastal wind storms over hundreds of years. Every time a gale broke off a crown, the trunk would produce another one. Each new crown had to contort itself to find an upward path to the sun around the main trunk."

The result is the massive trunks spread before us, each of them peppered with a myriad of crowns that stretch skyward. They resemble candelabras. Hence the name of this place: the candelabra grove.

In the death and madness of the apocalypse, we've found a tiny slice of magic. Standing beneath the ancient grove gives me hope. It's a reminder that not everything in the world has been rendered with rot and ruin. It's possible to live, survive, and thrive. If these trees survived the logging massacre and everything else that has come and gone over the last five hundred years, we puny humans have a shot at making it, too. We have a shot at turning into something beautiful. Someday.

"I'll be damned." Ben's shoulder brushes mine as he comes to stand beside me. "I've never seen anything like this."

"Really?" I tilt my head at him in surprise. "You've been all over the world."

"In the Middle East and Africa. Nothing magic out there." His voice drops to his usual grumpy mutter. "Just assholes and sand."

Caleb, who overhears, raises an eyebrow. "Still plenty of sand and assholes around here."

Everyone laughs. I relax into the moment, taking in the rare beauty. For once, we aren't running for our lives. We aren't hungry. We aren't slinking around zombies or fighting them.

Dry sky, ancient candelabra grove, and family. It's perfect.

"You know what this means, don't you?" Susan's eyes are bright as she limps past me for a better look at the trees.

"No. What does it mean?"

She grins over her shoulder. "The candelabra grove is the end of the Lost Coast. Usal Beach and campground will be right on the other side of the grove."

My mouth falls open. In my wonder of the grove, my brain hadn't processed this piece of information. It only takes a moment for the shock to turn to joy.

"You mean we made it? We survived?" Reed asks.

"You can say that as soon as we get to Usal Beach," Susan says. "Don't jinx us."

"It means you all completed your first ultramarathon." Pride fills me. I glance down at my watch and do a rough estimation of the miles behind us. "I think it's safe to say you guys traveled roughly thirty-three miles in twelve hours. That includes the time we stopped to build a fire and—" I throw a smile in Ben's direction "—kill a bear."

Eric lets out a whoop of joy. He and Reed slap high fives. They race down the trail. The rest of the group hustles after them, all of them energized by the first official finish line of our journey. This is a first ultramarathon for all of them.

The trail and its ancient trees swallow my people. I'm about to run after them when I feel Ben's hand close around mine.

I stay back with him. We haven't had a moment alone since our kiss over the bear carcass. It's unlikely we'll have another anytime soon.

"How long until Rosario's deadline?" he asks.

I hold up my watch so he can see it. It reads twenty-three hours and fifty-six minutes. Alvarez only has four minutes until Rosario's deadline. "I didn't want to ruin their moment by telling them. They survived hell."

Their accomplishment would be short lived, unfortunately. We may have reached the end of the Lost Coast, but we still have a long way to go.

"We'll get to Fort Ross." Ben puts an arm around my shoulders. "Alvarez will manage until we get there."

I let out a long sigh and lean into his solid warmth. "I know."

"Alvarez has survived this long without you to babysit him. He can hang in there another twenty-four hours. Or however long it takes us to get there. And we just survived the Lost Coast so quit sulking."

Ben is right. When I look up, he gives me his eye-crinkle smile.

"This thing between us," he says. "I'm not dropping it. Just so you know."

"You're not *dropping it*?" I raise an eyebrow at him. "I think that may be the most unromantic thing anyone has ever said to me."

"You know I'm not good with words." He huffs in annoyance, rubbing a hand over his face. "I'm trying to say I'd take a bullet for you, Kate. A thousand times over, any day of the week. You look after all the little shitheads, but all I want to do is look after you. You know how hard you make that? For fuck's sake, look at where we *are*." He jabs a finger at the trees around us, scowling. "You make it damn hard for a man who just wants to make sure you see the next sunrise, you know that?"

I stare up at him, emotion making my throat tight. I think in his own way, Ben just told me he loves me.

His scowl fades as I trace a finger down the stubble lining his cheek and jaw.

"That was a lot better," I whisper. "I'd take a bullet for you, too."

His eyes warm, that smile crinkling along the edges again. He bends down and kisses me.

His mouth may not be great with words, but as I stand in the circle of his arms, I realize it's definitely good at other things. He kisses me breathless, showing me just how much he cares.

I've so badly wanted this closeness with him. I resolve not to fight it anymore. I let the world fall away and lose myself in his kiss. There are no kids to tease us this time. It's just me and Ben in the candelabra grove. It's perfect.

My knees are weak by the time he pulls back. I wrap my arms around his neck, wanting no space between us.

He presses his forehead against mine, arms tightening around me. "I'm not dropping this. I mean it, Kate."

"You'd better not," I murmur. "I'm counting on you." I think I could drown in his gray eyes. The warmth in them leaves me as weak-kneed as his kiss. It's been a long time since a man has looked at me the way he does right now.

Ben kisses me one last time before breaking away.

"Come on," he says. "Let's catch up with the little shitheads before they blunder into a pack of zoms at the campground and get themselves bit."

I bark a laugh. "They know how to be careful."

"Sometimes. There's a reason you fret about them all the time." The gruffness of his voice is softened by his eye-smile again.

It warms me all the way to my toes.

We surge forward, running through the trees.

Together.

THE END

Want an exclusive novella about Alvarez?
Sign up and get a FREE copy of *Foot Soldier*:
subscribepage.com/footsoldier

Don't miss the series conclusion in Book 4, *Fort Dead*! Get it on Amazon at mybook.to/fortdead

Thanks for reading!

Printed in Great Britain
by Amazon

81295110R00236